STEVENSON'S TREASURE

STEVENSON'S TREASURE

BY

MARK WIEDERANDERS

To Edie,

Fireship Press
www.FireshipPress.com

A friend and fan of music! Enjoy —

Mark Wiederanders

STEVENSON'S TREASURE by Mark Wiederanders
Copyright © 2014 Mark Wiederanders

ISBN-13:978-1-61179-307-9: Paperback
ISBN 978-1-61179-308-6: ebook

BISAC Subject Headings:

FIC014000FICTION / Historical
FIC027050FICTION / Romance / Historical
FIC019000FICTION / Literary

Cover Work: Christine Horner

Address all correspondence to:
Fireship Press, LLC
P.O. Box 68412
Tucson, AZ 85737
Or visit our website at:
www.FireshipPress.com

NOTE TO READERS

Historical fiction derives its strength from historical accuracy, its grace from creativity. Thus, while I have been able to include some of the actual letters written between Robert Louis Stevenson and Fannie, many gaps remained. I did my best to write letters in the style, or at least the spirit, of these star crossed lovers, showing their thoughts and feelings as I imagined them. Those letters and portions of letters that are direct quotes from their actual writings are printed in italics. Fanny and Sam's telegrams about Hervey's desperate illness are also authentic, as are Stevenson's poem-excerpts. For further information, please read the Afterward.

DEDICATION

To Esta, John, Sarah and Annie

STEVENSON'S TREASURE

REVIEWS

"Drawing on prime sources, Wiederanders' debut novel captures both the depth and charm of one of the Belle Epoch's most unique couples; an absolutely sparkling read." – Persia Woolley, author of *The Guinevere Trilogy*.

"With intricately-rendered characters, rich international historical settings, and a warm humor simmering throughout its pages, STEVENSON'S TREASURE reminds us that while pirates, buried treasure, and split personalities can captivate, there is no adventure quite like the deep longing of the human heart." – Kim Culbertson, Northern California Book Award Winner for *Instructions for a Broken Heart*.

"STEVENSON'S TREASURE is an exhilarating ride through the Golden West as we follow Robert Louis Stevenson from France and Scotland to Monterey, California in search of love and inspiration. ... Wiederanders' style is richly descriptive, sensual with both a painter's sensibility (Fanny was an artist) and a writer's depth of character and detail." – Mary Burns, author of *Portraits of an Artist: a novel about John Singer Sargent*.

"In the first lines of Mark Wiederanders' captivating novel we are introduced to the eccentric, brilliant Robert Louis Stevenson through the eyes of the no less iridescent Fanny Osbourne, and from that meeting, the novel—meticulously researched by an author who has a sense of wicked humor to match Stevenson's own—plunges forward. Stevenson's early, absurd efforts to be a published author are almost impossible to juxtapose with his eventual fame, and he and Fanny seem to be in equal measure mismatched and fated. We follow with delight their careening efforts to figure out how to be—if they can be—together, and what that love life will or will not mean for Stevenson's literary life. A great and unexpected love story, beautifully and compellingly told." – Sands Hall, author of *Catching Heaven* and *Tools of the Writer's Craft*.

Chapter	Content	Page

Chapter	Content	Page

CHAPTER 1
Fontainebleau Forest, France
August 1878

Fanny Osbourne had not expected to fall in love with a penniless writer in bad health who was closer to her daughter's age than to her own. When they first met, his strangeness had put her off. What sort of man would go by his middle name—and insist that it be mispronounced? Now, two years later, she followed Robert Louis Stevenson down a twisting path beneath beech trees, aching to stay with him. In her dreams, every afternoon would be like this one, with filtered sun warming her shoulders as they strolled deep into forests, talked, sipped wine and made love.

Louis had immediately stood out from the other men at the camp who scurried around with easels and claimed they were Bohemian but, excepting their berets and paint-spattered smocks, were as ordinary as hitching posts. Louis—now with arms waving within his wreck of a blue velvet coat as he gushed about the canoeing trip they would take in the morning, and how they must stop in the village to buy a baguette and burgundy—had been honestly strange, madly funny, dying but self-denying, passionate, sensual, devoted, everything she wanted. She longed to reach her arms around him, quiet his chatter with soft words, and convince him of the reality of her situation.

Unfortunately, accepting the reality of *any* situation did not seem to be Louis's strong suit. Reaching a pond choked with yellow and white water lilies, she set her foot against the root of a weeping willow tree. "Louis!"

He turned to her. "Is something wrong?"

"This spot is as good as any."

He set up her easel and placed the stool on a firm patch of dirt. "Give me a minute to compose myself." He sat on a low branch of the tree, pushed his ridiculous Indian smoking-cap back on his forehead and folded his arms in what he, no doubt, considered a rakish pose.

She would sketch him first, and then tell him. Greedy, to capture him on a page that she would pack with her things and take out, later, to secretly savor when she was back in California with her husband. But it was all she would have of him, so she felt desperate to create something of beauty. Or if not beauty, she would at least render him with the competence gained in two years of study with some of the finest artists in the world, purchased at enormous cost, her husband's dollars being the least of it.

Feeling a bead of perspiration crawl down her neck, she loosened the chinstrap of her sun bonnet. What a ridiculous sight the two of them must be: she, barely five feet tall, dressed from bonnet to shoes in black, her flowing skirts failing to conceal her natural, hourglass figure; he, tall and too thin, wearing yellow linen trousers, big-knotted red tie, blue velvet coat, and an embroidered silk cap that flaunted every color of the rainbow.

First, his proportions. She formed a rectangle with her fingers and considered Louis through this frame, trying not to be distracted by the meadow behind him, where boulders jutted up like castles from the riot of flowers and the more muted tones of junipers and heather. His face was oblong, like a long stone hanging from an earring. Slight, trifling almost, but with unusual length from the eyebrows down to the chin. Long thin nose, and beneath it the wry grin that would be charming except the teeth were stained and a little bit crooked. She would draw him with lips closed. A gentle mouth, a boy's, really, except for the thin mustache above it. The nose a classic shape, slender like the rest of him. And the eyes. Sensuous and, unlike her husband's, utterly without guile.

"Are you certain that you are all right, Fanny? You look so sad."

She swallowed. "Don't talk, it distracts me." She took up a pencil and quickly sketched his face and its features in rough proportion to what she observed. Then she worked on the rest of him. The big coat with its wide lapels that dwarfed his shoulders pleased her. She added shading to suggest bulk until satisfied that her drawing captured the way he looked like a boy who had put on his father's coat. The humor provided by the coat might counterbalance the haunting strangeness of the thin face.

Now to the hands. He had propped one of them on a knee so that the fingers dangled downward. Long, lean and delicate, they were the fingers of a pianist or, perhaps, a masseur. Sinful fingers.

He smiled playfully. "I saw that look, Fanny Osbourne."

"What look?"

"Just for an instant, the grim look you've had all day gave way to a naughty grin."

"Nonsense." She dug in her purse for a cigarette paper and tobacco.

Louis relaxed from his pose, and they each rolled a cigarette. Fanny realized that her hands were trembling, so she held them to her sides while Louis struck a match. She wondered if the children were busy packing for the long trip home as she had asked. *Tell him now.*

Louis blew smoke to the wind and smiled. "What are you thinking, Fanny?"

She swallowed. "I'm thinking we should finish the sketch."

She continued in silence, fiercely concentrating on the details lest she burst into tears, first drawing the silly cap and adding scribbles for its embroidery. She drew, and re-drew, the eyes because she found them his most winning feature. Their soft stare managed to pierce her with their innocence. "Could you look elsewhere than at my eyes?"

He grinned. "No."

"Then at least close your mouth over those teeth."

He laughed. As always, the laughter brought on coughing but he soon quelled it. He composed himself, clamped his mouth shut but his lips quivered as if with the slightest provocation he would laugh again. Something in the pale, mock-solemn face provoked in her a deep longing and a profound sadness. She had an inkling of why, but suppressed the haunting thought, finding it obscene.

"What is it, Fanny? You're shaking."

She gripped the edges of the easel with both hands, took a deep breath, and opened her mouth—but could not find the words.

"Fanny?"

She swallowed hard and looked down.

"You are going back to California," he said flatly.

"I must," was all she could manage.

His arms were open for her when she collapsed in heaving sobs, holding her, rocking her as if she were a child, a ridiculous idea, she being eleven years older than he. "You won't be rid of me so easily," he said.

"Easily? Please Louis, no jokes."

"Who is joking? I shall come for you."

"No, Louis," she said, voice shaking, clinging to him, kneading his back, needing his soul, numb to the course she had set.

Soon thereafter, on a chilly grey day at London's Victoria Station, she clambered to the platform with her children to

4

board the train that would take them to Liverpool, where they would find a steamer bound for New York. Louis was there to see her off, having followed her from Fontainebleau to Paris, and from Paris to London, greeting her at the station with a big grin, which only made her final departure more painful.

Instead of having a few quiet moments together, the leaving was chaos. Lloyd, her tow-headed ten-year-old, had the carrying-tube of his fishing pole perched on one shoulder, swinging it this way and that while gawking at hissing steam engines and passengers in bowlers, bonnets and turbans who jabbered in a dozen different languages. The tube knocked one man's hat off before Fanny could guide the boy up the stairs to their compartment. She had no answer to his questions: "Isn't it great to be going home? Won't it be fun to see Papa again?"

Her nineteen-year-old daughter Belle, dark-haired and buxom, a younger version of Fanny in a yellow dress and bonnet was struggling to get Barney, her terrified pug, back on his leash. This lead to Louis chasing and diving for the dog before the beast might yap his way off the platform and be squashed by the gleaming wheels of the train. By the time Louis captured the dog and handed him to Belle, who turned to climb the stairs without thanking Louis—the girl adored her father and, thus, loathed Louis—the goodbye had to be short.

Louis gave Fanny a chaste kiss on the cheek.

"What will you do?" Fanny immediately realized the question was inadequate.

He gave her a wry smile. "Go for a walk. And you?"

She knew what she would do: endure seasickness for ten days on a steamer to New York, and then an even longer ordeal in a jouncing car on the overland train to San Francisco. She would have almost a month to mourn Louis and, as her childhood preacher in Indiana used to say, to consider the error of her ways. Then, she would put away her easel and dreams and try to be wife again to a man she had ceased caring about.

Louis pressed a scrap of paper in her hand. "A discreet address where you can write me. Can you give me one as well?"

The final boarding-whistle blew. She gave a slight shake of her head. Feeling hot tears on her cheeks she turned and walked up the stairs. Through the window of their compartment she watched Louis trudge away, shoulders sagging under a brown ulster with its collar turned up. As the brakes hissed and the train drew her slowly away from happiness, she stared at his back, desperately hoping that he would turn to her, but he did not.

CHAPTER 2
Walking

As Louis saw things, he had two choices: kill himself or go for a very long walk. After two days of drinking with his cousin Bob, which failed to deaden the pain of Fanny's absence but added a pounding headache, he chose the walk. Given the state of his lungs, a long enough walk would kill him anyway; should he live, a lively enough journal of his walking-travels might be published, and this might impress Mrs. Osbourne, wherever she might be. He made his way by rail and stage to the south of France, where, within a week, he found another female companion.

"She is young, spirited and beautiful," said Father Adam, a wiry old man in a flat-brimmed hat, frock-coat and gravy-spattered trousers, all of them black. "I have enjoyed her services for two years but, alas, must now give her up. She is yours for one hundred francs." He gestured to where she stood, silhouetted against a blue sky, in the marketplace of the pine-scented mountain town of Le Monastier.

"I'll pay no more than fifty." Louis looked around at the grave faces of other men in stained aprons who had left carts from which they had been hawking grapes, peaches and pears to watch the negotiations.

"I must have eighty. A sacrifice."

"She is too small. I plan to work her hard."

"She can take it! And you'll find none with as cheerful a disposition. Just look at her pleasing shape."

Louis had to admit that her petite curves were handsome and, judging by the way she kept turning to eye him as he walked around her, not letting him see her backside, she was charmingly modest. "Sixty-five francs, take it or leave it."

"Sixty-five francs—and one glass of brandy!"

"Done."

Father Adam slapped Louis on the back, and handed him the reins of what had to be the smallest donkey in France. The color of a mouse, she was little bigger than a dog.

Louis dug in his pocket for the money. "I shall name her Modestine."

The onlookers burst into applause. "To Modestine!" one of them shouted. "To the tavern!" yelled another.

Two hours later, Louis's new friends wobbled with him out of the tavern to see him off. First he had to pack provisions. He spread a canvas tarp on the grass and set down a quart of milk, three bottles of Beaujolais, an egg-beater, a cold leg of mutton, chocolate cake, sausage, black and white bread, tobacco, cigarette papers, matches, lantern, leather flask, a bottle of brandy, oilcloth, sleeping-sack, two changes of clothing, a revolver and cartridges, jack-knife, books, writing tablets, pens, pencils, and ink. He rolled the tarp into one lumpy ball and shoved it atop Modestine's pack saddle.

Father Adam frowned at the pack, which was larger than Modestine. "How far will you go?"

Louis looked to the south and the endless granite peaks and dark green valleys that stretched in the distance. "Across the Cévennes. A hundred twenty miles, I believe."

"Why?"

"Why not?" Louis tugged Modestine's reins. "Come along, dear."

Modestine did not budge.

8

Louis yanked harder. "Come. Come *now*."

The donkey seemed to be smiling with a sly, secret wisdom. The look on her face, with its dark eyes and determined underjaw, reminded Louis of a look that Fanny often gave him.

Father Adam slapped her rump. Modestine jumped forward. The pack slid down her side and she spun in circles, slinging sausage, cake and clothing everywhere as the villagers guffawed.

Three nights later, Louis had made it as far as Cheylard, shoving Modestine most of the way. He sat by the fireplace of a decrepit inn with his writing tablet balanced on his knees, drying out from a storm and bringing his journal up to date. Although exhausted and with blistered feet, his lungs had remained clear. Perhaps the mountain altitude helped, although the weather had not been dry. At the moment, a pelting rain hammered the smudged old window next to him and wind howled through the rafters. The innkeeper, his portly wife and five children wandered freely through the barn-like place to stare at the madman who had wandered in with a tiny donkey in the black of night. One daughter in particular, perhaps nine years old, in velveteen slippers and a floral-print house-gown, gawked openly at him while hovering nearby with a feather duster, swiping at spider webs while he worked.

He had plenty of misadventures to write about, including getting lost the previous day and stopping to ask two giggling farm girls how to rejoin the trail. One of them had stuck her tongue out at him. The second had pointed to some cows and said, "Follow them," a suggestion that had taken him even further away from his intended route.

He heard Modestine munching dinner in the very next room, the inn bedding travelers and their animals, conveniently, on the same floor with only a thin wall between them. "Once, when I looked at her, she had a faint resemblance to a lady of my acquaintance who formerly loaded me with kindness," he wrote. Might Fanny, on some

9

future day, read his travel book and cringe at being compared to a donkey? The thought made him smile, but only briefly. Would he ever set eyes on her again? Would she, perhaps as an old woman, regret that she had not thrown caution to the winds and stayed with her young lover in France, the man who so passionately wanted her? Such questions ran endlessly through his mind on the trail, at least at the times when he wasn't cursing Modestine or retying her pack.

Father Adam had told him that within a few days he would love Modestine more than his favorite dog. "Three days have passed," Louis wrote in his journal, "and my heart is still as cold as a potato towards her."

A shadow suddenly loomed over him and made him jump. The innkeeper's daughter had crept up behind him and was peering over his shoulder. She beckoned him with her finger to the corner of the room, where she lifted a chain from a hook on the wall and let down a small writing-desk.

"Thank you. *Merci*."

She perched on a nearby stool, grandly gesturing for him to continue his work. When he finished for the night, she had not moved. "Do you like to write?"

She frowned at him, and he repeated the question in French. She nodded.

He put the cap on his fountain pen, bowed and presented it to her. Clutching the pen to her chest she fled up the stairwell.

Two days later, he ate bread by a campfire behind the stone walls of an old Trappist monastery. The weather had warmed and he was glad to be camped outside, taking in a drowsy sunset that had formed above the limestone bluffs that ringed the valley. Modestine wheezed from the shadows of a chestnut tree to which he had tied her. When he ignored her she began stamping her feet. He sighed and broke up the other half-loaf of bread, and held the pieces in his open palms. She gently nibbled it from them, giving him her mysterious look and snorting contentedly.

By the sixth day of his journey, he was talking to her. "Love for you is a simple business. Cast those dreamy eyes on some handsome donkey fellow, toss up your tail and have him aboard."

Modestine shuddered.

"Point well taken, I apologize if I've offended you. But you know what I mean. In your love life you have nature on your side, whilst I have tradition, legality, marriage vows, a husband, dear children and all that pitted against me."

The weather remained calm and the sky blue as they trekked through the green valley of the Chassejac. Modestine marched agreeably through a handsome stand of pine, and did not so much as flinch when a farmer emerged from the trees like the pied piper, leading a sea of black and white sheep that surrounded them, neck-bells clanging as they bleated past. Louis took a moment to admire the packing system that he had devised and improved on, each day of their journey, by trial and error. Two large flower-baskets hanging down the sides of the pack saddle now held his belongings, an elegantly balanced rigging of which Modestine seemed more approving than the original single heap. When the trail steepened and became a series of switchbacks up the mountain of La Goulet, he tried to turn Modestine off the trail to take a shortcut, up through pines to the next link of the trail, but she came to an abrupt halt.

"Courage, dear!"

She turned and looked at him as if he were mad.

"'Tis hardly a hill, my sweet. *Go.*" He gave her a poke in the rear with a goad that an innkeeper at Le Bouchet St. Nicholas had made for him a few nights before.

Modestine jolted off the trail but seemed none too happy. "I'll bet my bank balance that some fool urged you to recognize your limitations, perhaps when you were just a wee lass of an ass. And you, dear Modestine, believed this fool."

11

She tossed her head back, not quite meeting his gaze but at least, Louis thought, indicating interest in what he had to say.

They stopped for lunch on a boulder-strewn plateau at the summit. Louis munched a cold bologna sausage and smoked a cigarette before giving Modestine her favorite meal, black bread crumbled up with chocolate cake. While swishing at black flies with her tail she nibbled the food, as was her preference, from his outstretched hand. When it was gone she lifted her fawn-like eyes to his, a look, he decided, of profound sadness. The look recalled that of his mother, on a day years ago when he had first heard the Limits-On-Life Speech...

He had been about seven years old. Lying in bed and stifling under its heavy counterpane, he tried to hear what the doctor was saying to his parents outside his bedroom door. He wondered what it would be like to be as tiny as the spider he saw high above him on the ceiling, able to slip through a crack to the next room, look down on the grownups and hear the words they were trying to keep him from hearing. He slipped out of bed, willed himself not to cough, tiptoed to the door and pressed his ear to it.

"One word can guide you," the doctor was saying. "Limits."

"Limits, sir?" his mother asked.

"You must limit what he does, limit what you expect from him, and, I must reluctantly say, limit your hopes that he will live to adulthood."

"He is our only child." Louis heard his mother begin to sob, and then a long silence broken only by a rustling sound, as if his father had drawn her into his arms.

"Go then, if you can give us no hope," his father's stern voice finally said.

"Of course, sir. Good day."

Louis heard the doctor's footsteps clatter down the three flights of stone steps to the street level of their richly appointed house in Edinburgh. Then, he discovered a wonderful thing. The doctor had left the flat stick he had used to press down Louis's tongue. He propped it near the tin soldiers that stood on the nightstand and reached beneath his bed for a bag of marbles. They would be perfect missiles for a catapult made by the tongue-stick. The weapon could destroy the phalanx of tin soldiers and their horses that were arrayed on the opposite nightstand.

He pulled back the tongue stick and launched a marble, which sailed in a nice arc but missed the soldiers and clattered onto the hardwood floor. The next try came closer, landing just beyond the cavalry. He was readying his next shot when the door opened and his father and mother walked in, he in his black frock coat and she in a long gray satin dress.

"Louis." His mother looked down with soft, beautiful eyes that brimmed with tears, surely the saddest look that any mum had ever given a boy. She threw her arms around him so tightly he thought he might smother.

"G' night, mum," he managed. When she stood, he bent another marble against the tongue-stick and arced it into the cavalry, sending three of the soldiers clattering to the floor. He laughed and cheered, but this made him cough.

"To bed with you." His father, strong, compact, and ruddy-faced, lifted the blankets as if Louis were unable to lift them on his own.

"Did you see my shot?"

"Yes, son. Cracking good." He pulled the blankets up to Louis's chin. After more long stares—he thought these would never end—they left the room. He pushed off the covers, coughing only a little bit, hoping to use the precious time before the fever went up again to massacre the cavalry.

Hours later, when he had long since returned to bed and the house was dark and silent, the door opened and he heard his nurse's careful footsteps, and then felt her touch his brow. "Not so hot, is it, Cummy?"

"Not so bad."

Mrs. Cunningham, thin but steely in both body and imagination, surely his favorite woman in the whole world besides his mother, bent over him and fussed with his bedding. He savored the sweetly burned smell of her starched blue dress that she always ironed for a bit too long, and the way her chest brushed his nose and cheeks. He felt an odd thing happening below the covers, his penis straining to attention. He wondered if Cummy felt this soldier pressing up through the blankets, and considered whether he should ask her about this mystery, which he imagined had something to do with how much he loved her. But a more important question came to him.

"Cummy, can we take a picnic to Greyfriars churchyard, and see the graves of the Covenanters?" This subject often got her telling him fine stories of the gory torture and executions of the Scottish martyrs buried there.

Tonight she disappointed him. "You're t' be kept in."

"Did my mother tell you that?"

"Aye, and your father, too. For your own good."

"They don't know everything. You've said it yourself."

"Only God and his angels do. Now let's pray to Jesus that he'll send an angel down with a big pet dragon, one that's friendly to little boys with rotten lungs who'll breathe fire in them and dry him out."

"Are there really dragons like that, Cummy?"

"Of course."

He did not believe what she had told him about the dragons. He did not believe the doctor, either, nor did he believe much of what his mother and father told him. He believed only what he chose to believe, and that way was seldom frightened. The only things that really frightened him were bad dreams, and if he stayed awake long enough he did not have them. Perhaps when Cummy finished her prayers and left him he would play with the soldiers until morning came...

Morning indeed came, just as it had done each day for the twenty years that followed until today, when he found himself pondering life with a doe-eyed donkey named Modestine. "Limits, hah! As you can see, dear one, I've not only survived but thrived. Seen every inch of Europe, or close to it, and sometimes by extraordinary means. When I met Fanny, my true love, although of course she has since abandoned me for a husband in California, but let's not discuss that at the moment, I had been canoeing through France. You've not heard that story?"

Modestine frowned intelligently.

"Then I shall tell it to you, since asses don't read. If asses did read, you could read all about that adventure when the book is printed. Because, oh dearest, my account of that adventure has been bought, just as my much-embellished journal of this little sojourn with thee will be."

Modestine stamped her feet.

"I concede your point—you believed that our time together would remain a memory for just the two of us. Have cheer, girl, being gossiped about isn't the worst lot in life. Oh no, the worst is being denied love."

She cocked her head, as if not sure she believed him.

Louis set water in front of her, which she loudly slurped as he continued. "This has happened so repeatedly that I have come to believe that it is my destiny, to be denied love and then go adventuring and write stories about the adventures. Trials and tribulations make one stronger, like heat tempers the steel. Consider yourself. You, dear girl, could have been an ordinary ass; well, not even ordinary, being so puny and clumsy. But when you fell into my care, I put you to the test, and now, you are proving your mettle."

Modestine loudly broke wind, then looked up from the bucket and gave him a sort of shrug.

Louis cinched up the packs and they set off, beginning a steep descent toward green meadows in the distance. With each step the air hung heavier and hotter. Modestine trudged with a kind of resignation, swishing her tail at swarms of flies. Louis took off his shirt and tied its sleeves to the pack saddle. Soon they had left the mountain pines behind, and walked in the shade of oak trees clinging to the hillside. Louis heard the welcome sound of water tumbling down through boulders. Rounding a hill he saw a cascade above them that foamed through a bend and rushed next to their trail, eventually widening to a river far below. "Won't be long, dear, and we'll take a bath."

Louis dreaded the end of their trip and picking up his mail. He did not dread the letters he was sure to get, from his parents, friends, and perhaps a magazine editor to whom he had sent stories. What he dreaded was the letter that he would *not* get—one from Fanny—yet he hoped with all of his heart one would be waiting, just the same.

Modestine veered toward the crystalline stream that with every step looked more inviting. Louis took off his straw hat and fanned his face. "You might ask why I decided to cross Europe in a canoe."

Modestine stopped and loosed a torrent of urine near his shoes.

"It started when I argued with my father about religion, saying I'd begun to doubt the literal truth of the Bible. When I told him I did not think anyone had walked on water, father got red-faced. I assured him that I believed Jesus was a great man, whether or not he actually hopped up from the tomb, but this sent father to bed, sick with worry for my soul. Soon he declared that I must live elsewhere.

"My cousin in Suffolk took me in, and damned if a neighbor, Mrs. Sitwell, wasn't one of the most enchanting women I have ever met, and certainly the most literary one. She'd a smile to put Mona Lisa to shame. Mrs. Sitwell did, indeed, sit well, with me, on long summer afternoons in the rectory where we talked about books. She was wife to a vicar, a drunken lout but a vicar all the same. Young fool that I was, I thought myself in love, and worse, that there was hope—after all, she had kicked the vicar out, making him rent lodgings while she lived in the rectory, where she held dinner parties for the likes of Sidney Colvin, Ed Gosse, and Henry James. She made me feel like I belonged!

"One day, after a feverish discussion of some clod of a writer, Anne Thackeray it might have been, I was looking over her leather-topped desk and into her eyes when she leaned toward me, and I leaned toward her, and our lips met. We kissed long and ardently while her breasts, the most tantalizing fruit since Eve's in the Garden, pressed against my chest. My hope soared. But when that one glorious kiss ended, she laughed at me and asked, 'Whatever possessed you to do that?' She insisted that I leave, and never come to the rectory again. So, I canoed through Belgium and France."

Modestine halted at the edge of the rushing water and swayed from side to side, her signal that if Louis did not soon get her packs off she would begin spinning again and flailing out his things, or perhaps ruin them with one wild leap into the stream.

He lifted the packs from her back and swatted her rump. She splashed in the shallows, kicking water on Louis. He peeled off his clothes, drawing a scowl from Modestine. With a whoop he jumped into a deep pool, loving the shock of the cold, cleansing water.

When he came up gasping, sunlight gleaming off the water reminded him of that canoeing trip, when a broken tree branch hanging low over the banks near Origny knocked him from his craft. He had been standing, enjoying the thrill of trying to keep his balance through a narrow, foamy stretch of the river, his mind straying to some lines written by Walt Whitman, envying the way the American described pastoral scenes like the one blurring past. Next moment he was tumbling in the river foam, lungs burning from the blow the tree branch had struck him, fighting for breath. The canoe, varnished so well that a French girl told him it looked like a violin, almost became his coffin. The linen suit and straw hat that had looked so jaunty, when crowds of farmers had cheered him off in Antwerp, now hung in tatters. Rain soaked him all the following week, and when it stopped raining, as he wrote in his journal, he had to dodge "the crop-headed children standing on bridges and spitting down." He had to hole up in a seedy hotel at Pontoise, halfway through his planned journey, to dry out his lungs and write up his adventure. When his mail caught up with him, there was a letter from his cousin, Bob, begging him to come for a visit to the artists' colony at Grez, in the Fontainebleau Forest, where Bob was painting landscapes and lusting after an American girl who had showed up for the season with her mother...

Louis scrambled onto dry land and toweled off while Modestine scratched her fly-bitten rump against an oak tree. "So you see, dear one, things often work out for the best. My travesty of an adventure, that summer, left me on the doorstep of a much grander adventure, although I'm not at all certain how that one will end. 'Tis the joy of it, right?"

Modestine gave a nod, either in agreement or showing her approval that he was putting his clothes back on.

Within a few days, Louis was in the main street of St. Jean du Gard, holding out his hand. A farmer, whose little cart stood horseless nearby, counted bills in his palm while Modestine cowered behind. "You won't be sorry," Louis promised, "she's remarkable."

When the stranger took the reins, Modestine looked confused, shaking her head as if to clear it, and then piercing Louis with her big brown eyes.

The farmer turned and gave a curt tug on the reins, clearly experienced in the ways of asses, for Modestine followed him at once, although her shoulders slumped and her head hung.

Louis hurried around the corner of a church, pushed his back against its brick wall and wept. When he had gone through several cigarettes, he trudged to the train station, feeling like he'd come from a funeral. It would kill him, he decided, to let even one more go whom he loved. He tossed his bag up on the train car and swung his leg up after it, his mind racing, already planning a new adventure, an outrageous one, dangerous almost beyond his imagination.

CHAPTER 3
Oakland, California
September, 1878

On her knees and shaded by a big straw hat, Fanny Osbourne weeded the planter box of roses that lined the front of her modest white house. Their scent was so dense, in the still, warm September air, that for a moment she felt nauseated. Sam had let them get unruly, and she doubted he'd done much more than toss a bucket of water their way, now and then, during the many months she was in France. She briefly considered cutting some of the prettier ones and arranging them in a vase for a table bouquet.

But today was Friday and she didn't have the time. At this very moment Sam would be on the deck of the *Bay City*, a side-paddle-wheel ferry, chuffing his way across the bay after his workweek in San Francisco and having a beer and cigar with his pals while they talked about events of the week: the dry goods place on the Embarcadero that had burned to the ground, and whether the Jo Boys had set the blaze. The ditches being dug to run cables beneath the streetcars, and the waste of tax dollars put to such a ridiculous purpose. The runaway hansom that had rolled and spilled a knot of German merchants onto Polk Street.

She washed her hands in the basin of the marble-topped washstand, looked briefly in the oval mirror and cursed two more gray hairs that had sprouted among her dense brown hair. Always, the gray ones were the thickest.

It had been a difficult week. On Monday she'd walked Lloyd to 5th Street for his first day at Lincoln Grammar School after a two-year absence, and so far, school wasn't going so well. In Europe he had worn black shorts and a beret to school, and after some tears and floundering become fluent in French; now, lessons in McGuffey's Reader and playing marbles in the dusty Oakland schoolyard bored him. Tuesday had brought an argument with Belle over Joe Strong, her latest love, a frighteningly handsome portrait artist. But how could Fanny disapprove of Joe—because he was passionate and impractical, like the man she herself had cheated with in France? What kind of mother was she, anyway?

On Wednesday she had packed ham sandwiches in a wicker basket and crossed the bay to meet Sam at his office on Kearny Street for lunch, something he had insisted she do once a week so that they could "grow closer." The trip waked her from the slumber of Oakland with its tree-lined streets running straight as hatpins and its neighbors who all looked the same. The salty breeze on the deck of the *El Capitan* ferry, the sight of a steamer chuffing in from Panama, and the swarming dock-boys at the embarcadero had quickened her pulse. And when the fog lifted, the sunlit houses pasted on the hills reminded her achingly of Paris—and Louis, who rose in her consciousness, day and night, no matter how hard she tried to suppress him.

They had lunched on a bench in Portsmouth Square while watching sailboats tacking in the bay. It seemed half the city knew Sam, handsome as a statue in his Van Dyke beard and blue suit. Lawyers in gray suits, sailors in cotton jerseys, Chinese vegetable sellers in straw hats, and saloonkeepers in aprons—all of them strolled over to tip their hats at Sam and "the pretty missus" sitting next to him.

Today was her day to Put Away Louis. It was her weekly ritual, handling the bits of him that she owned and then hiding them away: his red-and-green silk smoking cap; a hand-drawn map he had pressed in her hand that led to a weeping willow by the Loing River, where they had picnicked and made love; poems in his chaotic handwriting that he'd dropped by her plate at the dining table of the Inn Chevillon; a copy of his story, "The Suicide Club" on which he had scrawled "I adore you;" and a thought he had jotted after they'd argued, "To be in love is to be a pair of children, venturing together in a dark room."

Friday night came and went passably enough. Sam came home the tired breadwinner, tossing his bowler on the sofa, loosening his tie, and charming Lloyd with a little wood box that had secret compartments which he'd bought in Chinatown. He marveled over the stew which she knew as beef bourguignon, and, thankfully, soon went off to bed, apparently too tired to make love.

Saturday morning she left Sam at the breakfast table with his coffee and the *Oakland Tribune* to hike to the chicken ranch on 12th Street and buy a hen for dinner. When she got home she found him in the bedroom—and gasped. He had untied the tall art portfolio that she kept in the closet, propped it against the wall and was looking through her paintings, one by one: a peasant in a black cap working his way down a cobblestoned street with a heavy broom; the artists at their easels under white parasols in the garden; the stone archway and stairs that led up to the bedrooms at the inn in Grez...

"Why've you been hiding these, dear? They're good. Awfully darn good."

"Thanks, Sam."

"Here's an odd-looking boy."

She willed her heart to stop pounding. "Oh. That's Stevenson. One of them, anyway. There were two Stevensons there. Cousins. I told you about him."

"You did?" Sam pulled the sketch from the stack and set it alone against the wall, stepping back and folding his arms as if to admire it.

She wracked her brain, trying to remember what she had said about Louis. She felt herself blushing, and silently begged Sam not to turn around. The sketch itself was proof of her guilt: Louis, as he had looked that day by the river, smiling at her with knowledge so complete, in his soft eyes, that she might as well have added a caption, "My Lover in France." She had not so much drawn the sketch as caressed it into existence, and had made it so true that even now, maddeningly, she ached to be with Louis in the soft French sunlight again, or in a sudden downpour, or in a darkened bedroom anywhere.

"Sam, have you noticed how Lloyd isn't very happy to be back at the Lincoln Grammar School?" Usually, any problem of their son could be counted on to get Sam's full attention.

"Lloyd gave me quite an account of your friend."

"Oh?" She stooped to a throw-rug and hurried it to a window.

"Said you rode in his canoe and laughed. And that you sat with him by the fireplace and talked. For hours."

"A nice man. You know how entertaining the Scots can be." She thrust the rug out the window and banged imaginary dust from it.

When she turned back to the room, Sam was smiling oddly, his towering frame filling the space before her. "Strange how the nice man hasn't written."

She smoothed the rug on the hardwood floor, studying its jagged Eastern patterns.

"The mail's been full of letters from the other painters," Sam continued. "Bloomer and O'Meara and the rest. Not one from Stevenson, who writes for a living."

Sam strolled to the hutch and plucked a cigar from a silver canister. Fanny longed to just tell him the truth about Louis, now, and be done with it. He pushed the cigar into a desk-sized guillotine and cut off the end. "I wonder what's bothering Lloyd at school?"

She woke before dawn as she often did, with a hollow feeling and a sense of having lost her way to a destination she did not even know. Next to her Sam snored away like there was no tomorrow, on his back, arms flung wide.

As the dull light of dawn seeped through the window above the kitchen table she began another letter to Louis. She would not mail it; like the three others she had burned, it was just something she needed to do.

Dear Louis,
Come quickly to California, before I lose my sanity. Tell me that we are possible. Take me away, anywhere—

"What are you writing?"

Sam's voice from the doorway made her jump. "Just jotting some thoughts."

"Thoughts?"

"For a story to read at my writing class on Wednesday." Lying to him had become easier, but still gave her a sick feeling in the pit of her stomach.

Standing in his blue bathrobe, he stared down at her hands that she held over the letter as if shielding her naked flesh. "Bring it out on the boat and read it to me. I love a good story."

"Boat?"

"I was thinking it would be nice to go out on the water with my wife today."

He looked magnificent, rowing them away from the dock. Shoulders broadly framing a white shirt open at the collar, sleeves rolled above his strong wrists, smiling, his clear blue eyes watching her, the eyes that had been the envy of every girl in Fanny's high school in Indiana when she married him. He stroked in perfect rhythm, as he did every physical act, sweeping her past whitewashed boat shacks and the Oakland Bait Shop, then nosing them inland, following a long finger of the estuary along marshes toward murky eddies and thickets that grew in tangles along their banks.

An unsettling feature of a small rowboat, she realized, was how the rower and passenger were forced to face each other unless one of them turned, which Sam did only occasionally in order to steer the boat. His face was placid, unreadable, and she tried to assume a similar look as they continued in silence. Eventually they reached a wide pond that teemed with squawking ducks and buzzing insects, so deeply shaded by weeping willows that the water looked black. Letting the boat drift, Sam unscrewed the cap of a flask and took a long swig. He passed it to her but she shook her head. He took another swig.

"Let's go back, Sam."

He glanced around at their primordial surroundings and smiled. "If someone fell overboard out here and couldn't swim, it might be months before the body was found."

She stiffened, her hands involuntarily clenching the splintery bench while Sam took up the oars and continued rowing impassively, in rhythm. "Luckily, I can swim."

He leaned toward her until she could smell the whisky on his breath, lowering his voice to a whisper. "But how long could you stay above water?"

She'd had enough of his nonsense. "I stayed above water just fine in France without you, Sam," she said in a firm voice.

He released the oars and took another swig of whisky.

She snatched the flask from him and threw it far out in the water.

Sam laughed. "Read that story to me."

She glanced down at the writing pad in her handbag on the floor between her feet and shook her head.

He grabbed the pad and opened it.

She threw herself on him, tearing it out of his hands and flinging it into the pond while the boat rocked wildly, splashing them with water and almost capsizing.

They sat down, gasping, staring at each other in silence while the boat settled.

"I'm moving to Monterey," she said quietly.

"To do what?"

"Work on my painting. Jules Tavernier has moved there, and other artists from Europe."

"Is your Scotch boyfriend going to be there?"

"If you mean Louis Stevenson, he is six thousand miles away. And he's not my boyfriend."

"Then what do you call the chump you walked with and talked with and were so damn obvious with, that even our little son remarked on it?"

"What do you call the 'cleaning woman' who stayed overnights on Fridays while I was gone? Sam, you've cheated with other women since our honeymoon."

"They meant nothing. Nothing!" He clenched the oars, his knuckles white, and began moving the boat in what she hoped was the direction of home. "I work hard to provide everything you and the children need for a good, respectable life while you traipse off with your fancy friends and take up with some skinny boy!"

"He is not a skinny boy. He's a smart young man who is kind and caring."

Sam's rhythm broke down, the oars savagely slapping the water as he gritted his teeth, his face mottled with fury. "Caring! You call someone trying to break up a family caring? Have you taken leave of your senses?"

"Yes," she said softly. "Sam, I appreciate what you do for the children. I know you love them and... I'm sorry."

Suddenly he dropped the oars, slumped forward and propped his head between his knees. For a moment she thought he was sobbing, but when he turned his face up to her he was dry-eyed, his rage barely throttled. "I don't rightly care where you go. But I won't have my wife living like some whore while she raises my children. You want your freedom? Hell, I'll give you freedom! I'll file for divorce on the grounds of unfaithfulness. And I'll see to it that you get nothing. Certainly not my children. Don't you ever—*ever*—get it in your head that you'll get my children away from me."

Fanny bit her lip and stared out at the choppy water to avoid prolonging an argument she knew she could not win. He had played his trump card, the children. Although she could not imagine him caring for them by himself, if she wounded him further she had no doubt he would carry out his threat. In the eyes of law and tradition, she was a "fallen woman" and would receive worse treatment than Sam if a divorce proceeding became nasty.

In a stony silence, they returned to shore.

In the morning, when Sam came to the breakfast table dressed in a grey suit for his workweek, she set a cup of coffee in front of him. Cautiously she broached the subject again. "Sam. Nobody is trying to take your children from you, but we need some time apart. Monterey is a short train ride from here, and you could see us often enough. I could give the children a few months in a different town that they might enjoy."

His eyes narrowed in suspicion, but soon his expression turned bland. Taking a sip of coffee, he stood and gave her a thin smile. "Sure, dearest." Taking up his Gladstone he headed for the door.

Fanny stood under the trellised roses in front of the adobe she had rented, looking down Alvarado Street with growing annoyance. Belle had promised to be back an hour ago. Monterey's main thoroughfare looked like its usual sleepy self, paved in sand and lined by a mix of two-story Spanish adobes and low-slung clapboards with false fronts.

Men in bowlers waited for a stage under the porch of the Wells Fargo station, a saloonkeeper swept the boardwalk in front of his double doors, and a woman and two girls carried baskets from the General Merchandise Store.

Heading back in the house she heard a pounding of hooves and laughter, and turned to see Belle galloping up the middle of the street on her black pony, blue dress flapping, apparently oblivious to scattering chickens and staring men. What *really* annoyed Fanny was the sight of Joe Strong galloping next to her, one hand pressing a jaunty felt cap to his head as if he were some damn steeplechase champion.

The two reared to a stop in the wheeling fashion of the local vaqueros. Joe, sandy-haired, athletically built, dapper in a corduroy suit, swept off his cap, smiled what he must have imagined was his most charming smile and inclined his head. "Mrs. Osbourne. A pleasure."

"You were supposed to pose for me," Fanny snapped.

"That's why I'm here." In a flash of petticoats Belle swung off the pony and looped the reins around one of the Spanish cannons poking up from the sand along Alvarado Street that served as hitching-posts, although Fanny thought they looked like rusting penises. "Joe and I were riding," Belle continued, striding nonchalantly toward the front door. As if Fanny couldn't tell.

Joe, a portrait artist who now slouched in the saddle stroking his moustache, was one of Belle's more handsome beaus—just not marriage material. He seemed shiftless, earned a sporadic income, and judging by the greedy way his eyes followed Belle, his intentions were strictly carnal. Much to Fanny's surprise, as soon as Belle disappeared in the house Joe whipped an envelope from his coat and held it to her as if playing a trump-card. "I'm to place this in your hands only." He tipped his hat and rode off.

On the envelope she immediately recognized Louis's scrawl: "Mrs. Fanny Osbourne, Care of Joe Strong, Monterey, California, U.S." Joe had been at their artist colony in France, and Louis must have figured out how to use him as intermediary. Suddenly she felt giddy, but tried to hide her excitement as she walked inside.

Belle was waiting in the parlor. "What should I wear to pose? Mother, what's wrong?"

"Nothing."

"You want me to wear nothing?"

"What you're wearing is fine. Nothing is wrong." She led Belle up a wrought-iron stairwell to her studio, a high-ceilinged bedroom where the coastal sunlight spilled softly down from the windows onto their subjects. Usually these were still lifes: a bowl of roses, or some green peppers and a tomato picked from the garden. Today's subject would be a challenge, and not because of the usual difficulty of drawing any human form. The last time Fanny had sketched her daughter the girl had looked at the result and stormed from the room.

"How do you want me to pose?"

"You choose."

Belle turned sideways, thrust a rolled-up parasol over her shoulder and gazed out the window in a pose that Fanny thought was a bit melodramatic. It accentuated the bust line that, although covered by a blue dress buttoned to the neck, was still one of Belle's more notable features. A prominent bust was just one feature, along with a tiny waist, small stature and dark hair, that mirrored Fanny's features to such an extent that they were often mistaken for sisters.

"Hold still, honey." Itching to be alone and to read the letter that poked up from her handbag on the bed, Fanny hurried through the sketch, trying to capture the essence of Belle with dark scribbles and a few dashes in what could only be considered a gesture.

"Finished," she said after ten minutes.

"Already?"

"I'm not much in the mood for sketching today, I guess." Fanny took the sketchpad off the easel, closed it and set it on the bed, scooping up her handbag. "Actually, I have some business to attend." Under Belle's suspicious frown she crossed the cool tiles to the stairwell and hurried downstairs to her desk.

Tearing open the letter she saw Louis's familiar scrawl:

Dearest,

How is life at the edge of the known world? By now you must be established with the children and Big Sam and having a stupendous autumn or do they have such in California? I have a brilliant plan. Which is to make a lecture tour of the western United States, California in particular, topics to be determined. Should we chance to meet (insert laughter here) you can introduce me to friends as a Scottish academic you met in Europe.

What say you??!!!

Below the text was a childish sketch of a thin scholar in academic gown, monocle perched on his nose and the words "blah, blah, blah" spewing from his mouth toward a large audience that he had drawn as a sea of tiny circles.

For my sanity please write soonest and assure me of your existence. Vastly better send a telegram which is a small fortune at eight US dollars but if you value the ways of Boheme you understand that money means nothing. A comforting belief where my finances are concerned.

When my love is far from me
The undersigned feels all at sea
And all seems uncanny
When separate from Fanny.
Ever, RLS.

Belle's voice suddenly screeched from the bedroom, "You made me look like a streetwalker!"

Hearing Belle pounding down the stairs, Fanny turned the letter over on the desk, just before Belle burst into the room waving the sketch.

"You chose the pose, honey," Fanny gently tried, "with the parasol and, well, thrusting yourself forward."

"I did *not* thrust myself forward. You exaggerated the pose and made me look like a streetwalker! Why do you do this to me?" Belle headed for the front door but suddenly stopped. "What's that?" Another trait the two shared was an intuitive sense of when something was up—and Belle now stared directly at the overturned letter.

Fanny shrugged.

"Mother?"

"It's a letter from Louis. He's thinking about coming to California."

"And you want him to. You are thrilled," she said sarcastically. "No, not just thrilled. You are ecstatic."

"Belle, that is my business."

Belle's face reddened, tightening in an angry knot. "Not just your business. He's trying to get you away from my father. How can you possibly disapprove of Joe and me, when you sneak around behind Father's back to carry on with a man who's barely older than I am!"

"You are nineteen and he is twenty-nine. That's more than 'barely older.'"

"And you are almost forty," Belle spat back.

"That's enough."

"I know what it is—you're jealous! You'd like to be young and single too, but you're not!" Belle threw the sketch onto the floor, burst into tears and stormed out of the room.

Fanny retrieved the drawing and looked with a critical eye. She had to agree with Belle; it was a caricature of a top-heavy brunette who exuded sexuality but nothing else. How had her hands done such a thing? And how had her art degenerated so completely? It was as if, once she had given her love so completely to Louis, her powers of objective observation and artistic technique had evaporated.

She read Louis's letter again, and then sat motionless for an hour, a profound sadness coming over her as she knew what she must do. She reached for a pen and a page of her formal stationery, starkly white and bordered with sharp black edges.

> Dear Louis,
>
> If you value my life and yours, do not come. Find a good Scottish girl, one who is free to give you all that you deserve which is so much more than I could ever give you. I am sure there are many who would worship you! Know that I shall never forget you, but please do not attempt to contact me again.
>
> Love, F

She addressed an envelope. Numb to all sensation, her feet somehow found their way down the boardwalks of Alvarado Street to the little white U.S. Post Office where she dropped the envelope in the slot. On her way home her vision darkened as if a cloud enveloped her. She recognized that she was having one of her dangerous moods; the last one had come over her in France and had taken weeks to get out of, with the help of the mesmerist, Dr. Charcot. Idly, she wondered if death would come easier by hanging or cutting the wrists.

CHAPTER 4
Edinburgh—Winter, 1878

Dr. Balfour placed the cold brass cup on Louis's naked back and listened while the patient took deep breaths and gazed out the window of the bedroom in which he had grown up. The winter-bare tips of elms that reached up from the ground, three stories below, seemed to be straining to touch something of value in the bleak gray sky. The tall room with blue-patterned wallpaper was much too warm; as usual, the household servants had been too generous with the coal that smoldered behind the fireplace grate. Over the years Louis had grown bored with the little bald man in his black vest circling like a gnat, probing and sighing, always with the same findings and warnings. Finally the doctor gathered his stethoscope, tongue depressors and other instruments of torture. "I hear you've been on the go, Lou."

"Here and there."

"Your mother would be relieved if you'd stay put for awhile and start your law practice."

Louis thought of how ridiculous he had looked in the photograph taken a few years previous when he graduated law school, mugging in his barrister's robes and periwig, and how proud his mother had been of the frightening result. "I might take one more trip."

"It had better be to a high, dry climate. Perhaps to Davos —there's a fine spa there for consumptives."

"California is dry."

"California!"

"Yes. Getting across the American plains would make a fine travel essay."

"Louis." The doctor put his hands on both shoulders and looked into his eyes. "I say this not just as your doctor but as your Uncle Jack who cares for you. California might be dry, it might be beautiful, it might even be fascinating, if you could reach it. But given the shape your lungs are in, and the likelihood they'll bleed with any further provocation, I doubt you'd survive the journey."

Louis warily stepped into his parent's huge bedroom. Thomas Stevenson, waiting at a tea table, smiled and pulled out a leather-backed chair. "Lovely, isn't it?"

His father seemed to be gazing out the window at the same elms that Louis had seen from a slightly different angle from his own room. Despite the grim sky, Louis supposed the view had a certain beauty, the branches silhouetted against the tan stone walls of the stately homes opposite theirs, all of them with crisp, white trim. "Lovely, yes."

"Lovely, I mean, how we've been getting along since you've quit traipsing around the continent and come home."

Actually, Louis had been feeling intensely lonely, living with his parents, although relieved that they had given up arguing with him about religion or his choice of career.

"But I'm worried," Thomas Stevenson continued. "You've been so quiet. Brooding."

"Well..."

"Louis, I'm your father. If there's something wrong I'd like to know."

"All right then. I have fallen in love."

"Wonderful news! And high time you did, at least with someone worth telling your father about." Thomas Stevenson poked him playfully in the ribs. "Do I know the young lady?"

Louis shook his head.

"When will you bring her by? What's her name?"

"Mrs. Osbourne."

His father cocked his head as if he had not heard. "Is this one of your jokes?"

"No joke. I won't be bringing her by anytime soon because she lives in California with her husband and children."

A maid bustled in with a pot of tea and filled two cups while Thomas Stevenson looked like a pressure cooker about to explode. As soon as she left them, his father whirled on him. "I hope you've a good explanation for this."

"A simple one. I met a wonderful woman at Grez. She is gracious, artistic and beautiful. She laughs with me. I love her and I believe she loves me. She is already married. Unhappily."

Thomas seemed to be trying to control himself, sucking several deep breaths before asking, "Is it affection you have for this woman, or lust?"

"Quite a bit of both, sir."

His father suddenly stood and embraced him. "Son, we are all human. These things happen and I'm glad you've unburdened yourself. Fortunately, God forgives our mistakes, and by His example, I forgive you, too."

"Thank you." Louis knew that his father had meant every word. For as long as he could remember, his father had donated generously to homes for wayward women and other charities for the fallen of humanity, despite an inability to allow himself any lapses or waywardness.

His father pushed him to arm's length, his eyes moist, but narrowing. "Yes, Louis, I can excuse the indiscretion, the wayward impulse, but—having acted on the impulse, and having had time to consider what you've done and the harm such actions cause, *then* should you carry on with this woman, I cannot forgive. And I could never forgive a son who would torture his mother with worry and shame."

Louis soon realized that his two best friends had invited him to Hook's, their favorite tavern in Old Town, with an agenda in mind. W. E. "Teddy" Henley, the shaggy-bearded, tweed-coated, one-legged art critic who peddled Louis's essays to editors and other contacts in the literary world, set down his pint, licked foam from his moustache and got right to the point. "Afraid the word is out, Lou. How you're crucifying yourself with the American housewife."

"How I'm what!"

Charles Baxter, fair and clean-shaven in a corduroy coat, smaller in both size and volume than Henley, raised an eyebrow and smiled. "Those were your father's words."

Louis sighed. "So he asked the two of you to bully me."

Baxter took a sip of ale. "He puffed and blew about disowning you if you continue to carry on in this sin with an American. We all know your father tends to be heavy-handed, but in this case we agree with him. Lou, you have to break this thing off."

"I am leaving for California as soon as I am able."

Henley glowered. "Then how the hell can you complain about the morals of Robert Burns, hero of Scotland? To some people, that essay you wrote about his mistresses was a hanging offense, but people are buying the piece and I'm glad to have sold it for you. But if you carry on with a married woman, worse, an *American* one, as a man of letters you are finished. It's that simple."

"Nothing is that simple, Teddy, you know that."

They silently finished their ale, his friends looking like they drank at a wake.

CHAPTER 5
The Monterey Peninsula, California
August 1879

Looking out the railway car at an endless stretch of brown hills, Louis wondered if he had been talking to himself. Since leaving Salinas he had been mentally rehearsing what he would say to Fanny when he got to Monterey, and he might have gotten carried away. By the stares of the squirmy little girl in a yellow dress on the bench opposite him, he feared that he had not only been speaking aloud but also gesturing with his hands, a habit that others found disturbing. He winked and tipped his hat. The girl's mother, a stout woman in old-fashioned gray hoopskirts and a sunbonnet, put an arm around the girl and drew her closer.

Or perhaps they were just put off by his looks. He could explain that he had taken ill on the steamer to New York, been soaked to the bone for two days in New York while waiting for the train west, and developed an itchy skin-rash somewhere near Cleveland, but this might just frighten them further. When had he last eaten, was it yesterday or the day before? His appetite had left him sometime after changing trains in Chicago. By Ogden, Utah, he'd been so lightheaded that he could not write in his journal without becoming nauseated. Since then he had been trying to commit the strange sights and people he had encountered on the journey to memories that he could later put down on paper.

When he stretched his arms, he felt his linen shirt peel from the small of his back. He had read somewhere that Monterey was cooled by sea breezes but at the moment he was stifling. Perhaps the velvet jacket and wool tie had not been such a good idea, but the occasion of his reunion with Fanny, the one he had dreamed about for a solid year, demanded his best clothes. He shoved a window open and was blasted with smoke from the engine car, making him cough so hard that he could not lift his arm to close it. Another passenger hopped up, held one hand down on his bowler and slammed the window shut.

"Might we be nearing Monterey, sir?" Louis asked.

The car abruptly turned, tossing him to the right. In that direction he saw the hills fall away to a long, scimitar-shaped beach and the bluest bay he had ever seen. With a squeal of brakes the train slowed, chuffed along a ridge above the water, and eventually rumbled to a stop in a sea of sand. A brakeman threw open the doors. "End of the line!"

No city could be seen, just a few bleak buildings in the distance, and bumpy sand dunes with blue wildflowers clinging to them, all of it pounded by the sun above, which seemed even hotter now that the car had stopped. But passengers were smoothing skirts, gathering bags and heading for the door. He followed them outside where an assortment of hacks waited with their drivers behind tail-swishing nags. While he struggled to get his sea chest down from the luggage box the passengers began haggling with the drivers and climbing into buggies.

"Where you headed?" A driver in an open-necked shirt and brown suspenders frowned down from a one-horse buggy.

"I seek a woman in Monterey, a Mrs. Fanny Osbourne."

The driver held out his palm. "Two bits."

Louis was not sure he had heard. "Sir?"

"I'll git you there for a quarter."

When Louis produced the coin from his pocket, the driver helped heave the chest in the buggy. "What in tarnation you got in there, lead?"

"Bancroft's History of the United States, all ten volumes. My pleasure-reading. I'll admit, a bit heavy in the carrying as well as the reading."

The driver spit tobacco at his horse's flanks and snapped the reins. Within a half-mile they reached rickety docks jutting over the bay to their right and just before it an intersection of sorts, with a road turning inland. They took the turn, passed a tiny church and stopped at a plain, square building that stood alone in a weedy field. The driver motioned Louis with a jerk of his head to follow him down from the buggy and through the double doors of the structure's entrance, over which tall black letters proclaimed it the "Bohemia Saloon."

The smoky room was crowded with merchants in bowlers, fishermen in cotton jerseys and Mexican cowboys in sombreros, jabbering in several languages as they drank at a long redwood bar or played cards at small tables. The driver banged a spoon against a glass. "Anyone know the whereabouts of a Mrs. Fanny Osbourne?" he hollered over the din.

This set off side-discussions among the men as if they were playing a party-game to see who could answer first.

"Short woman with a couple of children?" one of the merchants eventually yelled back. "Has a tall husband who works in San Francisco?"

The driver forwarded the questions to Louis with a nod.

He felt his face flush. "That would be Mrs. Osbourne, yes."

The men now stared over their beer glasses with raised eyebrows and frowns. Were they friends of Sam? Perhaps they were staring at the red sores on his face from the rash he had caught in the railcar near Cleveland, when someone had thrown a filthy blanket over him during his chills and delirium. Or maybe they were just curious about his Scottish brogue and the foreign-looking cut of his blue velvet coat.

"The big adobe down Alvarado Street," the businessman said, "just back of the French Hotel. Has roses growing over the door."

The driver nudged Louis. "It would be civil to buy that man a drink. And one for me too, of course."

Louis stepped up to the bar. "Of course."

One hour and two whiskeys later, the driver was jouncing Louis down the sandy mud of Alvarado Street. They passed clapboard shanties, balconied adobes, and rusty Spanish cannon marking the street corners. Every chuck-hole the buggy hit made his head pound and his lungs ache. When he gasped for air, he started coughing and could not stop. The fog that had settled over Monterey, as thick as any fog he'd suffered in Edinburgh, didn't help matters. He fought a growing sense of panic; for the most important meeting of his life he had wanted to be in a healthy, confident state of mind.

Just beyond a ramshackle hotel, the driver reined in at a handsome, two-story adobe with trellised pink roses growing in profusion over the doorway. Louis climbed down from the wagon and walked up a flagstone pathway beneath the pungent flowers. Finally, after six thousand feverish, stomach-churning, bone-jarring miles he found himself at her door. He leaned against it to get his breath, willed his cough to be gone, his head to clear and his heart to stop racing. Then he knocked.

Fanny opened the door and gaped.

She was five feet of sheer beauty, although dressed a bit more matronly than when they had met in France, when like the other artists she had favored peasant blouses, scarves and berets. Now she wore a long, blue dress buttoned to the neck and trimmed with white lace, her dark hair pulled upward and pinned, with a few curls dangling over her small, perfect ears. The dark brown eyes smoldered with what he hoped was passion, although they might have been alarmed, too, darting up and down his face.

For a time, speech deserted him and all he could do was grin like an idiot. He took her in his arms, savoring her clean scent and the warm breath against his neck.

"Louis. Oh, Louis," she murmured. Eventually she pushed him to arm's length and frowned. "You don't look well."

"I'm just tired," he lied.

Ten-year-old Lloyd bounded in from a side room. "Mister Stevenson?"

Louis thrust out his hand. "Could this be Lloyd? You're a head taller than a year ago."

Lloyd gave a quick handshake and stepped back, gawking.

Her daughter whisked into the room in a clinging yellow dress. "Good God, what happened to your face?"

"Wonderful to see you, Belle. Just a rash I picked up, in Ohio I think."

"It's scaly like a lizard," Lloyd added.

Fanny took Louis by the hand and tugged him toward the sofa. "Sit down, Lou. I'll bring some salve."

This was not going the way he had dreamed. "I didn't come all this way for salve."

"But that's what you need." She jerked her head to remind him of her staring children.

Ten minutes later she was walking him out the door, his face a blotched mess of white lotion. She shut it behind them. At last they were alone beneath the roses. It was a fitting enough setting to do what he had come so far to do. Perhaps it wasn't the best time, but he'd never been one to endlessly ponder when it came to matters of the heart.

Louis dropped to one knee and tried to give his boldest smile despite the pull of the face-lotion. "Fanny, will you marry me?"

She looked confused by the question, perhaps even frightened, opening her mouth several times as if to speak while he wobbled on her flagstone porch.

The door banged open. Lloyd stood in the doorway, watching them.

"Mister Stevenson slipped, go inside dear, everything is fine." Fanny pulled the door shut while Louis lurched to his feet. When she helped him up, her eyes glistened. "I am already married, Louis."

"Of course you are married, but that can be changed. I know divorce will be difficult for you and the children but things will go wonderfully for us, I know this, I feel it in my heart, I vow it, please Fanny, don't lose courage now!"

"Is everything all right, Mrs. Osbourne?" A grey-haired woman in a black shawl frowned down at them from an upstairs patio of the next-door adobe.

Fanny leaned close to him with tears on her cheeks and breathed, "Please go."

He quelled an urge to shout at her. Go where? Imagining a dozen protests he could make, but too sick and discouraged to raise them, he turned and stumbled off down the barren street.

He woke on a bed of dirt, disoriented and coughing. He had hiked all of the previous day, getting the hell out of Monterey, following the stage road south to the Carmel River and then turning inland, away from the ruins of the stone mission and its weedy graveyard, stumbling up a long valley lined by ancient redwoods. Having eaten nothing for two days he had no appetite and no aim except to escape the fog. He vaguely recalled taking a trail up a mountainside, crashing through thickets and a canopy of twisted live-oak and emerging on a plain. There, he had seen a beautiful sunset—and collapsed.

Now in the dawn he saw that he'd reached a humpback ridge of primordial beauty, carpeted with sunburned grass, studded with scruffy pines and twisting madrones. He had no idea where he was, but reveled in the warmth of the sun on his back while, far below him, the long green slash of the valley disappeared to the west under a murderous fog.

Although his throat begged for water, from his knapsack he took a pen and bottle of ink. He would leave a letter for Fanny and one for his parents. Perhaps he would scribble a cartoon of him sitting on a mountaintop in California, laughing down at the fog. Or barking like a dog; what did it matter? He pushed away regrets, telling himself that he would rather leave the earth in this pretty place than slowly smother under blankets of fog, sickbeds and doting parents. It took all of his strength to twist open the bottle. The irony of it: having found the sun he was now burning up. He opened his notebook to an empty page but his vision blurred, and then turned to black.

The next hours or days he spent on his back, asleep or in delirium. He dreamed that he was very young, had run away from home and boarded a ship as cabin boy. The crew had turned out to be mutinous pirates; now, their chief and his mate were advancing on him, the mate aiming a musket at him. He thought it odd that pirates roamed the soft hills above the Carmel Valley, but in dreams, anything could happen, and surely this was a dream, wasn't it?

"Halloo! You up there! Stand up slow, whoever y' are," the chief yelled. Intriguing, how the man spoke more like an American than a pirate. Louis reminded himself to get this dream written in his journal. The two men got close enough so that their hats looked more like the floppy felt hats worn by California settlers than the three-cornered hats of pirates. As dreams went this was not a bad one, more of an adventure really, except that the pirate and his mate were now upon him.

"Looks like he ain't doing so good," the mate said, setting down what Louis now saw was a big Sharps rifle and looking him up and down. "Foreign, that's sure."

"Ain't no poacher, that's sure, too," the captain said, "being as he's up here without a gun."

"Can you talk, fella?"

Louis tried to say his name and assure them that he meant no harm, but could not make a sound.

The captain, tall with a white beard, Methuselah in denims and a plaid flannel shirt, stooped and felt for a pulse in his neck. "We'd best get him to the house." The man slid his arm under Louis's back and lifted. "Sack of sticks is all he is. Good Jesus, the man's starving."

The other man, younger, stocky and similarly dressed, picked up Louis's knapsack and peeked inside.

"No," Louis gasped.

"Just tryin' to help you. Can you walk?" They got on both sides of him and half-carried him across a tiny bridge, through a herd of goats with tinkling neck-bells and down a path toward a small cabin.

"We raise goats," the older one said, somewhat redundantly, Louis thought, which was his last thought before losing consciousness.

He woke in a girl's bedroom, judging by dolls propped in the windowsill and a pink laced quilt on the little bed he lay on. The rough beams above him and the knotty pine walls looked vastly different from the muted wallpaper, crown molding and high ceiling of his bedroom in Edinburgh, yet he took comfort from the innocent surroundings.

Two girls in gingham dresses stared from the doorway, probably sisters, both with blue eyes and straw-colored, home-cut hair. "Who are you, Mister?" asked the oldest one, who looked to be about ten years old.

"What's the matter with you?" the younger one added.

"Much," he mumbled, although it came out "mush" and drew frowns from the girls. "Love," he blurted, and then realized that he was not in his right mind and should not try to expound. In any case he was wracked with coughing and the girls ran from the room.

In the morning, Louis heard the clinking of tin cups as the ranchers seemed to be drinking coffee just outside his door. "I don't like going through someone's things," he heard one say.

"The man's dying," the old rancher answered. "Maybe we can get his kin up here, if we can find out who they are."

Louis heard his belongings—penknife, fountain pen, tobacco tin, journals and books—clatter onto a table but could not summon the strength to call out in protest. "You take the notebook while I look at the letters," the old man continued.

The men then seemed to be reading silently, or almost silently. "You have to do that?" the younger one asked.

"What?"

"Make that noise."

"What noise?"

"The mumbling."

"Only way I can read."

Louis drifted off, not particularly caring if he ever waked. He dreamed he was drowning in heavy surf just off a beach in Scotland. On dry land just ahead of him his father strolled with hands thrust in his waistcoat pockets, examining the foundation of one of his lighthouses. Louis tried to call out, but coughed instead. Something heavy was pressing down on his lungs. Breathing was impossible, so he tried to relax and let death take him quickly.

He woke to the clinking of goat-bells—and something sticky. His shirtless chest was coated with a dark oozing substance. The two sisters stared down at him. "Goose grease and moss. It cures everything, leastways that's what Pa says." The older girl poured a glass of water from a steel pitcher, set it on a nightstand and backed away. Lanky and with freckled cheeks, she would become a pretty woman, Louis decided, and an interesting one; the clear, matter-of-fact blue eyes reminded him of Fanny's eyes even though hers were brown.

"He says you're writing a dairy."

"A diary."

"What's that?"

"Something to help me remember my adventures. You will be in it."

Her eyes widened. "What's your name, Mister?"

"Louis, and yours?"

"Sarah Wright."

"I'm Dolly," her sister said, "and I know you're right sick, Mister Louis, but you've had my bed for three days." About eight years old, Dolly's face was rounder, her eyes smaller and perhaps more skeptical than those of her sister.

"'Twas not by choice, I assure you." Louis struggled up and reached for his linen shirt that hung on a bedpost, but his vision blurred and he lay backward on the bed. He floated to a different place... a frothy, warm surf. The two girls, smiling with what seemed a wisdom beyond their years, splashed into the water from a sunny beach in their long gingham dresses. Reaching him they took each hand in their little ones and walked him out to the firm sand.

When he woke they were in the doorway of the knotty-pine bedroom.

"You talk funny," Sarah said.

"Because I was at sea too long, working as a cabin-boy on a fine sailing vessel."

"Is that how you got sick?" Dolly asked.

"He said it was love," Sarah corrected.

Dolly put a hand on her hip. "If you were working on a boat, how'd you end up on a goat ranch?"

"Pirates."

"What?"

"They boarded us near the Cape, but alas, our powder was wet and we were overrun. They bound my hands and made me walk the plank, but I took a big breath, and floated, and washed up at the docks of Monterey." He pulled his shirt on, leaving the front open because of the goose-grease, and reached with a shaking hand for the glass of water.

Sarah turned to her sister. "Let's bring him something to eat."

Over a feast of buttered bread which the girls had cut in little squares, he resumed his tale of the pirates, taking it in impossible directions, pausing for the girls to bring lemonade and chairs that they placed at the foot of the bed. He learned that the older man, Anson Smith, owned the ranch. The girls' father, Jonathan Wright, worked for him while their mother was recuperating from an illness in Monterey.

After the ranchers clomped in from their day's work, poked their heads in the doorway and made brief introductions, Louis said, "You went through my things."

"To see if we could locate your kin."

"Then you know that my kin are six thousand miles away."

Smith cleared his throat and gave a wry smile. "Maybe so, but there's your friend who signs her letters 'F.' Maybe she could come up."

"I suspect you already know why that will not happen."

Wright frowned. "We patched you up and we'll feed you, it's the Christian thing to do. In the morning we'll hitch a team and get you to Monterey." He turned to leave.

Louis doubted that he could survive the foggy town, and more importantly, did not want Fanny to see him pale and sick again. "Your girls can't read."

"What?"

"We argued a point about pirates, so I opened a book on the subject to settle the matter, and showed them a sentence..."

Wright stared down at his feet. "There ain't many schools up this way."

"I've another solution."

Next morning, Louis began giving reading lessons to his small but lively class. In the afternoon, feeling strangely invigorated, he dug out his journals and began fleshing them out, adding observations and smoothing transitions. Comforted by the yellow glow of a gas lamp and the croaking of bullfrogs outside his window he worked late into the night, eventually dividing his journals into two sections. The one he had kept about the endless, stinking, below-decks voyage over the Atlantic he titled, "The Amateur Emigrant." The pages following it, its words jagged and frequently blotted with spilled ink, recounting his miserable, jouncing, fascinating ride by overland train he titled, "Across the Plains."

Two weeks of identical days were capped by meals of venison stew and corn bread. After the girls went to bed the men would retire to the porch, where Anson Smith would solemnly pour tin cups of whiskey and they would smoke while the sun sank below the hills. Smith told stories of marching with Fremont and chasing the army of Mexico all the way to Los Angeles. He told of a hanging in Salinas, and of being charged by a ten-foot grizzly.

Louis told of blood-feuds between the clans that perched in castles on every Highland crag, of men in kilts who fought to the death against the British at Culloden, and of pirates and shipwrecks, exaggerated nonsense that seemed to please the ranchers as much as their stories did him.

"How did love make you sick?" Sarah Wright asked one warm morning. She had finished reading several lines, haltingly, from *The Lady of the Lake* while flies buzzed in through the open window above the knotty pine table they used for their lessons.

"I love a beautiful woman but she is already taken."

Sarah pondered this while her younger sister dashed around with a straw broom, swatting at the flies. "Does she love you?"

Louis nodded.

"Then you better go try to win her, like those men in the poem tried to win Ellen."

Louis resisted an urge to throw his arms around the little sage and kiss her.

Cleaning up for the ride down to Monterey, in the mirror above the steel water basin he saw that color had returned to his cheeks. He had just enough time to start a letter to Ed Gosse in London:

> *I do not know if I am the same man I was in Europe. My head went round and looks another way now, for when I found myself over here in a new land, and all the past uprooted with one tug, and I neither glad nor sorry, I got my last lesson about mankind—*

"You ready in there?" Smith's voice hollered from outside the bedroom.

They drove him to Monterey in a buckboard wagon, stopping at the Bohemia Saloon to raise toasts, first to health, then to Scotland, and finally to Wright's daughters—who could now read not just verses from Walter Scott's volume that Louis left for them but from the King James Bible, the only reading material Louis had found at the ranch.

From the saloon Louis walked up and down the dusty streets on a blessedly fogless day, searching high and low for Fanny Osbourne. Everyone seemed to have seen the short, buxom woman who carried an easel and always wore fine starched dresses, but nobody had seen her today. He yelled up at the Mexican workers perched high on scaffolds who were whitewashing the Washington Hotel. He questioned two men in U.S. Navy uniforms who were patrolling the pier. He even asked women sweeping steps of stick-houses at the Chinese fishing village, describing Fanny's features with gestures and getting shrieks of laughter in return. Finally, just when the setting sun was turning the bay bright orange, a stage driver arriving from Santa Cruz said he'd seen a small woman carrying an easel down the beach toward Point Piños.

He found her standing before an easel on a windswept knoll, dressed in a flowing black skirt, white laced blouse and broad blue hat that flapped in the stiff onshore breeze. She had bound the hat to her head with a red scarf, knotting it under her small chin. In this getup she stared out at the lighthouse on Point Piños, dabbing brush to canvas as if this was something that every well-dressed woman on a beach in the middle of nowhere would do.

Louis came up behind her. "You've made an excellent big penis."

She turned to him. "A small lighthouse. You don't like it, I can tell."

He leaned to kiss her.

She threw down her brush, put her small, gloved hands on his shoulders and shoved him backwards. "Where on earth have you been?"

"A goat ranch."

"I didn't know if you'd taken off for Scotland, sank in a storm or had your throat slit. Can you get it in your skinny head that I worry about you? Not a word from you. Not one word!"

"I was being held against my will by a bear hunter."

"Don't fib. I'm tired of your fibs."

"Very well then, I was sick."

"You were sick when you got here."

"Well, after a hike I got sicker. Couldn't move for a time."

"Louis, this has got to stop. The wandering, I mean." She slumped into him and began to sob. He held her close, savoring the sound of the surf hissing against the sand and the feeling of her in his arms, mystified, as always, by her turns and moods.

That night in the cheap room he had rented in a ramshackle boarding house he dreamed of Scotland. The lighthouse of Skerryvore loomed before him, with huge waves rising from a stormy sea and crashing against the rocks at its base. High up in the tender's coop a bright candle flame moved back and forth behind the panes of glass. In the manner peculiar to dreams, Louis could see the man clearly through the storm, his father, pacing and staring accusingly down at him. The sea rose higher, swamping the base of the lighthouse. His father gave him a cruel grin before turning to face a massive wave that engulfed him and swept over Louis as well.

Louis smelled something sublimely feminine.

From where he lay on the floor he woke to see her sitting on his bed, fully clothed, reading his notebook by the light of a kerosene lamp. "How long have you been here?"

"It took some time to learn where you were staying. I had to ask around. Now people will be talking." She sighed and her eyes glanced around at the bare adobe walls. "Not even a desk to write on. And why do you sleep down there?"

He got up and sat next to her on the mattress wearing only the long undershirt he always slept in. "I write in the bed, and take my rest on the floor."

"Which of us is the more insane?" Tears welled in her eyes as she pressed against him.

He put an arm around her and kissed her neck. "I prefer you to sanity."

She pushed away from him. "Go back to Scotland, Louis."

"Not without you," he said tenderly, kissing a tear on her cheek. "I am here till we are one, with no restrictions, and to hell with anyone else."

"You're here for the impossible, then," she said between sobs.

He reached behind her neck and fumbled with the hooks of her dress.

"No, Louis."

He kissed her soft lips. He thrilled when her resistance melted, her mouth parted and her tongue touched his. Soon their breathing was ragged. She reached behind her neck and made quick work of the hooks. He pushed the dress off her shoulders. She stood and kicked off her dress, peeled down her garters and stockings until all five feet of her stood deliciously naked.

He pulled off his shirt and held her, feeling her curves against his skin and her tears on his neck. "Sam is coming tomorrow, on the afternoon train," she whispered, pulling him onto the bare mattress. Her soft brown eyes were inches from his, reflections, openings to her soul. Urgently they kissed again. He stroked her smooth, soft skin everywhere, no stopping, getting moans and wonderful caresses from her in return as he smelled her sweet hot shallow breathing, and they became one...

Fanny knew that she had lapsed back into madness when she agreed to go downstairs with him for breakfast in the sitting room. Her dress of the day before had been only slightly rumpled in their hurry to get it off and by its spending the night on Louis's floor. Louis looked like a vagrant, nothing new for him, in his faded black beret and wrinkled velvet coat that on the goat ranch had developed a gaping hole at one elbow. Nonetheless they sipped tea like any long-married couple, sitting by a window that allowed in the dull light of a foggy day and looked out on a garden of scrawny roses.

It pained her to see him so thin. "Let me buy you eggs."

Louis shook his head.

"You can't live on tea and toast. You'll get sick again."

"I can live on twenty-five cents a day."

"Look at you. You ask me to divorce my husband—"

"—A baboon!"

"You're starving and sick and can't even support yourself. How would you support a wife? How would you feed her children?"

He tapped the notebook on the table and grinned.

"People won't pay to read about getting seasick on a steamer," she said. "They won't pay to read about your train ride through Nebraska."

He shrugged. "I wrote those stories while delirious at a goat ranch."

"When will you get serious?"

"Never. Which is why you must marry me."

Should she explain the full extent of her madness—the visions, fits, and blackness that struck at random times and without warning? "Even if I wanted to divorce my husband, marry someone with no future and toss my children into certain poverty, there's this." She tapped her forehead.

"Do you think I care about a few strands of gray?" He kissed the spot.

"Not the gray hair, dammit. I mean, you don't want to marry someone with brain fever."

"Oh that."

"Yes, that."

"I thought you left it behind, in France."

"I don't leave things behind as easily as you do." She looked out the window to the garden where a swarthy Miwok laborer, naked to the waist, bent forward with a rope over his shoulder, dragging a bundle of firewood behind him.

It happened: faintness, nausea, tightness in her chest making it hard to breathe, her heart racing as unbidden memories flooded her consciousness....

CHAPTER 6
Paris—1876

Fanny stared at a naked man, oddly posed, leaning forward with a rope held over his shoulder as if dragging something. She was forced to crane her neck this way and that to see around the other students in tight-waisted dresses and their easels in the narrow studio lit by winter sun falling from high windows. As Monsieur Julien's academy was the only one that admitted women, it was crowded every day. If she wanted a better seat she would have to start getting the children up earlier, especially Belle, who took twice as long to get ready as she did, yet at seventeen was agile enough to jostle her way into a spot in front.

Fanny took another look at the model, drew two oblong haunches and then scribbled dark thatch between them. She had overdone the body hair, which gave her the giggles that she squelched when their instructor in a flat back hat, Monsieur Julien, began plodding among the easels to review their work. He stopped behind two Swedish sisters, frowning even though everyone knew the crop-haired blondes were the most talented. Next he stood behind Belle, staring over her shoulders at her easel. Fanny allowed a moment of motherly pride at the stylish way the white laces fastened down the back of the tight gray dress; she had sewn it.

Julien jabbed his forefinger on Belle's drawing. "And what is this, Mademoiselle?" he asked in strongly accented English.

"A moustache, Monsieur Julien."

"You have drawn curls on the tips. Look at him; at this distance the moustache is only a shadow. When you draw something your eyes do not see, you are lying!"

Belle's neck turned red, and Fanny knew there would be tears. She longed to take the girl in her arms and tell her it was all right, but it was time Belle toughened up. Good grief, at Belle's age Fanny was married and on her way to Apache country to raise children while her husband poked in the hills for gold.

In the afternoon, after they had tucked their sketchpads under their arms and boarded a jammed omnibus pulled by two brown nags for the ride up Montmartre, Belle was laughing again, especially when Fanny quipped that the naked models always seemed to be the ugliest. When the horses slowed and made the final ascent past spindly houses and wintry elms, Belle said wistfully, "I wanted to make one thing on him beautiful."

Fanny pulled on a rope to ring the bell for their stop. "A curl on the moustache, what a nice thought."

When they got to the steps of their little apartment on the Rue du Naples, Fanny was disappointed that Hervey, her four-year-old, was not standing as usual with his nose pressed against the window waiting for her. Although she was always tired, with an aching back after hours bent over her easel, nothing lifted her spirits better than the boy's excitement at seeing her. She opened the door. "Hervey?"

"Hullo, Mama," he said from his bed next to the wall.

"Were you sleeping?"

Kate, a stocky young American who watched Hervey during the day, stepped in from the kitchen. "He's been under the weather."

Fanny sat on Hervey's bed and felt his brow. Clammy, but thankfully no fever. Hervey was her most beautiful child, she thought as she regarded his wispy face, blond curls and the big blue eyes looking up at her. She kissed his forehead. "Are you hungry?"

"A little."

"Lloyd is buying bread from the man on the corner," Kate said. "I had to give him the last coins you left in the cup."

Fanny nodded, trying to look matter-of-fact. Kate should have been paid for the week's babysitting yesterday.

Lloyd bounded in with the loaf of black bread and dropped his wool coat on a chair. "The hook, Lloyd." He flung the coat onto its peg. Only eight, he already looked like a young man in his black beret and trousers, his school uniform. "How was school?"

He shrugged.

"That doesn't tell me much." Fanny took the bread to the cutting board and reached in a drawer for a knife.

"A boy from Cleveland said he's going to punch me. I'm supposed to give you this." He dug a piece of paper out of his trousers and handed it to her.

A bill for his tuition, stamped in red as overdue.

The truth enforced in Monsieur Julien's studio by day was purer than the truths Fanny wrestled with at night. After a supper of leftover chicken and the bread, she read a story to Hervey while Lloyd and Belle washed dishes. Finally, while Belle sat at the dresser in a flowered nightgown pinning curls in her hair and Lloyd studied a sheet of French vocabulary, it was time for Fanny to write letters home.

In this art she was the world's biggest liar.

"Dear Sam," she wrote, already lying. She dunked her pen in a well and pulled up its brass lever. She wondered what she could say that would be more significant than the news she had received about him: Mrs. McGrew, their next door neighbor in Oakland, had written that Sam had moved a blonde into the home, saying she was "the housekeeper."

"The children are fine," she continued. Not a big lie, but Hervey had been barely able to keep his eyes open during story-time, and now she heard him cough from his bed near the wall. She would send Belle alone to the studio tomorrow while she found a doctor.

"They miss you," she wrote. Finally, a simple statement of truth. She knew, too, that Sam missed them. He was a doting, indulgent father, always with a big smile for them, whose broad shoulders looked like they could bear any burden and protect against any threat. Every child deserved such a father, she supposed, or at least the idea of one. And the fact was, Sam paid the bills; his check would arrive in the next day or two, enough to pay for another month's rent, their simple meals and tuition. She supposed that Sam was fine with this arrangement; he could have his blondes, she could study art in Paris, and he could remain Papa...

...She had dozed off on the couch that, in the past month, had become Hervey's sickbed and her constant perch. His hoarse whisper, "Mama," jerked her awake. She leaned to the thin, pale boy whose blonde curls hung limp on his forehead and kissed his cheek, trying not to flinch at the swollen, draining sores on his neck.

"How is he?" Lloyd had come in from school and stood helplessly behind her.

"I'll fetch Doctor Simone," Fanny said.

"But Mrs. Osbourne," Kate said, "it's getting dark. Are you sure that—"

"Feed the children," she yelled on her way out the door.

Two long hours later, the heavy, thick-browed man opened his doctor's bag and began prodding the boy's chest and neck. Fanny appreciated the man's gentle touch and what seemed a genuine concern for the American boy whom he had already seen three times.

"Unfortunately, Madame, the glands in the neck have become badly inflamed. This gives the boy difficulty in breathing as his body tries to fight the fever. I shall leave a medicine to calm him, which may improve his breathing but at the further expense of his energy."

"You will return tomorrow?"

"I shall try, Madame," he said tiredly. "My patients are many."

She knew that Doctor Simone had already rendered more service than she could pay him for. "You must, Sir. You simply must."

When Lloyd and Belle had gone to bed, Fanny broke down and wept. She had been deluding herself in thinking that any day Hervey would get better. He was dying. She would fight for him until the end, but she knew it would come soon. He was too sick to get back to California; she had marooned him. All she could do was to send the children off to spend each day at school while she kept Hervey as comfortable as possible. She might keep a semblance of the normal life she had wrenched from them when she had packed them off for this self-indulgent escapade.

Two hours later, Hervey's soft crying waked her. "Blood, Mama," he whimpered.

Thus began horrors that soon increased in frequency: at random hours of day or night, membranes in Hervey's throat, nose, or ear would rupture, followed by convulsions in which the boy thrashed and kicked.

"Lie down with me," he would say after she had staunched the blood and he had calmed. When she did so, Hervey would rest his chin on her chest and immediately plunge into exhausted sleep.

She dashed off a telegram to Sam: "Impossible to move Hervey. Come at any price. Come quickly."

Fanny was not sure when Sam would arrive, but she knew that he would move hell and earth to get to his son. He was manly and sentimental where his children were concerned, traits that other women, maddeningly, seemed to find seductive. And, he was a frontiersman who rose to physical challenges.

Yes, he would come, but would it be soon enough to see Hervey alive? She had given him an entire bottle of quinine, a tablespoon at a time, to no effect. For days she painted his chest with a hideous brown substance that the doctor prescribed. The chemicals in it were so strong, she wrote one night to a California friend, "that everyone in the room is almost blinded by it." Still, Hervey weakened and the bleeding spells became more frequent.

During the doctor's next session of poking and prodding her listless son, Fanny hovered over the couch, desperate for encouraging signs. At length he gathered his tools, walked to the table and wrote a prescription. "Take this to Monsieur Belshé, the butcher."

"Did you say butcher?"

"The boy must drink a half-cup of fresh ox blood for a week. Then we shall see."

Fanny sat on the couch and stared at her open palms, for a time wondering if she was actually present with a French doctor mumbling bizarre plans for her dying son, or was she dreaming?

"I can barely get him to swallow water," her voice said.

"It is his only chance, Madame, and a poor one at that."

For a week, she brought home jars of blood and somehow got them down Hervey's throat. The thick smell of the ox blood hung in the cramped air of the apartment and mingled with the odors of infection and decay. Lloyd and Belle pinched their noses, and in their bedrooms quietly wept.

Sam's cable arrived from Liverpool: "I leave tonight via Dieppe. Reach Paris noon tomorrow. Telegraph about Hervey."

She dashed off a reply and gave it to the waiting telegram-boy: "Still living."

When Sam arrived on the apartment doorstep, his face haggard and his blue suit rumpled and dusty, she embraced him, for the first time in years grateful for his strength and military posture. When she led him inside, she saw him stiffen, most likely from the rank odor, and when they reached the couch he looked down and muttered, "My God."

Hervey's eyes opened and slowly seemed to focus. "Papa," he whispered.

"I'm here now, son." Sam knelt by the couch.

"Stay."

"Not going anywhere."

But after the first day, Sam the war veteran could not stomach Hervey's bleeding and thrashing spells, even though they had become feeble and shorter than the ones Fanny had lived through. While she kept vigil on the couch she heard the rhythmic clang, clang, clang of Sam's pacing on the wrought-iron landing while he smoked cigars, occasionally coming inside to stare with frightened eyes before retreating to the door.

"Sing to me," Hervey suddenly gasped during one of Sam's visits inside.

Sam had a strong baritone voice that he trotted out after brandy at social gatherings, but at the moment he looked lost. "What should I sing?"

"Anything," Fanny whispered.

"Mine eyes have seen the glory of the coming of the Lord," he began.

Hervey stared upward while Fanny gripped his small hand and Sam faltered through the rest of "The Battle Hymn of the Republic."

A late-season snow fell on the family while they hunched in dark coats and hats and followed Hervey's small white coffin to an open grave in the Saint-Germain cemetery. Sam had paid for a plot that could be leased for ten years; after that, he would have to come and claim the remains or pay more money. The thought of her son lying in this place far from home was more than she could bear, and she took flight; one moment she was standing with Sam and the children, each dropping a shovel of wet dirt down the hole onto Hervey's hideous box, and then she was back in the apartment, curled up in bed. It was as if someone had moved a switch and shut her down.

Miss Kate brought in bowls of soup that she did not touch. Sam appeared at her bedside, staring down with sorry eyes as if she were a sick pet. Lloyd and Belle with frightened eyes said bedtime prayers and kissed her goodnight. Once she clutched their hands in a death grip, not letting them leave her for an hour. She came to believe that her brain was swelling inside her skull, throbbing and pounding in an attempt to be free.

One morning, Sam tugged her upright. "Life goes on."

"I have brain fever."

"You what?"

She turned and stared at the wall until he left the room.

Later she rose, carefully made the bed and dressed. She found Sam on a wicker chair in the living room, paging through her sketchbook of naked men and bowls of fruit. She took it from him and folded it under her arm.

"Are you ready to quit this nonsense and come home?" he asked.

"There is no home."

"Your California home."

"Lloyd is pale. Don't you think Lloyd looks pale? The trip would kill him." She returned to bed, pulling the covers up on the black dress, black gloves and black cap of mourning that she wore.

Next morning Dr. Simone showed up at her bedside with his black bag of tricks. While Sam hovered, the doctor put a stethoscope on her chest, opened her mouth and pressed a stick on her tongue.

"Well?" Sam asked.

"Mrs. Osbourne is in the shock of deep grief. It is understandable."

"What about this 'brain fever'?"

"There is no such malady."

"You, sir, are a quack," Fanny said.

Dr. Simone took a notepad and pencil from his pocket. She watched his thick bushy brow tense as he scribbled, and then handed the note to Sam.

In the morning, Fanny felt nothing as the cab drove her along the River Seine where women strolled with parasols and men walked their dogs and children ran in the spring sun. She had not brushed her hair, and had fought off Miss Kate's efforts to change the dress she had slept in, barely allowing the woman to smooth out her rumpled dress. Sam had gotten Lloyd to help carry her down the stairs and into the waiting cab. She had seen Lloyd's eyes, terrified, when the driver snapped his whip and the horse sped her away from where he stood on the curb.

Sam sat opposite her and smoked, thinking God knows what. She stared past his face and out the window, feeling as if she were an insect looking out from a shell that was shaped like a woman. The cab turned onto a cobblestone lane and drove between rows of blossoming cherry trees toward the yawning gates of the Salpêtrière, a sprawling complex of squat buildings made of tan, massive stone. On one building a gray dome capped by a little clock-tower reminded her vaguely of a medieval cap she had seen in a museum with a tightening-screw on top that could be turned to torture the wearer and extract secrets.

The cab lurched to a stop outside the double doors of one of the buildings. Sam clenched and opened his fists and finally said, "Well."

He backed out the door, grasped her forearms and pulled until she stumbled out onto the cobblestone. "It's for your own good."

With a hand firmly on her elbow he guided her down a concrete path to the hospital doors.

"Salpêtrière. Funny name for a hospital. Know what it means?" Sam asked, tugging her down the whitewashed hallway of the ancient building.

Of course Fanny knew what it meant—saltpeter was the main ingredient of gunpowder—but she said nothing. Sam looked through an open doorway that they passed, then hurried her along. She had just enough time to glimpse, in a side room bathed in sunlight from tall windows, an old man suspended from ropes that were fixed to a harness under his shoulders. Approaching another doorway her eyes were stung by a strong-smelling chemical of some kind. She dragged her feet at that doorway, scuffing the toe of one black shoe to slow Sam's pulling and get a good look at a laboratory of some kind. In it, young men in aprons peered at jars of what seemed to be body parts and solemnly jotted notes.

An aide showed them to a chamber to wait for Doctor Charcot. In the yellow glow of a kerosene lamp swinging from a chain, she saw that the room contained only a cot and a wooden chair. Sam sat on the chair and waved her toward the cot, smiling pleasantly.

She backed into a corner instead, running her knuckles against the stone wall behind her. Sam softly whistled what sounded like "Camptown Ladies" and tapped his foot on the tile floor. Doo-dah, doo-dah indeed. She tasted blood. It occurred to her that she'd been chewing the inside of her cheek.

A short middle-aged man in a doctor's smock with slick black hair stepped into the room followed by a young man, most likely a student with a notebook. Sam hopped to his feet. "You must be Dr. Charcot."

The doctor gave Sam a brief nod before turning to Fanny and staring into her eyes for several silent moments. He leaned so close she could feel his breathing, which was measured and calm. She found his dark eyes probing, curious, intelligent. He reminded her of portraits she'd seen of Napoleon. Oddly, she felt comforted by this man of science who seemed to be regarding her with keen interest yet with no personal or moral judgment. She also felt an immediate sense of the man's commanding presence. When he placed his hands on her shoulders, she felt a pulse of energy as if a spark of electricity had passed from the steady hands. At his gentle push, she sat meekly down on the cot. Finding the spell he seemed to have over her disconcerting, she looked down at her hands, giving her full concentration to the act of pulling off her gloves.

"Thank you, Madame," said the doctor. "Please lie on your back."

She did so, again transfixed by the dark eyes that peered at her face, neck and bodice while he pressed here and there. The student hoisted the lamp down from its chain and held it close while the doctor squeezed the sides of her mouth so that her lips pursed open. Peering inside, he mumbled observations in French while the student recorded notes.

Dr. Charcot placed his hands below her ribs and pressed various places on her abdomen.

"Sir?" Sam stepped forward looking alarmed.

"I'm afraid you must leave," the doctor said. "I can examine and treat your wife but only if you are gone."

"But—"

"Go now." Sam slowly left the room. Hearing his footsteps echo down the hall and become faint, Fanny felt the tension in her back, shoulders and chest easing for the first time in weeks. She took no offense as the doctor probed and kneaded her belly, instead becoming drowsy. She found the rhythmic mumblings of "Negative, negative," followed by the student's pencil rustling on the page oddly soothing, and she dozed off.

Fanny spent the next several days sleeping more than anything else in the small, spare room they assigned her. A fat maid brought in a pot of tea and biscuits each morning, and at midday some cheese and bread. She and other women who had been left at the asylum for one reason or another were fed at long tables from common bowls of stew and vegetables. They passed bread, butter and tea like any group of ladies at a church supper. Besides a glumness of spirit and the pale looks of melancholy, the only real differences to Fanny between meals at the Salpêtrière and those in polite society were that the women wore white hospital gowns and none of them spoke English.

She was given work in the gardens, pruning the azalea bushes. When they provided her with steel hand-shears for the task she felt encouraged, because the ladies bent on killing themselves were given only bamboo rakes. Mademoiselle Francois, the stout matron of the gardens, taught her that azaleas were acid lovers, and showed her how to measure acid powder with water in beakers that reminded her of the laboratory she had glimpsed.

After toiling in the gardens, she would be led to a large metal vat like those farmers used to cure cheese. Matrons poured minerals into the steaming water, stripped off her clothes and helped her in. The baths, she was told, were designed to Doctor Charcot's precise specifications to produce healing of the spirit as well as deep sleep.

She did not feel especially troubled for the children. Although she missed them—especially Lloyd's boyish chivalry and Belle's flair—Sam would see to their needs; he'd always been better at that than he was at seeing to hers. In any case, one of the other women working in the garden told her that Doctor Charcot's strict policy was to keep patients away from their families, friends and the society that had made them mad in the first place; an asylum, after all, was a place of refuge.

On her fifth morning at the hospital, the fat matron brought clothes, neatly folded, and placed them on the bed. In French she said that this was to be a special day, and helped her don a white flowing blouse which smelled as if it had been freshly laundered and hung in the sun, and an ankle-length charcoal skirt. The matron carefully brushed her hair, tied it back in a bun and applied rouge to Fanny's cheeks.

Feeling more curious than afraid, Fanny followed the matron down a hallway to a paneled, high-ceilinged room illuminated by two tall windows that revealed a trellised garden of roses and vines behind it. Two dozen men in dark suits, high white collars and black bow ties sat in folding chairs arranged in a semicircle. The men stared at her from behind large mustaches, beards and spectacles as the matron led her in. Waiting at the head of the room, immaculate in a black double-breasted coat, with the air of a circus ringleader or head magician was Dr. Charcot. He bowed to her and gave a little stamp of his foot. Facing her he took both hands and smiled confidently, looking at her with his clear black eyes.

Never lifting his eyes from hers he addressed the men in French. "Mrs. Osbourne is an American wife and mother," she understood him to say, "who lost a young son and then fell into deep melancholia." The doctor squeezed her hands, his eyes bathing her with manly sympathy. Feeling safe in his hands, comforted by his eyes, and oddly detached, she looked past the doctor's face to the tall windows, and then down at the interesting patterns of light they shed on the rows of men in dark suits who stared so intently at her.

Dr. Charcot gently pried open her clenched hands and massaged her palms with his thumbs. His touch felt very warm, almost hot. "Look at me, Madame," he purred. "Only me. Look in my eyes."

While captive to his eyes she heard him drone on to the men but it was too much work to follow the meaning; he might have said the word "hysteria." When he stopped speaking, the floor creaked and one of the men cleared his throat. The air in the room became thick and warm. She heard Dr. Charcot's deep breathing as he continued to hold her hands and peer into her eyes.

"You become sleepy, Mrs. Osbourne. Embrace the sleep. Count your breaths with me but do not speak: one... two... three.... Good, now merely watch my eyes and listen as I say... four... five... six." During a long pause she heard the deep slow sighs of his breathing.

"By the time I reach ten," he murmured, "you will feel an overpowering need for sleep. Yield to it. Seven. Eight. Nine..."

Thoughts yielded to feelings: of comfortable bliss, of the warm glow of sun falling on her from the windows, and eventually, tingling skin as if she were in a bath containing exotic minerals. She sensed being observed by dozens of intelligent and competent men, a delicious sensation, strangely powerful.

On the following three mornings, she was taken to the same tall-windowed room and similarly entranced. Otherwise she was allowed to work in the garden, bathe and sleep. On the fourth morning she woke earlier, feeling rested and eager to get on with the day. Looking in the small oval mirror that hung from a nail above her bed she noticed that her nose and cheeks had acquired a tinge of sunburn from her hours in the garden.

The matron took her to Dr. Charcot's office, which was decorated with illustrations of the brain and skeleton as well as childish sketches of trees, flowers and women. Journals and notebooks were strewn over a large desk, and a full ashtray reeked of stale cigars. In a leather armchair, the doctor finished jotting a note of some kind, jabbed the pen in its holder, looked up at her and smiled. "It is time you leave us, Mrs. Osbourne, and also time that I explain the treatment I gave to you."

"Oh?" She fidgeted with the strap of her handbag while he paged through notes.

"You were splendid. My mesmerisms were productive for both you and my students." He took a thick cigar from a silver case. "Unfortunately, you live under the curse of most artists."

"Curse?"

"You are brittle, sensitive, and desperate for the world to adore you. It will not do so, of course, for your talent is minimal."

Fanny rose from her chair. "You know nothing of my talent."

"You contend! I am delighted at how much healthier you've become." Dr. Charcot motioned her to sit but she stayed on her feet while he lit the cigar, puffing thick smoke that hung in little clouds.

"I had a breakdown after the death of my son," she said, her voice catching, "yet you insult my art."

"I merely guessed about your talent. A scientific guess, nonetheless. If I say the same to one hundred artists, I am correct ninety-nine times." He waved through the cigar smoke at the sketches on the wall. "I once wished to be an artist, too. Now that I've grown up, I know that this," he said, waving expansively to indicate the entire Salpêtrière, "is my art."

She backed away, wondering if the doctor himself were mad.

"You have a tendency, Madame, to believe that all concerns you, only you, and your intense desire to be grand. Grand, even with the most petty sketch of an orange."

Tears stung her eyes. "You said that you would explain my treatment."

"While hypnotized, you were an intriguing and powerful presence. Charming, feminine, witty to a fault. Men kill for such a woman." He smiled. "Please, Mrs. Osbourne, sit down."

She did so, keeping the handbag on her lap.

"Although you grieve for your dear son, while entranced, you danced a ballet for us. You sang an aria from *The Marriage of Figaro.* You recited the Gettysburg Address that was made by your President Lincoln. All of these you performed convincingly, charmingly, with those sultry eyes and a bold smile."

"You made me perform like a circus tiger?"

"And what a tiger you were. Are," he corrected himself. "Because you see, Mrs. Osbourne, beneath the layers of grief and bourgeois motherhood you are the person who performed for us. You must send your husband home."

She was not sure she had heard correctly. "Sir?"

"For your health, pack him off, and soon. He is death. Art is life, no matter your paltry skill."

"But—"

"I shall order him to California." He waved as if shooing away a fly. "For you, there is a village in the Fontainebleau forest, Grez-sur-Loing, quiet and serene, precisely what you require. Artists spend their summers there. The Hôtel Chevillon will accept unaccompanied women if they have a reference." He jabbed his pen in the inkwell and scribbled a note on his official letterhead. With a flourish he handed the letter to her.

She stared at the letter, slowly absorbing what he had accomplished. A smile formed on her face, the first one for weeks. Quickly she stepped around the desk and kissed the doctor's cheek before hurrying out of the room.

CHAPTER 7
Grez, France—1876

Fanny sat at her easel in a balmy sun on the banks of the Loing River. Lowering her brush she backed away and considered her painting. Something was not right. She had captured the river that flowed before her, brown, glassy, quiet as a grave. She had gotten the vines that tangled in the mud at her feet right, too. The Grez bridge was pleasing enough, with the deep shading she had given the bottom of the arches and the ancient strength of their pocked, yellow stones. She was satisfied that the elm she had put in the left-foreground, with one delicate branch stretching over the water, counterbalanced the squat old bridge on the right. And yet...

She closed her eyes, loosened the knot in the ribbon under her chin that held her black bonnet in place, and tasted the thick damp air. When she opened her eyes she saw it—the evergreen on the far bank was too low and beaten-down. She dipped the brush to the palette, swirling in the yellows and blues until she got deep green. With jabbing upward strokes she grew the tree until it almost hit the top of the canvas.

She set the brush down and flexed her aching fingers. She found a clean strip of cotton among the ones she had brought to blot the canvas, and used it to dry her eyes. As usual, finishing a painting brought depression. The delicious abandonment of her being—to the mixing of colors, the study of the landscape and the slow, steady brush-strokes against the pleasing texture of the canvas—had put death behind her, or at least well off to the side. But it always returned, especially at night, after Belle and Lloyd had chattered and argued and gone to sleep in their cramped room at the inn. Then she would hear him. Sometimes a sob, sometimes a snuffle, sometimes even a whispered "Mama." Later, when sleep finally overtook her, she would see him, and would reach out to touch his soft curly hair, pixy face, and big blue eyes that stared so expectantly.

After gathering up her paints and brushes, she stood still and focused on the quiet eddy just before her, where she had seen him last week. Although underwater, his face had turned up to her, white as the underbelly of a fish, pleading with his beautiful eyes. Just when she decided to enter the water to join him, he had vanished.

As she passed quiet days and nights at Grez, the colony filled up with artists: Americans Walter Palmer, Hiram Bloomer and Will Low; a blond young Irishman, Frank O'Meara; a tall Scot, Robert Alan Stevenson; and two very proper American women, Margaret Berthe Wright and her daughter Marian. The visions of Hervey became less frequent and confined themselves to the middle of the night. Always he would walk to her with opened arms as he had when living, when he wanted her to pick him up. But when she bent to sweep him up he would vanish. Always the dreams—for she now recognized them as such, nothing more—woke her and left her heart aching.

Almost as strange were her mood swings. On a Tuesday she might be dumb with grief; by Wednesday she would be chatting with the other artists, and sometimes not just chatting but regaling them with stories of the mining towns where she and Sam had lived. Although enjoying these giddy moods, at nights she wondered about the sanity of a mother who had lost her beautiful son yet six months later would perform, as Dr. Charcot had called it, to a roomful of admiring men. She hoped that the ebullient moods were an aftereffect of being mesmerized in France rather than a sign that she was callous to the core and hopelessly defective in character.

Such a mood enveloped her after supper on a balmy July evening. She loved the splintery old dining room at this time of day, when they would push their empty plates and baguette crumbs to the center of the long table, pass cups of thick-smelling coffee and settle in for talk. Some of the men would have brandy, too, especially Bob Stevenson, the big Scot with a fine mustache who usually sat just to her left. They had thrown all of the windows and the half-door open to admire a particularly beautiful sunset, although Bob seemed more interested in other sights, waving a snifter stupidly in the direction of Belle. Belle was holding court at the end of the table, showing Tim O'Meara and his friends her sketch of a tree. The men were giddy over Belle's tree, and, no doubt, her firm young chest that, although wrapped in a lacy white blouse, was profiled against the twilight in the open half-door. Fanny would have to talk with her daughter about the shameless way she thrust herself forward while talking with the men over coffee.

"Don't you just love Grez in September?" Fanny asked Bob. "So much warmer than other places I've lived."

Bob, who'd had three glasses of Burgundy with dinner, was now trying to get Belle's attention by tossing an olive at her. "Virginia City," Fanny continued, "was so high and cold I didn't see a flower for five years. Only rocks and ore carts, and gunfights outside the hurdy-gurdy houses."

Bob raised an eyebrow but kept his gaze on Belle. "What the hell's a hurdy-gurdy house?"

"You, a man of the world, don't know what a hurdy-gurdy house is?" Fanny propped her feet on the rungs of Bob's chair, took paper and tobacco from her beaded handbag and rolled a cigarette. She knew that the men found this to be the most fascinating trick she'd mastered in Nevada.

Suddenly Belle screamed. A stork-thin man vaulted over the sill of the half-door and into the dining room, tripping, rolling and laughing like a madman.

"Louis!" shouted Bob, pulling the stork to his feet and clapping his back.

Bob dragged Louis around the table to shake hands with the men and give little bows to the women. Watching their progress while sipping coffee, Fanny was a bit disappointed by this young man Bob had talked so much about. His tan slacks had holes in the knees, a linen shirt smothered his skinny chest, and the sleeves of his blue velvet jacket were splotched with mud. Sandy brown hair hung in strings down a long thin face, cropped below the ears like he'd cut it himself. He seemed jovial enough, laughing when the men punched his arm or said something they thought was witty.

Bob had gotten him around the table and was pouring himself more brandy. "I'll bet we can scare up a chicken leg or two. Maybe even bread."

"I'm not hungry," Louis said, eyeing the empty chair on Fanny's right, "but coffee would be swell."

Fanny supposed that things could be worse than being trapped between the two cousins. Bob raised the snifter in a sort of toast to her face. "Last but not least is Mrs. Fanny Osbourne, a painter from the wilds of America."

Louis smiled at her with soft brown eyes, handsome eyes, really, or at least they were not as frightening as the rest of him. The three of them talked. Louis took an immediate interest in Virginia City, going wide-eyed at her tales of outlaws, card houses and women of ill repute. Bob, for the time being, stopped gawking at Belle while telling Fanny about the practical jokes the cousins had played in Edinburgh, all of them quite stupid.

Louis settled back and rolled a cigarette in the same style Fanny used, by crimping the paper in one hand and opening the tobacco pouch with his teeth. Fanny glanced down the table and saw that Belle, and for that matter the sixteen others in the room, were watching Louis with interest. Perhaps it was the young man's strange looks, or his wild enthusiasm over all that was said, or the frantic hand gestures he tended to make while talking.

Fanny flicked ash in a saucer. "Just what, Mr. Stevenson, are you doing in France?"

Louis reached for a candle with his long fingers and lit his cigarette. Fanny would kill to have fingers like those. "Canoeing." Louis began coughing and turned away. Abruptly he stood. "I should go out and stow it."

"I'll come along and admire your ship." Bob wobbled to his feet and threw an arm over Louis's shoulders. "You too," Bob bellowed at Fanny. "Come out and see the boy's damn boat."

"Fine idea, yes, please do come along and see Arethusa," said Louis.

"Arethusa?" Fanny drew on her cigarette, raised her chin and hissed smoke at the ceiling. She'd no intention of walking outside with drunken Bob and a coughing scarecrow. "You named a boat Arethusa?"

"After a poem, by Shelley." Again, the warm smiling eyes.

Fanny walked between Bob and Louis to the door.

"A literary sort, Lou is," Bob explained. "Writes essays about his travels. Sold one for a hundred pounds."

"Three," Louis said as they passed the old beams in the doorway.

"Three," agreed Bob, stumbling down the steps to the path outside. "He's sold three essays."

"No, I've sold one essay, for three pounds."

The moon shone down on them while they walked past the graceful elm branch. Fanny could hear the river, just ahead of them, lazily slapping against the banks. "I've written some things, too," she found herself saying.

"Splendid! You must tell me about your writing. And all about the American writers. Hawthorne and Poe and James

Fenimore Cooper. Oh Mrs. Osbourne, we'll feast on talk!" He kept staring at her while sidestepping through the mud toward the river.

"But Mr. Stevenson—"

"Louis. Please call me Louis. And you must draw me. I'll sit for you and you'll draw me while we converse."

"Tonight?"

"Are you out of your mind, Mrs. Osbourne? I'm much too tired. Tomorrow will be fine." Still looking at her Louis banged his head on the canoe that was propped against a tree. He sank to the ground, laughing while Bob roared and slapped his knee.

The laughing turned into wracking coughs. "Are you all right?" Fanny asked.

Louis struggled to an elbow and waved off her concern.

She stooped down to him. "Louis," she said, for some reason using his familiar name, "You're not at all well. What's wrong?"

He smiled up at her, fighting for air, and suddenly, *she* felt sick—dizzy, nauseous, her heart racing. Ghastly pale in the moonlight, his face was too familiar: thin, boyish, with long hair and a brave smile. It was the identical smile Hervey wore when he lay dying, a smile that, she knew, had been meant to comfort *her*.

"What the hell is it with you two?" Bob tucked one arm under Fanny's, grabbed Louis with the other and tugged them toward the inn.

Next morning, Fanny woke in a sweat in her room in the Hôtel Chevillon, bolted out the door and stumbled down the pre-dawn darkness of the hall to the commode, barely making it before vomiting. Returning to the room she checked on Lloyd and Belle, peering carefully at their sleeping faces in the dim light until satisfied that their breathing was regular and peaceful. Always when she woke from Hervey's visits in the pre-dawn, she knew she would be unable to get back to sleep. Pulling on a house robe she trudged downstairs, made tea on Madame Chevillon's stove and brought a cup back to the room. At her open window she sat on her rumpled bed, cradling the tea in her palms and breathing the humid summer air.

Someone knocked. Perhaps Monsieur Chevillon had come to present her slip of charges for the week. She cracked open the door.

"Bonjour," Louis Stevenson said cheerfully.

"Please, Sir, I—"

"It's a perfect morning for you to sketch me, warm in the garden but not too bright." He struck a dramatic pose, grinning, dressed up for the occasion in blue velvet coat, scarlet tie with a big sloppy knot and linen slacks.

She still felt queasy, and sensed that her hair was plastered every which way. "Perhaps some other time." She closed the door.

Later, when she sent the children down to breakfast, a scrap of paper lay on the doorstep. On it was a cartoon sketch of a thin man bowing contritely before a closed door while behind it a woman swooned onto a chair. "Please forgive my intrusion. RLS."

Ridiculous, vain, how the odd man with the haunting face and worn clothes signed the scrap with his initials! But she smiled nonetheless.

At the end of each week, Bob Stevenson would lug bottles of wine from Madame Chevillon's cellar, the artists would prop their week's work in the dining room and then circle the room giving critiques. The scathing remarks, witty comebacks and wine always turned Friday Reviews into raucous parties which sometimes helped lift Fanny's spirits. But tonight, seated in a corner chair, she found it an effort just to smile her hellos as the men passed.

"'Tis lovely, stunning," Bob announced, standing before O'Meara's painting of an ancient village church. "I would never have thought a cow-barn could be rendered with such precision."

O'Meara cheerfully thrust an obscene gesture in Bob's face. The two men turned to visit Belle's tree, giving the work what Fanny thought was undue attention while the girl stood by the easel, smiling and blushing. Soon three other men joined Bob and O'Meara to remark on the amazing color of the tree and its breathtaking majesty.

When Louis Stevenson strolled in, wearing an artists' smock but with sleeves that were wet, as if he'd been canoeing, he ignored the knot of men at Belle's tree, instead making straight for Fanny's painting of the Grez bridge. After a long viewing of it he walked to her. "Mrs. Osbourne, I am so sorry about your son."

She drew a sharp breath and looked again at her work. She had spent hours on it, trying to render it as accurately as her eyes saw it, and, truth be told, she was proud of it. Nothing in it was about Hervey, yet she supposed that it did have a brooding quality, a sense of melancholy. Louis had obviously heard of her tragedy, probably from Bob, but how had this interloper, this strange man eleven years her junior made such an uncanny connection between her art and her grief?

"Louis," she began, but did not know what she wanted to say.

He squeezed her hand and left to look at the other artwork.

Next morning she recognized his knock. "I'll let you in on a secret, Mrs. Osbourne, I'm an early riser, a bad sleeper, I mean. Why stay in bed when there is such life to be found outdoors?"

"Please, Louis —"

"I'll understand if you don't wish to sketch me, although I would do my best to make a superb subject. I don't pose for just any American mother who happens along."

"I'm not ready for that."

"Let's just stroll then."

Having slept better, she had risen early and was already dressed in her usual black. What harm could a stroll do? She followed him down the stone stairwell, out the door and down a dirt path toward the garden. "I expect you think me mad, Mrs. Osbourne, and I suppose there's truth enough in the charge, but you are by far the most interesting person in the chateau."

"I am?"

"To be perfectly honest, and you shall keep this under your cap, well, if you wore a cap that is, the other inmates at this asylum bore me silly. I love Bob, mind you, we're like brothers, we have the same name, Robert, although he is Robert Alan and I am Robert Louis. But even dear Bob can wear on a man, if you know what I mean. But you! You are the most fascinating woman of the Wild West I have known. Well, you're the only one I've known, but you paint, and you write, and this means that as a companion you are just short of perfect. Perhaps you *are* perfect, so please, Mrs. Osbourne, humor me with some harmless talk."

"What sort of harmless talk did you have in mind?" They had reached a small sea of big white umbrellas under which the artists would set their easels and work when the weather was right.

He held out a wooden lawn chair for her. "Any light topic would do. We could talk about art. Your art. Or, art in the abstract. For example, what is great art? How do you define it? Who are the three greatest artists alive, and why? That sort of thing."

"You're giving me a headache."

"Very well then. Tell me about Mrs. Fanny Osbourne."

"I hardly know you."

"Then I could tell you about Robert Louis Stevenson."

"All right." She reached for her paper and tobacco and began rolling a cigarette. "But I believe they start serving lunch at noon."

Louis threw back his head and laughed. Later, she realized that this was the moment of falling in love with him: the open, child-like laugh told her how completely he liked simply being with her, and had sent shivers down her spine.

CHAPTER 8
Monterey, California—1879

"Fanny," Louis said, frowning at her over the small table in the sitting room of Louis's hotel, where they were eating breakfast after spending the night together. "Fanny, are you all right?"

She had been lost in memories of Julien's academy, Hervey's death, her stay at the asylum, and the beginnings of her love for Louis; now, it was as if he had wakened her from a dream.

She pushed away from the table and walked for the door.

"Fanny!" he called.

She closed the door and hurried toward the docks on Alvarado Street, her small black pumps sounding as harsh as pistol-shots as they struck the hollow boardwalk. Hopefully he would not follow her; she did not want him to see the tears on her cheeks, nor did she want him to discern that she was already making her way to the train platform to meet Sam. By all rights she should go home first, take a bath, change into fresh clothes and wait for Sam to arrive by taxi. But the walk would do her good, and help clear her head of Louis and last night's relapse with him.

When she passed the big window of the haberdasher, a fat little man standing on a platform getting fitted for a suit seemed to leer at her and then nudge the tailor with his elbow, who stared at her as well. Monterey might have a saloon that called itself Bohemia, but it was certainly not France, where a little bit of stepping out of line was allowed, especially where love was concerned. She stepped off the boardwalk to cross to the other side of the street, in her distraction not realizing until she heard the yells of the driver that she'd walked into the path of a two-horse beer wagon. It narrowly missed her; she waved an apology to the cursing driver and walked onward, deep in thought.

She was now certain that her attraction for Louis—well, now she could admit it to herself, more than attraction—her weak-kneed, helpless, damn-all desire for him—had been a symptom of grief and madness. The precise mechanism, the *reason* for her attraction was too appalling to even consider. She would write to Dr. Charcot in France as soon as she had a private moment, lay out in detail what she believed was the explanation and beg for his guidance.

She waited on a splintery bench at the lonely platform in the sand dunes. While afternoon gusts blew sand in her eyes she stared at advertisements in a *Monterey Californian* that someone had left. "Come see our Neckwear and Elegant Goods!" one of them said. Another extolled the virtues of "Harnesses, Saddles & Silverwork!" A rectangle in the shape of a coffin had been drawn around the ad for Flanigan & Gallagher, Undertakers. This led to bleak thoughts about her sanity and future, which were not helped by the sight of a dead bird in the dirt a few feet in front of her and a line of ants tramping away from the carcass with bits of the entrails. When at last she heard the chuffing of the train and the angry squeal of its brakes during its final approach down from the bluffs, she dug a mirror, brush and rouge from her purse and made a quick, hopeless attempt to freshen up.

As usual, Sam looked unruffled and at ease when he stepped from the car in a blue suit and crisp maroon cravat. He tossed his cigar toward the gleaming wheels and swept off his bowler. "Gosh, dear, you look like you slept in your clothes."

Instinctively she smoothed her skirts, hoping he would not notice her blushing.

He guffawed. "Just kidding, my darling, just kidding." He put his arm heavily around her and she smelled the Bay Rum that he always splashed on his face.

Feeling like she might smother against his coat she pushed away from him. She smiled, trying for a lighthearted attitude she did not feel. "Welcome to Monterey."

His eyes were darting around at a motley collection of buckboards and hansoms that were loading passengers. "Hole of a town. Where are my children?"

"I don't know."

He beckoned one of the drivers with a furious wave. "What do you mean, you don't know?"

"Lloyd went camping with his friend Daniel and his father. I'm sure I wrote to you about his plans. Belle stayed last night with Nellie. So at this very moment I don't know if either of them is home, because for the past hour I have been here, waiting to meet my husband, Samuel Osbourne, at his train from San Francisco."

Sam frowned but appeared to have lost interest in the subject, tossing his Gladstone onto a buckboard and helping her up to a seat.

Louis walked, after she left him in the breakfast room—endlessly, aimlessly, it was all he could do when his heart was so full that his mind could not work. Tea and toast was perhaps not a fitting meal before a day's journey to nowhere, but as often happened when he was so thoroughly stymied, he felt neither hunger nor pain of any kind. He headed out of town, passing the Chinatown shanties and trudging west, up the long hill leading to the boot of the peninsula. Soon he sweated beneath the sun that broke free on the cypress-studded bluffs above the whitewashed cabins with red-brown roofs of the Pacific Grove Christian Retreat that stretched along Central Avenue. He plunged into the deep shade of a redwood grove and the sweet moldy scent of the huge trees.

Another climb along a row of Monterey pines took him to the forest atop the peninsula. Dense, primordial tangles of live oak, pine and redwood cooled him while he heard the crashing of surf from all directions. His lungs cried out for rest but he picked up the pace; perhaps the pain was punishment for the "sinful mad business," as his father had called it, that he had begun in France with Mrs. Osbourne. He wondered, should he collapse again, who, if anyone, would revive him this time.

He must have stopped for a nap in a bed of soft grass beneath a redwood, or had he passed out? It made no difference; when he woke, the sun had dipped low over the breakers. Still no fog, but what was this? Black plumes of smoke were rising above Monterey, and an acrid stench wafted toward him as if from some hellish marine crematorium. His curiosity drew him down from the bluffs toward the smoke. Soon he moved at a jog, gasping, but feeling euphoric. If he was to expire, it might as well be gloriously, on a beach pyre along with other burning martyrs to Venus who, by the smell of things, were being tossed to the flames on this day when Fanny was re-uniting with her husband.

Louis turned onto a deer path, following the smoke through sand dunes toward the beach. The smoke, now thick above him, smelled something like when his father cooked trout over an open fire in the Highlands, but magnified a hundredfold. He pressed a handkerchief over his nose and mouth but could not stop a hacking cough. Resting on a fallen pine trunk he heard a clanking sound.

"Stevenson?" Damned if it wasn't the saloon owner, Sanchez, now a marionette in black frock coat, gold-tasseled epaulets and tall white hat, and carrying a bugle. Behind him marched six other men with horns and drums.

"What's burning?"

"Humpback."

When Louis followed the band over a hill he was met with a scene that was part hell, part carnival, part organized mayhem. A forty-foot whale lay in the foam at water's edge while five sunburned men, their trousers and jerseys covered in blood, hacked chunks of flesh from its belly with axes and long flashing knives. A line of Mexican workers hurried the chunks to bonfires and pitched them into iron cauldrons where they steamed and sizzled. Men with long dippers made periodic sweeps into the sizzling pots and dumped the rendered oil into waiting barrels while at one fire, Indian women pitched guts and offal into the flames, causing the awful stink Louis had smelled from miles away.

Louis eased to the sand with his back against a dune, upwind from the burning, transfixed by the macabre sight which half of Monterey had turned out to enjoy. Men lugged picnic baskets and blankets, women in long cotton dresses followed with children, and dogs dashed around sniffing and lifting their hind legs. Chinese families in domed hats set their blankets separately from the whites, but all seemed to be enjoying the show. Trumpets of the brass band blared bullfight music. A mule pulled a gleaming black wagon with "Bohemia Saloon" stenciled in gold letters on the side, drawing cheers from men who dug in pockets and crowded around it.

"Stevenson!" Augustine Dutra, a Greek fisherman in a striped jersey and filthy straw hat whom Louis remembered meeting at the saloon, stumbled to him and shoved a bottle of whisky in his hand.

Louis tipped the bottle to his lips. "Exquisite." Privately he thought the rye tasted awful compared with the single malt of the Highlands, but he liked the pleasant burning of the liquid in his throat and the gesture made by the friend.

"How are things going with Mrs. Osbourne?" Dutra asked, sitting cross-legged next to him in the sand.

"Slowly, I'm afraid. Have you seen her, by chance?"

"Everybody in town knows she's holed up with Sam."

"They do?"

Dutra took another swig. Louis rolled a cigarette with shaky fingers, turning his attention to the band that was playing "Yankee Doodle" with all the aplomb of a team of morticians. Before Louis had finished the cigarette, an activity that helped ward off the burning-whale stench, Sanchez and his men had segued into a German polka. Weary, light-headed from the whisky that Dutra kept passing to him, Louis began to think the whale-blubbering a damned pleasant affair. He petted stray dogs, made faces at giggling Chinese children, and even shouted "Bravo" to the band after a dreadful but spirited attempt at a Highlands lilt.

He lay back, savoring a brilliant orange twilight, vowing to get every moment of the event down in his journal. Someone thrust a warm corn husk in his hand. "Tamale," said Adolfo Sanchez. "You need to eat, Looee."

Louis tiredly chewed the delicious crumbly meal as Sanchez and the band gathered their instruments and marched off over the dunes. The last sight before sleep overtook him was of the dead whale. Silhouetted in the orange twilight, violated, eviscerated, ribs exposed, it nonetheless seemed a living presence, rooted in the wet sand while the waves baptized it. The glassy eyes in the huge, spade-like head seemed to look directly at him. Closing his eyes, Louis thought it noble that the giant's flesh would fuel the brightest lanterns and make the finest machinery spin. He was certain there was a lesson in this, but was too tired and drunk to decide what it was.

A squawking seagull woke him. He was sweating beneath a horse blanket that some kind soul must have tossed over him, Dutra perhaps. The gull was pecking at the corn husk, a fierce sight when viewed at eye-level from three feet away. The sun, struggling through a high fog, was well above the brown hills to the east; he must have slept past nine. To the west, men in long rowboats with ropes strained to drag the whale carcass out beyond the breakers where, he supposed, it would be abandoned to the sharks. He rolled a cigarette, smoked, and got to his feet, coughing. Head throbbing, he struck off for town, resolved to spend the day writing.

He had just reached a field of sand and crabgrass next to the brackish Lake El Estero when he saw her. Or, more precisely, them: Fanny and a tall, bearded man who had to be Sam, strolling beneath a stand of Monterey Pines like any well-dressed American couple from San Francisco. Louis ducked behind a live oak tree to observe. Besides his headache he now felt nauseated, not just from last night's whisky but because Fanny walked with perhaps the handsomest man he had ever seen. Sam had golden-blonde hair, a well-trimmed beard, and the nose of a Greek god. He wore fawn-colored trousers, a blue coat with brass buttons and a crisp white shirt. Louis recalled Fanny saying that Sam had been in the Union Army, that men still called him "Captain," and Louis could see why. Louis realized that if circumstances were different and he had encountered a man like Sam in a train car or saloon, he would try to strike up a conversation. He further imagined that Sam would smile, offer him a cigar, and tell vivid stories of marching on the Confederates or scrambling for gold in Nevada—just the sort of stories that Louis would want to get down in his journal.

Fanny looked wonderful as always, today in a flat straw hat with yellow ribbon around the brim, pale blue dress, buckskin gloves and boots. New clothes, no doubt bought for her in San Francisco by her husband. She carried a folded parasol at her side that swung in rhythm with her stride. Louis noticed that each swing of her parasol whisked the sand with its tip, leaving a trail of pock-marks as the couple ambled toward a brood of mallards that quacked along the lake's edge. He longed to know what they were talking about. Love, and why it had fled them? Plans for a divorce? More likely it was something entirely banal; clothes that the children needed for school, or the price of oysters at Simoneau's restaurant. Louis took faint hope from seeing that Fanny swung her parasol in the space between them rather than out to her side, perhaps to enforce a distance between her and Sam.

Louis took a roundabout way to his lodgings, trudging back through the sand dunes to get to Alvarado Street. From Alvarado he cut through the rose garden of Mrs. Heintz, his landlady, hoping to avoid her notice by taking the back stairs up to his room. No such luck. The woman, wearing a black dress and crocheted shawl, shaped like a pot-bellied stove, loomed in his path.

"You missed breakfast, Mister Stevenson."

"Please forgive me, Frau Heintz. I was walking." He gave the Swiss woman the short bow that he knew she liked, wondering if he should also click his heels.

"All night you were walking? Come. I'll cook eggs and sausage. You need food."

"Perhaps tomorrow." He tipped his cap and bolted around her to the stairs.

Once inside his room he slammed the door and paced, kicking his bedding from its place on the floor against the wall, stopping at the steel basin to splash water on his face and then seeing his hung-over visage in the mirror. Sunken cheeks, mottled complexion, red eyes, hair every this way and that, velvet coat and linen shirt wrinkled, trousers stained with tamale sauce and sand. He was a human wreck and it was time he faced up to it. How on earth, in this deplorable condition, could he expect to compete with Samuel Osbourne, the Captain, father of his lover's children, Greek god incarnate? He wondered if he should give up all drink, sleep eight regular hours, eat his vegetables, and buy dumbbells, as his father had done for him when he was a boy to "put beef on that sunken chest," all for naught, of course.

He rolled a cigarette. No, he could never compete that way.

He threw open a window, climbed onto its thick adobe sill and sat, swinging his legs out over the weedy back field as if he were on a porch swing while he smoked. A better strategy than the hopeless one of improving his physical self, such as it was, would be to divine why Mrs. Fanny Osbourne had thrown all caution to the winds and become his lover in France in the first place. Then he could find every conceivable way he could build upon and strengthen that source of attraction.

He took pen and notebook, and wrote on the top of a fresh page "Why she loved me." After giving the matter some thought, he inserted two words so that the heading now read, "Why she might have loved me." He hoped that she had, and did still, but he supposed that if he were going to be completely cold and scientific about this exercise, he could not say for certain what was, or had been, in her heart. He thought about the balmy night on which they had met, a night in early September, three years previous.

He had dragged his canoe onto the riverbank of the peaceful Loing River just before sunset, and tiredly set it upright against a poplar tree to drain. Admiring the handsome stone walls of the Inn Chevillon before him, he wiped his damp forehead with a handkerchief and tucked in his shirttails, welcoming the thought of a good meal, seeing his cousin Bob, and sleeping indoors. His linen slacks and coat were muddy, his shoes wet, but they would have to do. He tramped through the garden and the artists' umbrellas that looked like giant mushrooms, pausing to peek through an opened half-door of the inn. The tableau that the opening framed for him was a parody of Da Vinci's Last Supper: men in paint-smudged cotton jerseys, baggy linen trousers, straw hats and berets sat at a long table, but instead of clustering on either side of Christ in the center, the artists seemed divided by magnets drawing their attentions to the table's ends. At one end a young woman in a sun bonnet and lacy blouse held half of the men rapt with smiles, giggles and flips of her dark curls.

The woman at the other end made Louis gasp—in appearance she was almost a twin of his hopeless flirtation of the year before, Mrs. Sitwell, the vicar's wife. Like Mrs. Sitwell she had dark hair and eyes, was short, buxom, and exuded a mysterious feminine energy that even at a distance seemed electrically charged. She seemed to be enjoying the attentions of the men, yet oddly, was dressed head-to-toe in black. A widow? By the way she rolled her own cigarette, laughed at something Bob said, and held her eyes unflinchingly on each person to whom she spoke, Louis perceived a strong, extraordinary woman that he would simply have to get to know. And the seat next to her was empty!

It was she, the mysterious woman in black, who inspired his grand entrance. Childish, to vault through the half-door and tumble, but effective. Predictably, Bob had guffawed and drawn him over to where he wanted to be. And at that long rustic table, he soon found himself revealing to Fanny Osbourne the details of his life, loves and aspirations that usually took him months or years to tell anyone else, if ever he did. He told about being the only child of a famous lighthouse engineer and a socialite mother, God-fearing Calvinists who had raised Louis to be anything but a writer. How he had spent his boyhood tramping behind his father on frigid windswept beaches as the surf pounded against the stone structures while Mr. Stevenson, as solid and square as his creations, took measurements. About how he loved his father's stories of seafarers, pirates, and Highland warriors but could not stay awake in any class related to mathematics or engineering. How his father had decided, reluctantly, that law would be an acceptable career. How Louis had somehow made it through the University of Edinburgh law school despite daydreaming through lectures, or ducking out of them to drink in Old Town pubs with brilliant but unruly friends who debated books and devised practical jokes on professors they considered pretentious. He even told Fanny something he had never shared, his belief that of all his father's disappointments in him, his deepest was Louis's frail health, unique among the many generations of sturdy Scots who comprised the family.

Through it all, the woman he had just met encouraged him with smiles and bathed him with the sympathy of her soft dark eyes. With small gloved hands, Fanny waved away a cloud of cigarette smoke as if dismissing any idea that his weakness bothered her. "You're a writer, Louis, a determined one. That's all that matters."

He restrained an impulse to kiss her. Instead, he touched her arm. "And how did you get here?"

She rolled another cigarette. "From Indianapolis, with long stops along the way in the Indian Territories, Virginia City, San Francisco and Oakland." Thus began a story that enthralled him, about life in the frontier among miners, card-sharks and Indians, raising her children while her husband Sam looked for gold. She painted the characters there—gamblers in ruffled shirts with names like Billy Bird, tobacco-spitting Wells Fargo Express drivers, purple-plumed saloon girls, and her daughter's Indian playmates—as colorfully on the canvas of his mind as those created on the page by the famous writer Bret Harte, who, Fanny said, was a friend-of-a-friend of hers in San Francisco.

Next morning, after she turned down his offer to pose for a sketch, they strolled through the rose garden, eventually sitting on an ancient stone wall next to Madame Chevillon's fat grey cat. "What is art, Mrs. Osbourne?"

"What artists create."

"All right then, what is great art?"

"What a few artists, but not I, create." Absently she swung her legs back and forth under the long black dress like a young girl, a gesture that Louis found hopelessly alluring.

Louis casually shifted to sit a little bit closer than the respectful two feet he had allowed between them. "Self-deprecation doesn't suit you, Mrs. Osbourne."

"But it's true. Bloomer sometimes creates it. Renoir. And Monet, always. I'm just a student, a pretender."

"Who told you that?"

"A mesmerist in Paris."

"Really?"

She looked down, frowning as if from a painful memory. He waited but she did not elaborate.

Frank O'Meara, the blond Irishman, strolled past them with an easel tucked under his arm. "Would it be all right if I sketch you while you work?" Fanny asked.

"As long as I can scratch from time t' time." O'Meara ambled to a spot before a graceful elm tree, his apparent subject, and set up his easel.

"Why would you want to sketch that sorry-looking Irishman, but not me?" Louis asked.

"Practice. So that by the time I sketch you, it will be great art." She kissed Louis on the cheek and hurried off with her easel toward an umbrella near O'Meara.

He touched the spot on his cheek, surprised and thrilled by the kiss.

The following day, cool and rainy, when breakfast ended and the others had traipsed off with easels, he lugged armchairs to the big stone fireplace in the dining room and coaxed her to sit with him. Again in a black dress, she propped an elbow on her thigh with an air of great boredom. "So. What will today's topic be, oh Professor Stevenson?"

"Love."

She fell silent for a few moments. "Love?"

"Yes. What is it?"

Fanny opened a cigarette paper and shook tobacco from her pouch. "Love is what I have for my family."

"Your family?"

"For my children," she said, after another pause. "But since you don't have children, you would not know that kind of love."

"True, I've never been a mother," he said with a laugh, "but I do love children. They show their feelings more

94

honestly than adults do, and their instincts are truer, being less muddled by all the civilizing we oldsters impose on them."

"Oldsters? Hah."

Louis lit a cigarette. "But we digress. What I intended for our topic today was the love between a man and a woman."

She blew smoke toward the ceiling. "Oh."

"What is it?" he pursued. "And what is great love?"

"When I was young, I thought I knew. What do you think it is?"

"What you fall into."

"An accident, like falling into a rabbit hole?"

"A glorious accident that you can neither ward off nor prepare for. A fall into a mineshaft rather than a rabbit hole, a cave gleaming with sapphires and rubies. In the case of great love, a cave glittering with diamonds."

She leaned forward to flick ash from her cigarette into the fireplace. "Like being lost in King Solomon's cave. A big adventure."

"An illogical adventure, perhaps a supernatural one that defies easy definition—and exists regardless of whether or not we were seeking it."

"For someone so young, you seem to have done a lot of thinking on the subject."

"In the last few days, Fanny, yes." He took her hand and squeezed it.

She squeezed back, shutting her eyes. "This cannot be, Louis." She took her hand from his, opened her eyes and looked into his with what seemed like pain, and, perhaps, great longing...

In his Monterey adobe, he looked at his list of items that had made Fanny love him. Awfully short; in fact, he had written one item: "Words." He took the notebook to his cot and propped his back against the chipped wall. If it was words that had drawn them together, he would have to spill out hundreds more of them, and not just say them to Fanny, but write them. And if he was to have any chance at wresting Fanny from Sam, he must write tens of thousands. If he could get not just two, but twenty-two essays written and sent to publishers he might generate a decent enough income to support her and her children. These would not only have to be good essays, but great ones that would rivet the attention of genteel European readers to the wonders that the young adventurer, Robert Louis Bloody Stevenson, would bring into their god-awful boring lives.

He opened the journal he had kept while crossing America by train. The whole sorry experience could, if he were clever enough, be cast as a hair-raising adventure story that would sell, especially to British readers who in recent decades clamored for tales of the American frontier. He spent an hour reading his entries about endless prairie landscapes, and about bumpkins who had nicknamed him "Shakespeare" and laughed at his bouts of coughing and his struggles to write while in the cramped, stinking car.

"I could not look but with wonder and respect on the Chinese," he had written. "Their forefathers watched the stars before mine had begun to keep pigs. Gunpowder and printing, which the other day we imitated, and a school of manners which we never had the delicacy so much as to desire to imitate, were theirs in a long-past antiquity."

Soon he despaired. Fanny had been right that most people would not pay for such drivel. These pages contained no great adventure, just a recounting of misery, much of it dully written. Perhaps his writing style had been sickened from the fat volumes that he'd read on the train, George Bancroft's *History of the United States,* which had informed him about the country but invariably put him to sleep.

He smoked two cigarettes, lighting one off of the other, inhaling deeply to dull the pains that had started again in his chest. He opened the notebook to his beginnings of a novel. In big block letters he had titled it:

ARIZONA BRECKINRIDGE, OR, A VENDETTA IN THE WEST.

After reading the nineteen pages of Chapter One that he had drafted, he crumpled it in a ball and flung it across the room, where it smacked against the adobe wall. The story had a hopelessly flimsy premise and wooden, unbelievable characters. Two hours of trying to write another beginning got him nothing but a headache and a coughing fit.

Perhaps writing a letter would clear his mind. He began one to Henley:

> *I get terribly frightened about my work, which seems to advance too slowly. I hope soon to have a greater burden to support, and must make money a great deal quicker than I used. I may get nothing for the Vendetta; I may only get some forty quid for the Emigrant.*

He set the letter aside; it, too, depressed him so much that he would finish it another day.

He paced from one end of the room to the other, kicking the wall in frustration. How could he ever survive as a writer, not to mention earn enough to support a family, should Fanny, for some reason unknown to him, decide to cast her lot with him? Besides these dark thoughts, and the night-bogeys who invaded his dreams and even, at times, bothered him while he was awake, another defect had plagued him since he was a child: his distractibility.

The past few hours were exactly like so many other times when he would seize a pen, turn his notebook to a fresh page and scribble an inspiration for an essay or story. The inspirations always came in a rush, sometimes in the middle of the night after a dream, but at other times in the broad daylight after a walk or a conversation with a stranger. Always, he started writing with certainty that the idea was brilliant. Then, after dashing off several pages, often twenty but sometimes as many as forty—he would hit a brick wall. His energy spent, the wellspring of his ideas shut off as quickly as they had begun, his excitement would fade, turning into depression. Try as he might, he could not summon the energy to draw the threads of the story together, re-spin them, or otherwise come to a satisfying result.

Always, the pain of seeing how far short a piece had fallen from his initially exciting vision of it hurt as much as the pain in his lungs. So he would lay the work aside and vow to finish it some other day. But on these other days, he'd have a different inspiration that consumed all of his available energy for its writing down.

He walked out of his room and down the oak planks of the stairwell to the adobe's *sala*, the reception hall. Although the airy room was deserted, Louis cherished the room for its bold Indian rugs on the floor and the life-sized oil paintings of Mexican *generales* and their *señoras* that hung on the walls. More importantly, the landlady always kept a tin pot of coffee simmering on the stove. He poured himself a mug of the coal-black brew and trudged back upstairs.

After lighting another cigarette and slurping down half of the coffee, he again took up the notebook and paged through it. Perhaps he could flesh out the impressions of Monterey that he had been jotting since his arrival. "The waves come in slowly," he wrote, "vast and green, curve their translucent necks, and burst with surprising uproar, up and down the long keyboard of the beach. Inshore, a tract of sand-hills borders on the beach. Here and there a lagoon attracts the birds and hunters. A rough, spotty undergrowth partially conceals the sand. The crouching, hardy live-oaks flourish singly or in thickets—the kind of wood for murderers to crawl among—and here and there the skirts of the forest extend downward from the hills with a floor of turf and long aisles of pine trees hung with Spaniard's Beards..."

Mrs. Heintz's knocking interrupted him. She marched in with a tray of toast, mounds of butter, strawberry jam, and three fat sausages. She set the tray down on the nightstand and waddled to the door.

"I can never repay your kindness, Frau Heintz."

"Eat. Clean up. Rest." She walked out and slammed the door.

Why did women insist on mothering him? He rolled another cigarette and smoked it down until its glowing tip burned his fingertips. The tobacco perked him up a bit, but after a few fitful starts he just couldn't find the words to complete his essay.

His mind, instead, kept returning to Fanny walking with Sam, and what it meant. He took one bite of the sausage, which was enough. Lacking taste, it consisted of white globs of fat that reminded him of the dead whale's blubber. He shoved the window open and tossed the sausage to the dirt below the stairs, where Mrs. Heintz's collie slept in the shade. The dog pounced within seconds, yapping up the ground-up offal.

Louis returned to the bed and notebook—and fell asleep. He dreamed, in a sweaty, daylight-sleeping way, of Scotland where he walked up from the beach near Aberdeen on a long, grassy link. A dead humpback whale waited for him, but with eyes that glowed with a light that grew more intense the closer he got. Fanny walked from behind the whale dragging her parasol in the sand. A heavy surf pounding onto the rocks below rose into a huge tidal wave that rolled in. Louis fought to get up and yell a warning.

He woke perspiring, his throat parched, sometime in the late afternoon judging from the sharp slant of the sun through the window above him. One sip of coffee was enough —sickeningly cold. He took up his pen and notebook, turned to a fresh page and dashed out his thoughts which, oddly, twisted effortlessly into a story, or at least part of one. His words told of a beautiful, mysterious, dark-haired woman walking with a man on the beach—no, not a beach, on the *links*. He realized that the landscape near the lake and estuary near Monterey where he had shamelessly spied on Fanny and Sam had reminded him of the sweeping expanses of sand that had been claimed and firmed by tough grasses in his home country. So, he set the story in Scotland. The woman in his story dragged a parasol in the sand between her and a man whom she loathed but who dominated her and controlled her every move. He was an ogre, very handsome but an ogre just the same.

He narrated the story in the first-person before he had given any thought to exactly who this narrator might be. He decided that there had to be some back-story, some intimacy between the ogre and the narrator. But the two shouldn't be friends; this would strain credulity. Old schoolmates, perhaps. Or, old roommates, yes, much better. The narrator, young, innocent, idealistic of course, comes upon the couple quite by chance, while hiking. He is mesmerized by the beauty and mystery of the woman, and sets out to liberate her and make her his wife—even at the risk of his life...

The words flowed furiously. He was interrupted only once in the early evening, by Mrs. Heintz, who came for her dishes and to check on him. The sausage was exquisite, he told her, secretly hoping the dog had not vomited it onto her kitchen floor.

He wrote a title in block letters at the top of the first page: "THE OGRE ON THE LINKS." He closed his eyes and imagined seeing the title and story in print. No good; although he liked the story that was so easily spooling onto the page, "ogre" lacked all subtlety. He drew heavy lines through the word and left the title, "_____ ON THE LINKS," and jumped back to where he had left the story, and kept writing. He was not one to fritter and ponder a word, or at least not in a first draft, and absolutely never on the rare days like today when someone else within him seemed to be doing the work. He continued to churn out words and smoke through the night until the story, twenty-six pages of it, was complete.

The sun had been up for well over an hour when he wrote "The End." He dashed a cover letter to Henley.

> *My Dear Henley,*
> *Herewith the PAVILION ON THE LINKS, grand carpentry story in nine chapters. Where is it to go? God knows. It is not bad...*

He bundled the manuscript with the letter, addressed it, and then realized the post office would not open for two more hours. He sank back on the mattress and closed his eyes.

Within minutes, he jerked awake with a new idea about what to do with the story.

He forced himself out of bed, scrounged for a clean sheet of paper, and despite his exhaustion, carefully wrote an invitation.

CHAPTER 9
The Reading

Fanny answered the knocking on her door on a bright October day. Largo, the town's messenger, a white-haired Indian with a tattoo of Jesus on his wrist, handed her a thin envelope. She pressed a nickel in his palm, hurried it to her bedroom and tore it open. On a single page, a sketch showed a thin man at a lectern, reading to an audience of two women in dresses and a schoolboy in shorts. Scrawled below it:

> Your presence is requested at the first appearance
> of R. L. Stevenson, in his first North American tour,
> reading a work far in advance of its publication.
> 25 October, 2:00 PM, Casa Bonifacio.
> R.S.V.P. soonest!

She laughed at the audacity of it, inviting himself to her house. Clever, too: on a Tuesday, when Sam was sure to be at work in San Francisco, Louis would march to the front door in broad daylight like a merchant or salesman, dressed up, she imagined, in his blue velvet coat and sloppy red tie. Far better to do that than meet her in a café or at the beach, which would set off another round of gossip. Already, on any trip to the General Store for a loaf of bread she could count on a long stare or two from a neighbor, or an elbow-nudge between two of them, and whispering.

On the appointed day, Louis was dressed exactly as she had imagined—no great powers of prediction were required, on her part, since he hadn't brought much of a wardrobe from Scotland to begin with. His hair vaguely parted and shining from recent washing, he stood in her parlor before his audience of three, Fanny in a deep blue linen dress, Belle in one of yellow cotton, and Lloyd in shorts and a striped fisherman's jersey. "Today I shall read my recent story, 'Pavilion on the Links'."

Belle sighed. "What are links?"

"And what's a pavilion?" Lloyd asked.

"A pavilion is a big cottage, often with a grand outlook of the ocean. Links is a Scots word for a beach that's been overgrown with grass."

"Oh." Belle crossed one leg over the other and swung it up-and-down.

Louis set several loose pages on an easel that Fanny had set up for the occasion. "I was a great solitary when I was young," he began, rather solemnly. "I made it my pride to keep aloof and suffice for my own entertainment; and I may say that I had neither friends nor acquaintances until I met that friend who became my wife and the mother of my children...."

Fanny liked the way he quickly set up the characters, setting and conflict: the narrator, hiking through a remote expanse of seacoast, happens upon a handsome man, Northmour, who holds a beautiful woman, Clara, captive in a pavilion. As if she were a pet, Northmour takes Clara out for walks on the beach where the narrator observes them.

After reading a few pages of his dark, moody story, Louis warmed to the task, seeming to forget his audience and surroundings. Like a schoolboy reading a drama and acting all the parts, his voice rose and fell depending on the situation. The characters seemed to live a few feet before his eyes, as if he were having a vivid dream. Soon, Fanny was swept into his fictional world, entranced almost as completely as when Dr. Charcot mesmerized her in Paris.

"...The girl walked faster when she was with Northmour than when she was alone," Louis continued, "and I conceived that any inclination between a man and a woman would rather delay than accelerate the step. Moreover, she kept a good yard free of him, and trailed her umbrella, as if it were a barrier, on the side between them. Northmour kept sidling closer; and, as the girl retired from his advance, their course lay at a sort of diagonal across the beach, and would have landed them in the surf had it been long enough continued. But, when this was imminent, the girl would unostentatiously change sides and put Northmour between her and the sea. I watched these maneuvers, for my part, with high enjoyment and—"

"You've been spying on them!" Belle blurted, jumping from her chair.

"What?" Louis stammered, his face reddening.

"On my mother and father!"

Fanny was mystified. "Belle, honey, I don't know what—"

"Mother, you do that when you walk with father—you drag your umbrella when you're cross with him!"

An awkward silence fell, broken only by the tick-tocking of the Seth Thomas wall clock.

"I can't believe this. I can't believe you and... him!" Belle thundered, pointing an accusing finger at Louis before storming up the stairwell so hard that pictures rattled against the walls. Lloyd stood and followed her.

Louis took up his pages. "I'll go."

"No," Fanny said. "I'll have a talk with them, but first, finish your story."

Louis wrapped it up: the narrator frees Clara from her bonds, psychological and otherwise, Northmour is allowed to board a ship and sail away, and the narrator and Clara look forward to a happy future together.

When Fanny walked Louis outside, he stopped beneath the rose trellis. "Give me your honest opinion. Hold nothing back."

"You should forget writing travel essays. Write more stories like Pavilion."

"Seriously?" He frowned down at his papers as if they might be counterfeit bills.

She took his hand that held the pages and pressed it to his chest. "Burn the others, they don't matter."

"Don't matter! 'Travels with a Donkey' sold, and Henley thinks 'Amateur Emigrant' has a chance."

"Like flogging a dead horse."

He grinned, reached up to pinch off a rose and pushed it behind her ear. "Since when has Fanny Vandegrift Osbourne of Oakland, California become a literary critic?"

"Make me a cigarette." She led him to a wrought-iron bench in front of a birdbath. He rolled one, gave it to her and lit it. When he'd made one for himself, he leaned in and touched it to hers. His soft eyes and boyish lips, inches from hers, made her want to throw her arms around him and whisper that they must find a spot, soon, where they could make love.

Instead, she backed away and drew on the cigarette. "Since being mesmerized by Dr. Charcot, I've done lots of thinking and reading about the mind. About our dark side."

He laughed nervously, sliding so close on the bench that his thigh pressed against hers. "Oh?"

She shifted beneath her blue dress so their legs did not touch. "We are icebergs. The part of us that people see, the tip that lives out in the sunshine, is our civilized part. But the philosopher Schopenhauer says that our truest nature, which reveals itself when we are mesmerized, is ruled by animal instinct, the same force that governs the behavior of spiders and ants. That larger, stronger, more important part of us, the unconscious, lives below the surface of the water—in the dark."

"I'm two people," he agreed, raising his chin and blowing smoke toward the bright blue sky. "It's me and this other fellow. He comes out in my dreams. And in my desire." He squeezed her thigh.

His touch was enough, even through the fabric of her dress and petticoat, to give her goose bumps. "The dark side contains our animal nature," she managed, "but also our creative abilities. We observe ordinary things and then, in wild mysterious ways, our mind mixes them to make a vivid painting, or in your case, a story."

"Usually it is you, Fanny, who accuses *me* of being the pompous one who gives lectures during casual conversation."

She tapped the pages on his lap. "Belle was right—you were spying on Sam and me. But that's where you got the details about the way that sorry couple walked together, with her dragging the umbrella in the sand, that gave this story life."

"I suppose. But the plot and characters came to me in a dream, fully formed."

When she shifted on the bench to turn and flick cigarette-ash to the ground, she again felt their legs touch. "Keep dreaming, Louis. Let your 'other fellow' roam. He makes art for you."

He brushed his lips against her neck. "I want you more than art."

"Go," she whispered hoarsely. "It's torture to continue this way."

"You tell me to listen to my dark side, yet you squelch yours. Is it because your children love Sam?"

"He's a good father."

"And you love him," Louis said softly, dropping his cigarette on the stone path and grinding it out with his heel.

"I love that he loves the children," she said carefully, "and they love him. He's father, he's papa, he's..."

"What I am not."

"Of course Sam is what you are not! Why would you want to be Sam?"

"Belle loathes me, and Lloyd is wary."

Fanny stood, knowing she should head inside and try to reason with her daughter. "It complicates things that Belle wanted you in France."

"What!"

"And you were the only man in the camp who didn't seem to lust for her."

By his baffled frown she knew he'd had no idea. "Oh dear God."

She kissed his cheek, turned his shoulders and gave him a gentle push toward the street. There, a burro pulling a hay cart sent up a cloud of dust. She saw Louis cough, and wanted to rush to him and give comfort, but turned to the house instead.

That night, Fanny had a vivid dream of her own: while she sat on a bench in a lush rose garden, a man stood before her, reading aloud from his notebook. She had no understanding of the words he spoke, nor could she see features of his face although she knew it was Louis. She rose from her chair like an automaton drawn to a giant magnet. In some mysterious, wordless way, the reader commanded her to remove her clothes, which she did without hesitation, dropping them to the ground. Overwhelmed by lust, she threw her arms around him, and he soon became, in that dream-way of sudden transformations, completely naked, his skin feeling wonderful against hers. Feeling his erection pressing against her, she pushed him onto his back on the garden bench, shamelessly spread her legs and lowered onto him, impaling herself and savoring the feeling of being filled with his warm, thick phallus. Thoroughly enjoying her dream, not wanting it to stop, she looked down at her lover while rocking over him and saw that he now had a face— Louis's, smiling and seeming to experience ecstasy as well.

But the face began to change. The moustache disappeared. The face softened and lost its manly definition until it became the face of a very young boy, perhaps Louis at the age of four or five. She backed away, muttering an apology to the child who continued to gaze at her with longing.

Suddenly the facial features became clear: it was Hervey, her dead son.

She woke, heart pounding, disgusted to find her hand between her legs and to feel the slickness of excitement there. Swinging her legs out of bed she rushed to the basin, washed her hands and splashed water on her face. She lit a cigarette and paced furiously on the cold tile floor.

No mesmerist was needed to decipher the meaning of the dream. How pathetic, damning, and obscene! In Grez she'd had visions of her beautiful boy, heard his voice, and believed that he had come from the dead to visit her. Utterly predictable, then, how she was drawn to a thin, boyish man who dropped into her life just months after Hervey's death and had been so attentive. Dr. Charcot, no doubt, would have plenty to say about this substitution, and might be able to treat her for it, but as Louis had said, Dr. Charcot was in France. She had put off Louis's marriage proposal with talk about his lack of earnings with which to support her family, but now she realized an even more important reason why they must have no future.

How could she tell him? Could she simply apologize to Louis for taking him, the embodiment of her dead child, to bed and using him so shamelessly? She had exploited his innocent idealistic nature, appealed to his literary interests, seduced him with her Wild West nonsense, performed for him by rolling cigarettes—oh my God, cigarettes!—that she had lovingly made, thrust between her lips and sucked; certainly the base, animalistic nature of that activity needed no explanation. She shuddered, thinking how much she had enjoyed oral forms of lovemaking with Louis, acts that Sam would not engage in, or at least not with her, because he declared them unnatural.

She opened her roll-top desk, took out stationary and pen, willed her hand to stop shaking, and wrote, "Dear Louis..."

CHAPTER 10
Rendezvous

Louis tore open the envelope and quickly read the short letter while Largo waited on the rickety landing outside his upstairs room. "Thank you, good man!" Feeling that life in California was good after all, he dropped every coin that he could dig out of his linen trouser pockets, a dime and a quarter, in Largo's palm.

"Too much, Lou-ee," the old messenger said, giving the quarter back, "you look like you should buy something to eat."

Louis's hopes soared even higher on the following morning, when he hiked south of town, passed the crumbling mission, and followed the directions in her note until he arrived at the place where, she said, she "urgently" needed to see him. Could there be a more romantic place to rendezvous than Hidden Beach? Behind where he sat in soft sand, granite bluffs rose like a high, horseshoe-shaped wall topped with pine, live oak and gnarled cypress and stretching a mile in both directions. In front of him, sea lions sunned on a tiny rock island while breakers rose from a bright blue sea and gently foamed around them. He decided that he adored this rocky little peninsula that the locals called Point Lobos. That would be Wolf Point, he translated, grinning to himself. If Fanny didn't think this beach was private enough, he would gladly walk further with her through this wild, lush Eden until they found one that was.

He took out the contents of his knapsack, a bottle of Chianti and a blanket, hoping she wouldn't find these props too obvious. In his eagerness he had practically sprinted to the beach from his lodgings and now he had time to kill. After smoking a cigarette he strolled to a tide pool and sat on his haunches for a better look. The yellow-green anemones, brown and orange starfish, and purple hermit crabs were larger, more vivid than those in Scotland. And in California, it seemed, the wildlife was more cheerfully deadly: hearing a splash he looked up and saw a sea otter just offshore poke its whiskers out of the water, roll onto its back and crush a mussel with its jaws.

After another cigarette he saw her making her way down the ridge in short, determined strides. In a gauzy white blouse and long blue skirt, dark hair ruffling in the sea breeze, she looked as exotic as the peninsula. Less exotic was the wicker picnic basket she lugged, big enough for a small tribe.

He waved the bottle of Chianti. "Welcome to Hidden Beach!"

"Hello, Lou." Fanny set down her basket and backed away from his outstretched arms.

"What's wrong?"

"Nothing." She gave a wry smile and lifted her head toward the ridge above them, where Belle and Lloyd were trudging down to join them, Belle fashionable in a blue sundress with an orange parasol over her head, Lloyd in khaki shorts and straw hat.

"Oh."

"I thought this would be a lovely place to discuss with you and the children my exciting plan."

"Oh?"

"Is there a reason why you only seem to be able to say 'oh' today?"

"No."

She opened the basket and pulled out fried chicken legs, forks, and a tin of potato salad.

He resolved to make a go of it, unfolding a section of the blanket to make more room. "Lloyd and Belle Osbourne," he said when they arrived, exaggerating his Scots brogue, "what kinds of mischief do y' think we might find here on the island?"

Belle sat on a flat rock, crossed one leg over the other and twirled her parasol. "Mother, do we have to picnic with this man?"

"Certainly you know that 'this man' has a name, Louis Stevenson."

Belle skewered him with her sharp brown eyes. "You wanted me in Grez. Don't pretend you didn't. Couldn't have me, so you settled on my mother."

"What!" Louis restrained an urge to utter obscenities at the girl.

Lloyd slapped at a mosquito on his neck. "Mother, what's Belle talking about?"

"I'm not quite sure." Fanny stood. "Louis, Belle and I need to talk. Could you entertain Lloyd for a while?" She took Belle's hand and tugged her down the beach.

"So. What sort of entertainment can we find? I suppose we could set fire to the Carmel Mission."

"Huh?" Lloyd blurted.

"On second thought, since adobe doesn't burn so well, let's go exploring. There's supposed to be treasure on Point Lobos. Gold and doubloons left by a band of vicious pirates."

"You made that up."

"Follow me." Louis set off on a path that wound up a rocky outcropping. "Stay close, in case we're attacked by a mountain lion."

He heard Lloyd sigh behind him. "We won't be attacked by a mountain lion."

"You never know, you see, because they stay hidden. One of them is probably creeping along behind us right now, up on that ridge, switching his tail like a tomcat does before pouncing on a mouse."

Pushing through some overgrown brambles, Louis heard Lloyd's footsteps catching up to him. He nodded ahead to a cypress on the crown of a hill. "A likely place they'd bury the bones."

"Bones?"

"Of the sailors the pirates massacred. Dashed their brains out on the rocks and buried 'em on the spot."

"What pirates?"

"The rogues who sailed under the flag of Black Dog. Or maybe it was Red Dog, one of the two. The pirates pretended to be ordinary sailors and worked aboard ship for an honest captain who was sailing here for treasure, but then mutinied when they got here, murdered the captain and his crew. But then, their fatal mistake: the pirates filled up on berries picked from those bushes over there, which are like a sleeping potion. In their stupor they were set upon by Indians, who killed and scalped them all."

"How do you know all this?"

"I read it in a guidebook somewhere, or was it a history book."

Lloyd gave him a long stare. "Let's dig for the bones."

They spent an hour poking in the rocky ground with pointed sticks, the only digging tools they could find. Red dirt soon filled their hair and coated their knees. A screeching flock of seagulls pelted them with droppings. Eventually, Louis leaned against a cypress, perspiring, trying to fight off the coughs that stirred in his chest, surprised at how long the boy flailed with the stick.

"There's no bones here," Lloyd finally said. "No treasure, no nothing, and these things don't work." He threw down his stick and folded his arms over his chest.

"Is great fun to imagine it though, isn't it."

Lloyd looked at him as if he were insane.

"What say we hike back to the beach and have lunch."

"Mister Stevenson, why did you come here?"

"For treasure."

"Don't lie."

"All right. I came to California for your mother. She is treasure to me. So you see, we have something in common."

"But she already has my father."

Louis peered up and down the trail, then along the cypress-dotted promontory and down at the beach. "I don't see him anywhere."

"You know what I mean."

"Yes, she is married to your father, but I'm sure you've noticed they don't spend much time together. You don't want lies and tall-tales right now, so I'll say it straight-out: I believe your mother would be happier if she divorced him. I'm certain he loves you, and he'll always be your father, but I hope that your mother will soon become my wife."

Lloyd wheeled and stalked away. Louis slowly followed.

When they got back to Hidden Beach, Fanny and Belle were eating lunch. Fanny frowned at their muddy knees. "What on earth have you been doing?"

Louis shrugged. "Searching for murder victims."

"He said there was buried bones and treasure," Lloyd said. "I want to go home."

Belle patted a spot on the blanket. "Have some chicken."

Lloyd plopped onto the blanket and glumly peered in the picnic basket. Louis took a seat near Fanny. All of them chewed drumsticks in silence until Fanny eventually said, "I spoke to Belle about my friendship with you, Louis."

"Oh?"

"I explained how a friendship can change and grow over time."

"Change and grow? You make us sound like a fungus."

"Must you always be silly, Louis? The story you read to us the other day gave me an exciting idea about our future."

"No need to make a speech, Fanny dear, just say what is on your mind."

"We can be more than friends."

"Good."

"We can have a professional relationship. You can show me your ideas and drafts, and read them aloud. I will give you comment about their worth, both as art and as commercial sales. In short, I propose to become your literary advisor."

Louis made the mistake of laughing.

She turned away, staring off toward the rocky bluffs. In the awful silence that followed, the back of her neck, beneath her pinned, upswept hair, had turned pink. "Come, children," she finally said, stooping for the picnic basket.

Belle and Lloyd quickly complied, leaving him alone on his blanket with the bottle of unopened wine. He watched them ascend the trail, Fanny in the lead, and saw them briefly silhouetted on the ridge before they descended from view on the other side. Resisting an urge to rush after her, explain and apologize—this would only make matters worse —Louis sat for another hour, watching the ocean wash over the rocks in front of him while insects buzzed around his head.

He uncorked the wine and drank straight from the bottle. His one consoling thought about the thoroughly botched day was that he hadn't laughed to belittle her. Laughing had been a nervous reaction, the culmination of months of frustration in both his love and his work.

He got to his feet, folded the blanket and set off. During the hike back up the steep, cough-inducing grade to the summit of the redwood-darkened road to Monterey, he mentally composed a letter that he immediately dashed out on a sheet of paper when he arrived:

Dearest,

Humbly beg forgiveness for not making suitable answer to your proposal during the family picnic. I would be honored to contract for your services as literary advisor, critic, confidant, etcetera forever. God knows I need your advice, as my father, W. E. Henley, Sidney Colvin, Robert Baxter, Ed Gosse and others throughout the civilized world have tried and, judging by my income, fallen woefully short. The forever-aspect of the above means this: for me to agree to your proposed contract for services, you must agree to the marital one.

All my love forever,

RLS

On a fresh sheet he jotted an inventory of current and planned essays that, he vowed, must be completed and sent off in a month. Finish a tightened version of "Across the Plains." Finish and send to Henley the impressions of Monterey he had been writing. Begin essays on William Penn and Benjamin Franklin. Rewrite his recollections of Edinburgh, before he forgot its gloomy haunts and denizens altogether. Finally, after catching up on his correspondence, each night he must spend at least an hour with Hazlitt's essays, copying them out one-by-one; it was the only way he knew to learn the style of a great essayist.

He turned to a fresh note page, drew ink into his pen and got to work.

He settled into a routine. In the mornings he walked down the creaky stairs to Mrs. Heintz's kitchen, paid a dime for a pot of coffee and a heavy German roll with butter. Thus fortified, he worked through the morning and afternoon, smoking cigarettes when the coffee and roll were gone. After each page was filled, he pinned it to the thick oak ceiling beam, trying to complete a line of them from wall to wall before quitting at 4:00 P.M.

Then, the event he eagerly anticipated, a walk through the squawking chickens and dust of Alvarado Street to the little white U.S. Post Office, just beyond the General Store. Today, as on most days, there were no letters. He hoped that his family and friends had by now digested the news of his coming to California and were churning out as many letters to him as he had written and sent to them. Considering the three weeks it took for European letters to reach his remote station, perhaps mounds of them would soon arrive.

On Friday, homesick and needing company, after the post office he turned onto a dirt path overgrown with fuchsias that led to the door of a weather-beaten adobe. A pull on a knotted rope unlatched the door and admitted him to an entry hall with whitewashed walls and a coat rack.

"The flea-bitten Scot is here to spend his quarter!" boomed a deep voice from the end of the hall. If Jules Simoneau were not Louis's best friend in Monterey, the man would frighten him. In a shapeless work shirt and baggy khakis, with a blocky build, hooked nose, white beard and chaotic hair, he looked like one of the fanatic martyrs Louis had grown up hearing about.

"Monsieur Simoneau." Louis swept off his beret.

"May I show you to our finest table?" Louis followed Simoneau into a low-ceilinged dining room hung with sketches of still-lifes and paintings of Greek goddesses. At one of the restaurant's four small tables, two swarthy men swilled Chianti and munched tomatoes.

Augustin Dutra, the fisherman, shoved out a chair for him. "Where've you been hiding?"

"Working, I'm afraid."

"The day that sitting around with a pen all day is working is the day I blow a hole in my boat, send it to the bottom of the bay and find a rich widow to care for me."

Louis speared a tomato slice with a fork. "Bad catch today?"

"I catch what I catch. Some days a half-ton of tuna, other days a bony shark. Today I caught a size-twelve boot."

The other diner, Francois, wiry, with a thick head of red hair, poured Louis a glass. "At the bakery, some days I bake big loaves of bread. On other days, I bake big loaves of bread."

Dutra held up his glass. "To fat fish and soft bread."

"Hear! Hear!" the others answered.

Simoneau brought another bottle of wine and sat, topping off their glasses. "You'll be drunk before the chili is served."

"My work is the same as yours, truth be told," Louis said. "Some days I write a shark, other days a jellyfish. Today I wrote a size-twelve boot."

"Never trust a Scot," Dutra said, and belched.

A dark woman in a bright cotton skirt and a blue scarf set bowls of chili before the men. Simoneau pulled her close and kissed her.

She whacked him with a spoon. "Just 'cause we're married, you don't do that in front of your friends," she said with a smile before heading off to the kitchen.

"I was thinking," Louis said, "when I was camping a while back, as I sat atop a glorious and pristine mountain, before I fainted and almost died and would have been consumed by hungry goats, about California. How she is a woman, a dangerous one."

"She's a whore," Francois said, sloshing more wine.

"Not a whore," Louis said, "although she does exact a price. Beautiful, raw, young, lush, curved, she draws you in and you can't get out. Scotland, an ancient beast, is darker and gloomier, but kinder."

They drank to that. Soon, Doña Martina brought slices of watermelon and brandy, and they lit cigars. Eventually,

Dutra and Francois said boozy good-byes and swayed out the door.

As usual, their chess game progressed slowly. An hour into the game, Louis toyed with his knight. "I shall have her. Whatever I must do, I will. There's no going home without her."

Fat cigar between his teeth, Simoneau scratched a match under the table and lit a candle. "You love her."

"Ridiculously."

"The question is, does she love you?"

"I believe so. She wants to be my literary advisor."

Simoneau's eyes followed Dona Martina, who wiped down a corner table and replaced its vase of droopy roses with fresh ones. "Love and business can mix, you know."

Louis drew on his cigarette and blew a smoke ring. "She says I should write from the dark side."

"The what?"

"The side of nightmares. Of primitive urges that take us beneath damp rocks where we slither and creep. The side of us that wants to burn flies with a magnifying glass, to tear our tormentors apart with bare hands, to pay whores and defile them."

"Jesus."

"Fanny thinks I should harvest stories from these grotesque places, but I prefer to write essays. Of course life is grim, evil is real, living things rot; I'm not stupid. But I prefer to look at life as a noble adventure, a quest, even if it's usually tilting at bloody windmills. Why wallow in foul thoughts?"

Simoneau set his cigar in the ashtray. "Why not?"

"Typical Gaul," Louis muttered.

Simoneau laughed. "Thoughts hurt nothing, Louie, only deeds. Let me ask you something. Have you ever hurt someone?"

"I hurt my father when I rejected Presbyterianism. I hurt my mother when I bolted Scotland to run after a married woman."

"I mean have you hurt someone so they bled or bruised?"

"I suppose I got a bit harsh with Modestine."

"Who?"

"A donkey. I'd still be trying to get across the Cevennes, had I not sped her up with a stick I used to prod her."

Simoneau threw up his hands. "Stevenson, you're the most harmless man I know. If you were to become a bit crueler, you might even be interesting. Now are we going to play chess or natter like spinsters?"

"I'll slaughter you in six moves."

"In six years, but only if I fall asleep and you cheat."

Long after midnight, Louis sat on the bare mattress with his back propped against the wall, dashing off a few lines to Henley in Edinburgh:

> ... *My health keeps along fairly; I do think it improves all the time; it had need, for I was pretty low at one time. Jules Simoneau is a pleasant old boy with whom I discuss the universe and play chess. He has been out of France for thirty-five years. Were you here you would find me in evenings installed in Simoneau's little whitewashed back room, round a dirty tablecloth, with Francois the baker, perhaps an Italian fisherman, Augustin Dutra, and Simoneau himself...*

When he finished and signed the letter, he added,

> *P.S. Do acknowledge the 'Pavilion' on return. I shall be so nervous till I hear; as of course I have no copy except of one or two places where the vein would not run. God prosper it, poor 'Pavilion'!*

In the morning, when he handed the sleepy clerk his letter and a nickel for postage, the boy handed two thick envelopes to him in return. He shoved them in his jacket, hurried out onto the boardwalk and grinned at a crisp morning sun. Luck was changing—he would allow himself a half-hour's detour to savor the rare missives. He sauntered to the docks, sat on a redwood bench, briefly marveled at the sidewalk paved with cross-sections of whalebones, and rolled a cigarette. He drew the wonderful thick smoke into his lungs and watched the fishing boats load their nets and set out toward the deep water beyond the bay.

He opened the first letter, from Henley. It opened with the usual banter, inquiring how "my dear mad Louis" was getting on at the edge of God's earth, then getting to the point.

I'm afraid I must admit to the view that California and California things are having a bad effect on your writing. "The Pavilion on the Links" is quite below the mark, although I have, as promised, sent it along to *Cornhill Magazine* for consideration. Perhaps it is due to your travails over Mrs. O but I must say, you've not come up with anything in America that is worthy of your usual keen wit...

Louis dropped the letter to his lap, took a long drag of the cigarette and looked out to where the horizon of the ocean blurred with the sky, fighting off a feeling that he might as well just give up. Coughing welled from low in his chest, yielding to light-headedness and nausea.

He forced himself to resume reading:

..."The Amateur Emigrant" and "Across the Plains," interesting in a prosaic sort of way, could well prove unsaleable. When you come home, we can finish *Deacon Brodie*. Plays, not essays or stories, will provide best income, and *Deacon* is a fine one.

Louis groaned; he'd been working on and off for two years with Henley on the drama about an ordinary Scottish cabinet maker by day who leads a secret life as a thief by night. The story, based on a sensational Edinburgh news event of the previous century that had culminated in Deacon Brodie's hanging, might at least follow Fanny's suggestion that he write from the "dark side" of life. But he had no plans to return to Europe without her, and even if he did, the experience of co-writing just the first act with bombastic Henley had exhausted and depleted him. He lit another cigarette, inhaling carefully, but the smoke that sometimes calmed him only intensified his queasiness.

The second envelope contained letters from his mother and father. He unfolded the thin, yellow stationery bordered in floral patterns first. "I pray to a merciful God that this letter finds you well," his mother had written, three weeks before. "My heart breaks at the thought of the privations you suffer, and the threats to your health of living in that remote, unfriendly land." After continuing for several paragraphs of motherly concern, she urged him to come home so that he could be "restored by a loving home and the comforts that a man of fragile health requires."

His father's letter, written on stark white paper, began with the subtlety of a meat-axe. "I have begged the help of your good friends to use what influence they might have on you to end this sinful mad business with Mrs. Osbourne. Is it fair that your mother and I should be half-murdered by your conduct?" The body of the letter became a tract on the teachings of both New and Old Testaments concerning the sanctity of marriage, morality and fornication. The final paragraph, which began with a softer tone, expressing love "for my dear, only son," offered to pay first-class rail and steamer passage home, but then stated that if the offer were rejected, Louis could expect no further support.

Louis ground out the cigarette with his heel, stuffed the letters in his jacket pocket and trudged toward his room. A stiff breeze blew sand and dried horse dung from the road into his face and eyes. When he reached the back stairway, a boy wearing a black cap and suspenders walked up with a yellow Western Union envelope.

Louis tore it open and immediately saw that it was from his uncle in Edinburgh:

YOUR FATHER CRITICALLY ILL STOP BEGS YOUR IMMEDIATE RETURN STOP PLEASE CABLE INTENTIONS SOONEST STOP GEORGE BALFOUR

CHAPTER 11
Change of Plans

Fanny yanked a straw hat off its hook on the way up the wrought-iron stairwell. She ducked into her bedroom, grabbed her easel and yelled down the hallway, "You about ready, Lloyd?"

Finally, she had come up with something to do with her son that he seemed excited about. They would spend the bright autumn day at the pier where he could fish, his favorite pastime, while she sketched the men in straw hats and jerseys setting out in their boats. Lately, Lloyd had been quiet and surly. She feared his growing away from her even if such was the nature of boys who were about to be teens.

Her thoughts were broken by shouting and banging on the door. Hurrying downstairs she saw Sam through the open doorway, magnificent in a fringed buckskin shirt and silver-spurred boots, holding up the reins of two black-and-white Appaloosas while Lloyd raced out yelling, "I can't believe it! I can't believe it!" and Belle threw her arms first around her father and then her new horse.

Sam tugged Fanny outside to a third horse, a white mustang. "His name is Clavel, the Spanish word for carnation. Perfect for you, the flower of my life, wouldn't you say?"

She didn't say. In fact she was speechless, forcing a smile in front of the children to hide her disappointment that her plans for the day had been shattered. Typical of Sam, to show up for the weekend unexpectedly and throw money at the hearts of the children, thereby underscoring her complete financial dependence on him.

She kept her horse behind those of Sam and the children as they rode the bluffs above Monterey Beach on the crystalline Saturday. The white sandy beach stretched below her on one side, edged by a foamy line of surf, while the black ponds of the estuary inched by on the other side. By the way he twitched and tossed his head, she knew her horse was itching to pass the Appaloosas that now seemed to strain to stay up with Sam's red roan. Eventually tiring of eating dust from the hooting, hat-waving threesome she gave rein to Clavel and, skirts billowing in the wind, quickly drew alongside them.

Sam reached over and grabbed her reins. "Whoa! Whoa, Clavel, whoa, Fanny Osbourne!"

"What are you doing?"

He reined in the horses and steered them to a ditch of brackish water on the estuary-side of the road. "Admiring the children we made," he said with a nod toward Lloyd and Belle, who raced ahead, "and wondering why you're dirtying their name with that Scotchman again."

For the second time that day, she temporarily lost the power of voice.

His bigger horse shoved against hers while the beasts slurped water. "People talk, you know," he continued.

Who had told him? One of the children? A neighbor? A saloon friend? "He's here to write a travel book about coming to America," she finally managed.

"That so. You going to be in it?" He gave her a long look, wheeled his horse and galloped after Lloyd and Belle.

At supper, cheeks tinged with sunburn, Belle and Lloyd sat at Sam's end of the table while he attacked fried chicken with his fingers and guffawed at everything they said. Eventually he puffed a cigar, called for brandy, and violently swirled the glass Fanny brought him before poking it between his moustache and beard.

After the house was quiet and Sam had tipsily sauntered off to bed, Fanny lugged the bath-water kettle from the stove to the bathroom and poured steaming water into the claw-foot tub. She tiptoed to the bedroom for her bathrobe. The gas lamp still burned on the wall above Sam, hissing yellow light onto his hair and beard as he sat naked with his back against the oak headboard. He patted a place next to him.

"I'm taking a bath."

He stood and grinned, apparently proud of the erection he waved her way. "Take it afterwards."

She trudged to the cherry-wood wardrobe and slowly hung up her dress. She turned off the gas lamp before taking off her underclothes, refusing Sam the pleasure she knew he took in staring at her naked skin. In bed she got his usual preamble, the scrape of his beard against her neck and a hand fondling her breast. When he grabbed between her legs she shoved him away. "Slow down."

He sighed but obeyed, moving his hand behind her neck, pulling her face toward him and kissing her. Sam had never been an awful lover, and he did seem to be trying, but she felt no excitement whatever from his ministrations.

Deciding she might as well get it over with, she splayed her legs.

He pressed himself in her dry cleft and began sawing back and forth against it in the sure rhythm he used when rowing a boat, perhaps hoping she might slicken enough for him to penetrate. As he doggedly continued she felt drops of his perspiration splat onto her chest.

"Sam, we could end this marriage."

She felt sudden cool night air on her flesh as his weight lifted off of her. The bed creaked as he rolled away from her, and she heard him breathing in heavy sighs, whether in sorrow or fury she couldn't say. Except for a dog yapping out on Alvarado Street and someone cursing at it in Spanish, the next minutes passed in deadly silence.

She swung out of bed, her bare feet cold on the tile floor. In the bathroom she tested the water with a toe and stepped in—still nice and hot. She tried to lose herself in it, sinking her back against the smooth slope of the tub, looking up at a brass vase of roses on the marble sink and, hanging above it, her painting of the bridge over the peaceful river at Grez. She lathered a sponge with soap, lifted it high and squeezed, savoring the suds raining on her shoulders and oozing down her back. She filled the sponge again, emptying it in front so that the warmth spilled over her neck and breasts. With intense longing, her thoughts went to Louis, and the first time they had made love...

She had moved with the children to Paris after the summer painting-season in Grez was over, and Louis had gone to London to badger his literary friends about getting more of his essays published. Planning to spend another winter in France—by now, she really did not care how many mistresses Sam paraded through their marriage bed in Oakland—she found a cheap rental in Montmartre, a climb of four flights on wooden stairs to a tiny one-bedroom apartment. For a week, Fanny caught up on her correspondence, Belle painted sensuous scenes of young artists, all of whom looked like O'Meara, the Irish painter she'd met, and Lloyd stayed glum, either because he missed his father or because they were miles from good places to fish.

Then, frantic knocking on their door. She opened it to Louis who stood on the iron landing in a threadbare tweed coat, clutching a beret to his chest and fighting for breath. "Was hoping this was the place." His eyes rolled back in his head, and he collapsed like a heap of sticks to the porch.

Fanny stooped down to him.

Lloyd appeared in the doorway. "Mr. Stevenson?"

"Help me get him inside."

They each took an arm and half-carried, half-dragged him in. In the small living room, Belle looked up from a dresser where she was putting on lipstick to gape. "Mother?"

"Let's get him to the bedroom." Under Belle's stare they continued through a doorway, dragging him onto the bed. When Fanny eased off his shoes and jacket Louis's eyes fluttered open and he gave a weak smile. "Sorry, love, I've no other place to go."

"What's wrong? Have you been eating?"

"Just need a little rest."

"Don't you ever take care of yourself?" She brought a damp cloth and smoothed the hair from his forehead. He smiled weakly, and closed his eyes.

Belle stepped into the room and whispered hoarsely, "You can't let him stay here!"

Fanny walked Belle out of the room and softly closed the door behind them. "He's desperately ill."

"He's always desperately ill. He's pathetic, mother. Can't you see, he just wants to be with you?"

"That's enough!"

"And if he has your bed, where are you going to sleep?" Belle waved at the room that was already crowded with cots for Belle and Lloyd, a table and chairs.

"On the sofa. Just for a few nights."

Lloyd frowned at the bedroom door. "I'll bet my father wouldn't like this."

One week to the day after Louis collapsed on her doorstep, Fanny returned from the baker to find Louis dressed and sitting on the sofa with his writing. "You look much healthier."

"As do you." He rose from the couch and kissed her forehead.

She set her handbag on the table and sat on a chair, modestly apart from him.

Louis smiled at her with the boyish grin and soft eyes that made her want to hold him. The look was also, somehow, an invitation.

"Louis, I..."

He walked to her chair and touched her shoulders. She rose, and found herself in his arms. "Lloyd and Belle—"

"Are gone for a few hours," he finished. "Belle to Monsieur Julien's to do sketches, and Lloyd to a shop that sells fishing tackle."

She allowed a kiss, which felt wonderful, and made her feel womanly and loved. The kiss turned into a second kiss. He took her hand and led her to the bedroom. "We're both mad," she said, locking the door behind them and kicking off her shoes.

The strength of her desire surprised her; she realized from her depths how much she wanted Louis to be one with her, to be inside her. Surprisingly, she found his thin body when unclothed to be strong and sinewy, not at all that of a weak indoor man. Perhaps his canoeing through Europe, or his childhood tramping to Highland castles and coastal lighthouses, had created the tough layer beneath the clothes. He was as tender and adoring as she imagined he would be, a vigorous, playful, intoxicating lover who took her to blissful heights and let her down gently, in his arms. For the remainder of their time in France he made love to her every day, if not with his body, then with notes, hand-drawn cartoons, and the wide-open smiles that displayed his startling view—that to him, she was everything...

Monday morning, Fanny had just finished setting bowls of oatmeal on the breakfast table for Lloyd and Belle when Sam in his blue-vested suit stepped in from the bedroom and set down his Gladstone. "All good things must come to an end—gotta catch the 7:55 to the city." He swept up the children for hugs, pressing a ten-dollar gold piece in each palm "to go out and buy something fun."

When he leaned to peck Fanny's cheek, he said in a pleasant tone of voice, "Pack for home. The rent on this place is due Friday, and I won't be paying."

CHAPTER 12
Decision

Louis stuffed the telegram from his uncle in his jacket and hurried out into a rain so heavy that Mrs. Heintz's chickens were hunkered down in their coops rather than pecking for worms in the yard. Soaked by the time he had run one block to Simoneau's restaurant, he found the proprietor on his back under a table, fiddling with one of its legs.

"One of these things is shorter," Simoneau explained, wriggling halfway out from under the table and glaring. "You're making mud of my clean floor, and you look like a ghost. What is it?"

Louis passed him the telegram.

Simoneau sat up and read it. "If you got on tomorrow's train, you could get to San Francisco in time to board an overland train by night..."

"... be in New York two weeks from today, book passage on a steamer, and if all goes well, be in London ten days after that. Then catch a train to Edinburgh, by which time my father might be dead."

"And so might you, from the looks of you."

"Or, I could find him in good health, ready to pounce on me with talk of sin and the devil. He so desperately wants me home that he might be lying to get me there."

"Your uncle would lie, too?"

"My father is a persuasive man."

Simoneau handed back the telegram. "I know you well enough, Louis, to know that if you believed he was in dire straits, you'd have thrown your moth-eaten clothes in a trunk and be headed east instead of standing here watching a clumsy chef fix a table."

Louis felt tears welling in his eyes.

Simoneau stood and put an arm around his shoulder. "But you love him."

"It's complicated, Jules, like every other bloody thing in life. He cares enough about me to lie, something that doesn't come easily to him, to get me back from the other side of the world. He is certain I'm ruining myself, not to mention going to everlasting flames."

Simoneau grinned. "But your backbone is strong. You are Don Quixote on his grandest, most ridiculous quest."

"But what if he truly is dying?"

"Life means making decisions in the face of uncertainty."

Louis made his way back on the boardwalks, staying beneath the eaves of storefronts, rain sluicing down the roofs all around him. When he got to the stairway to his room, Largo stood in the shelter of the opened door of the livery, waiting with a note from Fanny:

> Dearest Louis,
>
> I leave Monterey immediately for home because my husband demands it. Certainly you will understand that the children must have a roof over their heads and food to eat. As to your two-part proposal, may I have some time to think about it?
>
> F

Louis paced his room while he pondered the messages from the two persons in the world he loved the most. At worst, his father was dying and Fanny would stay married to Sam forever. Or, at the other extreme, his father could be in ruddy good health, and Fanny would leave Sam and marry him. Dozens of possibilities lay between these extremes, possibilities that could take years to play themselves out while he fought to survive with two rotten lungs—and editors who believed he was below-the-mark.

Looking out the window he saw that the rain had stopped. Sun peeked through the clouds onto the deep puddles on Alvarado Street and, further down the block, was trying to dry the wet streaks on the walls of the General Store. He took a deep breath and pushed open the door.

At the Western Union office he took a pen from its stand at the front desk, tore a page from the pad of telegram forms and addressed one to Uncle George in Edinburgh. After scrawling the text of a message, he dug in his pockets for seven dollars and sixty cents, almost half of all he owned. Before he could reconsider, he pushed the message beneath a wire screen to a clerk:

STAYING CALIFORNIA STOP FATHER BETTER
OR DEAD ERE I GOT HOME ANYWAY STOP RLS

*****

November, 1879

Propped in bed with his notebook, Louis bound the blanket tighter around his legs. Every morning he felt cold. He had rented the upstairs room cheaply, back in August, because it had no fireplace. Nobody had warned him that within a few short months, the ocean chill in Monterey would bite right through the windows, not to mention the socks, trousers, shirt and coat he wore beneath his one wool blanket.

For several shivering, indoor days he had subsisted on little more than the hope that Fanny would find a way to divorce Sam. To his impassioned letters sent to Fanny's

Oakland address he had received one chatty letter filled with news of the children. Lloyd had slipped from a tree and gashed his forehead, requiring a whip-snapping buggy ride to Dr. Bamford for six stitches. Worse, Belle had resumed her relationship with "shiftless Joe Strong" who lived in a San Francisco walk-up that doubled as his portrait studio. Worst of all, Fanny said her black mood had returned and that a recurrence of brain fever could not be far behind. Her only reference to divorcing Sam was to say the situation was "complicated."

Damn the word!

Louis's cough had become more than nagging; each episode made his throat and chest burn and was followed by a throbbing head. He wondered if the flecks of blood on his handkerchief would became a hemorrhage, and if, some lonely night, death would quietly take him as he lay in his miserable, crumpled bedding.

He shifted positions on the bed, turned his pockets inside-out and saw another pressing problem: money. Even rationing his spending to fifty cents per day—on average, anyway, some days living on coffee and cigarettes while on others he paid a dollar at Simoneau's for supper with wine— only four crumpled greenbacks, two quarters, three dimes and twelve Indian-head pennies remained of the hundred dollars he had borrowed from Charles Baxter before bolting Scotland. Unless he received a check from selling one of the dozen essays and stories he had sent from California, unlikely, given Henley's letters of scorn for them, he would starve. Given the frightened looks Frau Heintz had been giving him, he was already starving. But he would die before asking money from his father, who had supported him through college and beyond, even when Louis's biggest achievement had been canoeing halfway across Belgium, but who had made clear that Louis would not get a shilling should he follow the American mother to California.

He glanced through his work of the morning, nine pages of what seemed a silly story about a frontierswoman, Arizona

Breckinridge. The name had come to him while riding the overland train. To kill time, he had chanted American place-names that to him sounded magical, such as "Susquehanna, Minnesota, Arizona, Pensacola." Although his fellow passengers failed to appreciate the glorious rhythms, one of them telling him to shut the hell up, somewhere in the Rockies, Arizona got paired with the mining town of Breckinridge and became his heroine's name. Unfortunately, in six weeks he'd been unable to come up with a suitable story; now, had he a fireplace he would gladly burn the pages to warm himself.

He dozed—and dreamed of the warm summer sun he had felt at the goat ranch where he had almost died, and the warmth of the ranchers who had found him and nursed him back to health.

When he woke in the late afternoon, his back ached from being crumpled against the wall. Kicking off the blanket, stumbling to the mirror that hung over the metal basin, he winced at what he saw: a pale, almost beast-like face with eye sockets that had sunk deeper in recent weeks. Long strands of hair stuck every which way to his clammy forehead. He splashed water on his face and, with a varnished wooden brush his father had given him when he was a little boy, did his best to tame the hair.

He walked out into a cold fog.

At the Bohemia Saloon, the usual knot of evening customers were clomping mud onto the plank floors, drinking to a cold day of fishing or to warm sweethearts in Kansas City, Juarez and Shanghai. Behind the bar, the proprietor, Adolpho Sanchez, frowned from beneath his bowler. "*Que pasa?* Jesus in heaven, Louis, you look like you need a drink."

Louis whispered his idea to Sanchez.

Sanchez shrugged, pulled the cork from a whisky bottle and filled a shot glass. "On the house."

As Louis tossed down the cheap rye, savoring the warmth that slithered down his throat, Sanchez rapped on the bar with a glass. "This evening, gentlemen, as a special treat, a famous visitor to these shores, R. L. Stevenson of Edinburgh, Scotland, an author, adventurer, and performer, will entertain us with a story full of excitement, deep woe, beautiful women, and—"

Louis grabbed his arm. "That's sufficient."

"—all for the reasonable sum of a nickel a man!"

Sanchez dropped his bowler on the bar. The room buzzed as the men frowned, scratched their heads, raised eyebrows and debated the idea with friends. Someone yelled "Famous?" followed by laughter. Warily, they settled and lit cigars until a consensus mysteriously emerged. One man plunked a coin in the hat and passed it to the next man, who shrugged and paid as well. Louis's spirits soared; by the looks of things he might earn a dollar.

"The tale is about great love, interrupted," Louis began.

"The hell?" muttered a cowboy.

"Sure it's gonna be worth a nickel?" a fishermen shouted to guffaws.

Louis held up his hand. "And more. 'Tis a story of a good man pushed so far that he had to take the law in his own hands. Pushed so far that he committed a deed so foul, most God-fearing men could not imagine it."

Sanchez slid a mug of beer to him. Louis took a gulp and wiped foam off his mustache. "Arizona Breckinridge was a beautiful, dark-haired woman who came to San Francisco from Illinois after the Gold Rush of '49 with her new husband, Mr. Wellborn, whom she did not know well, or certainly not well enough. Wellborn had arranged the marriage with Arizona's poor but trusting parents quickly, his pockets full of glitter from the California gold fields and wearing the finest suit money could buy. He paid them a modest dowry, even more than one would pay for a fine horse, and promised to give her a life of ease.

"They settled in a small town near San Francisco; let us call it Happy Town, which turned out to be not at all happy for Mrs. Wellborn. To the townsfolk, Mr. Wellborn was a paragon of virtue, a church deacon and town mayor who raised money to build orphanages. In the privacy of his home, Wellborn proved to be a boor, and worse. After wolfing down the delicious meals his wife cooked, he complained that the soup was cold, the coffee weak, and the meat overcooked. Instead of encouraging her with words of love, he would ask why she grew uglier by the day. After downing three brandies he would march her to the bedroom, rip off her clothes, and savage her in every imaginable way. When he saw her tears he beat her, aiming blows below her soft face so the bruises would not show.

"Arizona—well, actually, she was born Hilda Smith, and at this point in the story her name is Mrs. Hilda Wellborn, but later she changed her name for reasons that will become clear—quietly bore his foul abuses and two children, a boy and a girl. Mr. Wellborn became a smiling papa who laughed and sang in their presence before sallying out to saloons where he bought whores, paid for slavish acts and beat them, too. And then strolled home where he waked his wife, mounted her like a stag in rutting season and beat her again.

"Mrs. Wellborn had one weakness, one escape, one sin: dime novels. She read how the heroes and heroines got out of every tight spot with dash, imagination and blazing six-guns. Perhaps this got her thinking..."

Louis sipped more beer and took his time lighting a cigarette, not having a clue where the story was headed. He noticed with satisfaction that the room had grown quiet and that many of the men sat forward on their stools.

"One day, at a general merchandise store she chanced to meet a young traveler from Europe who stopped to ask directions. A stain on his shirt pocket led her to ask boldly, 'Sir, how did that ink end up on your linen shirt?'

"He revealed that he penned adventures for a living. Intrigued, she stretched out the encounter, riding a short distance with him to help him find his destination, a small inn where he planned to lodge. If there is such a thing as love at first sight, it visited the traveler and Mrs. Wellborn. They talked for hours about stories, and about life, love, and all they held dear. 'Twas as if they had always known each other, that they'd been destined by the heavens to meet.

"The traveler made sure that he 'accidentally' met Mrs. Wellborn every day, by strolling the streets near her home and the stores she frequented; she, of course, ventured out constantly for this and that. Soon they crossed a dangerous line by planning the wheres and whens of their meetings. The adventurer declared his love for her, and she tearfully confessed that she felt the same.

"The young man explored all legal means of getting Mrs. Wellborn away from her vicious, hypocritical husband. He begged the police to investigate her beatings but they refused to be involved.

"One day, the ogre simply disappeared. The authorities at first suspected that he had committed suicide, but given his religious nature they soon rejected the theory. Next, they theorized he had left town, perhaps to escape a large debt he could not pay, but this idea, too, made no sense given his affluence and generosity. They eventually concluded that he had died of foul play, but having no clues or leads they closed the case."

Louis drained his second whisky and plunked the glass down on the bar. "I thank you, gents," he said and put on his cap to leave.

"You're sure as hell not leaving till you say what happened!" a patron hollered.

Another man slapped two bits on the bar to buy Louis another whisky.

Louis nodded his thanks and sipped the drink, silently but frantically dreaming-up a method of murder, which came to him while he rolled a cigarette. "The traveler," he at last continued, "posed as a visiting British industrialist who invited Wellborn to come aboard a ship anchored in the San Francisco Bay. There, he wined and dined Wellborn, flattering him every which way. After brandy he told him he'd arranged a visit by the most exotic, skilled woman of ill repute west of the Mississippi—who went by the name of Arizona Breckinridge."

"In fact, the traveler had laced Wellborn's food and drink with enough laudanum and arsenic to drop a grizzly bear. The last time he set eyes on his wife was when, barely able to keep his eyelids open, 'Arizona Breckinridge' was announced. And who should stroll in but Mrs. Wellborn! Who sadly shook her head, put her arm around the traveler's waist, thence to watch Wellborn give a ghastly look of utter shock—and drop dead.

"The lovers stuffed the body in a barrel, filled it with acid, weighted it with lead and rolled it overboard. Arizona—for that is the name she's used ever since—whose father was a tanner, knew the acid would dissolve the corpse long before the wood of the barrel rotted through. The only evidence of the foul deed that ever surfaced on the San Francisco Bay," Louis concluded, draining his whisky glass, smiling at his audience and pausing for maximum effect, "was a slick of foul-smelling brine."

The men laughed and applauded while Louis bowed. Sanchez tipped the jingling contents of the bowler into his palms, and Louis stumbled into the cold night.

Immediately on getting back to his room he wound the blanket around him like a mummy, propped his back against the scratchy adobe wall, and by the glow of a hissing gas lamp wrote the words to the story he'd told the men. Just before dawn he finished, lay down on the mattress and slept without so much as removing his boots.

He dreamed of walking in the estuary, rounding a tree and meeting Fanny and Sam Osbourne. Sam greeted him with phony kindness and inquired about his health. Louis tried to stammer "hello" but his face muscles were frozen. He began to grow taller and more muscular, a process that did not end until he was a giant and his muscles burst the buttons off his shirt. Sam, standing below him in miniature, blathered about the weather while Louis looked down like a hawk spying a field mouse. Eventually tiring of the little man, he plucked him up and tore him apart with his bare hands. Louis instantly became his usual size again, offered his arm to Fanny, and as they strolled away, she fit her thumb into his palm and rubbed, always her private sign that she wanted to make love.

He woke somewhat disgusted by the dream but also feeling an intense longing for Fanny to be next to him. Instead, his gaze was met by the pages he'd filled with the "Arizona Breckinridge" story that lay inches from his pillow. Cursing the cold he kicked off his blanket, lit a cigarette, read the first several pages—and was appalled by how stupid and trite the thing seemed, with plot-holes big enough to drive Sanchez's beer truck through. As if it were evidence of a crime he shoved the manuscript under the bed, trudged downstairs for coffee, and vowed to spend the rest of the day working on his essay about Ben Franklin.

Mrs. Heintz, wearing a shapeless gray dress, scarf and scowl, probably due to his unkempt looks, met him with a cup of steaming coffee. As he muttered his thanks she pulled a yellow envelope from her apron. "This came for you."

He ripped out the Western Union telegram:

YOUR FATHER IN GOOD HEALTH BUT SCOTTISH WINTER MIGHT RUIN YOURS STAY PUT CONFIDENTIALLY COLVIN

Greatly relieved, in his room he propped himself in bed with a fresh notebook on his knees, drew ink into his pen and worked for two solid hours on the Franklin essay. When he stopped to smoke a cigarette, he looked at the result: two pages of heavily crossed-out, blotted manuscript, all of it boring and tedious. He stood and rubbed his back. "Stodgy prick," he muttered toward Ben's portrait on the cover of a biography he'd been consulting.

He yanked the sash of the drapes, hoping that a dose of wintery sunlight might make a dull subject seem more interesting. Instead, the brilliant light set in bold relief the mess he should clean up: the muddy boots, dirty socks and shirts he'd tossed here and there, stray manuscript pages, some of them crumpled on the splintery hardwood floor, books stacked on the nightstand with dirty coffee cups and overflowing ashtrays. His gaze eventually fell on an odd item, a small canvas bag with a rawhide drawstring that Dutra had given him a few nights before that sat alone in the corner by the door.

After a dinner of pork tamales and rice washed down with beer, Dutra had followed him out of Simoneau's restaurant. "Take this," the fisherman said when they passed beneath the dark shadows of the fuchsias growing over the porch trellis.

The bag felt heavy. "I don't understand."

"There's been talk. Did you know, a husband who kills a man who's fooling around with his wife won't go to jail?" Dutra tapped the bag. "Learn to use that." Dutra had turned and walked swiftly away.

Today, a glance out the window at the bright autumn sun convinced Louis that he would feel warmer outside than in his room, and anyway, he could use a walk. He set off with the bag down Alvarado Street until he came to the Salinas road and turned inland, passing a pen of squawking chickens and a few stray adobes until he was well out of town. An empty whiskey bottle laying in a gutter caught his eye. He carried it by its long neck as he the road began an ascent into damp brown hills, making him gasp and perspire despite the crisp air.

Turning into a peach orchard, he ambled down rows of trees until he found one with a chest-high fork, and perched the whisky bottle in the tree. Stepping off twenty paces, he

untied the drawstrings and removed the contents of the bag
—a rusted .45 caliber Colt revolver and a handful of
cartridges. The gun looked like it could use a good cleaning
and some oil, but Louis wouldn't bother with that now. He
chose six of the least rusty-looking cartridges, pushed them
into the cylinder and snapped it shut.

"Die, Mr. Rye!" Louis laughed, raising the heavy gun in a
sideways stance like a duelist. He thumbed back the hammer
and pulled the trigger. The gun made a hollow popping-
sound. The bottle sat in the fork of the tree, unscathed. The
tree, for that matter, was unscathed, as was the hill behind it,
for Louis saw no dirt kick up, not one weed so much as
ruffled by his shot.

He cocked the gun and aimed more carefully, using both
hands. Again, only a muffled "pop." He suspected the
cartridges had gotten wet, perhaps on Dutra's boat. He
cocked and fired two more times with the same results.

Louis stepped to the bottle and held the muzzle against it.
"So, Osbourne, you've finally come for me!" He laughed,
pulled the trigger and—

An explosion and brilliant flash momentarily blinded him
as metal shards whooshed past his face. He smelled burnt
hair. Running his fingertips over his face he found nothing
left of his eyebrows and mustache. He stumbled off toward
town, his ears ringing until, eventually, he heard faint
squawking of blue jays in the pines along the road.

Reaching the Bohemia Saloon he made straight for the
washroom. Looking in its oval mirror he had to laugh.
Dozens of holes, the largest of them big enough to poke a
finger through, had been burned in his linen shirt. His skin
beneath the shirt was dotted with powder-burns that now, he
noticed for the first time, had begun to throb. The front of his
hair had burned off and what was left of it lay plastered to his
forehead in jagged curls, the overall effect being something
like a shrunken head he'd once seen in the British Museum,
only bigger.

Finding the barroom quickly filling with a late-afternoon crowd, Louis edged through knots of drinkers to find Dutra, in a striped cotton jersey and sailcloth trousers, with one foot propped on a stool while drinking a mug of beer with some similarly dressed fishermen friends.

"Jesus, Lou, what happened?" Dutra asked.

"Your gun."

"What!" Dutra pulled Louis by his tattered sleeve to the bar. "Hey Sanchez, bring two shots straight-up for the Scottish gunslinger."

The proprietor, in his white shirt, black vest and apron, gravely stepped to them with a bottle of whiskey, raising his eyebrows at Louis while he poured.

Louis told how he had repeatedly fired at a bottle from twenty paces and gotten only popping-sounds from the old gun, until he moved closer for "the execution" whereupon the gun exploded.

"That gun of yours was rusted shit," a fisherman told Dutra, "the barrel so choked that it blew."

"Did you take out the cleaning rod?" Dutra asked Louis.

"The what?"

"Oh good Lord, I always left a cloth and a cleaning rod in the barrel when I stored the thing."

Sanchez shook his head and poured Louis another shot. "Here's to taking out the cleaning rod!"

The men at the bar lifted their glasses, guffawed, and begged him to repeat the account of his target-practice for some suspendered farmers who hurried over to the bar to see what the laughter was about.

Later, at Simoneau's, the Frenchman whisked Louis to a table and yelled for Dona Maria to bring broiled salmon and sangria, on the house. Midway through the meal, Simoneau escorted a wiry man in a grey vest, black tie and red suspenders to the table. "Louis, meet Crevole Bronson, chief editor of the *Monterey Californian*. Mister Bronson, may I present Louis Stevenson, a writer of considerable renown."

"Oh?" Bronson seemed to be frowning doubtfully at Louis's singed hair while the men shook hands.

Louis stood respectfully, extending his hand. "I've sold some essays and a story or two."

Simoneau pulled out a chair for Bronson. "Louis writes like an angel, or at least the Scottish version of such. But the kitchen beckons; I'll leave you gentlemen to chat."

After leaving the restaurant, Louis dashed home, light-headed, pumping his fist as he passed through Mrs. Heintz's garden and raced up the stairs to his room. He tore a sheet of paper from his notebook, grabbed a pen and sketched a thin man with a notebook tucked under his shoulder and a pen clenched in his teeth, chasing a fire wagon. Below it he scrawled:

> My Dearest Fanny,
>
> You may now call me Robert Louis Stevenson, newshound. As of one hour ago, I am a salaried reporter for the Monterey Californian.

Deciding that less information was better, especially leaving out the part that his salary was only two dollars per week, he closed with,

> All of my love, RLS.

At five minutes before eight on the following morning, Louis waited on the boardwalk at the door of the newspaper office on Alvarado Street, a one-room operation among a row of small businesses that rented space in a low adobe. Louis wore his one wool suit, beret, a linen shirt that he had spent the previous afternoon washing and ironing, and purple knit tie. Bronson had told him the office opened at eight sharp, and the man had seemed like the punctual type, so when eight o'clock came and went, Louis began smoking cigarettes and pacing until, at twenty minutes past eight, a white-haired Chinese man in a black vested suit and skullcap walked up and pushed a key in the lock. "You Stevenson?"

"Louis Stevenson, yes."

"Mister Bronson says have Stevenson come in and do everything."

"I don't understand." Louis followed the man through the doorway to the dimly lit office that smelled of ink, machine oil and mildewed paper.

"Mister Bronson sick," the man said, yanking a cord of the window blinds to let in the morning sun. "He says have Louis write copy, set type, take ads, you know. Everything." He waved his hand at the tiny office that contained one desk covered with notes and billings, stacks of newsprint rising along the walls and a typesetting machine.

"The other reporters?"

"Ha. Just you and Mister Bronson. You want tea? My name is Chan."

Louis sat at the editor's desk and, after a few minutes of sheer panic, began digging through the letters to the editor, orders to place ads, bills and the like. He figured out that Bronson had coded them with a checkmark if they had been attended to, an exclamation mark for items needing immediate attention, and a question-mark for items that needed investigation. One stack of letters had no marks on them at all; these, Louis concluded, Bronson had not even looked at yet. Louis decided on a course of action. He would start by reading and putting what he hoped were the appropriate marks on the new correspondence. In what remained of the morning he would write ad copy from the new orders he had read. In the afternoon he would write his very first article, a lively piece, he hoped, about the virtues of restoring a roof to the Carmel Mission.

The morning went according to plan. He was a dynamo of activity—well, by Monterey standards, anyway, plowing through the stack and guessing about what mark to put on each item. For his first creative act, he wrote an ad for a new hardware merchant, touting an "extensive selection of the latest implements for all farm and household needs," agonizing for a half-hour over the word 'implements,' finally replacing it with 'tools,' mindful of the literacy level of the readership.

At noon, Jules Simoneau and Adolpho Sanchez strolled in. Simoneau tipped his beret. "Stevenson, the famous reporter."

"*Hola*, Louee, Sanchez said.

"How did you know?" Louis asked.

Simoneau shrugged. "News travels. Come with us to lunch."

"I should stay and man the office."

Chan, who had been oiling the printing press, wiped his hands with a rag. "Mister Bronson always closes for lunch."

"Civilized man," Simoneau said. He and Sanchez took Louis by the arms and marched him out the door to a wagon in the shade of a pine tree, where its black horse swished at flies with its tail.

Sanchez walked to a barrel in the back. "Lunch," he announced, pulling several huge beer steins from a canvas bag and setting them under the tap.

Bronson did not return until Thursday. Guided by handwritten instructions and copy that Chan brought from Bronson's house each morning, Louis managed to compose Friday's edition. Besides pages of inane advertisements and announcements, and a story Bronson had sent about a hanging in Sacramento, Louis had drafted two pieces of his own, one of them about the Carmel Mission.

He was editing for the tenth time this latter masterpiece when he heard the floor creak and turned to see Bronson standing over him with red, puffy eyes. "Good to see you back, sir."

Bronson sneezed into a damp handkerchief. "What've you got?" He snapped up Louis's draft and glanced it over. "It'll put 'em to sleep." He turned to a new page.

"But Mr. Bronson—"

"I like this piece you call 'Lunch'."

"You do?"

Bronson loudly blew his nose, shoved the handkerchief in a vest pocket and read, "While doing our level best one day last week to present an acceptable paper to our patrons, a vehicle was drawn up in front of our office door and descended from it Adolfo Sanchez, who immediately unloaded a staving thing from the rear of the delivery. An examination proved that there was a vent in it that distilled a white fluid and which after being allowed to stand for a few minutes, changed its color to a beautiful amber. Tasting it we found it very palpable—so much so that we tasted several times... The beer was from the brewery of Lurz & Menke of Salinas, for whom the Sanchez Bros, of the Bohemia, are agents. No better article is to be found in the State; Gentlemen, our respects."

Bronson grinned. "Now that, Stevenson, is writing."

Louis walked home with two silver dollars in his pocket, enough, if he ate light meals and skipped all wine except the glasses Simoneau sometimes poured free of charge, to subsist for another week. Dark clouds were blowing in from the Pacific and settling over the town. Merchants in aprons and bowlers brushed the week's dirt out onto the boardwalk and shut their doors against the coming storm.

The climb up the stairs to his room made him gasp; then, the gasps turned to violent coughing. He stumbled to the bed, suddenly very dizzy, and angry about it because he had planned on buying supper and then getting three good hours of writing in before sleep. Lying on his back, studying a spider web with several dead yellow jackets tangled within it on the ceiling, he realized he had no appetite. But neither had he an ounce of energy left for writing.

When his head cleared enough for him to sit upright, on a clean sheet of paper he wrote:

"Dearest, just one question: WHEN?"

He doodled a cartoon sketch below it, knowing that Fanny liked them. When he dipped the pen in the ink bottle and lifted its lever he heard a sucking sound. He would have to buy ink tomorrow, or what passed for it in California, a weak, brown substance that was outrageously priced at thirty-five cents.

He had just enough strength left to address the letter, walk downstairs and leave it at Mrs. Heintz's desk with an effusive note asking her to mail it. Clinging to the handrail, pulling himself more than stepping back up the stairs, when he got up to his room he collapsed, fully clothed, onto the mattress.

That night a heavy, blowing rain sounded like it might take the roof off of the tired hotel. Long after midnight, with a loud crack the oak tree in Mrs. Heintz's garden split in half, certainly a bad omen. He lit the gas lamp and a cigarette and saw by his fob that it was 3:40 AM. He stood to pour a glass of water and immediately felt dizzy. He didn't like the new sharpness of the pain in his lungs or the gurgling sound when he breathed.

At least, he thought, stubbing out the cigarette and laying back on the mattress, he no longer felt cold; the storm, Bronson had told him before closing the office, was blowing up to them from the tropics. He imagined flying on a magical carpet to a tropical beach, lush with coconut trees and a stretch of powdery warm sand where he could wiggle his toes, feel the gentle trade winds and breathe freely.

He coughed more violently, and lost consciousness.

CHAPTER 13
Oakland—November, 1879

Fanny opened the front drapes to look at the mess the storm had left. Finally, at midmorning the sun was trying to peek through clouds after days of wind and rain, but that was the only good news. Broken branches from her weeping willow sprawled among the thorny stumps in her rose garden that she'd recently pruned for the winter. Pine needles choked the gravel on the path to the door; it would be a dreary, on-her-knees job to clean them. Soggy pages from the *Tribune* plastered her picket fence, blown from the neat stack she had set out for the trash-boy. Worst of all, a once-stately elm that had arched over the street had come down. Its huge root ball, unearthed from the mud, lay on her side of the road with the trunk stretched all the way across, blocking passage in either direction.

She took up a feather duster, climbed a chair and attacked the spider webs in the corners of the ceiling, forcing herself to go about her day, fighting a growing panic that she was even more shut off from the world than she had felt before the storm. Her routine had been numbingly quiet: get the stove going and strong coffee made, cook oatmeal for Lloyd, and get him trudging off to school by 7:40. Then, on days when she felt up to it, write letters or, more rarely, paint a still-life. Seldom did she see Belle until 10:00 A.M., the girl now staying shut in her room and making only brief appearances before heading out "to meet friends."

Sam had come home just once, late-Friday from his San Francisco office. He had hugged the children, strolled to the bedroom and opened a suitcase. "I'll need a few more things. Won't be bothering you on weekends anymore." He began packing socks and shirts in silence.

"Sam, I—"

He slammed the suitcase shut. "You took up with the sick Scottish boy again."

"It's a little more complicated than that."

He yanked the suitcase off the bed and turned to her, his face mottled fury. "How is sleeping with another man all over France more complicated? How is starting up with him in California, where my children live, more complicated?"

"Keep your voice down, Sam."

Too late—Lloyd and Belle stood gaping at the open door. Fanny hurried to them, trying to think of something to say, while Sam hurried past them and out the door with his suitcase. Belle stalked away, slamming herself into her bedroom. Lloyd pressed his hands to his sides, tears running down his cheeks, stiffening as Fanny put her arms around him. "I'm sorry honey, I'm so sorry."

Now, a week later, Fanny finished with the spider webs and climbed down from the chair. Belle suddenly stepped from the bedroom hallway wearing a felt hat, wool coat, grey dress and clutching a carry-bag as if she were leaving on a trip. "Meeting a friend," she explained, stepping around Fanny and heading to the front door.

Fanny knew this meant Joe Strong. "To do what?"

Belle shrugged. "Go on a boat ride. G'bye." She hurried outside, slamming the door.

Fanny resisted the urge to throw open the door and holler at the girl. Instead, she watched through the window as Belle tiptoed around the fallen elm, turned toward the Oakland docks and sauntered off.

She had never wanted to consider her daughter a trollop, but lately had begun to wonder. Her fears had begun in Monterey; no, even before that, in Grez, when Belle quickly became the male artists' chief object of lust. She had teased the men with tight bodices, given them saucy smiles and the poses of a cat in heat. Fanny had chalked all that up to a seventeen-year-old's curiosity mixed with inexperience. But in Monterey, the girl—well, at twenty, the young woman—aided and abetted by shiftless Joe Strong, had apparently crossed the line from innocence to experience.

Fanny had caught them standing on the porch, kissing and running their hands up and down each other's backs. She had doused their fires by simply opening the drapes and staring until Belle stormed inside and Joe slinked away. But this only seemed to provoke Belle into coming home later, alone, with no explanations offered, after she and Joe had been together doing God knows what. Then, one afternoon shortly before they moved home from Monterey, a headache had brought Fanny home early from a stroll with her sketchpad to find Joe Strong and Belle lying on the sofa, clothed, but with the cad's hands roaming under her petticoats.

After Joe's red-faced departure, Belle had ended a tearful argument with, "Mother, if you keep bothering us, I'll run away."

That had stopped her, terrified her, even, and led to days of black, lonely moods. Eventually, she arrived at the most appalling realization: she would rather have the girl, whom she once considered her closest friend, a trollop and living with her than a trollop and gone from the house. For fear of alienating Belle, in the two weeks they'd been living again in Oakland Fanny had not so much as mentioned Joe, even though she knew that he had moved to San Francisco and opened a portraiture studio; she had seen his advertisements in the *Tribune*.

Fanny took a broom outside and worked on the debris on the porch. She hoped, at least, that Joe had the sense to wear a sheath when violating her daughter. She jabbed the broom at a big spider scurrying out from a crack, the mere thought of Joe taking advantage of Belle's affections making her blood boil.

Fanny, at least, had been a virgin when she married at the age of seventeen. The images of that night—a stormy one, too, in Indianapolis—flooded her memory...

...What a deliciously wicked feeling, being naked in bed with a man! She had always been a good girl, had always helped her mother and father with chores and done well in school. Now, in the bedroom of the little brick house that Lieutenant Sam Osbourne had already bought for her, she was eager to indulge her curiosity about the Way of All Flesh. She would show Sam that although she was only seventeen, and small—almost a foot shorter than he—she had plenty of love to give. She had no idea what she should do except press her hips up at him, cling to his strong back and keep whispering how much she loved him.

Sam, blue-eyed, blond-haired Sam, the best-looking man in Indiana, took care of her lack of experience—and then some. While kissing her deeply and pressing his tongue against hers, he slid a hand down to cup her breast. What a heavenly sensation when he gently teased her nipple with his thumb! When he moved his face down and suckled one of them like a baby, she was shocked but, also, awfully pleased by the warm, moist sensation. His hand slid down her belly, brushed the wispy hair of her pubis before finding the moist cleft and sliding inside, there finding her button of pleasure. She was shocked that he knew about that spot! Yes, he was one smart man, and not even twenty years old. She just knew that theirs would be a marriage of passion and excitement.

In the dim lamp light she looked at his stiff penis jutting from a patch of golden hair, and imagined it a thing of beauty, although, truth be told, its thickness frightened her. She closed her eyes when he pressed it against her and worked it inside. She thrilled at the way it filled her even though it hurt, something that of course she had known to expect during her first time.

When white light flashed through the window above the bed followed by a crack of thunder, she opened her eyes. Raindrops pelted the roof above them, filling the air with the sweet smell of water on the sun-baked earth, which mixed with the scent of the juices they'd made where their naked bodies met. All of it added to her bliss at being in Sam's arms.

He thrust harder, making the brass bed creak and bounce.

Another bolt of lightning and answering thunder, closer this time, lit the room and glinted against his cavalry sword that he had slung over the bedpost with his trousers. He ground away, hurting her a little more. She hoped he would end soon because the big drops of perspiration that fell from his face onto her face and neck were not at all romantic, and as he plunged and sawed she worried that her tight opening might be fearfully torn.

"Easy, Sam."

He groaned, slowing a little.

She shifted under him, remembering how perfect he had looked a few hours ago: blond hair with a hint of curl at the tips, perfectly trimmed beard, square-shouldered, resplendent in his blue Union coat, brass buttons, sword, fawn-colored trousers and black boots. Sam Osbourne had made her the envy of Indianapolis. She was no longer little Fanny Vandegrift, shunned by the girls and tagging along with the boys to climb trees after school. Today, she'd been drunk on the envious stares of the other girls: at her lace-collared, satin wedding dress, at her dark curls stylishly looped above each ear, at her radiant smile when Sam slipped a ring on her finger.

Above her, Sam's face tightened in what she imagined was ecstasy, his eyes staring but not at her, as if he were somewhere else. This reminded her of something that bothered her: Becky Blaisedale, a friend from high school, had come through the reception line and kissed Fanny's cheek. Sam had taken Becky's hand and kissed it. Nothing out of the ordinary, of course, but his eyes had gone to Becky's and lingered until Becky giggled and moved on, and his eyes had followed her. Becky had a fine shape, to be sure, and Sam had a healthy man's tendencies, so it was an awfully little thing to be disturbed about. And it didn't seem romantic or loyal to be recollecting such a thought when, for their first time, Sam gasped and relaxed on her.

She patted his sweating back. "I love you, Sam Osbourne."

"And I love you, Mrs. Osbourne." A gust blew open the drapes and sent raindrops down on them.

She giggled, thinking how romantic it was to have her husband's manly body over hers during a wild storm.

"I want to get us out of Indiana, soon's I can," he muttered, getting out of bed and stepping to the window. He lit a cigar. She remembered the room filling with smoke and making it difficult for her to breathe, and Sam continuing to stare out the window...

...Fanny shut the door and stacked the broom in a corner, having done as much as she could face, for one day, in the way of cleaning up after the storm. She walked to the stove to brew more coffee, reflecting on the fact that her marriage to Sam had begun to end on its wedding night. Part of her, the intelligent part, had sensed it was doomed from the time he had smoked and stared out the window in Indianapolis. She hoped Belle would not repeat the mistake she'd made with Sam; with luck, the fling would run its course without pregnancy, and Joe would move on before Belle foolishly married him.

By midnight, with the wind again gusting outside and bumping branches of the willow against the eaves, Fanny had bitten her nails down to the quick and was pacing the parlor, shooting glances out into the dark as if they could bring her daughter safely home. She considered pulling on her boots and venturing out to the police station on 16th Avenue to report her daughter missing, yet knew, in her heart, that Belle was safe and probably indoors, somewhere —with Joe.

Vainly trying for a sense of calm, she walked to her bedroom, sat at her cherry-wood dresser and took out her box of rag rolls. Brusquely she began twirling them into her hair; perhaps tomorrow she would walk out and have coffee with a friend. When she got the first layer of rags out of the box and in place, her fingers found a scrap of paper that had been tucked inside. Belle's neat, firm hand had written:

Dear Mother,

It is time you know that Joe and I were secretly married on August 9 in a private ceremony at the Pacific Grove Retreat. I did not tell you beforehand because I knew you would not approve. We kept our wedding a secret because we had no means to get a place of our own. Now that Joe is doing well in his business, I am joining him in San Francisco where we can live as man and wife. Please address mail to: Mr. & Mrs. Joseph Strong, 7 Montgomery Avenue. You of all people should understand that I had to follow the command of my heart, even though I knew my actions would hurt someone I love—you, mother.

Isobelle

P.S. Please don't be angry at Papa! He was in on our secret—Joe asked him for my hand and he was wonderful. He helped us find a place to rent and stuffed my purse with twenty-dollar gold pieces

Fanny set the note on the dresser and smoothed it with trembling fingers. Her gaze fell on Belle, smiling at her from a framed photograph that had been taken in France. Pressing the frame to her chest, she hurried it to the parlor and smashed it against the fireplace. She sunk onto her knees, sobbing.

"Mother?" Lloyd stood in his yellow pajamas in the hallway, rubbing sleep from his eyes.

"Go back to bed."

"Are you all right?"

"Fine, your mother is just fine."

Later, after a vain attempt to repair the ruined frame, she paced. Her rage had frightened her; was she losing her sanity? She decided that Belle's elopement had not unhinged her; in fact, she admired the girl for her bold move. No, the heart of it was her daughter's disloyalty: Belle had confided in Sam. And damn the man—he had not only graciously accepted her choice, but offered his support. How she wished Belle had confided in her; then *she* could have been the one to show a mother's love! But would she have done so? Could she have?

Next morning, while Lloyd was at school, the postman delivered one thin letter, addressed in Louis's almost illegible scrawl:

"WHEN?" he had written in tall blocked letters. Beneath the word he had sketched a thin man and shorter woman, locked in an embrace, with a pounding heart suspended in the air just above them.

She took a long, hot bath. After putting her curled hair stylishly up and fastening it with a scrimshaw comb, she pulled on a maroon skirt and ruffled white blouse. Stepping out in a cool bright sun, savoring the taste of the rain-washed air, she walked around the fallen tree toward downtown Oakland. By 11:00 AM she knocked at the door of an office on 14th Street.

A handsome, dark-haired man with a neatly trimmed beard and receding hairline, impeccably dressed in a green vested suit, opened the door.

"Hello, Tim," she said, trying to sound as if she had just happened by.

His shocked expression gave way to a grin. "Mrs. Fanny Osbourne, what a pleasure. It's been far too long. Where have you been?"

"Are you busy, Mr. Rearden?"

"Never too busy for you." He looked her up-and-down for longer than she would have liked before offering his arm and whisking her inside. *Be careful*, she thought as he escorted her across a gleaming hardwood floor and through an office decorated with an American flag, a California Bear Flag and, behind a large oak desk, a photo of Rearden and Bret Harte grinning on the docks of the San Francisco Bay.

He tugged an armchair that rolled smoothly out on casters and used two hands to ease her into it. "Are you ready to resume our writing lessons?"

Before going to France, weekly meetings with Rearden, who for some reason considered himself more of a writer than a lawyer, had been a welcome escape from Sam, the children and the tidy house. They would meet in the basement of the Oakland Public Library, where he would plod through her short stories as if they were great works of the western world and offer trite editorial suggestions, all the while flirting shamelessly. Back then, she'd been impressed by Rearden's friendship with the famous Mr. Harte. Now, after dozens of witty, manic discussions of the world's great writers with Louis, and the total intimacy with him that had developed, she would rather go to weekly tooth extractions than to more sessions with Tim Rearden.

She smiled. "Actually no, I don't have time for stories right now. I came to talk to you in a professional capacity."

"Problems?"

"Sam."

"You've always had problems with Sam."

"And I want to end them. End us," she corrected.

He raised his eyebrows. "It's nice outside, now the storm's passed. What say we stroll?" He jerked his head toward a cabinet where a shriveled woman with gray hair in a tight bun was thumbing through files. "More private," he added in a hopeful whisper.

Rearden steadied her arm as they walked up and down boardwalks of the bank and the general store, doing their best to stay out of the muddy street, heading toward the docks a few blocks ahead. Already he seemed to be wearing a hopeful look, she thought, wondering if confiding in Tim, of all people, had been such a sound idea. But who else could she enlist to help her in what would surely be a battle pitting Fanny Osbourne, housewife, against Samuel Osbourne, beloved War Veteran, loving father, employee of the court, Charter Member of the Bohemian Club and general Man-About-Town?

"Divorce is a serious business," he said unnecessarily, steering her toward a whitewashed bench where pigeons pecked at breadcrumbs. He waved, scattering them in a noisy beating of wings, then took out a handkerchief and polished a spot on the bench. "What does Sam think about this?"

"He doesn't know yet."

Rearden nodded as if that's what they all said. "What do you think he'll do?"

"Threaten to take the children, accuse me of adultery, take the house and leave me in poverty."

Rearden took a black cheroot from his vest and struck a match. "Is he right?"

"Right?"

"About the adultery." She noticed what seemed like a salacious gleam in his eye.

"That's none of your business."

"You are wrong, Mrs. Osbourne. If you're to be my client, it is very definitely my business. Who was the lucky man?"

Fanny stood. "I need to be getting home."

"Why now?"

"My son will be getting home from school."

"What I meant was, why divorce him now, after putting up with Sam all these years?"

"I suppose..." Suddenly her voice caught. "I suppose it's because I've been shut out by those I love. Sam a long time ago, yes, but now Belle, too, and I seem to be losing Lloyd. And Sam seems to be helping to engineer it. To ensure that I will be alone." She turned away from him, tears running down her cheeks. She felt Rearden's arm gently wrap her shoulders.

"This new man, do you love him?"

She nodded.

"Surely your boy doesn't get back from school at noon. Let me buy you lunch. You can tell me all of it."

That night after Lloyd went to bed, on a sheet of her fine, black-bordered stationery she wrote:

> Dearest Louis,
>
> I have consulted an attorney. It will be difficult, perhaps hell, but I am prepared to divorce Sam in the hopes of living honestly. As to our future, I regret to say that my love for you might have been spurred by a mental aberration that is too appalling to put in writing—I should be locked in an asylum or convent. I beg you, write to me, write more than cartoons, write beautiful thoughts, for I need them.
>
> Love, F

CHAPTER 14
Moving

He woke slowly, disoriented, at first believing he was home in Edinburgh. The feeling of weakness and the damp clothing from uncounted days of fever was familiar, but the voice yelling to him was not his father's. "Stevenson. *Comment ça va?* Monsieur Stevenson! Louis, answer me, are you alive in there?"

"Yes," was all that Louis could manage.

"*Mon Dieu*, boy, are you not eating again?"

Louis heard something large lumber up the wooden stairs, bang open the door and clomp toward him. White-bearded Moses in a blue work shirt and khakis suddenly loomed above him. The face lowered, smelling of *chorizo* sausage and with frightened-looking eyes. A ham-like hand felt his forehead. "Jesus but you're a mess," Jules Simoneau muttered.

The bulbous nose and wide brow in front of him began to blur. "Just tired."

Strong arms shoved under him, and the room spun upside-down. Suddenly he was an animal carcass, hanging over Simoneau's shoulder, approaching the doorway and floating through it...

... Louis felt something cold pressing on his chest. "Stop. Please, stop that," he croaked. His eyes slowly opened and

163

focused on a small man hovering over him with slicked-back hair, oiled mustache, starched collar and black vest.

"I'm trying to help you, Mr. Stevenson," said the man.

"Oh. Dr. Heintz," Louis muttered, recognizing his landlady's husband, a dour man from Luxembourg, who was sliding a cold stethoscope around his chest. "How long have I slept?"

"Two days here, and God knows how many before that. You are very ill, I'm afraid."

Louis wondered if doctors the world over said obvious things, or perhaps it was a case of déjà vu, waking feverish in a bedroom of velvet-covered chairs, rose-patterned wallpaper, crackling fireplace, and thick crown molding, all of it stunningly similar to his home in Edinburgh.

"You are fortunate that Mister Simoneau found you when he did, and carried you to my home where it is warm. And where it is clean," he added with what seemed a disapproving scowl.

Mrs. Heintz carried in a teapot. "See if you can take some tea with honey and lemon."

Louis struggled to a seated position against a carved headboard. On the wall opposite him a clock door sprung open and a wooden bird cuckooed ten times. "I could be in the Black Forest," he mumbled.

"You could be dead," Mrs. Heintz said. "Now drink, Louis. Slowly."

"Your lungs filled with fluid," Dr. Heintz said, while Louis sipped tea with a wobbly hand. "The coughing expelled some of it, but also triggered a hemorrhage. The bleeding has stopped, for now, and the warm room is helping to dry you out. But you could have bled to death, or drowned in the fluid of your lungs. If you continue to ignore the needs of your body, you will die. I am sorry, friend Louis, but this is fact."

"Is it." Louis reached for his trousers that lay on the bed and pulled a tobacco pouch from one of the pockets.

Dr. Heintz snatched the pouch from his fingers, reminding him of a thick-browed, Germanic version of his Edinburgh schoolmasters in the way he shook his finger and continued lecturing: "Your room is chaos. Wet clothes heaped about, books and papers all over the place, bloody handkerchiefs on the floor. All so you can carry on with that married woman."

Louis lay back on the bed. "Immorality kills, is that your point?"

"The entire town is talking. We can't have it. As soon as you are healthy enough, you must leave."

"Does it make a difference that I deeply love 'this woman' who in fact is named Fanny Osbourne, and that her husband is faithless and loveless, and that I want nothing more than to make her as respectably married to me as Martha Washington was to George?"

Mrs. Heintz bustled in the room and clattered the teacups on a tray. "What Herr Heintz is saying, Louie," Mrs. Heintz said gently, "is that we can't have you dying here because you're a nice boy, with a mamma and papa over the ocean who care about you. We couldn't live with ourselves if you die in our hotel."

"I couldn't live with myself, either."

"If we were home in Europe," the doctor continued, "I would insist you go at once to Davos, in Switzerland, a town that is high, dry, clean, and has a fine spa for consumptives that is isolated from all corruptions of the flesh. No drinking and no tobacco are allowed. Your miserable body would have a chance to heal."

"Sounds dreadful."

"But since we are not in Europe, your only hope is to take a train south to Los Angeles. The town is no more civilized than Monterey, I'm afraid, but from there you can travel one day by stage to the east where there is a vast desert. I shall refer you to a spa where I have sent other patients with acceptable results."

"Why not just shoot me?"

Mrs. Heintz bent over and kissed his forehead. "Is for your own good, Louie." The rustle of her starched black dress and its iron-burnt smell reminded him of his nurse, Cummy, making him suddenly homesick and even more miserable.

They left him. He felt the piercing ache in his lungs that always followed prolonged attacks like this one and the weakness of limbs that accompanied it. He lay sleepless through the morning, mind racing, restless to get back to his writing and, especially, to get to the post office to retrieve any mail.

In this last wish he did not have to bother. Mrs. Heintz bustled in at midday and slipped an envelope into his hands. Seeing it had been addressed in Fanny's neat, small script, he tore it open and quickly saw her glorious words, "prepared to divorce Sam." Life indeed was worth living! He ignored his exhaustion, forgot all pain and wrote her a rambling, effusive, messily scrawled letter of love and excitement. Poorly written, he knew, and with too many exclamation points and all-upper-case letters, but she had asked for a thorough letter and it certainly was that.

For the rest of the week Louis forced himself to eat all of the lentil soup Mrs. Heintz made, the sweet rolls she got at Schmidt's bakery, as well as the hearty food that the Simoneaus brought from the restaurant. He got out of bed and urged his body to strengthen. On the first day after waking he only managed to pace in the room. The following day, he walked a few circles around the old plaza, sagging onto a wrought iron bench in front of a large adobe when he needed rest. Although he breathed heavily, he smiled at the crisp dry weather, low winter sun and blue sky. By the third day, he moved back to his room at the French Hotel.

In the mirror he saw that he was still pale and thin, but he mugged some daring smiles and heroic poses and decided he was ready for a new adventure. He snatched his shirts and slacks from the chair and tied them in a ball. He carried them almost a mile to the Chinese village to be washed and starched. He gave notice to Mr. Bronson, who shook his hand, and insisted on paying him "two weeks' severance."

Louis found the Bohemia Saloon packed, that Friday night. Simoneau was there, of course, shoving a drink in his hand. Bronson tipped his bowler while Chan, his assistant, gave Louis a little bow. Dutra and the fishermen grinned at him with their sunburned faces. When Louis stepped onto the creaky flooring and headed to the bar for the last time, Sanchez banged a glass for quiet. "Boys, here's to Lou. May he dry out in the desert and come back healthy in the spring!"

"Here, here!" the others yelled, downing their shots with neat flicks of the wrist.

In the morning, Jules Simoneau and Dona Martina waited outside the French Hotel when Louis walked outside in his battered velvet coat, dragging his trunk to the street. While Dona Martina kissed Louis's cheek, Simoneau threw his arms around him. "Promise me you'll write," the bearded man said.

Louis smiled. "Only if you will."

Dr. Heintz, in a three-piece blue suit and bowler, hurried out of the house and yelled final instructions in Louis's ear while Simoneau heaved Louis's trunk onto the back of a hansom. "South to Los Angeles, then a stage to the Mojave Spa. Give them this." He pressed a folded page into Louis's hand.

In Salinas, Louis grabbed the strap of his trunk and dragged it fifty paces through the dirt, gasping to get to the correct side of the Southern Pacific platform in time for the train he wanted. Within minutes he saw the cowcatcher and belching smokestack of the locomotive making its approach. He thrilled at the sound of the hissing steam and squealing brakes as the train pulled to a stop in front of him.

He shoved his trunk onto the steps and climbed aboard the train—*northbound.*

Riding in an open cab to her house, Louis found Oakland to be a town of sober black carriages, wide, straight streets lined with poplar trees, and modest wood frame houses. The stocky driver nudged him. "Corner of Eleventh Avenue and East Eighteenth Street is just ahead. Which one is it?"

Of the homes sprinkled near the intersection of the dirt roads, Louis recognized Fanny's cottage from the way she'd once described it: small whitewashed frame house with dark brown shutters and trim, a row of roses and Spanish dagger plants in front, and a big weeping willow drooping over the eaves. He pointed out the house to the driver, wondering if Fanny might be gone, because the front drapes were drawn and nobody seemed to be stirring except—

"Keep going, sir!" Louis commanded in a low voice.

"Huh?"

"Just go."

The driver snapped his whip and they clattered past a tall, straight-backed, handsome man in a blue greatcoat and black hat—Sam Osbourne—who was tying the reins of a fine red roan to a rail on the side of the house. Sam glanced up and for the briefest moment seemed to look directly at Louis, who sank lower in the seat and turned away.

Louis doubted that Sam had guessed his identity—the two had never met, although Fanny may have had sketches or photographs that Sam had seen—yet the gaze had been unnerving. A sad and weary gaze of one who had suffered, of a man who had lived some of his life in hell. The hell of marching in the Civil War, perhaps, followed by marrying an exceedingly bright young woman he had never understood who had born him children, gone to France—and now wanted to take all away from him?

At that moment Louis felt very small. He made a snap decision to lodge across the bay in San Francisco. "To the Ferry Wharf, please," he said to the driver.

CHAPTER 15
Casting Lesson

"You could lie," Tim Rearden said, poking his fork into a broiled salmon steak and cutting off a piece with a bone-handled knife.

Fanny glanced at the well-dressed patrons to her right and left at Pierre's, a white-table-cloth restaurant that she could not have afforded on the allowance Sam gave her, and replied softly, "About what?"

She appreciated being treated to a nice dinner, but didn't like the offhanded way Rearden was plotting the dissolution of her marriage. She wondered why she had never been put off before by the sheer perfection of Rearden's sculpted black beard, expensive three-piece suit and ocean-blue tie.

Rearden smiled. "When he accuses you of adultery, just say 'No, I didn't do it.'"

She pushed a juicy bite of steak around her plate with a fork, not having much appetite. "You, an attorney, are advising me to lie in a court of law?"

He shrugged. "This isn't a sack race at the church picnic, dear Fanny. It's war. Winner takes the children."

"Child. Belle eloped with a cad. All I have left is Lloyd."

Rearden grunted while chewing his salmon. He took a sip of coffee, sighed and set it carefully back in its saucer. He unfolded a linen napkin and dabbed at his lips.

"Or," he continued, pausing and leaning toward her, "I could scare the bejesus out of him. Threaten to bring in testimony from a dozen saloon girls, misled secretaries and assorted mistresses that Sam's plugged."

How she hated the way he said it. "In this town, you think anyone would care?"

"Sam would. He likes being Captain Sam, Civic Leader. Testimony from a string of trollops wouldn't help his standing any. Problem is, Fanny..."

"The problem, Tim?"

"I'd lose a friend. A powerful one."

She tried to discern his expression; did Tim Rearden, Attorney at Law, really care about Sam Osbourne's friendship, or think him powerful? "It would seem to me," she said carefully, "that telling the truth about Sam's infidelities, whether or not you call it 'scaring him,' would be more to the point than lying about mine."

"I'll consider doing it then."

"You'll consider it?" She wished she hadn't raised her voice because the men dining at the next table were staring.

Rearden smiled and set his fork and knife neatly alongside his plate. "I'd lose Sam as a friend, but that would be a small price to pay for what I might gain. The truth of it is, dear Fanny, I value your friendship much, much more." He reached across the table and put his hand over hers. "Our friendship can deepen and grow."

Fanny pulled her hand away from his. "Are you suggesting..."

"I'm suggesting *everything*." Rearden gave her an oily smile and reached for the check.

Fanny stood, feeling like she might throw up.

On the following morning, she sat at the kitchen table, struggling to describe her situation in a long letter to her parents in Indiana. Filling four pages with pain had not helped her mood any. She set down her Cross fountain pen and massaged her fingers; she'd been pressing down too hard. She peered up through the window and its happy flowered drapes and saw fog so thick that she could barely make out the droopy branches of the orange tree Sam had planted several years before. The Roman numerals on the Seth Thomas clock, hanging on the wall before her, said it was past ten o'clock. She had accomplished nothing except scrambling eggs for Lloyd, who had hurried out to play with a neighbor boy. She had not even brushed her hair, but that could wait. And anyway, why should looks matter, when she had nothing planned but finishing a letter and chores?

She took up the pen again, put it on the page but paused. How could she explain why she hoped to divorce their son-in-law, handsome Sam Osbourne, pride of Indiana, who had given them lovely grandchildren, supported their daughter through lean times and good, protected her in fierce environments and was now a respected official of the San Francisco superior court? How could she relate that Timothy Rearden, whom she had once described to them as a brilliant lawyer, writing teacher and friend, now wanted her body in exchange for his services?

The letter could wait. She snapped the top onto the pen and took the pages to her bedroom, where she shoved them in a drawer of her roll-top desk. Her eyes fell on the edges of the canvasses she had brought home from France that she had stacked along the wall behind it. Setting these on her patchwork-quilted bedspread, by the dull light from the small window above it she turned through the paintings of barns, churches, still-lifes and portraits until she found an unfinished painting of Lloyd, standing on the banks of the Loire with his fishing pole. She had captured something about his expectant face, tousled hair, and outstretched arms that greatly pleased her.

For the first time in weeks, she found herself humming as she set up her tripod, opened the drapes of all three windows to catch what light there was, and mixed paints. Unlike life's events, art was under her control; with enough perseverance, she could make things turn out right. For a solid hour she worked on texturing the flesh tones in Lloyd's face and arms, adding a shadow beneath the tree and ripples on the river, and suggesting a gleam where the sun struck the wet fishing line. She would surprise him with it when he clomped in for lunch.

Heavy steps on the porch—certainly not Lloyd's—made her flinch, and the brush smeared the gleam in the fishing line. The door swung open and Sam swept in, dressed in a straw hat and dungarees.

"'Lo, Dear," he said as if he'd just been out for a quart of milk, instead of the four weeks it had been since he had last come home to get his things.

"You scared me."

He leaned down to peck her cheek and his eyes fell on the painting. "That's good of our boy."

As if hearing his cue, the door banged open and Lloyd charged in, throwing his arm around Sam. "Papa!"

"I was just admiring a painting of my favorite boy."

Lloyd glanced at the canvas. "I'm a lot bigger now."

"Yes, well, we should get to work on your form."

"Form?"

"Of your cast. I've got a perfect fishing spot picked out, you're gonna love it, but today we'll just practice." Sam was already leading the way to the back porch, Lloyd close on his heels. She heard the fishing poles clatter and the back door banging shut.

She pulled on a coat and headed after them.

Sam dragged a wash tub to a corner of the yard, took Lloyd's arm, and the two paced through the fog. Although Sam was in an open-necked linen shirt and Lloyd in a striped cotton jersey, the two seemed happily oblivious to the cold. "One, two, three, four five..."

At ten paces, Sam uncoiled line from his reel and in perfect rhythm, of course, rocked the bamboo pole back and then forward, arcing the hook gracefully toward the tub.

"Good one, Papa! Let me try."

Standing silently by the back door, Fanny watched Lloyd make a cast.

"Easy, son. It's all in the wrist, let me show you." Sam put his arms around him, clamped his hands over Lloyd's, drew the rod back and then snapped forward.

Fanny burned with envy. With no effort at all, Sam hit bulls-eyes every time he aimed at Lloyd's heart. "Honey," she yelled, "don't you want a jacket today?"

Lloyd ignored her.

"No sense just standing on the porch," Sam yelled. "Want to give it a try?"

She shook her head, shoving her hands into the pockets of her blue wool overcoat. "I'll just watch."

Sam swung the rod back and paused. "I'm thinking Lloyd and I will go fishing up in Napa. There's a nice stream there that's chock full of golden trout, lots of 'em over a foot."

"Oh boy! When, Papa?"

Fanny stepped toward them. "Napa? There are lots of closer places to fish. There's a pier two blocks from here."

"Pier, hell." Sam flung the line forward. The weight clanged into the tub. "The boy needs adventure. In fact, where I'm thinking of fishing is on a ranch. When he gets bored with fishing, he can go riding."

"Just how long of an adventure do you have in mind?"

Sam reeled in the line and set the pole in Lloyd's hands. "Try a few on your own, son." He thrust hands in pockets and strolled to her. "I might buy the ranch," he said, giving her an icy smile. "Lloyd will live there and help out. You'd be welcome to visit."

"No, Sam."

"Your old friend called on me. Rearden. Told me your plans for the future."

"Sam, I—"

"Don't worry, we'll keep things real amicable." He turned to watch another cast. "Good, son, now you're getting it!" He slapped Lloyd's back and headed for the gate.

"Papa?" Lloyd ran after him.

"Got business, son. Keep practicing." He flashed Fanny a smile and sauntered out the gate to the street.

She walked inside to the kitchen, where her painting of Lloyd stood in a shaft of sunlight, its colors bright and happy, mocking her. She put the caps on her paint jars and stored them in their case. Feeling tears wetting her cheeks, she set the canvas and the easel in the closet. From outside, she heard a clanking sound and Lloyd's happy yell as the fishing weight hit the tub.

She lay awake until long after midnight in the brass four-poster in which she had slept with Sam for so many years but which now felt bleak and threatening. Although it was a cold night she felt clammy in her nightgown, smothered by the blankets, frightened by what Sam could do, and terrified of growing old and alone. When at last she slept, dreams tormented her: Hervey, smiling up from where he seemed stuck in the mud beneath the water in the Loing River... Lloyd's face taking the place of her dead son, wide-eyed, struggling to breathe, drowning, and Fanny unable to move from where she stood on the riverbank to save him... Louis's face appearing, laughing idiotically as he coughed in spasms, drowning, vomiting blood into the water and clouding it so darkly that she could not see him.

When she woke, Lloyd stood frowning down at her bedside, dressed for school and with his hair combed. "Bye Mama."

She tried to get out of bed, stop him and cook him a proper breakfast, but was unable to move.

CHAPTER 16
San Francisco—December, 1879

Louis nursed his after-dinner brandy, thinking if the short German standing on the orange crate by the front window did not start playing his accordion soon, he would pay his bill and leave. The few dozen other patrons at Donnadieu's Restaurant at 425 Bush Street seemed to feel the same. They twiddled with their waxed mustaches, thumbed the brims of the bowlers and bonnets held on their laps, and pulled fobs out of vests to check the hour. A waiter was already making his way around with a dessert tray. The steaming bowls of apple-raisin pudding smelled delicious, but Louis had already blown the day's food allotment of fifty cents for the dinner of venison, mashed potatoes, a half-bottle of Burgundy, coffee and brandy.

"Apologies, gentlemen, and ladies, too," the German said with a bow, "but my fiddler is not yet come. Patience please."

Louis rolled a cigarette and closed the autobiography of Benjamin Franklin that he had been reading. He could only take Franklin's exhortations toward virtue in small doses; besides making him feel like a failure, the preachy volume reminded him of his father, and that brought on waves of homesickness. He lit the cigarette, brushed crumbs off the plaid oilcloth, opened the small notepad that he always carried and began writing.

STEVENSON'S TREASURE

My Dear Colvin,

I am now writing to you in a café, waiting for some music to begin. For four days I have spoken to no one but my landlady or to restaurant waiters. This is not a gay way to pass Christmas, is it? And, I must own the guts are a little knocked out of me. If I could work, I could worry through better. But I have no style at command for the moment...

Louis wouldn't bother to tell Colvin of his biggest frustration, Fanny, and his lack of hearing from her in the week since he had rented lodgings in San Francisco. For practice, he tried to think of his situation in American idioms: although she was just a few miles over the bay "as the crow flies," he was not a crow—by ferry and foot she was almost two hours away, too far to "just drop by and say hello." Perhaps lodging in San Francisco had been an overreaction to arriving at her Oakland home and finding Sam. But Louis also felt more at home in the hilly City with its twisting narrow streets, restaurants, theatres, and saloons compared with the flat, bland, straight-streeted suburbs on the Oakland side of the Bay.

A commotion in front of the room distracted him from his letter. Four men slapped on their hats and headed for the door. Monsieur Perot, the restaurant's owner, standing by the cash box made a cranking motion with his arm toward the German.

"Very well then, I play alone, only me will you hear," the musician announced. The man crushed out a polka. Bad as the music sounded, Louis felt a pang of sympathy for the sweating Hun and clapped enthusiastically when he finished. The chap was a kindred spirit, a performer of art; was he really any different, in level of skill, from Louis? Dropping two quarters plus a ten-cent-tip on the oilcloth, Louis concluded that kindred spirit or not, the food in San

Francisco had reached a higher stage of development than its music.

Outside, he turned up the collar of his velvet coat and shoved his hands in its pockets for the short walk uphill to his apartment. What fool was it who had first passed him the news, while he was shivering from pub to pub in Edinburgh, that California was warm and balmy? He admired the window display of flutes and guitars at Sherman and Hyde's Music Store, and then gazed with envy at the plush overcoats and furs worn by those in the queue to buy tickets at the California Theater across the road.

Reaching the door of 608 Bush Street, a wood frame building so narrow and dilapidated that it might blow down in strong wind, Louis tried to slip inside to the stairwell undetected, but could not suppress a cough.

"You got a warm room upstairs but you go walkin' in the cold," his landlady said in a thick Irish brogue.

"Hullo, Mrs. Carson." He stepped past a squat, blue-eyed woman with a broad forehead standing in the doorway of her ground-floor lodgings. "Has the mail come?"

The climb up rickety stairs to the second floor made him cough so deeply that he stopped, clinging to the handrail.

"Look you here," she said, clomping up the stairs behind him and shoving a San Francisco *Evening Bulletin* in his hands. "Strawberry Creek in Berkeley froze over. It snowed in Napa. Breakin' records for cold, but my tenant Looeey Stevenson is wandrin' about like he's tryin' to kill himself. When there's mail I'll send Robbie up."

In his room he saw that she had let herself in, set a fire behind the small grate and hung up his clothes. Why was it that he seemed to inspire nosy mothering everywhere in the world? Today, however, he thanked God for Mrs. Carson, the warmth in the room and his fortune at finding cheap lodgings that suited him. The room's two narrow windows on the northwest wall cast about as much sunlight as San Francisco had to offer on the little table that served as his writing desk, and green shutters reminded him of rooms in Paris.

He had just tossed the newspaper on the table and kicked off his boots when the door banged open. "Letters!" shouted four-year-old Robbie. The little blond boy in perpetually muddy corduroys tossed several envelopes at Louis.

"Thank you, kind sir." Louis thumbed through them, kept two that were addressed to him, one from Joe Strong and one, hallelujah, from Fanny, and gave the others back to Robbie for delivery to other tenants. He pried open the boy's fingers and placed a wrapped taffy in the palm. Robbie grinned and raced out.

He tore open Fanny's letter but Mrs. Carson barged in. "She's going to be the death of you, Looey."

"Beg pardon?"

Mrs. Carson put her hands on her hips. "Don't play dumb with me. The one you told me about, your fiancée. She's playing with you, and you're the one's payin' for it. A man can die of lovesickness, you know. If she lives just over the bay, why won't she see you? Leaves you sitting in Mrs. Carson's place while she makes sausage of your heart!"

"Sausage?"

"Now tell Mary Carson about her. Everything. I know how to listen."

"Indeed you do, but I'm afraid there's not much for you to hear. Fanny is a lovely woman, a bit large, well, three hundred seventy pounds and six feet tall. She worries that our first conjugal act may be the end of me because, you see, she insists on being the one on top. But her temper and persistent madness may be more to the point."

Mrs. Carson pressed both hands over her ears. "No! No more filthy nonsense from you!"

Louis raised his voice and continued, "She's married, ten years older, and already has a brood of children."

Mrs. Carson walked out shaking her head.

Louis tore open Fanny's letter, which was brief. After expressing hopes that Louis was "happy and well," she asked if he could "please meet with Mr. Rearden, my attorney, Tuesday at 10:00 AM at Frank's Place on the embarcadero." She closed with "Love, F" which he thought a hopeful sign.

Joe Strong's letter was also short. "Don't be a stranger! A lively time if you stop by our palace any eve, 7 Montgomery Avenue. Belle and yours truly anxious to see you. Joe."

The fire had burned down to embers, but Mrs. Carson had left an oak log and a hatchet in the wood box. Louis shoved open a window, set the log over the sill and swung the hatchet, burying it in the wood. He slammed it down several more times, causing the walls to shake. Finally, the log split with a satisfying crack.

He heard a window open. "Hey up there," a voice yelled, "what the hell you tryin' to do?"

Louis tried to shout an apology but started coughing. Sitting on the bed to get his breath, he eyed Ben Franklin's book, open on his table, and the pages of notes he had scribbled. Feeling just a moment of guilt, he pulled on his boots and jacket. Boring Ben could wait.

He headed a few blocks down Bush Street toward the bay, cheered by the sight of hansoms dropping off couples at restaurants, laborers trudging home through alleys, and men ducking into saloons; all of it brought back memories of his carefree student days in Edinburgh. His mood rose higher when he rounded a butcher shop, turned up Montgomery, and saw a three-story apartment looming just ahead. Its long green awning over the entryway, iron balconies, and artists bustling in and out with easels made him feel like he had been transported to Montmartre.

He made it up a wrought iron stairwell to the second-story without coughing and tapped on the door of Number 7.

"Lou!" Joe yanked him inside and thrust a brandy in his hand. Belle, barefoot and wearing a blue felt house-robe swept in from a doorway to smother his neck with kisses.

They tugged him into a long room with big windows that overlooked the shiny cable car tracks on Montgomery Avenue. A fireplace, Story & Clark upright piano, bench and music stand waited for revelers at one end of the room, while a tripod, camera-box and curtained background at the other end would be Joe's photography studio. Stacked along the wall opposite the windows, canvasses in various stages of completion gave off the rich scents of oil paint and turpentine. The subjects of these paintings included sober businessmen, their wives in lace dresses and, most spectacularly, a reclining nude painting of Belle.

Louis's gaze had lingered too long. "Do you like me?" she asked.

"Stunning. Where will you display it?" It reminded him of paintings hanging in barrooms from Edinburgh to Monterey, with the purple plume held strategically between the legs an especially artful touch.

"Over our bed!" she squealed. "Not that Joey needs any inspiration." She draped herself around Joe and slobbered a kiss on his neck.

"Yes, well I wouldn't advise showing it to your Mum."

They both thought that was grand, laughing and stumbling to a bright blue couch opposite a chair in which Louis sat. "So, how is San Francisco treating Lou the writer?"

"Not as well as it seems to be treating Joe the portrait artist." An understatement, he thought with a glance around the spacious den and a peek at Belle's leg, bouncing on her knee while she pawed Joe's thigh.

Belle tried to roll a cigarette but spilled most of the tobacco onto the floor. "You'll stay for supper."

Louis wondered if it would be bad form to get on hands and knees and scrape up the precious stuff.

Joe threw open a window. "Supper at Strong's!" he hollered to nobody in particular. "Lou Stevenson's here from Edinburgh!"

"Shut the window," Belle slurred, "the wind's blowing right up my robe."

Joe winked. "She was posing when you arrived."

Belle pouted. "Bring more brandy, dear."

Joe headed to another room for a bottle. Belle spread her robe primly over her legs. "Mother blames me, you know. Me and Joe."

"For what?"

"For eloping and causing her latest breakdown. She always has someone to blame. Maybe soon it'll be your turn." She poked the cigarette between her lips and waited while he struck a match. He hoped she wouldn't set her hair ablaze when she rocked forward toward the flame.

"Perhaps you overestimate your effect."

"What's that s'posed to mean?"

Louis lit a cigarette for himself. "I might be the one who is distressing her, by pushing for a divorce."

"I don't really blame father," Belle said. "For having girlfriends, I mean."

Louis wondered where the disjointed conversation was headed. Belle blew smoke toward the ceiling. "We can help each other. I know you like Joe. Convince mother to accept us."

"And?"

"And I'll do what I can to help your cause."

"Why the change? Not long ago you accused me of 'wanting you' in France."

She giggled and tossed her curls with a flip of her head. "I wanted you to want me, I guess."

He noticed tears welling in her eyes. "You love your mother."

"Life is so complicated."

"How I know."

Within a half-hour the room was pleasantly noisy with neighbors that included two poets, several artists that had found their way from the Fontainebleau to San Francisco, and various wives and girlfriends. Last to arrive, Jules Tavernier showed up in paint-spattered trousers with a steaming duck in a pan that he propped on his shoulder. "Provisions I picked up in Chinatown," he announced to cheers.

Before the night was over, Louis had drunk too much, the nude of Belle had been hung with twine from the chandelier, and Louis had been made an honorary member of the San Francisco Bohemian Club. "Come over to the library," said one of the more sober-looking guests, Virgil Williams. "You'll love it."

Next morning, Louis set off toward the docks on a clear, breezy day, walking behind a gaggle of bankers in black vests and crisp linen shirts who peeled off at Market Street talking about the killings they'd made in Nevada silver. On the pier he slipped past stevedores easing crates off of barge cranes and eventually found Frank's Place, a lean-to on the embarcadero consisting of a sloped tin roof over three long tables and a tiny kitchen in the back. There, a Chinese chef fried eggs, oysters, ham and beef steaks with frightening, undercooked speed, tossing them onto plates at a bench where a waiter hurried them out to patrons. Louis searched the crowded tables of longshoremen in dungarees, merchants in suits, and uniformed firemen who looked like they'd just gotten off the nightshift.

A solid man in a three-piece suit and Van Dyke beard waved Louis to a seat across from him. "Timothy Rearden," the man said, extending a hand. "I've heard so much about you, Mr. Stevenson."

"You have?" Louis sat, trying to recall what Fanny had told him about Rearden. "You gave her writing lessons."

Rearden dug his fork into a plate of eggs-and-oysters he apparently had already ordered. "I'm afraid she has more talent with a paint brush."

The dismissive comment annoyed Louis. "Actually she's a smart listener and critic. She's helped a story of mine enormously."

Rearden smiled thinly. "Was it published?"

Louis put a cigarette in his lips and struck the match in a long arc that forced Rearden to back away. "I understand you'll be handling the divorce."

An aproned waiter showed up with pad and pencil. "Sir?"

"They make good San Francisco hash," Rearden said.

Louis eyed the oily mixture on Rearden's plate. "Tea and toast, please."

An argument broke out near them about someone who had lost a poker game and was supposed to pick up the breakfast bill but had skipped out. Two men jumped from their seats and ran for the exit shouting, "We'll get him!"

Rearden watched until the pursuers were outside, smoothed his lapels and then turned back to Louis. "Divorce is no simple matter, Stevenson. You have no idea."

"Yes, I do."

"I've advised Mrs. Osbourne to take her time." Rearden's face suddenly grimaced and then relaxed, a tic that repeated several times during their breakfast. "She needs money."

"Don't we all."

Rearden's eyes seemed to scrutinize Louis's worn slacks and velvet coat. "You might think it great sport to live on pennies a day as a starving artist. But I've known Fanny for longer than you have. She plays at being a Bohemian, but she won't live in rags, nor will she dress her children in them."

"I never believed that she should."

The waiter slapped a plate of toast with a slab of butter on it and a mug of tea in front of Louis, who stubbed out his cigarette and took a bite of the toast.

"The laws of California require a man who is in the midst of divorce proceedings to provide full support to his wife and children," Rearden continued, "even if they live separately from him, until the date the divorce is final. Fanny can live quite well, apart from Sam—if things are kept the way they are."

Louis dumped two spoonfuls of sugar in the tea, hoping it would taste better than its mottled color suggested. "So you've told her to drag it out. You would consign her to a purgatory of indefinite separation so that she can, as you call it, live well."

"Sam has agreed to let her and the children continue living in the Oakland house. Despite what you may think, he's an honorable man. He wants to do the right thing by Fanny and would make any sacrifice for his children. She'd be mad to hurry through the arrangement." Rearden patted his lips with a napkin. "I've advised her to live quietly with the children in a manner of utmost respectability," he continued, giving Louis another frown of disapproval, "while things run their course."

"Meanwhile, what would you advise me to do, Mr. Rearden?"

"To be honest, you should go back to Scotland. Let her sort things out. If at the end of all this she is inclined in your favor, she can cable you."

The tea being as bad as it looked, Louis did what the firemen next to them in their brass-buttoned coats were doing, dipping toast in it. He took a bite and chewed. Suddenly, it all added up. "You have feelings for her," Louis said, raising his voice above the din of the other conversations, "No, more than feelings—you have *designs* on her!"

Rearden smiled at the firemen and merchants near them, some of whom had stopped eating. He pushed back his wooden chair. "I think your imagination is getting the best of you, Stevenson." Rearden snapped up the check and stood.

Leaving the embarcadero, hands thrust in coat pockets, Louis walked past booths of dangling chicken carcasses in Chinatown to his favorite place to think, an iron bench in

Portsmouth Square. He should not have been surprised by Rearden's motive to "help" Fanny; with her small stature, busty figure and smoldering eyes she was eye-catching; provocative, he supposed, to men like Rearden even if she did not intend it.

After smoking his fourth cigarette, coughing on each one, he got out his notebook and tried to write, thinking it might distract him from his ruminations and gloom. He dashed out a new chapter of *Arizona Breckinridge*. In this version the heroine, having gotten away with the murder of her vicious husband, instead of marrying her lover, tells him that she must spend the next ten years doing penance within the confines of a religious retreat. The lover loads his revolver and contemplates suicide...

Louis slapped his notebook shut. The main character was wooden, two-dimensional at best. Why could he never write a female character, was it because he had grown up without a sister? More importantly, writing had not distracted him from his real concern. He stood and hurried for the Ferry Building.

He knocked and, eventually, yelled at Fanny's door. Lloyd opened it looking pale and frightened.

"What's wrong?"

The boy shook his head and shrugged.

"Where's your mother?" Louis stepped around Lloyd and walked through the parlor toward her bedroom. When he saw Fanny curled on the bed in a floral-print robe, clutching a brass-framed photograph of Belle to her chest, Hamlet's Ophelia came to mind. The glass in the frame was broken, but seemed to have been crudely repaired with tape that ran in a jagged pattern over the glass. Several sketches of a very young boy with curly hair—Louis had never met him, but this had to be Hervey—were scattered on the bed near her.

"Fanny?"

She stared blankly up at him. "Brain fever."

Louis turned to Lloyd. "How long has she been this way?"

Lloyd swallowed. "A week."

"Why aren't you in school?"

"She won't let me go to school," Lloyd said, his voice shaking. "Says I might catch something and die, or get lost. How can I get lost in six blocks? I've never been lost." He began sobbing.

Louis put an arm around him but Lloyd yanked away.

Louis circled the bedroom throwing open the window drapes. "Lovely outside, isn't it? I think we should pack sandwiches and have an adventure."

While Fanny held up her hand to shield her eyes from the sun, Lloyd looked at him like he'd lost his mind, too.

"Fanny dear, please make haste to the pantry. Surely there's cold chicken there, or roast beef for sandwiches. Come sweetheart, time's wasting."

To his relief and astonishment, she rose without a word and walked to the kitchen.

"Jackets, Lloyd, and see if there's a spare one for me. And fishing poles. Do you have bait, perhaps a can of worms? Word on the docks is that the perch are hungry devils today."

Dwarfed in a pea coat, no doubt Sam's, Louis rowed the family's boat away from the docks, grinning at Fanny and Lloyd, who huddled opposite him with baleful expressions, Lloyd clutching his bamboo fishing pole. "Cast out, Lloyd, no need to wait. You can troll for the big ones."

Lloyd dug in a tin can of dirt for an earthworm, baited a hook and cast into the water.

Louis smiled at Fanny. "You can make cigarettes."

She sighed, looking at Louis with a wistful expression from beneath the flat straw gardening hat she'd slapped on, her dark eyes moist, unfathomable. "Louis, I appreciate what you're trying to do, really, but—"

He gently pushed his finger over her lips. "No talk, dear, cigarettes."

He stopped rowing for a moment, patted his pockets and came up with matches, which he handed to her.

Lloyd reeled in. "Nothing bites here."

"You be captain then, lad, row us to where they bite whilst I keep your mother company."

Louis stood and helped Lloyd to the forward bench, where he sat and took up the oars. Louis stepped to the rear bench, making the boat rock and splash until he sat down next to Fanny. Louis noticed Lloyd stroking with a fine, strong rhythm for his size, most likely trained by his father. The boy turned them inland, heading slowly along the tangled thickets on the shoreline as they inched up the estuary.

Louis turned up the coat collar against a cold wind. He coughed. And again, harder, after which he smiled and shrugged.

Eventually they were in a remote, quiet pool surrounded by trees and thickets. Fanny exhaled smoke. "Sam once told me if someone fell overboard out here, the body would never be found."

"For God's sake let's speed things up, any way we can."

"I can't row any faster," Lloyd whined.

"I was talking to your mother, about the divorce." Louis shivered and then convulsed in long, hacking coughs.

Fanny held him and gently stroked his back until he calmed. "If we married," she said softly, "what a pair we'd be."

Lloyd took several quick oar-strokes and grounded the boat on a mud-bank. "This is where they bite. Sometimes."

Louis tipped his cap. "Catch us dinner."

While Lloyd occupied himself with casting and reeling, Louis said, "I talked with your man Rearden."

STEVENSON'S TREASURE

Fanny gripped the bench, knuckles white and trembling. Suddenly she turned and vomited over the side of the boat.

CHAPTER 17
Words

Louis and Lloyd fidgeted on overstuffed armchairs in Dr. Bamford's waiting room. Opposite them, a wall clock ticked away the seconds while in the corner a potbellied stove clanked and overheated the room. Louis was fascinated by two wall decorations: the doctor's gold-lettered diploma from the Harvard Medical College and, less impressive, a photograph of the pear-shaped, mustachioed doctor himself wearing baggy breeches, knee socks, and brandishing a golf club as if he had just used it to conquer the army of Genghis Khan.

Louis opened his notebook and tried to jot an opening paragraph for his essay on Ben Franklin. Hopeless. Turning to a fresh page, he sketched a couple cowering in a boat while a boy frantically tried to row them away from a huge whale with a fish-hook stuck through its lip that chased them with open jaws. When he solemnly passed the sketch to Lloyd, he got a brief smile before the boy resumed his watch of the door.

Finally, it opened. Fanny stepped out with a dark bottle of medicine and a glum expression, followed by Dr. Bamford in a black vest that did its best to squeeze around an ample girth. The doctor, whose string-tie was partially untied and with what Louis hoped were stray breadcrumbs stuck to his moustache, smiled at Lloyd. "And how are you, young Mister Osbourne?"

"Fine, sir," Lloyd mumbled, unconvincingly.

He ruffled Lloyd's hair with his knuckles. "Don't you worry, your mother is going to be all right." Bamford shifted his gaze to Louis and raised his bushy eyebrows.

Fanny stepped forward. "This is my friend from Scotland, Louis Stevenson."

"I see." The doctor took Louis's extended hand, guardedly, Louis thought.

"Mister Stevenson is a writer," she quickly added, "making a lecture tour of the western United States."

"A lecture tour, how wonderful." Dr. Bamford shook Louis's hand. "I must say, Stevenson, you don't look terribly well yourself."

"Bad lungs. Comes and goes."

The doctor frowned. "From the looks of you I'd say you're short of red blood cells and in need of some bed rest, at the least, until your body makes more of them. You might have to miss a lecture or two, but each of us has just one life here on earth that the good Lord gives us."

"A shame, isn't it?" Louis smiled, guiding Fanny and Lloyd out the door.

Outside, they walked to the edge of the boardwalk where her horse-and-buggy was parked. "Well?" he asked.

She sighed. "Looks like I'll pull through."

He helped her onto the bench and took the reins while Lloyd hopped in back. "What did he say?"

She glanced at the bottle of medicine and put it in her handbag. "He said this stuff would make the symptoms better."

"The symptoms of brain fever?"

"Let's not talk about it right now."

Louis turned the collar of his coat up to guard against the brisk afternoon wind coming off the bay. He snapped the reins and they clattered off, passing quiet offices and storefronts.

Fanny tightened the scarf around her neck. "There's another problem."

"Oh?"

"I paid the doctor my last ten dollars."

"Did Sam stop his support?" Louis almost hoped this was true because it might speed her divorce.

She shook her head. "He didn't stop it, but lately he's been stingy. No more stopping by with gifts or paying the stray bill here and there. I'm not going to beg him. I need groceries and he won't be sending his check for two weeks."

"Sounds like it's time for R. L. Stevenson to support his intended family, then. Shouldn't be a problem. Any day, I'm expecting payment from a number of sources." They passed the brick library and general store in silence except for the steady clip-clop of the roan horse. He reined in behind several hacks at the dock, glancing up at *The Alameda* paddle-wheeler making its approach while boys with thick ropes waited. Handing the reins to Fanny, he dug in the bottom of his coat and brought up a ten-dollar gold piece he had kept for emergencies. Smiling as if it were a pittance, he kissed Fanny's cheek and pressed it in her palm.

The morning dawned bitter cold, but he would not waste time lighting a fire. He washed his face with icy water and combed his hair, wishing he could afford a haircut before visiting news editors. He hoped that the gaunt face staring back at him from the mirror would not frighten them. Perhaps this was yet one more virtue, looking very hungry when seeking employment. He knotted a black tie over his best cream shirt, fearing its wooly bulk was too European looking. He pulled on his velvet coat and practiced poses that would hide the threadbare elbows. Taking a last look in the mirror he thought that the effect was of a starving Left Bank artist rather than a reporter, but it would have to do. He took several newspaper clippings that he had written in Monterey and headed out into the cold.

Fortunately, Louis had to walk only two shivering blocks to the four-story *Chronicle* building on the corner of Bush and Kearny Streets. When he entered its grand, diagonal-facing entrance and explained to a receptionist that he was an "experienced newsman looking for work," he was referred to a pimply reporter, who led Louis back to a little desk near a stack of brooms and dust mops. Pimples dropped a half-eaten cinnamon roll onto the desk and thumbed through Louis's columns. Eventually, the young reporter said he didn't like the way they were written.

"Could you be more specific?" Louis asked.

"Not really." The boy pushed the clippings to Louis, turned away from him and bit into the cinnamon roll.

Next was the *Evening Bulletin* at the corner of Montgomery and Merchant Streets. On entering the sprawling, rickety building Louis immediately felt comfortable in its chaos. Secretaries, reporters, typesetters and editors, all in shirtsleeves, yelled across the room at each other and bounded up and down stairwells. Louis politely asked a janitor where the editor might be. The man jerked his thumb upstairs. "City room."

Louis found a graying man with a handlebar mustache under a skylight, sorting through a sea of papers spread on a table. A nameplate on the desk said that this was George K. Fitch, Editor. Louis tried an earnest smile. "Mr. Fitch?"

Fitch glanced up. "Whatever you're peddling, I don't need any."

"I am Robert Louis Stevenson of Edinburgh, recently a reporter for the *Monterey Californian* and widely published in Europe. I have written about my adventures with a donkey in the mountains of France, a desperate ocean crossing in steerage and a journey with emigrants across the wilds of America. They could be published serially, and I think your readers would thrill to the exciting—"

"All right, all right. Leave your clippings and check back with me in a couple days." Fitch made a fly-shooing gesture and turned back to the clutter on his desk.

Louis practically skipped back to Bush Street. He would be a paid writer again, a newshound! Meanwhile he would go to his room and write essays until midnight. He felt light-headed, though, and remembered that the roll and coffee were many hours ago. He hailed a Chinese boy pulling a steaming cart across Kearny and bought two pot-stickers for a nickel. After eating the savory lumps where he stood, he set a fast pace up Bush Street until again he felt dizzy. He slowed, and soon had to stop altogether when seized by a fit of coughing.

"My darling Fanny," he scrawled on a scrap of paper as soon as he had reached his cold room, "all money problems soon to be solved!" He sketched a thin man running for a building labeled "Evening Bulletin" with a notebook under his arm and a pencil thrust over his ear, against the backdrop of the tall San Francisco hills. He shoved the scrap in an envelope and addressed it.

He took a break to light a fire and smoke three cigarettes before copying, word-for-word, three Hazlitt essays—he simply must improve his writing style—and then dug out Poe's "The Tell-Tale Heart" and copied the first ten pages. Next he took a stab at rewriting, for the ninth time, his first chapter of "Arizona Breckenridge." Setting that aside, he dashed out two scenes for his play, *Deacon Brodie*. At 2:00 AM he wrote a brief letter to his friend Charles Baxter. "I have great fun trying to be economical. As good a game of play as any other." Great fun indeed. He begged Baxter to sell all of the books Louis had left in Edinburgh and send the proceeds. This might keep him going for two additional weeks.

Fully clothed, he rolled himself in his blanket and collapsed for three hours of fitful sleep.

For days he buried himself in work, smoking countless cigarettes and turning out thousands of frenzied words. He re-drafted his essay on Ben Franklin, roughed out articles on William Penn, Henry David Thoreau, and even jotted an opening sentence to one about Yoshida Torajiro, the visionary who tried to bring Western civilization to Japan. He outlined three new chapters of *Arizona Breckenridge* and the climax of *Deacon Brodie*. Having little appetite he skipped his twenty-five-cent noon meals altogether, and instead cinched his belt an inch tighter. Wouldn't Benjamin Boring Franklin be proud of his thrift? He refused to be discouraged by the dim views of his friends toward his California writing; what could they possibly know about American tastes?

Louis stepped into Editor Fitch's office on the appointed day feeling weak and queasy. He had been living on too much coffee; how he wished he'd chewed a crust of bread on the walk over instead of smoking two more cigarettes.

Fitch pushed up his eyeshade and squinted at Louis as if a snail had left a streak of slime on his desk. "Frankly, Stevenson, your writing bores me. But now and then you turn a phrase, and my grandmother was Scottish so I'll give you a break. Restaurants."

Louis wasn't sure he had heard correctly. "Restaurants?"

"You're a world traveler; fine, compare our restaurants to the ones in London and Paris. Give me some scintillating pieces, splash 'em with local color, you know."

Louis didn't, but nodded.

Fitch shoved some newspapers at Louis. "Here are samples."

"Might I ask how much you'll pay?"

Fitch took a cigar stump from an ashtray and shoved it between his teeth. "If I love your first piece, I'll ask you to write a second. If I love that one, I'll give you five dollars for the two."

Ignoring exhaustion, a persistent headache and sharp pain in his lungs, Louis forced himself out of bed before dawn for the next week so he could make it to several restaurants during breakfast. He sipped the coffee, noted the décor (the presence of tablecloths and clean spittoons being sure indicators of an upper-tier establishment), and talked with customers over their morning newspapers. After scribbling his impressions, he moved on to several more places for their midday meal. He tried to suppress his coughing spells, and knew that his clothes were getting shabby, but the real reason he was thrown out of several of the better eateries was that he could not afford to buy their food. Still, by week's end he managed to finish two articles, dropped one of them off with Fitch and treated himself to brandy and a cigar. He walked up Bush Street feeling elated, certain that tonight he would successfully rewrite the *Arizona Breckinridge* chapter that he had read the night before and hated.

The climb up the stairs to his room left him feeling weak and rubber-limbed. Thank God Mrs. Carson had set a warm fire. He pushed the stacks of manuscripts on his bed aside. A ten-minute nap was sure to revive him...

Next morning a pounding on the door woke him. When he got out of bed he was so dizzy he had to cling to the doorknob to stand. A message boy handed him a note— Fanny was waiting for him at the Pine Street Coffee House!

Fanny was eating a sweet roll by the front window when he got to the little place on Fifth. She looked wonderful in a yellow dress, with hair swept up and held above her ear by a wooden comb. "Louis! What is it?"

"Sorry if I look a fright, I overslept."

"You're not well."

"Well enough to have done one article for the *Bulletin*, three essays on American founders, seven letters, one chapter and two short stories since we last met. Now was that any sort of greeting?"

She leaned forward, and he kissed her cheek.

"Much better."

She felt his brow and frowned. "Let's get you on the ferry and back to Dr. Bamford."

He tried to give a carefree grin. "Not necessary. Now tell me, what brings you across the bay?"

She shrugged. "Just missing you, I guess."

Louis could tell something was on her mind, and waited for her to continue, but she lapsed into silence, pushing her breakfast roll around the plate. "Even if I can get free of Sam," she finally said, "you may not want to marry me. Not after what the doctor told me."

"What are you talking about?"

"Dr. Bamford thinks my black moods are hysteria," she said quietly. "It's a Greek word meaning—"

"Womb, I know."

"He thinks I could be starting the change of life. Earlier than most women, lucky me. I won't be able to give you children. I know how much you love them, Louis, and, well, maybe you should find a younger girl."

"Never." He moved his chair around the table and put his arms around her while she softly cried. Under the stares of other patrons, he eased her up, left coins on the table, and steered her out of the restaurant. He walked her to 608 Bush Street, where, miraculously, Mrs. Carson seemed to be out of the house. They tiptoed upstairs, she, red-eyed from weeping, he, pausing once to gasp air. What a pair indeed.

In the room he stoked the fire and pulled the shades. She was gazing around at the stacks of books, unfinished manuscripts and clothes that covered the floor, shaking her head. "Will you ever change, Louis?"

"No." He drew her close to him. As one, they stepped to the bed and eased down together, snuggling for warmth and murmuring words of love.

He kissed her, stroked her neck and began unhooking her dress, but he felt her stiffen. "What's wrong?"

"Dr. Charcot used the word hysteria, too, but he thinks my problems are of the mind, not the womb. That I love being onstage and worshipped by men."

"A smart man. I certainly worship you..." He struggled with the hooks, breaking one.

She pushed him to arm's length. "But it's more complicated than that. More perverse."

"Perverse? Fanny, what say we save this discussion and get our clothes off?"

She stood frowning for a moment, fists clenched over her chest... and then, with a sigh, reached for him. While she clung to him he somehow got the rest of the hooks undone and pushed down her dress. Suddenly she was the feverish one, yanking at his belt, getting his trousers off, and tearing at the buttons of his shirt. Finally they were naked in bed, gasping.

Blessedly, the weakness of lungs deserted him in his urgency and she responded, soft, accepting, gasping, open, and, eventually, noisy.

He doubted that he would ever understand her completely—brain fever, hysteria, change of life, and what was this "perversion" all about? He did not care, and their age difference, to him, was a blessing: he knew he would die long before she did. But rather than spoil things by sharing the morbid thought, he increased his efforts until the little bed creaked and bounced.

"Mister Stevenson!" Robbie's voice called. "Ma said you aren't supposed to chop wood up there anymore!"

"Quite right, Robbie," Louis yelled, "No more chopping wood." Louis and Fanny giggled like children, but continued their lovemaking more quietly. When they finished, Fanny pulled the blanket to their chins and they dozed in each others' arms.

He woke alone, in the middle of the night from a strange dream: huge letters appeared on a blank wall before him,

"W-O-R-D-S." Heart pounding, he swung his legs out of bed, ignoring the shock of the cold floor on his bare feet, felt his way to his desk, and opened the shutters above it to let in the moonlight. He was certain the dream contained the solution to the log-jam that his life had become in California. Recently he had learned, when his dreams were this vivid and left him so completely awake, to get aboard the runaway train of feverish thoughts that inevitably followed. Usually, he ended up in an exciting new destination, although, of course, there was the occasional wreck.

He lit a lamp, rolled a cigarette, and began walking the narrow space between his bed, against one wall, and the stacks of books and manuscripts that had grown up along the opposite one. He knew the pacing across the hardwood floor in the Bush Street apartment—from the desk and tall window at one end to the knotty-pine door at the other, a distance of twelve feet—would disturb the tenant below him, but he also knew that he did his best problem-solving on his feet.

For an hour, the dream's meaning remained coded and elusive. Words were his life, his soul, his chosen path. They were what had won Fanny's heart in the first place. Then, an image from his childhood danced through his consciousness —the rows of tin soldiers he had arrayed for battle on his bedspread when he was supposed to be sleeping.

All at once it came to him: words would be his soldiers, his army, his artillery in a war as he chose to fight it. As usual, the broad shape of a solution came to him before the details, but he knew the work he must do to flesh them out.

He took out a pen, the remains of a bottle of rich India ink that he'd brought from Europe and saved for a special occasion, and began writing a drama. He, Robert Louis Stevenson, was the main character. Fanny Osbourne was his love interest and Sam was the antagonist. He knew the desired end of the play because it was the same ending as "Pavilion on the Links": the ogre, Sam, releases the woman he has held captive and leaves the scene, allowing Louis to build with her a new, happy future.

The beginning of the drama had already been written in life: Louis and Fanny meet and fall in love, each bringing baggage to the stage. Louis's baggage included life-threatening illness, paltry earnings, and a tendency to be too slap-dash and spontaneous. Fanny bore the deep grief of losing a child, was desperately attached to two living ones, had bouts of madness that she called "brain fever," and was stuck in a marriage to a domineering, philandering husband. The many conflicts and complications of the plot easily flowed; he simply wrote the events of the past few years as he and Fanny had lived them.

The climax of the drama—the Final Conflict—remained to be written. This is where he was on dangerous, shifting ground. He had never tried to write a drama as he was living it, with an ending that he supplied, and then bring the actors onstage and hope they played their parts as written. He did know that from an early age he was an observer of others, fascinated by what they loved and fought about. He had listened to their dialogue, tried to ferret out motives and wondered where conflicting desires would lead. To write stories, he cast these elements into a pot and stirred, sometimes using a dream—or a nightmare—to do the mixing for him and yield unusual results.

Morning came and went as he imagined and recorded ways in which he might clash with Sam and triumph. In mid-afternoon, the sound of young feet pounding up the stairs interrupted him. The door banged open and Robbie burst into the room in his scruffy denims and cap. "No mail, Mister Stevenson!"

"You're just the man I want to see." Louis dug in his pocket and came up with three crumpled dollar bills. He pressed one of them in the boy's hand. "Bring me a turkey sandwich and coffee from Donadieu's. Keep the change."

Robbie whooped and dashed off, thrilled at the prospect of a fifty-cent profit.

Louis lit a cigarette and turned to the hardest work, crafting a resolution to the conflict that he desired while taking into account the needs, personalities and histories of his main characters. They might take the plot in endless directions when given their prompts. Some of these directions would require forceful countermoves and dialogue from Louis in order to steer the plot away from an undesired or even disastrous ending. He would have to draft at least the likely directions the conflict might take, his reactions to them, and then rehearse how he would deliver his lines.

Robbie came back with the food and coffee. Louis set his play script aside for thirty minutes while he ate, smoked two cigarettes and paced. He decided that his drama would take place on two sets, the first act at Joe and Belle Strong's apartment and the second one in Fanny's Oakland house. He rewrote accordingly, finishing a solid draft before looking out the window to see the winter sun, orange, hazy, a fog-burner, setting over Nob Hill.

All that remained before the next day's performance was to memorize the play and the many twists and turns it might take, a task which he began during eight more cigarettes. He had developed a working knowledge of the entire package by 8:15 PM, but was forced by his lungs to take a break. The first coughs were ordinary, although sharp; due, he supposed, to all of the smoking. Then, without warning, internal membranes rent and began leaking, as he thought of it—how he hated the word hemorrhage. He tried to be patient and calm while sitting with head against pillow against wall, but the bleeding continued. One handkerchief filled with bright lung's blood, then two before the leakage slowed.

Two more hours and the taps shut off, or mostly did, with just a little spotting in a third handkerchief when he coughed. He made the mistake of looking in a mirror and seeing a face the color of his grandfather's corpse, three days after death. Yet Louis felt very much alive, just a bit weak, but he'd been so before. He had waited and dithered far too long; nothing would make him postpone the Big Performance.

He stepped to the window and looked outside. At eleven o'clock, the peaceful scene reminded him achingly of what he saw from his bedroom window as a child in Edinburgh: street lamps softly glowing, a lone hack driving slowly past, and two well-dressed men exchanging laughs on their way home from an entertainment. Above the narrow buildings jutting precariously up from the San Francisco hills, a sea of bright stars evidenced an unusually dry night, certainly a good omen. Pulling on his velvet coat Louis walked unsteadily outside in hopes that taking the dry air would sooth his lungs. Resisting an impulse to roll a cigarette, like a mad ghost of the King in Hamlet he walked and muttered his lines for hours, undeterred by a black cat that jumped down from a fence and dashed in front of him and, later, a mastiff chained in a muddy alley that barked savagely as he walked by.

At 3:30 AM, satisfied that all was as ready as it could be, he struggled up the stairs to his room, picked his way past the piles of manuscripts and, fully clothed, collapsed on his mattress.

CHAPTER 18
The Drama

Louis shoved his hands deep in his coat pockets while walking down Bush Street on a clear, chilly morning, avoiding a broken whiskey bottle in front of the dry goods store that hadn't opened its doors for the day. He turned up Montgomery Street, passing a little butcher shop where the proprietor stood inside the storefront window in a bloodstained apron, hacking at a side of beef that slowly twisted on a rope. It occurred to Louis that the stop at Joe and Belle's apartment would be something like a Shakespearean induction, a brief scene to warm up the players and audience—in this case, one and the same—for the conflict to come.

By 8:30 AM he stood on the second-story iron landing and pounded on the door of Number 7. Belle finally opened it, looking uncharacteristically dowdy in a blue cotton robe and moccasin slippers, with what was probably yesterday's swept-up hairdo sagging and flattened on one side, her face mottled, puffy, and scowling.

"We were asleep." Despite the curt greeting she quickly admitted him, the result, Louis concluded, of his correct costuming: the parted hair, crisp linen shirt, confident red tie and grey bowler hat of a man who would be taken seriously. He followed her into the long room they used as a studio,

203

with Joe's partly finished portraits standing like mute sentries along the walls.

"Well?" she asked with a yawn.

He placed the invitation that he had addressed in block letters to "Mr. Samuel Osbourne" in her hand. "Make yourself presentable and hurry this to your father. Do your best to put out any fireworks and convince him to come."

"But I..."

"Time is ticking. After giving him the invitation, you and Joe must get to Fanny's house by noon, where we'll all wait for your father. If you go along with this, you'll soon be back in your mother's good graces." Louis smiled, trying to exude a confidence he did not feel.

Belle folded her arms and frowned. "All right," she finally said.

After giving her and bleary-eyed Joe their simple dialogue, and briefly rehearsing it with them, Louis rushed for the docks. He arrived just in time to board the 9:10 ferry to Oakland, clambering up the ramp behind a horse-drawn hearse and a large family of weeping Italians dressed in black. Not a good omen, but so far, all had gone according to script.

At 11:00 he knocked on Fanny's door. When she opened it he was relieved that she looked like her usual, well-groomed self in a soft gray dress, hair brushed up and held over the ears with scrimshaw combs that contrasted nicely with her dark eyes. Evidently her melancholy, brain fever, hysteria, or whatever else her dark moods could be labeled had fled, at least for the time being.

He smiled. "I've invited Sam to a meeting."

She pressed a hand to her mouth. "You what?"

"Invited him to discuss our future." He kissed her cheek and stepped past her, into the parlor, admiring its handsome front window, deep blue sofa and armchairs. A bit formal, he thought, but it would do for Act I. "He will be here this afternoon. I apologize for the short notice but wanted to complete our business before Lloyd comes home from school. May I?" He motioned toward the sofa.

She did not move. "What makes you think Sam will show up?"

"Wouldn't you, if for no other reason than curiosity?"

He sat on the sofa, pulled the pages of play script from his beaten valise and patted the cushion next to him...

Act I.

At 1:15, right on schedule came a knock on Fanny's door. Louis opened it to Belle and Joe Strong, and breathed a sigh of relief that their clothing hit just the right note for the performance, she in a demure navy dress with white buttons up to the neck, and he in the same sort of charcoal suit and bowler that any successful San Francisco businessman would wear.

"Fanny dear," Louis called, ushering them into the parlor, "look who's come for a visit."

Still on the sofa, Fanny turned her back on them and seemed to stare out the window.

"Mother?" Belle asked nervously.

"Say your opening line," Louis mouthed.

Belle cleared her throat. "Mother, please forgive me for marrying Joe behind your back."

Fanny stiffened, the back of her neck trembling ever so slightly.

"Fanny," Louis said gently, "Joe is a fine husband for your daughter. I have never seen a couple so... excitingly happy together. He is hard-working and his business thrives."

All watched Fanny for signs of softening. Nothing.

"In fact," Louis continued, "the finest work in Joe's studio, the most striking thing he has ever created, is a painting, in loving detail, of his wife."

Belle shot him a horrified look. The line was not in the script; what little devil in him had made him say it? Now, if mother ever consented to speak with daughter she would want to see the bawdy thing.

"Yes," Joe said, seizing on what he must have sensed was an opening. "I remember you sketched her several times in France. She's difficult. Well, I mean, as a subject, because she has these splendiferous, um, features and is a little bit short and, well, so am I, so in that way we make a good match, but what I meant to say is that it is tough to render her in the beautiful, I mean outstanding and wondrous beautiful beauty that she has. And she got this from you, her mother, that much is most certain, Mrs. Osbourne, and I just want you to know that I love her deeply, and, well, we plan to make grandchildren for you, heck, we've already been working on that and I hope you come around to the view that —"

Belle clapped her hand over Joe's mouth and laughed nervously. "Just quit while you're ahead, honey."

"Point being, Fanny," Louis said quietly, "Joe is an artist and doing well by it. There is no crime in marrying one, however uncertain the wages. Rather, I suspect the timing of the wedding, perhaps, was a problem for you." He stroked Fanny's back, at a loss for any other argument he could make.

After a long silence, during which the three of them exchanged nervous, what-do-we-do-now glances, Fanny mumbled, "She is difficult, all right. Easy to sketch, but otherwise difficult." She slowly stood and turned to Belle, eyes brimming with tears—and, certainly, Louis thought, love.

Belle opened her arms. "Mother."

Fanny took her daughter in her arms. Both women began to sob.

Joe headed toward the front door. "I'll buy us a bottle of champagne!"

Louis shook his head; the last thing he needed was alcohol in the room during the second act. "Lemonade and chicken sandwiches. Shall we go to the kitchen?"

Fanny ignored him, cooing and caressing Belle, who snuffled in her arms like a five-year-old; certainly, Louis thought, mother-daughter love was one of life's most powerful and mysterious essences.

Eventually, Fanny composed herself and led the way from the parlor and through a pair of swinging doors into the kitchen.

Louis quickly concluded that the informal breakfast table, cheery window with red-checked drapes above it that looked out on an orange tree, and cozy warmth of the cast-iron stove would be a good setting for Act II. He sat at one end of the table with his back to the wall, and arranged his players around it: Fanny to the left of him, beneath the window; and Joe and Belle opposite Fanny. He left the chair directly across from himself, at the head of the table, empty. With the double-doors just a few paces behind this chair, when Sam took his seat the setting might seem tight and closed-in. But the size would work better than the parlor, which would have allowed Sam to just walk out the front door if things became heated.

While they waited, Louis skimmed the script, satisfying himself that although the players had garbled some lines, so far they had successfully brought the plot to the right place at the end of Act I.

Act II began at 2:15, again with Louis answering a knock at the door.

Samuel Osbourne always made a commanding entrance. Looming in the doorway, wide shoulders thrust back in a trim blue suit and vest that as usual gleamed with brass buttons, he grinned with his head cocked back in a skeptical attitude as if he was about to be admitted to an exotic but disreputable circus.

Louis extended his hand. "I am glad you could come on short notice, Mr. Osbourne."

Sam brushed past Louis as if he was not there. "Nice being invited to my own house."

Louis refused to be provoked, stepping in front of Sam and leading the way into the kitchen.

"Papa!" Belle rushed from her seat and threw her arms around him.

"Hullo, sir," Joe said, standing and pumping Sam's hand.

"Sam," Fanny said quietly, remaining seated.

Belle sat and motioned her father to the empty seat next. Sam remained standing, towering above the rest of them. "Is there something I don't know about? Did someone die?"

"In a manner of speaking, yes," Louis said.

Sam pulled a whisky flask from his coat. "Anyone want to join me in a nip?"

Joe reached for the flask. "Don't mind if I do."

Louis saw Fanny and Belle exchange frowns, and he resisted an impulse to restrain Joe from taking the flask. A dilemma: trying to over-manage events might drive Sam from the room, but if Louis gave no direction, things could quickly get out of hand.

"Anyone else?" Sam wobbled a bit when he leaned to retrieve the flask, and a flush on his neck and cheeks suggested he'd been drinking all the way from San Francisco.

"This wasn't meant to be a drinking party, Sam," Louis said.

"Then let's talk about this person who died." When Sam sat heavily in the chair, something made a clinking-sound, yet another prop, Louis feared, that was not in the script.

"Actually, nobody died, not literally, anyway," Louis said carefully.

"Then somebody tell me why you summoned me here on 'a matter of urgency' so great that I was supposed to drop everything on moment's notice and come to this sorry place."

Belle touched Sam's arm. "Papa, I think—I mean, Joe and I both think that everyone would be happier if you'd give Mama a divorce."

Joe nodded and grinned, perhaps overplaying his role.

Sam looked down at the table and traced his finger on its varnished surface as if checking for dust. "So, sweet daughter, you've deserted me."

Belle swallowed, tears welling in her eyes. "I'd never do that."

Sam sighed and unscrewed the flask.

"Samuel," Fanny said softly, "maybe you've had enough to drink."

"You're one to lecture about bad habits," he shot back, taking a long swig and banging the flask down on the table.

Louis placed his hands, palms-down, on the table. "Fanny is no longer happy with you. Please release her. Do the honorable thing."

"You seduced my wife and now you're trying to take my children away," Sam hissed. "What would you know about honor?"

"Nobody's taking me away," Belle said, laughing nervously, "except my husband." She leaned on Joe's shoulder and hugged his neck.

Sam tipped his head at the couple and gave them the briefest smile. "All right, I stand corrected. But there's Lloyd. Where is my son, anyway?"

"*Our* son," Fanny said, "is where he is every day, at the Lincoln Grammar School. I would think you'd know by now."

Sam stiffened as if he'd been punched in the gut.

Louis nudged Fanny and frowned his disapproval. Dammit, why had she added that last unscripted phrase? She had agreed with his general approach—to be congenial and nudge Sam toward dissolution, not provoke him. Louis decided to skip the various rational arguments for divorce that he had planned and jump ahead. Taking two cigarettes from the pocket of his linen shirt that he had rolled earlier, Louis held one out to Sam, who ignored it. "Fanny's attorney is asking a very high price for his services, one that she has refused to pay."

Sam snorted. "Tim Rearden? Would think he'd work cheap. I always figured he was in love with her."

Louis reached for a cigarette. Joe Strong struck a match and held it while Louis leaned in and puffed. "Exactly the problem, Sam. It seems the price Rearden has set for his legal services is to have Fanny in bed."

Sam's eyes narrowed. "I'll kill the snake."

"You're not going to kill anybody, Sam," Fanny said, "but you should know that I want out of this marriage so badly that when Rearden made clear what he wanted, I didn't just kick his groin and storm out of his office."

"Jesus." Sam took another swig from the flask.

"You asked who died," Fanny continued. "What died is our marriage, a long time ago, even before I went to France. We pretended for years that it existed. Through it all, you've provided for the children, and I'm grateful for that, but now it seems you just want to control me."

"I am certain you are a better man than one who simply wants to hold on to Fanny and prolong her misery," Louis added. "So please, let her go. Give yourself a fresh start. There is such a thing as forgiveness, reconciliation, and—"

"Shut up!" Sam roared, slamming back his chair and lurching to his feet. "I didn't come here for a sermon from some half-baked fool who took advantage of my wife in her time of grief! Who followed her back from Europe to carry on with her right under my nose! Someone who would take my only living son away! What kind of a monster are you, Stevenson?" Tears welled in Sam's bloodshot eyes as he loomed above them, swaying.

Louis leaned forward and mashed out the cigarette in an ashtray, desperately wondering how to refocus what had become an appalling drama. When he had written his lines the night before, he had thought them incisive; when spoken, they sounded trite and patronizing, even to his own ears. He had deserved Sam's tirade. All he could think of to say was, "I am sorry for the pain I have caused you."

"You know nothing about my pain. Nothing!" Sam reached under his vest, drew an Army Colt .45 from his waistband and set it on the table.

"Papa!" Belle gasped.

"Sam, put that old thing away," Fanny said, her voice shaking.

Louis considered making a wild grab for the gun, but Sam lifted it and cradled its barrel as if it were made of gold. "No, I'm beholden to this old thing; it's seen me through hell." Silence fell as Sam stared at the weathered, octagonal barrel and picked at spots of rust.

Eventually, a chair creaked as Joe shifted forward. "Wouldn't mind another sip from that flask, Sam."

Belle smiled weakly. "Good idea. Perhaps we could all have a drink, Papa."

Sam ignored the requests but shifted his gaze reluctantly, it seemed, away from the gun to stare at each person sitting at the table. Louis now felt the room indeed much too small and airless, and it granted no escape except the double doors —yet Sam stood with his back to them, glowering down, a trickle of perspiration making its way down his forehead. Louis could only guess at the thoughts running through his mind. "You suffered," he finally tried. "Greatly. In the war I mean."

Sam snorted. "Nothing you'd know about."

Fanny stood. "Put the gun away, Sam, and I'll make us some tea. Or coffee if you'd rather."

"Sit."

She quickly did so.

Louis laughed nervously. "When I tried shooting one of those, I couldn't hit a bottle from three paces. In fact it blew up in my face."

Sam peered at Louis as if looking through him. "You're like a skinny boy I grew up with, his name was Willy. Always had his head stuck in books because he could never do anything else right. He died next to me, in a cornfield..."

Louis opened his palm upward, beckoning Sam to keep talking. "In the war, you mean."

"On a hot day in August," Sam rambled, seeming to lose himself in a memory. "We couldn't see who was shooting at us, the stalks were so high. First rifle fire, and then cannon, cut big swaths of corn, and men fell, pouring blood, and some who weren't hit were on their knees shitting themselves or trying to hide under the dead ones, but we just kept going forward, Willy and me, he was running next to me and then he was down, the back of his head gone..."

Sam shook his head as if to rid himself of the memory. "I could kill you for what you've done, Stevenson, and a jury would call it 'justifiable homicide.' But I'm an honorable man, even though when I made it out of the cornfield I kept running till I got back to Indianapolis, and told some lies, and got myself attached to a home unit at a desk job. I should have been shot for desertion. Maybe that would have been better for everyone."

Sam aimed the gun at his own temple.

"No, no, no," Belle whimpered.

Sam thumbed back the hammer... but the swinging door behind him suddenly banged open, and a young voice shouted, "Papa!"

Sam reactively shoved his elbow backward, sending Lloyd and schoolbooks sprawling onto the floor.

Fanny threw herself over Lloyd and held him as he cried. Sam set the gun on the table, got on his knees, bent his face close to Lloyd's and said in a small voice, "I'm sorry son, I didn't mean it, it's all right, everything's going to be all right."

"What is wrong?" Lloyd blubbered, "What is it?"

"We were having a serious conversation, but it's over," Fanny said, motioning to Louis, who carefully tucked the gun away in a drawer. She stood and offered a hand to Lloyd, but he shook his head, sitting up with his back against the wall instead.

"Give us a minute," Sam said, sitting down on the floor next to Lloyd and putting an arm on his shoulder.

Fanny walked the rest of them out to the parlor, where they stood by the sofa and waited in silence.

Eventually, Sam, ashen-faced but composed, came out from the kitchen and walked toward the front door. He paused by Fanny. "Rearden won't be bothering you anymore. I'll tell him I'm standing down. You'll have what you want."

"Thank you," she said, eyes moist.

Sam shifted his gaze to Louis, standing next to her. "Fact is, Stevenson, I can't hate you."

"Nor I, you," Louis said to Sam, who was already trudging out the front door looking smaller, somehow, than when he had arrived.

Halfway to the street, Sam turned and gave Louis an icy grin. "Beginning now, it's up to you to support this woman you love so much. Yesterday I was laid off my job."

Louis closed the door, leaned against it, prayed his thanks that his childish, contrived scheme for moving Sam off of dead-center had somehow succeeded. He also prayed that he could quickly find some income. He hoped that the dizziness he felt was due to the profound events of the day, rather than his lungs getting worse. Fanny wrapped her arms around him, pressed against his back and shook with sobs.

CHAPTER 19
Requiem

On Friday, Louis staggered past the cluttered desks of young reporters in rolled-up linen shirts and pinstriped vests who dipped pens in inkwells and scrawled on legal pads in the sprawling *Evening Bulletin* newsroom. Reaching the center, he slapped down a stack of pages on Editor Fitch's desk.

The newsman's eyebrows wrinkled, but his eyes did not look up from his eyeshade. "What the hell's that?"

Louis leaned on the edge of the big desk to get his breath. "Twelve more stirring articles about San Francisco dining establishments."

"I'll give 'em a look and get back to you in a couple weeks." Fitch made the fly-shooing motion.

"No!" Louis slapped his hand on the desk, making Fitch jump. "I'm sorry, sir, but you must look at them now. My wife-to-be is without support, and will soon be starving."

"Jesus in heaven," Fitch muttered, squinting up at him, "you don't look so great yourself." With a heavy sigh he shoved aside some copy he was reading and turned to Louis's pages...

On Saturday, after writing to Fanny and dropping the letter in a Post Office box on Geary, Louis felt so dizzy that he had to spend the rest of the day in bed. He forced his back against the wall, opened a notebook on his lap and began penning changes to Damned Deacon Brodie, as he had started to call the play which Henley kept urging him to send.

At some point he must have fallen asleep, because hours later he woke with vertigo and an awful taste in his mouth to find the room dark and the fire out. He slept again, coughing so hard at times that it woke him, whereupon he would struggle upright long enough for it to subside, and then prop a pillow behind him and doze off. When he woke in the morning, he barely had enough strength to change into a dry undershirt and climb back in bed.

Next morning he woke with so much fluid in his lungs that he feared drowning in his sleep. He wanted desperately to keep churning his five thousand words-per-day average of the previous week, although the sane part of his mind—an increasingly small place, he admitted to himself—knew this goal was madness. His head pounded, his limbs ached, and frequently, now, the coughing brought on the sweet taste of blood. He resolved not to complain—he would simply write in bed to the limit of his endurance, until the weather warmed enough for him to open the windows and dry out his lungs. Meanwhile, any day now, he was certain to get good news about a barrage of manuscripts he had shipped to Henley. He clung to the hope that a few more sales, plus setting a wedding date with Fanny would sustain his soul if not his wretched physical being.

And yet, in his lightheaded state that at times approached euphoria, he began to wonder what death would be like. Long ago he had rejected his father's belief, endlessly pounded into his head by Mrs. Cunningham, of an afterlife filled with flames. How could an all-knowing and loving God be vengeful toward the weaknesses of humans, whom He seemed to have created for his own amusement? He wrote to Ed Gosse in one of these philosophical moments that "death is no bad friend; a few aches and gasps and we are done."

The first day in February came. Could spring be far off? For days he had not risen from bed, but in lucid moments kept writing—in the daylight, essays and stories; at night, by gas lamp, letters to friends that he illustrated with silly sketches and poems. To Colvin he composed what, at 2:00 AM, at least, seemed witty. He drew a sketch of a grave that he labeled, "my tomb," and under this added:

Robert Louis Stevenson
Born 1850 of a Family of Engineers.
Died _____.
Home is the sailor, home from sea,
And the hunter home from the hill.

You, who pass this grave, put aside hatred; love kindness; be all services remembered in your heart and all offences pardoned; and as you go down again among the living, let this be your question: Can I make someone happier this day before I lie down to sleep?

He set down his pen, sunk back on his pillow and pulled the blanket to his chin. Reaching to turn off the lamp, he laughed—there were so many manuscripts stacked on the floor that he might not get out of the room even if he had the strength. With a light-headed sense of having one foot in that dark, next world, and an intense longing to have Fanny next to him and in his arms, he drifted off...

CHAPTER 20
Taking Him In

Pacing in the barn-like San Francisco Ferry Building on a foggy February morning, in a grey dress, long blue coat and fur-lined gloves, Fanny thought it strange that Louis had not been waiting when she stepped off the paddle wheeler. With his stork-like build and eccentric choices in clothing, usually the blue velvet coat and maroon beret or, in winter, a brown, cavernous Ulster offset by his bright silk smoking cap, he would be hard to miss. Nonetheless she walked for miles on the harsh brick floor, circling clumps of merchants in suits and bowlers, Chinese families in straw hats and tunics, and even a farmer pulling a cart of caged chickens in her fruitless search.

The letter she had received a few days after their showdown with Sam had been gleeful, running on, as Louis was inclined to do, about days spent at the Bohemian Club library and the "fascinating chaps" he had met there, and gloating about earning twenty-five dollars from news editor Fitch for "scribbling inanities about restaurants." He had enclosed a check for twenty of them for "the family's needs," and asked when they could get together to plan their wedding.

By return mail she had thanked him, pledged her love, and promised to ferry over the Bay and have lunch with him the following week. The excitement of waiting for their Big Day, she assured him, made her feel like a young, first-time bride. For their lunch date, she had urged him to spend a nickel on a trolley ride to the Ferry Building rather than walk through the cold, but knowing Louis, he would probably have walked anyway, perhaps accounting for his tardiness.

After smoking three more cigarettes and staring at men of all sizes, clothing styles and nationalities who set foot in the building and failing to see Louis, she hurried out onto the Embarcadero, turned up Market and then onto Bush Street. By the time she reached his lodgings she was imagining the worst.

She pounded on the door of No. 608. A short, dowdy woman who had to be his landlady, Mrs. Carson, eventually opened it and scowled.

"I'm here for Mr. Stevenson."

"And you are?"

"Mrs. Osbourne, his fiancée," she said, brushing past Mrs. Carson and walking up the stairs. She rapped on the door to Number B and got no response. "When have you last seen him?" she asked Mrs. Carson who stared from the bottom of the stairwell.

"I'm afraid he's not been well." The landlady clomped up the stairs, pulled a brass key from her apron and shoved it in the door. When she swung the door open, Fanny hurried past her into the room.

Fanny did not know whether to laugh or cry at the stacks of books and manuscripts, grown even taller since she had last seen the room, which she dodged to get to his bed. "Louis!"

His face lay slack and bloodless in the dim light. Long strings of hair splayed against his cheeks, and the rest of him looked like a sack of sticks in human form. Yanking the sash of the window shutters above his bed provided enough light for her to see his chest barely rising and falling. She shoved her arm under his neck and raised his head, feeling his faint breath against her cheek, smelling a rank odor of infection and illness. "Louis, wake up, we were going to have lunch, remember?"

Faintly he smiled, his eyes fluttering open. His lips, white and chapped, moved as if he was trying to say something, or perhaps to swallow, but instead closed his eyes and seemed to drift into unconsciousness. She turned to the landlady, who stood with folded arms in the doorway. "I beg you, Mrs. Carson, go to Seven Montgomery Street for my daughter. Hurry!"

Mrs. Carson hesitated for a few seconds, then set her jaw and turned. Hearing footsteps clattering down the stairwell, Fanny turned her attention to Louis. The next hour was a blur of actions that came to her naturally, having nursed children through ailments both minor and lethal, in surroundings more primitive than this. She hung a pot of water over the fire. She stripped off his linen shirt, trousers, socks and underwear, all of them soaked-through from what must have been a raging fever. Lifting and turning him, she tugged fresh clothes over his head and onto his arms and legs. With the warm water she swabbed his face and brow.

Joe and Belle showed up with a chubby, fresh-faced doctor in tow who poked Louis, looked down his throat and listened to his chest. He proclaimed that he might have influenza and possibly consumption. When he tried to sell her a general elixir, "sure to make him feel better," she ordered him off the premises, having vowed after Hervey's death never to trust the concoctions of a doctor she did not know. By the same reasoning, she felt an intense need to have him home—in *her* own home, nowhere else.

"Joe, help me stand him up. Belle, bring that brown ulster and look around for some gloves and a cap." While Joe kept Louis upright, she and Belle managed to get the coat, kid gloves and a woolen cap on him.

While Mrs. Carson held the door open, they half-carried, half-dragged Louis out of the room. "I'm not helpless," Louis mumbled while his feet slipped and flailed on the way down the wooden stairs.

Getting him out the door and into the fog, Fanny and Belle propped Louis between them while Joe dashed up and down the street yelling "Taxi! Need a ride for a sick man!" to sparse traffic—two men who walked by with their hands thrust in the pockets of long overcoats, and a beer wagon straining up the street toward Nob Hill, its two Clydesdales clashing hooves against the wooden cleats that had been driven into the street for better purchase. When a lone cab finally clattered around the corner of Powell and onto Bush but failed to stop, Joe jumped in front of it, causing its horse to rear and its driver to curse, but getting them a ride to the Ferry Building nonetheless.

Blessedly, a baggage boy on the boarding ramp of *The Alameda* looked their way while they struggled to get Louis aboard, dashed below decks and returned with a stretcher and another helper who looked like a cook. Louis smiled deliriously and tipped his hat at them, but weakly resisted their attempts to get him onto the litter. Finally, with his thin legs jutting at odd angles like an injured grasshopper, Louis let them carry him past the splashing paddle wheel to a stairwell while muttering to deckhands, "Merry Christmas to all, and to all a good night."

They took him down to the warmest spot onboard, a small, darkly paneled barroom, lowering him to a wooden bench opposite a lineup of men in black suits downing shots of whisky, who gave brief looks of alarm before returning to their glasses. "I need some sugared tea, and quickly, sir," Fanny said to a dour-looking man behind the bar.

To her surprise he hurried to comply, producing hot water from a pot over a small stove behind the bar, pouring it into an empty beer mug and steeping a sifter of black tea. After what seemed like the longest three-mile boat ride in her life, during which she managed to get a half-cup of the liquid down Louis's throat, they loaded him on a hack parked by the Oakland Ferry Wharf for the bumpy but brief ride to her home.

Draped over Joe and Fanny's shoulders he stumbled up the dirt path to the porch of her house. "Dead," he muttered as they bumped him up the small white steps. Fanny followed his heavy-lidded gaze to the long planter box before the front window in which a row of cyclamens, having produced lush purple blooms through the fall, now lay flat and blackened, victims of the winter frost.

The front door swung open. She was momentarily stunned by Sam, impassively holding the door with Lloyd beside him, until she remembered Sam saying something about coming today for a visit. If Louis felt any concern over Sam's presence he did not show it, perhaps needing all of his strength and concentration just to draw ragged breaths while they helped him through the parlor and into her bedroom. They sprawled him on the bed, got his head on a pillow and stretched out his legs on her quilted bedspread.

"I'll go for Doc Bamford," Sam said from the doorway.

"Thank you," she whispered.

"And I think it best if I take Lloyd to my place for a while."

She gave Sam a sharp look but soon decided that the matter-of-fact expression behind the golden beard bore no malice. She nodded.

Dr. Bamford arrived within a half-hour, clad in a black vested suit, string tie and muddy boots. He listened to Louis's chest, squeezed open his mouth and pushed a stick on his tongue for a better view. "How long have you been consumptive?"

"Forever," he muttered.

The doctor touched the bones of his ribcage. "How long since you've had a good meal?"

Louis gave a thin smile.

"The fevers and sweats?"

"A week or so."

"Oh, Louis!" Fanny exclaimed.

The doctor had Louis spit in a small jar. He swirled the contents as if they were a glass of fine brandy, held the jar up to the window and examined its contents. He pulled Louis's eyelids down and stared. "Rest, son." Louis lay on the pillow and closed his eyes.

Dr. Bamford took Fanny into the hallway. "Mr. Stevenson's got three problems—consumption, starvation and malaria. I suppose I don't have to tell you that any one of them could kill him."

She shook her head, trying to stop her lips from trembling.

"A man bleeding from the lungs needs to be still," he continued. "You're lucky he didn't die when you moved him over here."

She set her jaw. "I assure you he'll now be still. Tell me exactly what I need to do."

He instructed her on Louis's care, giving her a bottle of quinine and another one filled with a vile-looking brown liquid. Eventually, he took up his black bag, and she escorted him to the front door. He cleared his throat. "Sam told me the whole situation."

"Dr. Bamford, you've known the family a long time. I assure you that—"

The doctor held up his hand. "No explanations needed, Ma'am. I'm a doctor, not a priest, so I make no moral judgments. But Sam's a strong man, and this boy isn't."

"Louis is stronger than ten men, in his way." Sudden tears stung her eyes.

The doctor gave her a kindly smile. "I can see you love him. All I mean to suggest is that you might want to marry him as soon as possible, if you want to have some time together." He tipped his hat and walked with his black bag to a waiting buggy.

Fanny closed the door, struck by how her life had abruptly shifted from wondering, a few short weeks ago, if she would ever be free to marry Louis to wondering, today, how long he would survive. After Joe and Belle embraced her and left to catch the last ferry to San Francisco, she stepped to the bed and found him asleep, his breathing sounding reasonably clear, and his face even wearing a faint smile. How young and innocent he looked—and, she suspected, would always look, whether he lived another day or another thirty years. Youth, playfulness, and boyishness were Louis; death was not.

Suddenly she remembered the disgusting thought that her love and desire for him had somehow welled-up from her deep love of her lost son. She looked at the young man's face on the pillow, and saw something else besides boyishness beneath the skin: steel. He was *absolutely not* a four-year-old innocent, but a man who had crossed a stormy ocean and barren continent for her, had given up all that was comfortable and safe just to be with her and have her. Dr. Charcot and the other learned men could have their views, and she would have her Louis—alive.

She got a pen and notebook from the roll-top desk by the window, pulled her sitting chair close to the bed, kicked off her shoes and propped her feet against the mattress. Spreading her skirt across her knees, she opened the notebook. With the gas lamp on the wall softly illuminating his face just a few feet beyond her, she began writing:

> Dear Mrs. Stevenson,
>
> Because you and I have much in common, I hope—no, I don't hope, I <u>know</u> that you will understand why I am writing to you about your son and the steps I am taking for his health and happiness. What we have in common is our love for him, you as his mother and I as his future wife. I have often thought how his absence must tear at your heart, as it would mine, because he brings so much joy to every room he enters, every person to whom he speaks, every

gathering he joins, and to every person he pens a letter.

I am sorry to say you will not be getting his witty letters with their happy illustrations for a while. Louis is very ill, a fact that is the immediate cause for this outpouring from one mother's heart to another. Today, I took him into my home so that I can care for him; God knows—as I am certain you do—that Louis does not care very well for himself. He cares for his art, for ideas, and for others more than he cares about his sleep, his next meal, his lungs and his comfort. His neglect was such that he surely would have died, had I not found him in dire condition and taken him in. I vow to you that when I am his wife, the neglect will cease. I shall do all in my power to see him through the current illness, to provide loving care while he recovers, and to be vigilant lest setbacks occur. I hope this vow will provide you comfort that may, in time, overtake the misgivings which you and your esteemed husband have had about our most unusual courtship.

In time, I shall be delighted to meet you and Mr. Stevenson, as I have heard so much about you, all of it glowing! Please do send by return mail a photograph of yourself or other small items by which I might know you better.

Affectionately,

Fanny

Before she could reconsider, she folded the page into an envelope, sealed it and addressed it to 17 Heriot Row, Edinburgh, Scotland.

She became his fiercest nurse and protector. She allowed no visitors, not even Joe or Belle. She made sure Louis had no excitement of any kind. She hid his notebook and pen in a cedar chest below a pile of blankets. She gave up her bedroom and hovered outside its door, sleeping on the sofa.

She administered spoonfuls of the medicine, morning, noon and night. She fed him soft bread, noodle soup and mashed potatoes so that nothing hard or sharp would disturb his throat. Finally, although not a particularly religious woman, she prayed.

She soon noticed that the word had spread: Mrs. Osbourne had brought a young man into the house in broad daylight and was keeping him. Neighbors whispered, pulled their children close, or turned their backs when she walked out to buy bread or eggs. One day she caught Rodney Henry, a red-headed boy about Lloyd's age who lived two houses down, staring into her bedroom window when she threw the shades open to catch some precious sunlight. When, a week after Louis's arrival at the house, Sam brought Lloyd back to Oakland to "stay with his mother," Mrs. Henry gave excuses for why Rodney could not play with Lloyd. The fact that a divorce decree was issued ending the marriage between Francis Vandegrift and Samuel Osbourne did nothing to mollify the disapprovers; if anything, it inflamed them. She did not care.

"You're going to kill me," Louis muttered, sitting up in bed in a grey bathrobe when she took a banana and glass of milk to his room on a rainy March afternoon. "I'll die of boredom, or if I don't die, I'll hang myself."

"We have to get you away."

"Good. I was hoping you'd come to your senses and un-cage me."

She set the tray of food on the bed and sat next to him. "I don't mean turning you loose to work your way back to exhaustion. I mean we have to find a place for you to live that's hot and dry."

"My father might suggest hell." Louis peeled the banana and took a bite.

"Perhaps you underestimate him."

"He's disinherited me, and refers to you in letters, dear Fanny, as 'sinful mad business.'"

She laughed. "Well, the sinful mad business says it's time for your nap."

"My God."

"No, your angel." She smiled sweetly, kissed his cheek and walked out of the bedroom, locking the door behind her.

After a month of her care, he had gained a few pounds around the waist, a fact that she confirmed by pinching him. She brought in a fresh loaf of bread. "I'm fattening you up for the wedding."

He grinned. "I'm fat enough. Let's marry tomorrow."

She buttered a slice of bread for him. "I was thinking May would be lovely."

Louis sat up in bed. "How could you afford the bread? What have you been living on?"

"Sam's been helping. He got his job back with the court."

Louis frowned, as if remembering something. "Was Sam here when you moved me in?"

She nodded.

Louis sat down on the bed. "Bring my writing things. God knows I'm healthy enough."

After six weeks he was back to rising early and getting dressed for the day. "Today I'll battle the garden," he announced on a warm April morning, marching into the parlor in a broad-brimmed hat and huge leather gloves. She watched from the window while he strode out to the tool shed and came out armed with a spade. He attacked the weeds and dead flowers in the planter box on the porch, throwing dirt everywhere in the process, including his neck and back.

The day's mail included a letter for him that had been forwarded from his San Francisco address. When she showed him the envelope he propped the spade against the house and tore it open. He read the letter silently, smiled and sank to his knees in the dirt. "Hallelujah!" he shouted to the sky. He grabbed handfuls of dirt and tossed them into the air. "Hallelujah!"

"What is it?"

"Take that, oh ye of little faith! Take that, Henley and Colvin!" He shook his fist vaguely eastward, in their direction. "Leslie Stephens bought 'Pavilion on the Links' for *Cornhill Magazine*. He's paying five pounds for it. Hah! He says it is a grand good tale, despite what Henley and those other turds said." He threw his arms around her and ran his muddy hands up and down her back.

"It's a wonderful story, worth more than five pounds. It's far better than anything you've hacked out for the newspapers."

"'Hacked out,' do you jest? I've been paid by two top-notch newspapers for my work. Certainly that says something."

"Hmmm." She did not have the heart to tell him his Monterey newspaper job had been secretly rigged by Jules Simoneau, who passed a hat each Friday to the many patrons who were fond of Louis and then gave the collected coins to Editor Bronson, who used them to pay Louis's "salary" of two dollars per week.

Later, while Louis sat on the bed with muddy trousers, recovering with a cup of tea, Fanny worked the pedals of her Singer sewing machine, steadying an edge of light-blue satin while feeding in a long strand of lace. When someone rapped on the front door, Louis rose with a groan to see to it, returning with a yellow Western Union envelope which he eagerly tore open, perhaps in hopes of another sale.

"Well?" she prodded.

"'Count on me for two hundred fifty pounds annually,'" Louis read, striding over to where she sat. "'Have mailed a letter to explain. Father.'"

"Louis, that's wonderful. What a relief."

"He turned the thin sheet over in his hands. "What on earth could have possessed him to forgive me?"

She shrugged.

Louis's eyes narrowed. "How did he know where to send this?"

"Perhaps the letter he's sending to you will explain."

"You wrote to him!" Louis, red-faced, walked in little circles, tangling his foot in yards of lace that spilled down from the sewing machine. He tried to shake his foot loose and kicked the wall instead.

"No, I did not write to him. I wrote to your mother. And why not?" She stood from the little sewing machine table and faced him. "Sometimes I wish you would grow up and face reality."

"Reality? Reality is bleeding lungs. Reality is death. I don't need reality, thank you very much!"

"But you need to eat and you need a roof over your head. Louis, I'm doing what I can to keep you alive."

"I loathe begging."

"I did not beg. I told her how much I loved you." She reached for the wedding gown she'd been trying to finish and held it up to him. "But if you'd like, I can throw this away."

His large brown eyes peered directly into hers, and a smile formed on his lips. His arms drew her to him, and she felt his deep sigh. "Of course you'll not throw that away."

CHAPTER 21
Becoming Mrs. Stevenson

"Stop fidgeting," Louis said in the cab, squeezing the gloved hand she had been using to smooth her satin dress and check that the hair she had carefully pinned beneath a sloping grey hat was staying in place. "You are absolutely beautiful."

"So are you." She smoothed the lapel of the charcoal-grey suit he had borrowed from a friend at the Bohemian Club. The coat fit surprisingly well, its padded shoulders and double-breasted elegance making him look almost his age. The trousers were too loose, though, as all trousers tended to be when hung on Louis, making the fabric bunch around the belt. More than making up for this minor flaw was the huge smile he had worn all the way from Oakland while he repeated, "I can't believe this, I just can't believe it," over and over again during the journey.

Her gaze strayed out the window to the pedestrians on Market Street who seemed in no hurry, under a warm May sun, to get inside restaurants and offices. The steady clip-clopping of the horse pulling them past the tree-lined parade grounds of Union Square brought a sudden, unbidden memory of a dream-like ride through Paris with Sam, when a cab had taken her down a tree-lined street to a lunatic asylum. Fighting the thought that another one of her black moods could someday plunge her into madness again, this time as Mrs. Stevenson, she clutched Louis's hand. Surely misreading her action, he squeezed back and murmured, "I can't believe it. I just can't believe you're going through with it!"

"Louis, would you just shut up?" She smiled into his eyes and kissed his big grin.

They stopped on Post Street in the shade of a white spire rising above St. John's Presbyterian Church. Seeing Dora Williams waiting in the open doorway of a small brick parsonage in a green dress and purple-plumed hat, Fanny's fears vanished. Her oldest and most forgiving San Francisco friend, Dora had agreed without hesitation to serve as one of the two witnesses required for a legal wedding ceremony. "So glad you two could come," Dora said with a laugh, embracing them.

An ample, grey-haired woman in a tent-like brown dress appeared behind Dora.

"Mrs. Scott," Louis said, "I would like you to meet my fiancée, Fanny Vandegrift. Fanny, this is Reverend Scott's wife."

"We do the small ones here in the parsonage," Mrs. Scott announced, leading the way through a dim hallway to a small, book-lined study where she nodded to some stuffed chairs set before a heavy desk. They sat and, for want of anything better to do, stared at a heavy walnut crucifix hanging on the wall for what seemed like far too long, but might have been five minutes. "Bill?" the pastor's wife finally hollered down another dim hallway.

Reverend William Scott, with the bushy white hair, beard, and fanatical stare of an Old Testament prophet, stuffed into a backwards collar and black suit, lumbered in from somewhere down in the bowels of the house. Gravely shaking hands with Louis he asked in a thick brogue, "Well boy, have y' made it to the end?"

"The end?"

"The end of *An Answer to Bishop Colenson*?"

"Oh, your book. No, afraid not. There was just too much to savor in the earlier chapters." Louis nudged Fanny, and she noticed a mischievous smile on his lips. Two weeks previous, he had gone out alone for several hours and come home saying he'd found the perfect clergyman to perform the wedding, a Scottish Presbyterian like his father with a library chock full of fat theological volumes. The two men had "hit it off famously" due, Fanny had assumed, to their heritage. Now she suspected that Louis, who tended toward the theatrical, wanted his wedding to be performed if not by God himself than by someone who was a passable stand-in. Worse, the clergyman fancied himself a writer.

"What did you think of the earlier chapters?" Reverend Scott persisted.

"It seemed as if you set out to answer the bishop in precisely the way he needed to be answered."

Mrs. Scott creaked to the desk and flipped open a ledger. "Bill?"

The Reverend gave her a sharp look and sighed, as if the poor woman simply could not appreciate intelligent discourse. "The State of California requires certain information for your license. Name, nationality, that sort of thing."

Fanny reached for a pen that stood in its inkwell, but Mrs. Scott snapped it up and smiled. "I shall do the writing. Mr. Stevenson gave me his vitals when he was here last, but the only item I have for you is your name. Your city and state of birth, please?"

"Indianapolis, Indiana."

"Date of birth?"

"The tenth day of March."

"In the year..." Pen poised, Mrs. Scott waited, eventually frowning up at Fanny.

"Eighteen sixty."

Louis turned to the side and shook with either laughter or coughing.

Mrs. Scott cocked her head. "But Miss Vandegrift, that would make you only nineteen years old."

"It would, wouldn't it."

"One can't help but notice, ma'am," Reverend Scott said, "that y' look more... mature in years, shall we say, than Mr. Stevenson, and he is twenty-nine."

"You've sniffed me out. I didn't want to embarrass my beloved Louis but yes, he's a younger man. The birth year I just gave you is twenty years after my actual one." She sighed and leaned her head heavily on Louis's shoulder. "He is a saint, taking me on in my situation."

"Your situation?"

"My first husband didn't last."

Reverend Scott's thick eyebrow wrinkled. "I'm afraid I don't understand. Do you mean, you are..."

"She's a widow," Louis said.

This time Dora Williams turned her back to them, her plumed hat shaking so violently from her silent laughter that it almost fell off.

An enormous black-and-white cat suddenly leaped onto the stuffed arm of Louis's chair and stared with rheumy eyes. "Seems our third witness has arrived."

"Perhaps we should get on with it," Fanny said.

Reverend Scott opened a book of services and cleared his throat. "Dearly beloved..." When he got to the part asking Fanny if she would take Louis "for richer or poorer, in sickness and in health," she couldn't help noticing that Louis still looked much too pale. Her voice caught when she said "I do."

They exchanged simple silver rings, and kissed.

"Come in, newlyweds, the champagne is on ice!" Joe Strong hugged Fanny, shook Louis's hand and pulled them through the doorway of his Montgomery Street apartment. Inside, a party was in full swing that included the usual Bohemian and artist crowd. "Hey, everyone," Joe shouted, "my mother-in-law just got married, and to guess who?"

Virgil Williams, a balding, pleasant-looking man in a blue vest, handed his wife Dora a drink and pounded Louis's back. "I guess Lou!"

Charlie Stoddard, the poet, with a cigar clamped in his teeth, slid onto the piano bench and banged out "The Old Grey Mare She Ain't What She Used To Be" while drunken voices laughed, slurred along to the end and then raised their glasses to Louis and Fanny.

Belle emerged from the smoke and crowd in a clinging yellow dress and embraced her mother. "I do wish you had come," Fanny said.

"You could have held the cat," Louis added.

"I'm sorry, mother. But happy for you."

Fanny flinched at the explosion of a champagne cork blowing loose in the next room. Joe hurried out with a tray of bubbling flutes and offered them around.

Joe raised his glass. "To Mr. and Mrs. Stevenson!"

While the others drained their glasses, Fanny strolled to the canvasses stacked along the window-side of the long room. She recognized two portraits of Stoddard that Joe had done, one in which he was dressed as a monk, and in the other, a cavalier. Further along the wall, a grim-faced, white-haired, black-suited man seemed to glare at her, and next to it, a painting-in-progress of what must have been the man's portly wife smiled with what seemed self-satisfaction beneath a tangle of black curls, obviously a wig. Fanny wondered if she would look as ridiculous in her old age, and whether or not Louis would live long enough to sprout grey hair.

"Joe is good. Too damn good." Jules Tavernier had come up behind her with his pretty wife, Lizzie. "Makes two hundred or more per portrait. I'm lucky to get half of that for my landscapes. How's Lou doing with his scribbling?"

"Fine Jules, just fine." And Louis did seem to be doing fine with the scribbling, just not in earnings. She supposed it wasn't the time to tell Jules that if Louis's rate of earnings during nine California months continued, he and Fanny would soon be begging bread on the Embarcadero next to the other vagrants.

Charlie Stoddard strolled over. "Where are you lovebirds going to live?"

She paused. It had become a sore subject, Louis favoring Denver for its high, dry climate, and she wanting to stay in California.

"Somewhere warm and cheap," Louis chimed from behind her.

"I'd say hop a steamer to Hawaii or Tahiti."

"We won't be going that far," she said.

"Why not? Living in the islands is dirt-cheap, once you get there. You sure as hell don't need many clothes."

"Charlie, we need to be practical."

"I'll loan you *Typee* and *Omoo*, Lou. Melville's books about the south seas."

By the way Louis grinned, Fanny knew he would devour the books, and probably would want to take his father's allowance and board the first ship.

Virgil Williams appeared with a fresh bottle of champagne and filled their glasses. "Get thee to a mountainside above Calistoga."

Louis frowned. "Where?"

"The spa-town in the Napa Valley. It's just a few hours by train and ferry. You can hike up to silver mines and be drenched in sun while you look down on vineyards and meadows. Buy a decent Cabernet and drink it sitting in mineral hot springs. You could stake a claim and have land for free, who knows. You'll love it."

She saw Louis brace an arm heavily against the back of the sofa, and noticed, beneath his fascinated expression, how pale he had become in the past few hours. "We must be going," she announced, adding with a demure smile, "It's our wedding night."

He nodded, smiling.

Walking past Joe's paintings on the way to the door reminded her of something. "But before we go," she said to Joe, "show me that painting you made of Belle. The one Louis called your best."

Louis coughed. "No, no, Fanny, there's no time for that. Tonight is our wedding night!" He shoved his glass in Joe's hand and tugged her toward the door.

"What's wrong with you, Louis?"

"Drink up," Joe said, giving the glass back to him, "while I get the painting." He stepped to a closet and pulled out a large frame that was covered with a sheet. He set it against the wall opposite the big windows. Standing beside the canvas like a circus ringmaster, pausing and for some reason grinning at Louis, Joe pulled the sheet away with a flourish.

"It's an unusual pose, Belle, but very pretty." Fanny did not think it the best-ever painting of her daughter, but of course would not say this to Joe and Belle, who were smiling at each other as if sharing a private joke. Perhaps their joke had something to do with the way he had posed her, reclining on a sofa and holding a cup of tea in the middle of her lap, a faintly suggestive pose—were it not for the brown, ankle-length, buttoned-to-the-neck dress that obscured her most notable features.

CHAPTER 22
Honeymoon

They left San Francisco in a thick fog, ferrying to Oakland and then boarding a California Pacific Railroad car for the one-hour ride north to Vallejo. She had dressed smartly for their first trip as Mr. and Mrs. Stevenson in an ocean-blue dress, grey kid gloves, and black felt hat with the brim rolled on one side and topped with an artificial rose. Louis sat with his long legs pressed close to hers in his idea of natty tourist attire, a green Tyrolean cap, his blue velvet coat and big-knotted red tie. On his knees lay his ever-present journal that he occasionally jotted in, when he wasn't staring out the window at the scenery, which he seemed to find fascinating.

She followed his gaze outside as the train rumbled around a marsh, taking them into bright sunshine and sending ducks into flight. Climbing a pass of green, sunlit hills, the train's steam whistle sent stray cows stamping and bawling away from the track.

She saw him scribbling in the notebook again. "Are you writing about the ducks, dirt or cattle?"

"Everything, all of it, every beast and twig. Even you, my sweet, will be chronicled."

"Chronicled?"

"A lively account of our honeymoon, dear Mrs. Stevenson, in a place called Calistoga among mine shafts,

239

bears, mountain lions, and with Black Bart the outlaw on the loose is sure to appeal to the genteel readership of R.L. Stevenson, recently of Scotland, Monterey and San Francisco."

She sighed. "Is that what I am, an adventure?"

He scrawled a few more words, snapped the notebook shut and smiled into her eyes. "The grandest one of all. I still can't believe it." He slid his hand onto her yellow cotton sundress and squeezed her knee, a gesture he seemed to enjoy but which she found a bit startling.

She slid her hand high up his leg and squeezed, making him jump and sending the notebook to the floor. He dove, laughing, to retrieve it just as the brakes squealed and they lurched to a slow, grinding stop. She poked her head out the window and looked forward past the bonneted and bowlered heads of other travelers who were doing the same. Just a few feet ahead of the locomotive's cowcatcher the tracks ended on a ramp overlooking the muddy shallows of the Carquinez Straits. The *Julia*, a ferry with railroad track mounted down the length of a massive flat deck, waited to take them across to Vallejo, a sleepy collection of white buildings in the distance. It would be a long wait; on a sign staked on the loading ramp someone had scrawled, "Closed until 7:00 AM Good Nite."

Louis hopped up and gamely filled his arms with their lunch basket, notebook, satchel, assorted volumes and smoking things they'd strewn about the car. She smiled. For her new husband, the more complicated, convoluted and challenging a journey, the better. In Paris, Monterey, San Francisco, or anywhere else, he would venture miles out of the way for a look at a teetering house on stilts, or a site where foul murder had taken place, or where a vicious animal was tethered or, for that matter, where anything unusual was rumored to be found.

"What now?" she asked as a cloud of black engine-smoke caught up to their car, poured through the open windows and enveloped them.

Coughing, Louis nodded toward the window. "The Frisbie."

"The what?"

She followed his gaze to a dilapidated wood-frame inn with Frisbie House lettered on one side. "Our inestimable lodgings."

Conveniently, they entered the hotel, if it could be called that, through a bar that smelled of wood-rot and vomit. Louis bought a bottle of Sauterne before their climb to a second-story room of knotty pine walls, one sticking window and a creaky bed. He seemed in great spirits, whistling as he lit a fire behind a tiny grate and opened the wine, while she stepped to the window to admire the view of a marsh teeming with bullfrogs.

Somewhere during their second glass, she was laughing. It may have been the way he kept saying, "Isn't it grand? Isn't it just grand?" about their adventure together, or perhaps it was sitting alone, finally, with him on the bouncy bed. But his brown eyes danced, his every cell seemed vibrant and his mood was infectious.

As one, they set down their wine glasses and undressed. Their lovemaking was unhurried, lacking in the urgency with which they had attacked things when they were mere lovers, but doubly rich as Mr. and Mrs. Stevenson. Louis was youthful, tender but vigorous—she had a fleeting thought that with each mile away from fog he gained ten minutes of staying-power—and she eagerly joined him in glorious, shuddering, gasping spasms of relief.

"Isn't it grand?" He murmured one last time over the croaking of the bullfrogs.

"Yes Louis, it is grand." They kissed and drifted to sleep in each others' arms.

At 6:00 AM she woke to what she first thought was the cry of a wounded animal, but eventually realized was a male voice, elsewhere in the hotel singing what might have been opera. On the pillow next to her, Louis opened an eye and smiled. "I love you," he said, just before someone down the hall hollered "Shut the hell up!" at the opera singer.

By 9:00 AM they were across the straits and rumbling off the ferry's deck-tracks toward the adobe train station in Vallejo, where they transferred to bright-red cars of the narrow gauge bound for Calistoga. As they clacked north through the Napa Valley with its oak-studded pastures, tidy white corrals and vineyards circling the hills, Louis announced each station they passed, drawing out the names on his tongue as if tasting a rare wine: "Napa." "Yountville." "Oakville." "Rutherford." "St. Helena."

"Yes, Louis," she said each time, snuggling close to him.

Eventually they rode beneath the imposing hulk of Mt. St. Helena, and a small town of white cottages and a train station came into view. "I don't suppose you, born in America, would know the origin of the name Calistoga."

"No, Louis." She knew how much he liked to play tour guide and to display his vast knowledge of everything, learned mostly through books. "Please do tell."

"I shall. Sam Brannan, the Mormon of San Francisco who built this rail line and put the town on the map, after snatching the Napa valley from the Indians, of course, sought to establish a tourist destination that would appeal to the San Francisco bourgeoisie. So he combined the name California with Saratoga, the tourist spot of the New York elite. Hence Calistoga."

She patted his arm. "Louis, I don't know what I would do without you."

He grinned.

Louis hired an open cab to take them through the town on Lincoln Street, passing boardwalks and the false fronts of the General Store, the Magnolia Hotel, Kong Sam Kee's Laundry and several saloons. Beyond town the road narrowed and wound through stands of oak and low green hills, eventually emerging on neat rows of cottages, palm trees, a strong sulfurous odor, and straw-hatted tourists lounging under umbrellas or playing croquet.

"Stop," Louis yelled.

For five extravagant, idyllic days they stayed at the Hot Springs Hotel. They slept late, and shared coffee on the veranda in the shade of the little palm before the door of their cottage. They strolled through Calistoga in the warm sun, had their photographs taken, bought ridiculous-looking cowboy hats, rode ponies to geysers and to a petrified forest. In the evenings they dined on beef steak and soaked in the hot springs. At her insistence, Louis kept his writing notebook closed. Instead, each night they read aloud to each other over coffee, Louis his favorite scenes from *Moby Dick* and Fanny from *Madame Bovary*. They made love at odd times, sometimes quickly, before going to breakfast, at other times solemnly, and after dinners almost elegantly, perhaps, she supposed, because the act was now legal and took place in a proper hotel. She loved his touch and thrilled to the sheer joy in his eyes when they were together in bed.

"Folly," he said after one of these sessions, using a nickname of his invention that he seemed to think was mighty clever, "I am in sheer heaven just being with you, but must get on with my writing."

She nodded. "I can't believe you've gone so long without it." She kissed him. "Actually, I'm eager to set up our household."

"Excellent. I know of the perfect place."

"Oh?"

"I was chatting with Morris Friedberg, the proprietor of the hardware store on Lincoln Street, nice man, a Russian Jew, actually. Seems Mister Friedberg knows a driver of immense reputation hereabouts named Foss, who knows every nook and cranny, rock and stream, that sort of man, and—"

"Louis," she interrupted, not especially in the mood for one of his long discourses, "would someone who deals in nuts and bolts be the best person to give advice about perfect places?"

Foss was a man of fierce handlebar mustache and three hundred pounds who, Louis later told her, was renowned for his impatience, poker face and speed. In the space of thirty terrifying, whip-cracking minutes he got them, by buckboard wagon, several miles up a twisting canyon road, throwing Fanny from side to side and nauseating her in the process. She was just about to ask if they could get out and walk when Foss spit a stream of tobacco past her ear, reined in the sweating horses and pointed up a rocky hillside. "There 'tis. Silverado. You can live up there for nuthing."

Fanny craned her neck to look up a rock-covered path that disappeared high up the hillside in a tangle of thickets and live oak trees.

"Big silver mine that's run out," Foss continued. "Company left it coupla years back, lock, stock and barrel to dig somewhere else. Hell, there's cabins up there in the trees, snug as a bug. All the rabbits and deer a man could shoot. Could run around nekked, for all the company you'd get!"

Louis's face had that lost, dreamy look. "Why that's fantastic! Fanny, isn't that fantastic?"

"Very fantastic. But Louis, I've had my fill of mines. Virginia City, don't you remember? Rocks, and ore carts, and..."

"...whorehouses and gunfights. But this is different. This would be *our* mine. We'd be king and queen of the realm. King and queen of Silverado, no less!"

"I don't see how you'd get up there."

A half-hour later they had picked their gasping way a half-mile up a dry creek bed to a clearing in a stand of madrone and pine trees. At the foot of a hillside sprawled a large boarded-up cabin that was partly covered by thickets of Manzanita and poison oak. Sturdily built, she thought, but forlorn-looking. A narrow-gauge track climbed like a surgeon's stitches up a hill above the cabin to a six-foot gash near its rocky top.

"That has to be the mineshaft." While she waited with hands on hips, Louis clawed on hands and knees up the steep, rock-strewn slope to the gash, sixty paces above her, and climbed in.

"Be careful!"

She waited what seemed a long time until he finally emerged, hands and knees muddy and wearing a big grin.

"Well, what's in there?"

"Glittering gold, silver, jewels and buried treasure." He scrambled down to where she stood.

"Seriously."

"Seriously, there's plenty of mud. What else, I've no idea. Too dark. But there'll be plenty of time to explore."

"Or break your neck. Louis—"

"Isn't it glorious?" He threw out his arms as if embracing the entire settlement.

"That's not the first word that comes to mind." She had always imagined that after they married, Louis would want to live in a sophisticated city such as Paris, London or New York, surrounded by writers and artists.

Louis lowered his shoulders to an ore truck that squatted on the track and pushed but could not budge it. Beneath the shade of a huge pine, a blacksmith's forge and a stamp mill were covered in rust and moss. All around lay chunks of quartz the size of grapefruits, as if an angry troll living in the mineshaft had hurled them out at intruders. The setting, the trees, the dilapidated dwelling, and the abundant sun in the clearing had a certain beauty, but depressed her by its rotting sort of solitude.

"I can build a writing desk," Louis rambled. "Better yet, two of them, one for outdoors and one for my office."

"I'm not sure that building things is your calling."

"And we'll use the mineshaft as a wine cellar."

"If we don't fall in. Louis, we'd better get back down to the road or the driver will leave us."

"Let's take a look inside the cabin." He used a downed tree limb to pry at the board nailed over the cabin door, gritting his teeth and straining until it came loose with a loud crack. They carefully stepped in.

"Watch out," she said as Louis picked his way across broken floor planks in the dim light, dodging weeds growing up through the gaps. He got to one of three small windows and managed to get its shutter open.

"Oh God," she gasped. A shaft of sunlight pierced the dust hanging in the air and revealed old newspapers, wood chips, straw and stones strewn everywhere.

Louis seemed fascinated by scraps of paper that had been left on a splintery table beneath the window. He held one up to the light. "John Stanley paid twenty-five dollars and seventy-five cents for his board from April first to April thirtieth. I wonder where John Stanley is now?"

"There's poison oak sticking up out of the floor right behind you, Louis."

He stepped forward along the wall and yanked open the shade of a second window, continuing through a dormitory of twelve bunk beds at the end of the room. "We'll have plenty of room for visitors."

"Visitors? Louis, the place is a dump. Uninhabitable."

"It's a palace!"

A week later, she woke in their bed—a platform of a bunk bed that she had softened with pine needles and a blanket—to the sounds of a cracking whip, curses and barking. She joined Louis, who had risen early and now sat with his journal at the creaky mine's desk, to peek out the window. Just below them on the hillside, Foss stood in a buckboard wagon laden with three passengers and assorted goods, flogging a team of black horses up the dry creek bed toward their cabin. Joe, Belle and Lloyd clamped hats to heads as the wagon lurched up the last several feet of rocky incline and bounced onto the clearing.

She threw on a bathrobe and followed Louis outside, where Lloyd stood next to Foss's wagon and stared at the cabin. "Welcome to your new home."

Her son's eyes widened in either awe or fear. "My what?"

A yapping dog, vaguely a spaniel, left the horse's heels he'd been nipping to sniff Louis's shoes and lift his hind leg over them.

"No, Chuchu!" Belle climbed down, knocked dust from her yellow sundress and embraced Fanny while the dog ran circles around them.

"Choo-choo?" Fanny asked.

Joe smiled at the dog and bowed to kiss Fanny's hand. "A wedding gift from our house to yours. Belle named the beast for the way we got him to Calistoga."

"Clever," Louis said.

Foss unceremoniously dumped the stuff in the wagon onto the dirt: three trunks, two crates of books, several sacks of flour, a bundle of six-foot two-by-fours, a hammer, saw, nails, and a partly assembled woodstove that clanged and bonged as it hit the ground.

Fanny followed Lloyd, who walked away from the others and was staring at the rusted mining implements, ore cart and cabin with a grim expression. "Is something wrong, honey?"

"What am I going to do up here?" he muttered.

The day, for Fanny, at least, did not improve as it wore on. Foss left them, promising to return in three days to extricate Joe and Belle. Fanny took a pitcher to what she thought was a lovely spring of fresh water behind the cabin and found the spring filled with mud. Eventually, Louis found an ancient pick and a broken-off shovel lying in the dirt near the mineshaft. While Joe sat in the shade of the pines with his sketchpad, pontificating on the virtues of laboring outdoors, Louis flailed away at the spring, almost braining Chuchu several times in the process but eventually digging out enough of the mud to provide the group a few glassfuls of brackish water for the night.

For dinner Fanny sliced four green apples for the five of them. At least Joe had had the good sense to pack six bottles of claret. They consumed three and one-half of these before, at Louis's suggestion, they built a bonfire in the clearing with pine branches and told ghost stories.

"This one's for Lloyd," Louis said, adopting a thick brogue as the firelight danced on their faces while they sat on stones in a semi-circle around the flames. "Y'll like it, lad. I call it The Body Snatchers." Unfortunately, his tale about a team of Edinburgh cutthroats who sold fresh bodies to the medical school, accompanied by screeching howls and drunken screams, courtesy of Joe and Belle, seemed too much for Lloyd, who became very quiet and pressed close to her as the burning logs spit and crackled.

"Could we do something else?" he asked in a quavering voice when the story ended. All she could think of was to tell stories of family fishing trips, all of which involved Sam—and now it was Louis's turn to fall into stony silence. Finally, at midnight they stumbled into the dusty bunk-room, spread their bed rolls over splinters and passed into a sleep disturbed only by the frantic croaking of bullfrogs.

Three days later, Fanny sat at a tiny table sewing up holes in Louis's trouser-knees. Nearby, Belle shoved shirts and underclothes into a trunk while Joe sat in a far corner making finishing touches on a sketch. When hollering and whip-cracking outside signaled Foss's arrival, sending Chuchu yelping in frantic circles, Joe tore the top sheet from his sketchpad and presented it to Fanny with a flourish.

She held it up to a window for a good look. "Why thanks, Joe. I like it even more than the dog."

Fanny envied Joe's uncanny knack for detail. His drawing had captured both the look of the cabin's interior and the way her life was passing within it. Rough-hewn, cramped walls were topped by splintery ceiling beams and roofing-joists that criss-crossed high in the darkness above the newlyweds. Louis had been placed in a superior position, sitting in an upper bunk with his back braced against the wall, writing in a notebook and seemingly oblivious to all else. His bride had been drawn sitting on the floor below him —her head appearing literally at his feet—while she bent over the table with needle and thread. Not shown in the sketch was Lloyd, who had gone outside and around the hillside to shoot tin cans with his .22 rifle.

As the summer dragged on, each day hotter and dustier than the one before, Lloyd retreated around the hillside for longer and longer stretches of shooting. She worried about him, not that target practice would hurt anyone in this remote spot, but by the way he kept to himself and scowled whenever she touched, laughed with, or sat close to Louis. She was certain her son was not only disquieted by their union, but sorely missed his father as well.

"Do you suppose he would mind if I join him?" Louis asked as they sat at the little table finishing tea and the rifle shots began.

"Wonderful idea, Louis." She kissed his cheek and nudged him toward the door.

He hesitated, frowning. "I'm not sure. The rifle range is his preserve."

"Go."

Minutes later, he came back grim-faced and sat on his chair.

"What happened?"

"I asked if I could have a go at the tin cans, but he said his father had given him the gun on his birthday, and wouldn't approve of me touching it."

"He'll get over it." Privately, she was not sure he would.

By the way Louis stared down at his cold tea, she knew how deeply Lloyd's rejection had hurt. How sad that Louis craved to be Lloyd's father; by an irrefutable fact of biology, he was not and never would be. Powerful feelings of love welled up in her for her husband's big, boyish, sentimental heart, no doubt his most fetching quality. She leaned over the table toward him, put an arm around his neck and caressed it. "Well, at least when he's out there shooting, we know where he is."

Blam. Blam.

"We certainly do."

"We could use that time," she whispered, pushing her breasts against him.

Dear Louis still did not seem to get her meaning—at nights, their privacy in the one-room cabin was nil—so she reached down and tugged at his belt.

He jumped up, his long legs banging the table and upsetting the teacups. While they hopped around unbuttoning her dress and his trousers and flinging them onto chairs and bunk beds, she was pleased with herself at coming up with the plan. Finally on this dreary hill she had managed to reach him! And when he got off his undershorts it was abundantly clear that Louis was pleased as well.

They fell onto their bunk. She savored his kisses and playful caresses, and soon lay on her back, eager to receive him, not caring about the way her head pushed at an odd angle against the end of the bunk. And in her bliss, when Louis lowered into her she ignored the pine needles that jabbed her from the homemade mattress.

Unfortunately, after such fine beginnings, the sound of the rifle banging away outside seemed to have a less-than-stimulating effect on Louis's doing the same, indoors. And when there was a long pause between rifle shots, both of them were distracted by the realization that Lloyd could walk through the cabin door at any time. The afternoon activity was wrecked beyond saving when Chuchu ambled over and began licking Louis's heels, and when she started giggling and could not stop.

The dog was worthless—no, worse than worthless, for he liked to urinate on her hat, sundress, an expensive pair of kid gloves, and anything else that bore her scent and had not been hung up out of his range. Louis, of course, immediately fell in love with Chuchu and got the thing fat with bread crusts that he offered as rewards for learning tricks. For his part, the dog never got beyond a half-assed sit-and-shake.

After supper, Louis would put his head in a book or play tunes on a flageolet that he had brought from Scotland. He was not a natural musician and the dog, stupid in every regard except music appreciation, would eventually lift his snout toward the sky and howl every time Louis tooted on the little woodwind. This often sent Lloyd outside to stand in the darkness and throw rocks in the general direction of the bullfrogs.

With Lloyd surly and Louis in his own world, the only other source of human contact on most days was Rufe Hanson, a greasy-haired brute who lived over a neighboring hill. Rufe would show up at odd hours on horseback with a dead deer for sale, poking the carcass that was slung bleeding over his saddle to demonstrate the meat's tenderness.

Her belief grew, as their days above Calistoga dragged on, that Louis was happiest living in a fictional world that he created with his mind and then described with his pen. The portions of his journal that he read aloud to her told of vast beauty, fascinating persons, and grand adventure— concerning an experience that she saw as living in the dirt.

"I don't think this will need much of an edit, Folly," he said excitedly when she strolled out of the cabin on a stifling afternoon to find him sitting on a tree stump in the clearing, writing in his journal. He was shirtless, with beads of sweat trickling down his back creating a damp spot on the top of his trousers. "I'm going to call it *The Silverado Squatters*."

"A squatter, is that what I am?"

He laughed. "And I as well. I sent a few pages of it to Virgil Williams in San Francisco. He knows a friend who knows a publisher who, Virgil assures me, is certain to pay well for the book. Isn't that exciting?"

"I don't know if I like the idea of the world reading about our honeymoon. And I do think you could lighten up on your writing schedule a little bit, so that we could enjoy more of just being together."

"Not if I'm to be breadwinner." He returned his attention to his notebook.

"At least your father's funds give us a little bit of a cushion, wouldn't you say?"

Louis stiffened but did not look up. "My father's funds always come with strings attached. You'll see."

Each day, Louis seemed to grow stronger and more content. When he took breaks from his writing, it was to hammer empty tin cans into "sculptures" on the blacksmith's anvil, build a wine rack and install it in the mineshaft, and walk the half-mile down to the toll house for mail. He wrote pages upon pages in his journal, humming and sometimes even cackling as he worked. She was grateful for his happiness, and especially for his improved health, but could not stop her own growing sense of frustration, loneliness and despair.

It dawned on her, during one particularly lonely day, that they were halves of an hourglass: when one was filling, the other seemed to become sicker or more melancholy. In time, the empty, sick one would again be restored to health—but at directly proportionate expense to the first one.

By mid-July, she spent more and more of each day curled in the bunk. "I'm sick," she told him on a scorching afternoon.

He frowned down at her, feeling her brow. "What is it?"

"Migraine headache." True enough, although she recognized that this was just one symptom of her brain fever that had returned with a vengeance.

He brought a handkerchief that he had dipped in the cool spring and pressed it to her brow. Sitting with her on the bunk, he massaged her neck and held her hand. After an hour of his sweet attention, she indeed felt better—and told him to go about his business.

"Are you sure?"

She nodded.

"I'll hike down for the mail. And I can finally post double-damned *Emigrant*, too." He tucked the packaged manuscript under his arm and headed for the door.

An hour later he strolled in and tossed an envelope to her. "From Mum."

"Your mother wrote to me?"

"I believe that's what a letter from Mrs. Thomas Stevenson of Edinburgh suggests." Grinning, he hung his straw hat on a peg and sat next to her on the bed.

Her eyes raced down the neatly formed paragraphs that had been written on soft, scented stationery, her spirits beginning to lift as the implications of the words sunk in.

"Well?"

She set the letter in her lap. "She wants to meet me."

"Of course she does, dear."

Fanny smiled. "She invited us to come to Edinburgh for a visit."

Louis's laugh sounded nervous. "For a visit? Do you have any idea what traveling from California to Europe entails?"

"Yes. I've done it, remember? With small children."

Louis hopped down from their bunk and began pacing. "But I've been making such fine progress. *Silverado Squatters* could be a success, right here in the States, with just a bit more time in which to hone it, and there's *Arizona Breckinridge* to finish, and myriad essays, and—"

"You can work while we sit on the train and the steamship."

"If we can afford them. Good God, Fanny, it would cost more to get to Europe than I'll get from selling a book."

She swallowed. "Your father is wiring first-class fare."

He stopped pacing. "I won't accept."

She stepped in front of him, put her hands on his shoulders and looked in his eyes. "Yes Louis, you will. If you love me, get me off this godforsaken hill."

Next morning she woke to the sound of Louis banging their trunks onto an empty bunk and snapping open the clasps. With frightening speed and no organization whatever, he began stuffing them with clothes, books, manuscripts, letters, silverware, photographs and the various odds-and-ends of their brief married life.

"Mama, what's wrong?" Lloyd's sleepy voice called from his bunk bed at the end of the room.

"Nothing's wrong, honey. We're moving."

Lloyd hopped from bed and rushed over to her bunk in his flannel pajamas, staring down with bright eyes beneath his short blond hair that stuck up in various directions from sleeping. "Home? Are we moving home?"

She paused. "Sort of."

After mashing down the trunk lids, one of which he sat on to get shut, Louis opened the cabin door. "I'll hike down and hire Rufe."

By next afternoon they were checked in at the Hot Springs Hotel. Big Rufe Hanson, as always poker-faced behind his thick mustache and brows, heaved their trunks, boxes, bedrolls, camp lanterns and handbags inside their room, soon covering the small floor. After pressing some bills in his hand and bidding him a pleasant "Goodbye," Louis walked around their goods, sat on the bed and stared at them.

She sat with him and caressed his neck. "Louis, I know you hated to leave."

Eventually he gave a little shrug. "I'd best catch up on some correspondence."

"Good idea."

While Lloyd propped his elbows on his rollaway bed and played solitaire, she tackled a difficult letter to Sam, explaining that Louis's parents wished to meet her and Lloyd, and that this would require taking Lloyd abroad for a few months. She assured him that Lloyd would enjoy a visit when he got back to the San Francisco area, within the next few days, before leaving on their trip. Privately, she wondered if they might settle in Europe indefinitely, perhaps in Italy, southern France, or one of the other warmer regions, but would not raise Sam's ire about such a possibility until it was a definite plan.

She wrote a second, careful letter to Louis's mother. saying how excited she felt at the prospect of finally meeting her, then adding,

> *I do so earnestly hope that you will like me, but that can only be for what I am to you after you know me, and I do not want you to be disappointed in the beginning in anything about me, even in so small a thing as my looks.*

She interrupted her letter to rummage through the stuff on the floor until she found a photograph that had been taken on the afternoon of their wedding, when she wore her sloped hat, dark dress and a silver cross around her neck that, she was certain, displayed her in a serious light. She held it up to Louis, sitting up in bed with his writing. "Would this be a good picture to send to your mother?"

"Perfect. Looks like you're dressed for Sunday School."

She put it in a large envelope with her letter. "We'll post these in the morning so they'll beat us to Europe." Already feeling worlds better since coming down to civilization, she challenged Lloyd to a game of Hearts.

CHAPTER 23
Meeting the Parents

Standing on the forward deck of the *City of Chester* as the ship steamed through a light mist toward the belching smokestacks and hodgepodge skyline of Liverpool, she felt like she might have to lean over the rail and vomit. Not because of the sea rolling beneath her; seasickness had seldom bothered her. Rather, Fanny churned with worries, one of them being that Louis's parents would not like her. That morning she had spent hours in front of the mirror. She hoped to impress them as a stylish bride capable of caring for a household that included their chronically ill only son about whom, she knew, they constantly worried. She had pulled on a soft, flowing, light grey wool dress with white buttons to the neck, a wide-brimmed blue felt hat and white gloves. She had talked Lloyd, now fidgeting behind her, into wearing a wool jacket and bowtie. But she could not shake the fear that they would take one look at her—which would happen at any moment, for Louis had said they would be on the deck of the tugboat that was now chugging out of the harbor to meet them—and think "older woman" or, God forbid, "seductress."

Her much greater worry was Louis, leaning on the deck-rail next to her in his worn brown ulster. His expression was game, as always, the brown eyes wide beneath a jaunty straw hat that was beaded with moisture from the mist. But the cast of his skin, and the deep coughs that she knew he had been trying for days to suppress, frightened her more than anything she'd seen on the voyage. With each day of their complicated journey, first off of his dear mountain to San Francisco, then across thousands of miles of dreary prairie to New York followed by two weeks on the roiling Atlantic, his face had turned whiter and his cough deeper.

The tugboat, now just a few hundred yards away, tooted its whistle, the ship let out a return horn-blast and the travelers cheered and waved handkerchiefs. Louis squeezed Fanny's arm and pointed out his short, thick father and slender mother on the deck of the tug, both of them wearing hats that obscured their faces, at least at this distance. "Colvin has come too," Louis said as the boat drew closer, waving at his parents and the slight, younger looking man standing next to them. Stepping to the side and gesturing to her as if he were a circus master, Louis hollered, "My wife! My wife, Fanny!"

Their greeters on the tug, which was quickly drawing up to their ship, began nudging each other and waving back.

Deck hands on the tug threw a fat coiled rope, receiving hands on the steamer tied it down, and the slack in the rope snapped tight. The lurching ride toward the docks allowed a shouted conversation between the parties from a distance of forty feet.

On the tug, Colvin, in a trim tweed coat, raised a bowler hat from his head of wispy golden hair. "Welcome home! Home to the civilized world!"

"You haven't aged a day, fool!" Louis yelled back, and then turned to cough.

"Hello, Mrs. Stevenson!" Fanny yelled.

Louis's mother, who wore an expensive-looking, ankle-length coat and matching beaver hat, seemed startled by the yell, but smiled back; Fanny hoped her silence was simply due to European reserve.

"Hello back to you, Mrs. Stevenson!" Louis's father boomed, grinning broadly and shattering her theory of reserve. Thomas Stevenson wore an old-fashioned brown waistcoat and bowler hat; the face underneath was solid, the nose square, the skin ruddy, every feature the opposite of Louis's.

Fanny pulled Lloyd forward. "This is my son, Lloyd!" Lloyd waved uncertainly.

"Were you coughing, Louis?" Thomas yelled, and then, shifting his gaze to Fanny, "Has he been sick?"

She did not reply while Louis waved off the question.

When they docked, the initial meeting went well enough, with lots of hugging, back-slapping, and tearful expressions of how glad everyone was to see everyone else. The elder Stevensons seemed perfectly pleasant, with Thomas far less reserved and Margaret more beautiful than photographs had suggested. Fanny did not like the way Sidney Colvin seemed to be scrutinizing her, though, while gazing down his nose with a faint smile.

"You've a healthy lad there," Thomas said to her, nodding at Lloyd, who was bounding around, scattering flocks of pigeons while men in skullcaps pushed carts heaped with trunks down the ramp.

"Thank you."

Margaret Stevenson stepped closer to Fanny. "Poor dear, you must feel like a rare bird on display."

Fanny tried to smile confidently. "A little bit, but it's wonderful to finally meet you."

Margaret touched her sleeve. "You must be anxious to get your clothes."

"My clothes?"

"All boxed up for the voyage?"

"Yes." Fanny supposed it was not the time to tell her mother-in-law that she was wearing one of the best dresses she owned, and that she had sewn it herself.

Thomas Stevenson squired them all to dinner at a dockside restaurant of deep red carpeting, brass candelabras, and featuring roast duck. Lloyd wandered off just before their meals came in silver serving dishes, triggering commentary by Thomas about how bored the fine lad must be, stuck at a table with stuffy adults. Their tuxedoed waiter said to Louis, "A blond lad has been running up and down the stairs creating a fuss. Is he your brother?"

Colvin laughed uproariously and slapped Louis on the back. Fanny smiled, but the mistake made her feel ancient. Louis set down his linen napkin and excused himself to find Lloyd.

Thomas leaned to Fanny, his gaze following Louis out the doorway. "How long has he been ill, this time?"

She lifted the lid from a porcelain sugar dish and said cautiously, "A few weeks."

"Mrs. Stevenson and I would like to see him treated."

"He has been, sir. Dr. Bamford, my doctor in Oakland, helped him through his last bout."

Thomas patted her arm. "But I mean really treated—by the finest care money can buy—at the colony for consumptives in Davos. It would mean living in Europe for a while, but I would gladly pay for it."

"Louis was thinking of Denver or the California desert, where it is warm and dry."

Louis's parents exchanged a look as if she had suddenly loosed an obscenity. "Don't you see, dear," Margaret Stevenson said in a friendly tone but with her jaw tight beneath her cream-colored skin, "if he could get a lasting cure he could put this behind him, behind you, behind all of us?"

Their conversation stopped when Louis walked in with her son, whose collar had come open and the little tie now dangled off to the side. "I caught up to him on the second landing," Louis gasped, smiling but leaning on the table while he got his breath. "No harm done."

Silence reigned for several minutes as they went to work with knives and forks on the dark oily fowl that lay centered in each dish.

"We could share recipes," Fanny eventually blurted to Margaret.

Margaret's smile looked uncertain.

"I make a great lemon pudding," Fanny continued, nudging Louis playfully with her elbow, "and a claret jelly that your son likes."

"Mother's servants do her cooking," Louis said softly.

Fanny stared down at her dismembered duck. "Oh."

Thomas lifted his wine glass. "Here's to our charming daughter-in-law, who, by the way, speaks very good English. For a foreigner, anyway." He winked at Fanny.

"I do think America is part of the civilized world, Mr. Stevenson," Colvin said, "parts of it, anyway."

Louis clinked his glass against his father's. "You and mother should go home to Edinburgh. Ahead of us, I mean, and get our rooms ready. I have business in London."

"Indeed," Colvin chimed in, setting down his wine glass and dabbing his neat moustache with a napkin.

Thomas frowned. "Ah yes, the writing business. That reminds me, Louis. The travel book you sent..."

"*Amateur Emigrant*?"

"You said in a letter that it will be published."

"This autumn, yes."

"Would you like it to be a sellout?"

Louis cocked his head. "Of course, sir, that's what every writer wishes."

"Good. I'll buy every copy."

"I don't understand."

"It's an embarrassment. Lively writing, don't get me wrong, son, but all of the suffering and starvation, the traveling with peasants and chickens across America is beneath the son of Thomas Stevenson. So whatever you've contracted to have printed, I'll buy from the publisher. In fact I'll pay even more for them to stop any further issue of it."

"What?" Louis jumped up, bumping the table and spilling wine onto the white tablecloth. "Why do you want so badly for me to fail?"

"That's the last thing I wish," Thomas said. "Now please, son, sit down, you're getting worked up over nothing."

"Nothing?" Louis leaned on the table, turned to the side and coughed.

Fanny stood. "Good night, Mr. and Mrs. Stevenson, we're very tired. Come along, Lloyd." Lloyd dropped a duck leg he'd been chewing and stood.

"Such a long trip, you poor dears," Margaret said.

Thomas clutched her sleeve, motioned with his eyes toward Louis, who had handkerchief to mouth, and mouthed "Davos." Fanny put her arm around Louis's shoulders and steered him toward the door.

Fanny peered out the train window at the sooty sky, the rows of cheap brick homes with their sad little gardens, drainpipes and heaps of rubbish along the tracks on the approach to London. It was not the triumphant entry into Louis's world that she had imagined, back when they had talked about his career after meeting at Grez. She had imagined being ushered by Louis to soirées full of smiling, witty, welcoming writers and publishers, much like the artists at Grez, only better-dressed. She had not imagined a stocky father-in-law eager to quash books and consign them to live on a mountain in Switzerland. And if Sidney Colvin, stroking his goatee on the opposite bench while looking down his perfect British nose at her and runny-nosed Lloyd sitting next to her, was any indication of Louis's other literary friends, she would rather be back in California.

In London the family got out at Victoria Station and took a short cab ride to the Grosvenor Hotel, where Louis paid with a roll of pound-notes that Thomas had pressed in his hand upon parting, urging them to "treat themselves." She and Louis kicked off their shoes and sat on the purple bedcover of a soft bed while Lloyd yanked open the tall window drapes. They stared in silence at Buckingham Palace, Westminster Abbey and the River Thames in the distance.

She must have dozed off, because she opened her eyes to Louis's pale face looking down at her while gently shaking her shoulders. "The concierge is getting a cab for us." She splashed water on her face at the basin, tried to hide grey hairs under her sloping felt hat, and quickly applied fresh makeup.

After they had been dropped off at the Savile Club and were standing in the doorway to the dining room, Louis began wildly patting his pockets. "I left my watch in the cab!"

While Louis was somewhere on the streets of London trying to chase down the hansom, Fanny had plenty of time to get nervous about meeting W. E. Henley. She eventually spotted him—it had to be Louis's friend, over six feet tall, with bushy red eyebrows and a wild beard—circulating among the men at their tables. He seemed out of place in the room graced by Grecian columns, glittering chandeliers and oil paintings of poets that peeked down from the walls. His worn tweed coat strained against the buttons when he walked, or, rather, hopped, from table to table with the help of one crutch. The trousers at his left knee were sewn shut, but even without that foot he got around with frightening speed. The men in high-backed chairs seemed to receive him warmly, or perhaps they had to, when he stopped to lean on each table, exchange words and slap backs. Henley did seem to speak Queen's-English, from bits of his speech that she could hear, although at one table he delivered a punch-line in French. At this, the men in monocles and black ties banged down their glasses and cackled and seemed to think him witty beyond compare. When he finished making the rounds with the men, he turned to the doorway and lurched directly toward her wearing a wide grin. Fanny couldn't help staring at the empty trouser-leg and at the crutch that seemed so worn and scuffed.

"You must be what Stevenson got in California," Henley boomed, loud enough for the entire dining room to hear.

Fanny inclined her head a fraction of an inch. "And you must be what he left."

"Ha, ha, she's quick, good! Hello Mrs. Stevenson, and welcome."

She offered her gloved hand. "Mr. Henley, I've heard so much about you."

"I certainly hope you didn't believe it." He tugged her hand with surprising strength toward the back of the room, stumping his cane down with the free hand. "Where in God's name is Louis?"

"Henley!" Louis shouted from behind them. Henley dropped her hand, pivoted on the cane and the two men were in each other's arms, bear-hugging and back-clapping and laughing uproariously while she stood in the center of the room under the huge chandelier, ignored for five minutes while the men exchanged laughing inanities.

"He's here! The skinny sod is here!" Sidney Colvin rushed up to the other two men, and damned if the three fools didn't join hands and dance around in a circle.

There passed what felt to Fanny like a very long dinner. The two friends asked her all the polite questions, where she grew up, the ages of her children, how she liked England so far, and was she enjoying her standing rib roast? And she politely answered, commenting on the lovely old room, the interesting portraits hanging on the wall, and not saying that the meat had been ruined with overcooking. Louis beamed the whole time, obviously proud of both her and his friends, and most likely, Fanny thought, certain she was having as good a time as he seemed to be, which she was not.

After they had finished their dinners, an aproned waiter appeared with brandy. Louis swirled the liquid in his snifter and sipped. "Truth is, I'm not sure where we'll live. Possibly back in California. Or Colorado, for the mountain air."

Henley raised one eyebrow at Fanny, as if she were to blame for giving Louis such bizarre notions. The room had gone quiet except for the clinking of silverware being put on trays and the subdued conversations of the few groups that were left. The men pushed back their chairs, drank, and gossiped at length about friends she did not know. Fanny looked at the wall beyond them, following the floral patterns all the way up to the fat crown molding at the ceiling. The friends trimmed and licked cigars while Henley launched a witty discourse on why he had loathed Louis's California stories.

"'Pavillion on the Links' is brilliant," she said firmly, stopping the diatribe and drawing stares.

Henley poured more brandy for himself. "Plays, Louis. That's where the money is. Just one hit play and you'd have enough to write in peace for another five years, and feed the brood to boot! You should put everything else aside and get *Deacon Brodie* ready for production."

Louis puffed on his cigar. "Ready for whom? You've been pushing that idea since before I left for California. If it's such a fine concept, why haven't you been able to attract a producer to back it?"

Touché, she thought, observing how glumly Henley looked down in the brandy he swirled and then tossed back in one gulp. She got a paper and tobacco from her handbag and rolled a cigarette. Henley stared while she poked it between her lips and lit it in the flame of the candelabra. His smile was icy. "Perfect, Louis. She is absolutely perfect."

She turned her admiration on a busboy who was putting their plates on a tray. Without getting a drop of grease on his white shirt he was able to balance each piece of china on top of the pink duck bones of the one beneath it in an artful sort of tower. Louis's low coughing startled her. She saw him peek at his handkerchief before pushing it in his pocket. Fanny reached for her handbag. "I'm tired, Louis."

"Sakes, it's not even midnight," Henley said, "and I haven't seen my friend in a year. Truth be told, I was beginning to wonder if he'd ever drag himself back from the colonies." He laughed and clattered his wooden leg against the table, a habit that was getting annoying.

Louis tried to give a carefree smile. "Another half-hour?" He put his hand over hers but it felt clammy. The corners of his soft brown eyes were bloodshot.

She pushed back her chair and stood.

"Perhaps we boys can continue," Colvin said with a grin.

Louis stood, swaying from either drink, sickness or both, grabbed Henley's cane and held it up like it was a sword, "To the hotel!"

Fanny said very little during the rest of the night. She did not have to, for the three friends regaled each other for another two hours in their hotel suite. After checking on Lloyd in an adjoining bedroom and finding him asleep, she sat in an overstuffed armchair in a corner while the men passed around a bottle of wine and told stories of stupid things they had done together in the old days. Eventually, she dozed off.

She woke to the sound of coughing, and saw Henley and Colvin drunkenly patting Louis's back. When the coughing subsided he tucked away his handkerchief and excused himself to go for a glass of water.

As soon as he stepped out of the room, his friends stole glances at her and apparently believed she was asleep, for they began whispering. She caught snatches of their conversation:

"How old, did you say?"

"Old enough to be a grizzled one, isn't she?"

"...acts like his mother for god sake..."

"...bit of a bumpkin..."

"... his ruination..."

The conversation abruptly stopped when Louis walked in.

Fanny stood. "I'm going to bed."

He smiled. "Gosh, dear, have the boys been ignoring you?"

"Not at all." She glared at Henley and Colvin until the men looked away, and then left them. In the bedroom, she lay on the soft bed as the sounds of laughter and easy conversation between the friends resumed. So this was to be her role in what she dreamed would be the heady world of Louis's literary friendships—that of aging spoiler. She cried softly into the pillow, until she heard a chair clattering against the wall and more coughing. Rushing to the sitting room she found Colvin and Henley stooped over Louis, who was on the floor, struggling up on his elbow and mumbling "No fuss now, please, 'tis nothing." She knew the act well. It hit her: his friends were huge, worm-like parasites who grinned and laughed while sucking the life out of him. If she was to have Louis alive with her for very long, she would have to get him away from them.

"Go," she said, "you've done quite enough for him already." When they hesitated, hands in pockets, she threw the door open. "Get the hell out of here!"

As the men fled, she hurried to Louis and helped him to bed.

CHAPTER 24
Davos, Switzerland—Winter, 1881

Of the many doctors in black suits and vests who had examined him over the years, Dr. Ruedi of the Curhaus at Davos was surely the most thorough. After an excruciating day of being prodded, poked, and asked to produce samples from every orifice, Louis and Fanny sat in an office decorated with photographs of reedy consumptives in bloused-out trousers, white shirts and ties walking single-file on a narrow trail above an alpine cliff. Louis tried to place the scent hanging in the room, deciding it was either preservative or after-shave balm. Across a large desk from them, a red-cheeked, mutton-chopped physician carefully centered a sheaf of papers in front of him.

"So, Mr. Stevenson."

"So?"

"There is no consumption."

"None? I thought the town was full of it."

The doctor chuckled as if indulging a child. "You have chronic pneumonia that has damaged the surface of your lungs, a tendency toward bronchitis, and a slightly enlarged spleen. No consumption."

Fanny, in a deep blue dress, hat and gloves, leaned forward. "Do you mean, sir, that all of these years my husband was just plain sick? That he can have a long vigorous life?"

"Answer to question number one, he has been more than just plain sick, he's been very sick. As to his future survival, it is largely up to him."

Louis took a cigarette from his coat. The doctor's long fingers shot across the table like a hawk on a mouse. He crumbled it between his fingers and tossed it into a rubbish can. "Like many of the English—"

"Scottish, actually, sir."

"You lead a life of dissipation. Here you shall not. Here, you will learn to work against your illness, to take the fight to it, and most importantly, to squash your self-pity."

"Would that be 'squelch,' perhaps?"

Fanny kicked his shin.

The doctor pushed a page before Louis. "Read and sign, please."

Louis read aloud: "Rule one, I shall drink a quart of fresh cow's milk each day. Rule two, I shall drink one and one-half glass of Valtellina wine per day. Rule three, I shall take vigorous exercise in the fresh air each day. Rule four, I shall refrain from cigarettes and all forms of tobacco. Rule five, I shall refrain from foul language and thought. Rule six, I shall enjoy my days."

Louis solemnly dipped a pen in a brass inkwell and moved it to the page but began shaking, at first with silent laughter, but then it burst like a damn. He doubled over in paroxysms of shrieking, snorting, hysterical laughter that almost caused him to fall off his chair.

Fanny squeezed his arm. "Louis!"

He knew others were put off when this happened, but at times he just couldn't stop. Eventually, he calmed enough to sign. "If I break the rules, flog me with strudel!"

Dr. Reudi did not seem to think this was funny, nor did Fanny. Louis was well aware that others thought him juvenile at times, but couldn't help laughing again. This time he felt sharp pains in his chest when the laughter turned to coughing. Fanny tugged him out of the office while Dr. Ruedi shook his head.

Louis sat in a lounge chair on a long, outdoor balcony of the Belvedere Hotel, the cavernous but cheerless lodgings where Dr. Ruedi insisted they lodge because it was where "the British" stayed. The heavy blankets swaddling his outstretched legs, leather coat, gloves and knit cap pulled low over his ears made him feel as if he peered out from a cocoon. Several other bundled patients sat in a row of identical chairs next to him, peering beyond a cast iron rail at the Tinzenhorn and other peaks that ringed this beautiful valley of sickness.

Louis tried to ignore the layer of snow that whitened his moustache and coated the floor of the porch like icing on a fine confection.

"Might you tell me, good sir," Louis said to a man a few chairs down, who he had heard speaking English, "what we are doing here, exactly?"

The man's bushy eyebrows and doughy face, smothered by a fur cap and ear muffs, knit into a frown as if the question was a difficult one or had never occurred to him.

"I mean," Louis pursued, "What's the purpose of it?"

The blue tight lips on the doughy face opened a crack. "To take the air. If you get better, they'll make you sleep out here."

Noting the red-tipped noses and ears of the others, Louis quelled a moment of panic. "I thought we were to exercise."

The man nodded toward a distant mountainside, where figures stumbled like drunken ants, dragging toboggans uphill while near them, dark heaps of passengers plunged downward.

Louis fought the urge to roll a cigarette—or to scream obscenities. The Englishman let his head loll onto his chest and soon was snoring, the exhales making puffs of steam.

They took the midday meal with perhaps one hundred others in a barn-like dining hall of long tables down which platters of roast beef, black bread and steel pitchers of cream-flecked milk were passed. Most residents sat in wooden folding chairs, with the others heaped in large wicker wheelchairs, baskets of humans on tall spoked wheels. Thus fortified, with Louis irritable for black coffee and a cigarette, they bundled in ankle-length coats, ear muffs and goggles and trudged out for exercise.

Soon, Louis, Fanny and Lloyd stood atop a long, icy hill. At six thousand feet above sea level, barely able to draw breath, Louis eased onto a toboggan while Fanny, standing behind it, clung to a handle to keep it from sliding away.

While Louis worked to get his knees, jutting up like a grasshopper's, to lay flat so that Lloyd, hovering over the craft, could lower onto it she asked, "Are you sure about this?"

He patted the seat in front of him. "Come Lloyd, let's mush."

Lloyd dropped onto the toboggan and it lurched out of Fanny's grasp. He screamed all the way down as the snowy landscape blurred by and Louis's legs flopped and banged against the snow. At the bottom of the hill they hit a bump and were tossed into a snow bank.

Louis scraped a coating of snow from his goggles and clomped over to pull Lloyd to his feet. "Capital. We just need a bit more technique."

Spitting snow, Lloyd glared up at Louis, who imagined that the boy had to be cursing the bad fortune of having such a sickly, ungainly stepfather thrust on him.

"What say we try again." Louis took the towrope and dragged the toboggan uphill.

As the sun fell behind the tall peaks, they trudged back to their lodgings behind a dozen German consumptives who pulled scarves tighter around their necks, coughed and muttered what most likely were the same dreary thoughts Louis was having about life in a valley of dying people.

That night he had no appetite for writing essays or for his history of the Scottish Highlands, but he took up a pen and wrote the first stanza of a poem he had composed during the day's activities:

They had at first a human air
In coats and flannel underwear.
They rose and walked upon their feet
And filled their bellies full of meat.
They wiped their lips when they had done,
But they were ogres every one.

One week later. Louis shoved another log into the fireplace. Lloyd had gone out to play with the son of a patient from Liverpool and Fanny was at Dr. Ruedi's office, having decided that since she was stuck in a colony for consumptives she may as well get diagnosed. Louis had shunned the day's activities—which were the same every day —in hopes of getting some writing done. He thumbed through the essays he had published earlier in *Cornhill Magazine*, at Henley's suggestion that he might have a chance of publishing them as a collection. "Walking Tours" and "A Plea for Gas Lamps" were nicely written but overly sentimental, reflecting the influence of Hazlitt more than he had realized when writing them. "Apology for Idlers" he now found sophomoric; he would reserve judgment about "Ordered South," "The English Admirals," and "Child's Play" until he had had a good night's sleep because their effect on him now was to make him yawn. He disliked reading what he had written in earlier years—far more interesting, he thought, to be writing fresh material—which, in Davos, seemed impossible. He wondered why, after seven solid days of not smoking, eating tons of beef, drinking gallons of milk and getting daily exercise in dry, sub-freezing air, he had been unable to write one new word, but pushed aside the idea that he was hopelessly blocked.

He wrote a letter to his father, asking that he send more books to add to the thigh-high stack that had already accumulated in a corner. The old man had seemed ecstatic about his plans for a grand history of the Scottish Highlands; Louis was so happy to have found a way to please him! At last, a way to repay this man who had paid so much for his care, and who had suffered so much embarrassment due to Louis's "sinful mad business"—needlessly, of course, but suffered nonetheless—and of whom Louis was very proud. Louis hoped that someday, somehow, his father would also be proud of him.

He listed some volumes his father might be able to send:

Dr. Walker's Economical History of the Highlands.
Reports to General Assembly from 1760 to 1780.
Dr. Robertson's General View of the Agriculture of Inverness.
Dr. Smith's General Survey of Argyll.
All Mrs. Grant of Laggan's Works and her life.
The Engineers. Wade, Burt, etc.
Duncan Forbes of Culloden.
Boswell and Johnson...

Louis set the letter aside and rolled a cigarette; certainly one wouldn't hurt. After several inhalations of the lovely smoke he plunged onward, coming up with another half-dozen books. As boring as the project now struck him, he would write the history, write it thoroughly and write it well. The work, the burying of himself—how he hated that phrase, thinking of the acres of crosses in the cemetery for consumptives he'd passed that morning—in the thick volumes might keep him from thinking about his problems of late: his poor productivity, Fanny seeming bored to tears, and Lloyd making noises like he wanted to head back to California and live with his father.

The door banged open. Fanny rushed in, sobbing. "Fat. He says I'm fat!"

He took her in his arms and nuzzled her neck. "Now that's a silly thing to say."

"An entire day of tests to see if the great Herr Doctor Ruedi would have something to prescribe for my black moods and brain fever, and after it all, the only thing the imbecile says is, I need to lose weight."

Louis noticed that she had, in fact, put on a few pounds since leaving San Francisco. Her long dresses now bulged a bit at the waist and bodice, a change perhaps made more noticeable because she was short, but he wasn't particularly concerned. "If it's any consolation, he tells me I need to gain. So I'll eat the fat, you eat the lean and we'll be Jack Sprat and wife."

"That isn't funny."

"Why not, my dear little butterball?"

"You've had it, Stevenson!" She swung her purse, narrowly missing his head. She chased him around the coffee table in the tiny room, smacking the back of his head with her open hand and pinching his bottom.

He armed himself with a pillow, shoving it at her like a shield and taking wild swings. Both were laughing and screeching when Lloyd walked in.

"Help, Lloyd!" she hollered. "Help me kill this maniac!"

Shaking his head, Lloyd silently walked past them to his room.

Next evening when they returned to the room from supper, Louis stooped to pick up a telegram-envelope that had been pushed under the door. He opened it and read:

BRINGING MY SON BERTIE TO DAVOS FOR TREATMENT STOP SITUATION DIRE STOP MIGHT

STEVENSON'S TREASURE

YOU ARRANGE A ROOM FOR US IN BELVEDERE
HOTEL STOP EVER YOUR FRIEND FRANCIS
SITWELL

They arrived within the week from London. A fog clung stubbornly to the valley floor all day, turning the surrounding peaks into huge vaporous sentries. Hands shoved in his ulster while he waited on the hotel steps, Louis heard hooves clashing against cobblestone moments before a black cab took shape in the mist and reined in. Mrs. Sitwell slowly emerged from the passenger compartment. The woman who, a few years ago, had been the object of his desire now took the arm he offered looking beaten-down, her face wan, lips pinched white, gray hair pulled tightly under a beaver hat, her once-lovely figure obscured by a rumpled sable.

If Mrs. Sitwell's transformation was a bad dream, Bertie was a nightmare. A breathing skeleton wobbled in the door of the cab, glazed eyes staring at the hotel, and then with a sigh slumped into the waiting arms of Louis and a nurse who had materialized with a wheelchair. They got the eighteen-year-old seated in the chair, not too difficult, because although of medium build he couldn't weigh more than eighty pounds. The sunken face gazed at Louis as if looking out from the next world. He muttered "Louis" without smiling, and the assistant rolled the tall spoked wheels up a wooden ramp and into the hotel.

"I'm so sorry," Louis whispered to Mrs. Sitwell as they followed the wheelchair up the ramp.

She turned to him. A wistful look? A fond remembering of those carefree summers in the rector's study, flirting and discussing books? She nodded and went inside without saying a word.

Louis did not follow, because he simply did not have it in him to accompany the obviously dying boy he had always thought so bright and lively into the tall stone building that

276

would soon be the boy's tomb. He walked out into the fog until he reached the brick wall of a church. He pushed his back against it, with shaking hands got a cigarette lit, and wept.

"I am supposed to be healing, and perhaps the body is better, but when can I leave this place?" he wrote to cousin Bob that night.

> *The mountains are about you like a trap. My fellow residents are a whole crew of kind of gone-up, damp fireworks in the human form. There is no escape from them, well, besides the obvious, and I'm not ready for that one.*

Each morning over the next weeks he woke nauseous, wondering if Bertie had died overnight, or if not, if he would die that day. On some days, a second round of nausea would hit him at the thought of visiting the boy and spending time with his desperate mother.

"I'm going to the Sitwell's," Fanny announced one morning, giving him a look that said she would do that duty for both of them. Louis swallowed and nodded as she left him.

When she returned, he could not even ask the question. "He's a little better," she said. "Dr. Ruedi thinks it would be good to take him tobogganing."

"What?"

"It's something you could do for him, Louis."

Next morning, when Louis had collared a reluctant Lloyd and walked him to Mrs. Sitwell's room, Bertie lay sleeping on the sitting-room's sofa with head thrown back and legs splayed like a dead accident victim he'd once seen who had been thrown from a horse near Edinburgh. Mrs. Sitwell smiled and said, in a jovial, sing-song voice as if absolutely nothing was amiss, "Bertie, Louis and Lloyd are here to take you tobogganing. Won't that be fun? Come now, wake up, we mustn't keep them waiting."

Bertie did not move.

"Bertie? Louis Stevenson is here!"

Both of them looking at the comatose face, Louis gently touched Mrs. Sitwell's shoulder.

"He smiled, Louis. At the sound of your name. Did you see how he smiled?"

Louis tried to sound reassuring. "Perhaps we'll toboggan another day."

At nights, Louis expanded his cheating on the cigarette-rule. He would roll one before lugging a volume of his father's Highlands books to his writing desk and opening it to Page One. After smoking the cigarette to the nub, he would wait for the inspiration to strike him to turn the book to page two. If he could get through five pages he would reward himself by rolling a second cigarette.

Hearing tub-splashing sounds one night from the bathroom, Louis got all the way to four cigarettes and twenty pages of an appalling treatise on the casualties at the Battle of Culloden.

"You're looking better these days," Fanny suddenly said, padding out in her nightgown and sitting in an armchair. "A better skin tone."

"Yes, good. Thank you, dear."

"Why ruin things by smoking?"

He tried to mask his guilt with a smile—and noticed she was chewing something.

He hurried to her. "You're cheating, too, Fanny Vandegrift Osbourne Stevenson!" He snapped the remains of a buttered croissant from where she'd tried to hide it in her lap and examined it. "You're supposed to be eating less, and I'm supposed to be eating more, so..." He popped it into his mouth.

"You are a sadist, Robert Louis Stevenson. There shall be justice!" She dashed to the desk, snapped up Louis's tobacco pouch, shoved open a big window and threw it out.

"My God, but you are frightening."

"No, it is awe, darling. I inspire awe." She stood on her tiptoes and kissed him.

Her lips parted softly and he felt her tongue darting against his. His response was immediate; unfortunately, the lack of privacy in their hotel—Lloyd's small room adjoined theirs and he, like Louis, had begun to stay up late at night, reading—had kept times of lovemaking to nil. Thus Louis was thrilled when Fanny in her nightgown tiptoed to Lloyd's door and pressed her ear to it. Eventually she seemed satisfied that the boy was asleep, because she stepped to Louis, grinning.

She lifted her nightgown off her shoulders, tossed it in a corner, and stood wonderfully exposed, her soft breasts and rounded hips illuminated by a yellow gas lamp on the wall behind her. Her eyes meeting his, she smiled and thrust back her chin as if she was a stage star. Giggling, drawing out the show, she searched for a match, struck it and lit a single candle on the dresser. She stretched up to turn off the gas lamp and joined him in bed. Finally, urgently and vigorously, they pleased each other. Louis took satisfaction from the fact that he was, in fact, healthier since coming to this awful place, as judged by a thicker tumescence that felt wonderful when he slid it inside her.

Next morning came a frightful pounding on the door—a bellman with an urgent message that Mrs. Sitwell needed them.

They stepped into her room, passed a huge oil painting of the Alps—as if, Louis thought, one couldn't just look out the window—and found Mrs. Sitwell sitting on the bed next to Bertie's dead feet. She appeared to have gotten as far as combing her hair and putting on makeup, but still wore a house robe of yellow and white daisy patterns. Behind her, a breeze through an open window rustled the wisps of hair that had always fallen so beautifully over her small earlobe.

After an awkward silence during which they looked at the corpse, then at Mrs. Sitwell's frightened face, and strove to think of something to say, she broke the silence with a dreaded cliché. "He's at peace."

Louis thought he looked anything but. On his back, skin whiter than the linen sheets tucked neatly across his sunken chest, head back, mouth gaping wide like a bird waiting to be fed, small brass spectacles still perched over staring eyes, Bertie looked nothing to Louis except dead. A mirror hanging on the wall behind him doubled the view of death.

Fanny sat on the edge of the bed and put her arm around Mrs. Sitwell. "I am so sorry. Believe me, I know. I know..."

Louis eased down on Mrs. Sitwell's other side, trying without success to avoid bumping Bertie's leg. The bed creaked and sagged, and for a moment he feared they would all crash with the corpse to the floor. Mumbling sympathies, stroking her graceful trembling neck, aware of Bertie's glasses seeming to focus on him, Louis remembered Mrs. Sitwell saying once how Bertie looked just like him.

A gurney on tall spoked wheels rumbled into the room. Two attendants in crisp white shirts and black vests bowed and waited for them to stand, which Louis and Fanny did, but Mrs. Sitwell flung herself on Bertie. "So beautiful, Bertie, dear one, so beautiful, Jesus will have you, suffer the little children to come unto me," she raved, kissing his cheeks and forehead and leaving bright red smudges on his alabaster skin.

Eventually, Mrs. Sitwell allowed Fanny to gently pry her off of the body, and sobbed in her arms as the attendants loaded the hideous gurney and clattered out. Louis felt utterly helpless for the rest of the day, as he and Fanny attempted the impossible, which was to console her.

Late at night, when sleep finally took Louis, aided by a half-bottle of claret he'd smuggled in under his overcoat, he dreamed of being alone with dead Bertie. The brass spectacles made the bloodless face look intelligent, as if the corpse were trying to discern something about his visitor. Louis stepped closer. Bertie grinned. Suddenly the face was no longer the dead boy's, but his own. Louis tried to flee, but his legs would not move. He grabbed the corner post of the bed on which Bertie lay and tried to steer himself sideways, toward the door. Instead, the bed drew him closer...

In the morning Dr. Ruedi, in a black suit and homburg, frowned across his shiny desk at Louis and Fanny. "If you leave us now, Mr. Stevenson, you do so against my advice—against my many years of medical experience, against science, against all of my better instincts."

Louis shrugged. "Better than what?"

"Excuse me?"

"You said against your better instincts. What are they better than?"

"You make light of a life-and-death decision."

Out of habit, Louis patted the pocket of his blue velvet coat, checking for cigarettes. "I am leaving just the same."

"Then I urge you, go to Denver. It is as high and dry as Davos, and has a fine spa for consumptives. I practiced there for several years, you might know. Denver's a bit uncivilized, though it does have an opera of sorts. But you've experienced the western states too, I understand."

"We have," Fanny said, without smiling. Louis was well aware that she had had her fill of Western saloon-towns; even her choice of clothing—at the moment, a black satin dress and loose-fitting grey tweed overcoat she had left on during the meeting—looked European compared with the cottons and light wools she often wore in California.

The doctor rummaged in his desk. Eventually he spread on the desk several photographs of himself standing with the same kinds of bundled-up, sickly patients sitting on lounge chairs as Louis had seen in Davos, but in this case, western-looking cabins and the Rocky Mountains loomed in the background.

"I was thinking more along the lines of Paris."

Dr. Reudi wiped his brow with an immaculate handkerchief, smiling. "I never know when you are joking, Herr Stevenson."

"I don't always know, myself. But I do know that if I don't get away from sick people, I'll die."

The doctor slapped his palm onto the desk. "But you've become healthier! A few more months here, and—"

"My writing has gone down the sewer and my soul is in danger of joining it." Louis stood and offered his arm to Fanny.

"Please, Mr. Stevenson," Dr. Reudi called as they headed to the door, "consider carefully what you are doing!"

CHAPTER 25
Spring & Summer, 1881

Paris. Fanny pushed aside the letter she was writing to Louis's parents and flexed her fingers. His sleeping face, just a few feet from the desk in their cramped hotel room, looked jaundiced in the light of the low gas lamp. But Lloyd's face, in a cot along the wall also had a yellow cast, so perhaps the gas lamp's light was the culprit and not Louis's poor health.

Her eyes moved back to the letter and the litany of complaints she had written. Two months in Paris had been much too long, a disaster. None of their artist friends were around, having either moved to America or fled south due to the unusually cold spring. The editors to whom Louis had sold a few stories had not paid him. Taxes on the Oakland house, now her responsibility, were overdue, requiring them to wire twenty pounds to Joe Strong and beg him to pay the bill. The bank to which Louis's father, on Tuesday, had wired fifty pounds of his allowance were holding the funds until Wednesday, but their hotel, or what passed for it, demanded payment before they could leave. And they really wanted to leave the stinking Hotel St. Romain—literally stinking since the sewer pipes backed up, some days previous. The snotty desk clerk berated Louis about their bill every time they walked past, yet was taking his sweet time to fix those pipes.

"It's my flannel shirts," Louis had declared, earlier that day.

"Your what?" Sometimes Louis's insights and connections of thought escaped her; they had been looking at loaves of bread on a street vendor's cart.

He picked up a loaf and dug in the pocket of his Levi denims for a coin. "The hotel clerk does not like me because I wear flannel shirts. He is anti-American."

She smiled to herself; for some reason, Louis had taken to wearing plaid flannel shirts and denims in Paris like a Forty-Niner, whereas in California he had worn the berets and linen shirts of Left Bank artists.

Now she pulled her night-robe higher on her neck against the chill and tried to think of what more to say in the letter. She longed to be back in Davos, and wished she had recognized the symptoms of Louis's most annoying disease—Running Off—when he abruptly decided to leave Dr. Reudi's care. Louis had forever been running off: from schoolrooms to explore graveyards, from Mrs. Cunningham's care to play in Old Town alleys, from law school classes to carouse with friends, from Mrs. Sitwell's dining room to canoe across Belgium in the rain. He had run off to hike with a donkey when she had left him three years ago in Europe, and had run off to the hills above Carmel when she put off his marriage proposal. Now, he'd run off a Swiss mountain at the very point when Dr. Reudi had begun to put him in better health.

His health, by far her biggest worry, had slipped ever since Davos, first from a runny nose to a head cold, then from a cold to a chest cough, and finally, three days ago, the coughing had brought flecks of blood on his handkerchief. In desperation she had summoned a doctor.

She drew ink into her pen and resumed her letter:

The doctor was a sort of swindle altogether, his only anxiety seeming to get Louis to go away and leave his twenty francs; he didn't look at his chest, or make the slightest examination. That was just the way poor Bertie was treated...

She pushed the letter aside—too grim and carping to be an "objective" report of Louis's condition that she had promised to send each week. Perhaps she could write a more diplomatic one in the morning, if she could quit worrying about him long enough to get some sleep. A witty account of his hard work to earn a living might entertain his mother and father, excepting the fact that his output remained nil. He would sit for hours with pen in hand—and write nothing but the beginnings of Something Grand. But his writing mimicked his legs—thin, and prone to bolt when frustrated. Possessed of a vast imagination, he could finish only short stories and essays. Some brilliant ones, yes, she would give him that, but if he was to reach his lifelong goal—to live on his writing—he would have to stay put through the creation of long-form pieces. He had churned out tens of thousands of words since she'd met him but could not finish one novel. He made bold starts, fleshed out gorgeous characters, wrote beautiful descriptions of setting—and then got bored, frustrated, or both, and began hatching a different story.

She turned off the lamp, felt her way to their bed and climbed in. If Paris had been a disaster, where next? Louis had mumbled something about going to London. Good God, London, with its snobby Savile Club and his literary friends. She now knew them as leeches, parasites, a band of the boring, the walking dead who seemed to want Louis dead as well. When would this stop?

When daylight came, Louis was up before her, throwing on his ratty-looking purple robe to answer a knocking on the door. A boy in a grey cap handed him a thin envelope and waited for a coin, which took Louis a search through pockets of hanging coats and trousers to come up with, as they were down to their last few. She sat up in bed as he opened the envelope and silently read a single sheet of paper. "Well?"

He handed it to her and began pacing as she read the words of a telegram:

BRAEMAR IS HIGH CRISP MAJESTIC AND SCOTTISH STOP BOOKED MRS MACGREGORS COTTAGE FOR HOLIDAY STOP WILL YOU JOIN US STOP EVER YOUR LOVING FATHER

She got out of bed and took her robe off its hook. "Where is Braemar?"

Louis stifled a cough and stopped pacing long enough to light a cigarette. "In the Highlands. A few days north of Edinburgh."

"Louis, for god sake, Edinburgh is wet and drafty enough. And he wants us to go *north* of there?"

"It's the highest town in Scotland. Granted, it's not Switzerland, but with some luck the air will be drier than in this reeking place." He puffed on the cigarette but began coughing so long and hard that she took it from his fingers.

"Louis. We should either get you to a hospital—"

"Not a chance," he interrupted, sagging onto the bed.

"Or board the first train back to Davos."

Louis waved dismissively. "Braemar is a lovely old town. There's a castle to explore, and—"

"No." She sat next to him, puffing furiously on his cigarette.

He stumbled to his feet, snatched the cigarette back from her and took a small puff. No cough. Grinning as if he were now in perfect health, he yanked open the blinds of their one window, letting in the grey light of a rainy day. "In Braemar I can sit with father, open those Scots history books he sent and dash off the book I promised him. Not the epic he has in mind, but a little book stuffed to the brim with Highlander blood and glory. It would please him."

She heard something stirring in the shadows next to the wall. "What's there for me to do in Braemar?" her son suddenly asked.

"Lots of things," Louis said. "Glorious things."

Lloyd swung out of the cot in his pajamas and strolled to the rain-streaked window. "Like what?"

"Well..." Louis paused to cough, this time, she suspected, to buy time while wracking his brain. "Fishing!" he finally boomed. "The river is teeming with the biggest trout in the world."

*****

Pitlochry, Scotland.

Louis had slept during most of the long journey by train, ferry, and, eventually, a stage coach that rumbled north through Scotland toward the Highlands, waking now and then to drink cups of tea and honey that Fanny offered. "Exhausted," he muttered during one of these awakenings, during their first day on the coach to Braemar. "Would you mind if we stop and rest for a night or two?"

Now—more than two weeks later—Fanny sat opposite Louis at a card table in an upstairs dormer room in a creaky farmhouse they had rented in the hills near Pitlochry, a town nestled in the hills a day short of Braemar and known mainly, Louis told her, for whiskey distilleries. Although incessant rain hammered the roof just above them, a well-stocked fireplace had kept them warm enough. In the enforced quietude of no friends and nothing to do except sleep and write, Louis had regained a measure of health. Enough, anyway, to have hatched his latest scheme: writing a book together. For three nights they had huddled in the little room in near darkness, Louis and the Fanny at the table with a fat candle between them, each scrawling in a notebook while Lloyd sprawled at the fireplace, stirring the embers and shoving in a log when he wasn't dealing himself games of solitaire.

Louis, wearing his tattered Indian smoking cap and a striped fishing jersey he had bought in a saloon in Monterey, looked up from his writing. "I've a job for you, lad. It pays well."

Lloyd's blond head swiveled from the flannel pajamas he wore while propped on his elbows. "What kind of job?"

"Junior literary critic. I'll pay a shilling if you listen to a story and give me your opinion of it."

"Sure." Lloyd turned toward him and crossed his ankles.

Louis stood, gathering the pages in one hand and the candle in the other. "It is called 'Thrawn Janet.' A highlander story, fitting for this fair region."

He began reading in his usual way, solemn and stiff, but with each phrase he picked up the pace and force of his delivery. Within ten minutes he seemed to exist within a story-world, his face a skull above the wavering candle as he adopted a distinctive voice for each character's dialogue, letting each page drop to the floor after he had read it. Unfortunately, at about twenty minutes into the performance, when Louis turned to pace the other way, she caught a glimpse of her son—who was yawning. Louis, obviously unaware he had lost half of his audience, plunged on, his voice rising in pitch and volume:

"The guidwives up and claught haud of her, and clawed the coats aff her back, and pu'd her doun the clachan to the water o' Dule, to see if she were a witch or no, soum or droun. The carline skirled till ye could hear her at the Hangin' Shaw, and she focht like ten; there was mony a guidwife bure the mark of her neist day an' mony a lang day after; and just in the hottest o' the collieshangie, wha suld come up for his sins but the new minister..."

"Louis," Fanny interrupted, seizing her chance during a slight pause in the reading, "I'm afraid Lloyd isn't getting the dialect. Could you back up, explain some of the words, and catch us up on the action so we can better enjoy the story?"

Louis stopped his pacing and frowned. "Catch you up?"

"Lloyd doesn't understand the words," she added.

"Oh. Yes of course, I'm sorry..." Louis stooped to the floor, picked up the pages and fumbled to put them back in order.

Lloyd hopped up, his young face knit in fury. "Mother, I didn't say I couldn't understand!"

"You can admit it, honey," Fanny said, "don't feel bad, I didn't get all of it either."

"I'm going to bed." Lloyd stalked out, slamming the door.

Louis sat and stared down at the pages in his hands as if he had accidentally killed a favorite pet. "Would it help if I talk with him?"

She sighed. "I'll do that."

Louis fished in his pocket and put a coin in her hand. "Give it to him."

She walked down a narrow hallway and found Lloyd sitting on a cot in a small store room that he had made his bedroom. She tried to put the coin in his hand, but he crossed his arms over his chest, tucked his hands under his armpits and turned away. "He didn't have to pay me."

"He likes you, Lloyd, and wishes you liked him, too."

Lloyd turned half of his blond head toward her. "I like him fine. I just wish he wasn't so... foreign."

She put her arm on his shoulder. "He's trying."

Lloyd shook off her hand. "Trying to sell his stories. I know."

"Yes, he's trying to sell stories. He's also trying to include you in his life. While he tries to stay alive."

Lloyd made no reply.

"Good night." As she walked out of the room, her eyes fell on the ends of several envelopes poking out from beneath

Lloyd's pillow, and recognized the handwriting and return address—letters from Sam in California.

In the dormer she followed the glow of a cigarette to a wicker chair, where Louis stared at the embers in the fireplace, his clammy forehead pasted with limp strands of his long hair. She pulled a chair close to him. "Make me one."

He rolled a cigarette, and leaned toward her so she could light it off of his. "I'm a failure," he muttered.

"Nonsense. 'Thrawn Janet' is wonderful. Finish reading it to me."

He shook his head. "I've been stupid with Lloyd. It needs more attention, being a stepfather, I mean. If only I knew what I was doing..."

They smoked in silence for a while. "When you read your story," Fanny eventually said, "I was frightened."

"Good. That's what a 'crawler' is supposed to do."

"I was frightened about something else. Terrified, as a matter of fact. My fear is that you have too much passion for what you do."

"That's not possible."

"I believe it is. Your passion to write makes you oblivious to everything else. To others, to eating, to sleeping, to health. Your passion could kill you."

He waved dismissively, took a long drag on the cigarette and flashed his big, carefree grin. "If I have too much passion, you have too much Indiana. We'll balance out. How goes 'The Shadow on the Bed'?"

"Slowly." She would not admit that she had put aside the hopelessly contrived story she had begun, and instead had been writing a letter to his mother.

Later, while he slept in their bedroom, she tiptoed back into the dormer, lit the stub of a candle, and finished it. She explained that they were unlikely to reach Braemar for another week or more—which should not present a problem, as Louis's father had rented the cottage through the fall, and was still in Edinburgh, designing lighthouses—and mentioned her fear that Louis would relapse if exposed to more travel, more excitement, or more wet weather. She tried to finish on an upnote, stressing how dearly Louis looked forward to seeing his mother: *"...I think it must be very sweet to you to have this grown-up man of thirty still clinging to you with his childlike love."*

CHAPTER 26
Braemar, Scotland

Fanny did not know how much longer she could stand being stuffed in the cold, jouncing coach. They had been on the road for hours, winding through gales and sluicing rain on the road following the Clunie River up the Cairngorm Mountains. Looking out the window at a black sky, wind-bent pines, and red-and-black peaks looming above them she felt a growing sense of gloom.

Louis, who had been dozing next to her, roused long enough to poke Lloyd's arm. "Just wait. You'll be out in the sunshine, fishing in no time. There's an old saying in Scotland, 'If you don't like the weather, wait, for it will soon change.'"

Fanny had heard the same expression in Indiana and every place she had lived. She tried to smile, but part of her longed to grab Lloyd's hand, dash out the door and take the first steamer back to America. Abruptly the coach tilted upward and her back pressed into the bench as the horses' hooves clashed on the rocky road outside, pulling for all they were worth.

"The final climb up Glenshee Road," Louis offered.

The coach eventually leveled and they began to descend. During a hairpin curve she was thrown against the window, and caught a glimpse of a quaint village in the green valley below them. Her mood brightened at the thought that Thomas Stevenson had promised to bring along his servants to keep the fireplaces lit and do the cooking.

They clattered onto the cobblestone streets of a village of stone cottages, sturdy inns with colorful heralds jutting over their doors, two steepled churches, a butcher shop, a gushing stream with a millwheel creaking on one side of it, and an ancient bridge, all of it set against a craggy mountain that swirled with green and rust colors like a scoop of exotic ice cream. Smoke gushing from brick chimneys was blown flat by the wind, as were the oilskins of a few hardy residents scurrying between buildings.

After a long bend in the road, they pulled up by a long stone wall. Louis climbed out in the rain and held an umbrella out for her while rain sluiced down his neck. Walking backwards with the umbrella he led her and Lloyd through a gate and down a mossy path. "Welcome to the Highlands."

The cottage looked at least two hundred years old, with peaked roofs and thick dormer windows rising above two stories of tan stone. To one side, the white steeple of a village church loomed as if to protect them. A long, wedge-shaped lawn sprawled on the other side of the cottage, enclosed by an ancient stone wall.

A casement creaked open. "Good God, son, get out of the rain!" The front door opened and Thomas Stevenson hurried out to embrace her, shake Lloyd's hand and clap Louis on the back. Two servants materialized with umbrellas and escorted them inside.

In the parlor, stuffed armchairs and a sofa were set on a big Persian rug before a fire that crackled behind a large grate. In the far side of the room beneath a tall window, two aproned maids dusted a gleaming dining room table and set it with formal china. "You newlyweds can have the bedroom in back," Thomas said, leading them and Lloyd down a narrow hallway. "Your boy can take the one upstairs."

At the end of the hall Thomas nodded to the open door of a bedroom. Louis walked through, but banged his head on the low doorframe and staggered onto a four-poster bed. "Damn the little people who built this place!" At least, Fanny thought, the featherbed on which he sat rubbing his head looked soft, although the oil painting hanging near it, of a Highlands laird posing with a fowling gun and dead pheasants, seemed a bit much.

Louis kicked off his shoes, coughed, and lay back. "Wouldn't mind a short nap."

Thomas took her and Lloyd by the elbows. "I'll show you where Lloyd will sleep." As soon as they were in the hall, he said quietly, "I've a physician coming in the morning." He must have seen Fanny's skeptical look because he added, "A village doctor, yes, but a good one."

"Louis should be back in Davos," she said.

He sighed but said nothing, leading them up a polished wood stairwell to a low-ceilinged bedroom of timbered floors, whitewashed walls and dormer windows. She wished that she and Louis had been given this room, removed from the rest of them. She looked down from one of the windows on the lawn, groomed as if for croquet, and the Cairmgorm Mountains in the distance. "You've got a nice view from this room."

Lloyd gazed out with a pinched expression. "It's awful out there."

She followed his gaze out a different window that overlooked Glenshee Road, where a bare-headed villager chased in the mud after a tam that must have blown off. "They say the Queen rides by every few days on her way from Balmoral to the Braemar Castle. Maybe we'll see her."

"Who cares about a queen." He kicked off his shoes and curled up on the bed with his back turned to her.

She retreated downstairs to her bedroom and sat by the window while Louis slept, worried by his pale face, hoping he would recover enough to find something, anything to do to cheer up her son. Fishing? One look outside at the sluicing rain, wind-bent trees and mud quashed that idea, at least for the foreseeable future. She opened the book she had been reading on their travels, *Great Expectations*. A thin figure in a spider-black dress bustled in, sat on the bed and touched her cheek to Louis's forehead. It could only be one person. "Mrs. Cunningham?"

The woman glanced briefly at Fanny, frowned as if something was out of place, and then returned to Louis, loosening his collar.

"Cummy," Louis muttered, his eyes fluttering open.

"He's always called me that, 'Cummy,' just like he's always tirin' himself out and getting ill." She slipped her spindly hand under his neck and pressed her ear to his chest, an action that Fanny thought bizarrely intimate. "Doctors can do what e'er they wish, but I know this, a week in my care, he'll pass for well. You're the American."

"His wife. Fanny Stevenson."

Mrs. Cunningham kissed Louis's cheek and stood. Her eyes looked Fanny up and down, and she grimaced when her gaze reached the book in Fanny's lap.

"Is something wrong, Mrs. Cunningham?"

"We wear our finest for Sunday meals," she said, and walked out.

When a bell jangled elsewhere in the house—probably a dinner bell, for god sake—she roused Louis, who mumbled that she should eat without him. She pulled on gloves and a blue felt hat; the dress of grey muslin that she had traveled in would have to be good enough. After hurrying upstairs to pester Lloyd into a clean shirt and bow tie, they shuffled to the dining room.

Margaret Stevenson, dressed ankle-to-neck in a deep green dress with black gloves, rose from the table and rushed to embrace her. "Welcome, oh you poor dears, all that travel."

Thomas, at the head of the table in a starched collar and charcoal waistcoat, patted the empty seat next to him. "Louis wrote that you raised the boy a good Presbyterian," he said with a wink at Fanny. "Sit down, Lloyd, so I can put y' through your paces."

Lloyd walked to his seat like a man to his hanging.

"Pay no attention to him, child," Margaret Stevenson said, smiling.

"Is Louis sleeping?" Thomas asked.

Fanny nodded, taking the seat between Margaret and Mrs. Cunningham. "He should never have left Davos."

Margaret smiled. "We need to see him now and then too, you know."

Thomas nodded at Lloyd. "Do us the honor of asking the blessing."

Lloyd reddened, swallowed, bowed his head but said nothing.

Fanny reached across the table and patted his hand. "I'll do it. Let us pray. Lord, bless this—"

"I didn't ask you, Fanny dear," Thomas interrupted. "If my designee does not offer a prayer, then I get to choose someone else." He grinned, as if this were a party game of which he was especially fond. "Cummy?"

Mrs. Cunningham clenched her hands in a fist at eye level and pressed her forehead to it. "Let us all pray. Dear God in heaven, God of all that is great and good, God of all martyrs including the Covenanters, forgive us our weaknesses, both physical and moral, and restore our Louis to health if it be thy will. Bless this food to thy use. We thank thee for bringing this loving family together again at last, Amen."

"Amen," Thomas said. "Well done, Mrs. Cunningham."

Fanny began to think it would be a very long month. During the dinner of lamb stew, dark bread and burgundy, Thomas asked Fanny about her childhood. She tried to describe growing up in a red brick house in a Midwestern town on the edge of a vast frontier where she learned to sew, read Dickens aloud with her father, and win pony races against the boys.

He seemed to relax a bit. "Did you ever see Abraham Lincoln?"

"No, sorry to say." She spooned some peas, trying to think of some common ground. "But we lived next door to the church where Henry Ward Beecher, the abolitionist, preached. He baptized me, in fact."

Thomas raised his eyebrows. "I heard Mr. Beecher speak in London once. Seemed a devout man, although I've since read that he thinks Darwin's theory of evolution offers no threat to Christianity, and of course I disagree with him on that."

"Why?"

After a long harangue about the Bible being the literal word of God, "and thus of course we didn't descend from monkeys," Thomas leaned back in his chair and asked if she would like more wine. While a maid poured, Fanny steered the conversation to safer ground, her years in the mining towns. "The air was so cold and so clear in Virginia City," she said, this time without rolling and smoking cigarettes, "that you could see a hundred miles in all directions." By the time she described gunfights in the card parlors, the garish madams who donated to church fundraisers, and the burials at boot hill, Thomas was puffing away on his pipe and egging her on with questions. Fanny decided that he was a hot air balloon, soft on the inside but unpredictable, whooshing this way and that, lacking control. Although Mrs. Cunningham, who was served at the table by the two maids as if she were a member of the family, kept a prim look throughout, Margaret Stevenson raised her delicate eyebrows, made little gasps and pushed her gloved hand to her chest at what Fanny supposed were the shocking parts, and thus seemed to thoroughly enjoy the stories as well.

Next morning, she again made her way to the dining room without Louis, who slept through the breakfast bell and barely mumbled when she tried to rouse him. She and Lloyd took their seats just as Thomas launched a spirited devotional reading from the book of Exodus, about Moses and the burning bush, while plates of hotcakes and bacon cooled before them. He then passed-off to Cummy, who offered another rambling, passionate prayer, during which Fanny stole a glance at Lloyd, who looked as if he might run screaming into the rain.

Promptly at 9:00 A.M., Mrs. Cunningham opened the door to Doctor MacDonald, a short man with a walrus mustache. She hung his dripping, ankle-length oilskin and hat on pegs and whisked him down the hallway toward Louis's room.

"Don't worry, lad," Thomas said with a nod toward the dining room window that framed another dreary scene of muddy streets and pouring rain, "you'll be out fishing in no time. There's a saying in Scotland, 'If you don't like the weather, wait till tomorrow, it'll change.'"

Lloyd rolled his eyes. Thomas cheerfully went on to discourse about Louis's health, how the doctors in Scotland were as good as any on the planet, and how Louis needed to settle down and take better care of himself—as if Fanny didn't know.

When at long last Dr. MacDonald emerged from the hallway, she hurried to the bedroom where Louis was buttoning up his shirt. "Well?"

Louis kissed her cheek, tore a sheet from his notebook on the bed and scrawled on it with a pencil. He held up a sentence written in big block letters: "I cannot talk for a week."

"What!"

He wrote another sentence: "And then I can speak only in the mornings."

"What kind of quack would say that?"

More scribbled words: "One who thinks the ruptured blood vessels of the throat and lungs need rest from coughing and quacking."

"What will you do all week?"

He shrugged and scribbled one word: "Write."

She supposed that activity would be nice—for him. "What am I supposed to do, sing hymns with your father?"

He grinned and wrote: "We can play chess."

"What about Lloyd?"

Louis wrote: "Let me ponder that."

For the next several days, while Louis slept or sat in bed, writing, Fanny played Rummy with Lloyd, listened to Thomas's Bible devotionals, smiled at Margaret's prattle about the Queen on holiday just down the road at Balmoral, endured Cummy's skeptical stares, and wished again they had never left Davos. Louis won all five of their chess games, usually after taking ridiculously elaborate detours, as he did in every part of his life, before putting her in checkmate.

One morning, she walked into Lloyd's room and caught him hurriedly tucking something under the blankets. When she sat on the bed, he edged away, causing a rustling sound. "You must have memorized those letters by now."

He glared. "He wants me to come home and live with him in San Francisco."

She considered dashing off a letter to Sam Osbourne warning him that he had no idea how to care for a child and would quickly grow frustrated with the task. "Would you like that?"

Lloyd nodded.

She thought better of arguing with him. "I smell breakfast." She headed to the door and waited.

"Go ahead. I'm not hungry."

She found Louis in his ratty blue bathrobe sipping coffee with his parents in the dining room. He still looked pale, and occasionally coughed, but he had begun whispering from time to time. Thomas and Margaret Stevenson, as always, seemed solidly overdressed, he in a sturdy brown waistcoat and she in a blue satin dress. While the maids set hotcakes, orange marmalade and bacon on the table, Louis leaned to Fanny and croaked, "Why the long face?"

"Lloyd wants to live with his father in California."

"Admirable," Thomas said.

Fanny paused in stirring cream in her coffee cup. "Why admirable, Mr. Stevenson?"

Thomas spooned marmalade onto his pancake and spread it with his knife. "Too many sons don't care to be with their fathers. They ignore their fathers' counsel, and act like their fathers are a big bother."

Louis stabbed a sausage with his fork, cut a large bite and chewed furiously. The meal proceeded in silence except for the clinking of knives and forks, the creaking of chairs and Thomas snapping open his newspaper, *The Aberdeen Journal*. Louis soon stood from his mostly uneaten plate of food and walked out.

Following him to their bedroom, Fanny found him rummaging through an old wardrobe, yanking out a pair of ancient black hip boots, an oilskin coat and a wide-brimmed rain-hat. She sat on the bed and watched while he pulled on trousers, and then struggled to pull on the boots that were several sizes too small. "What on earth do you think you're doing?" she finally asked.

He shoved his arms into the oilskin and slapped on the hat that was so large it settled down on his ears. "Going fishing."

She stepped between Louis and the doorway. "Not on your life."

Louis put his hands on her shoulders and gently moved her out of his way.

She followed him down the hall and up the stairwell to Lloyd's room, where Louis was greeted by Lloyd, still in pajamas, staring at his strange clothing as if he were from another planet. "You'll find rain gear in the closet," Louis whispered. "Come, boy, I hear the big ones are biting."

"I'm not going fishing in *that!*" He jerked his head toward the dormer window that was being hammered and streaked by the never-ending tempest outdoors.

Louis smeared at the window pane with his sleeve and peered out. "I'll grant you, it is a bit damp, but the afternoon might be perfect."

"I doubt it," Lloyd muttered, staring down at the bedspread.

"Meanwhile, I've a better plan. There's a gift shop in the inn, just a few paces through the rain, and of course I'm flush with coin. Throw on some clothes, bring some oars and we might get there."

Fanny tugged Louis's sleeve. "Are you sure about this?"

Lloyd sighed and shuffled to a chair where his trousers and cotton jersey lay in a heap.

Knowing Louis would not be kept in, Fanny wielded a huge umbrella that she found in the cottage, squishing in high boots through the mud on Glenshee Road in her long overcoat behind Louis and Lloyd in their oilskins and soaking straw hats, failing to keep either one of them under it. To her surprise, as they crossed over the gushing river on the Clunie Bridge, a steady line of coaches clattered past them bearing men in topcoats and women in coats worn over flowing white dresses. Just ahead of them, under the awning of a three-storey inn of grey stone, the "Fife Arms," a crowd of townsmen in woolens and tams mingled with tourists in expensive-looking overcoats and bowlers. As they reached the crowd, a tall man pointed up the road and yelled, "It's her —the old lady!"

All eyes fixed on a black coach-and-four that rounded a curve, approaching on the Aberdeen Road from the east, the direction of the castle at Balmoral. The tall spokes of the coach gleamed as the horses drew it sedately along. Queen Victoria, ancient, dignified, wearing a long-sleeved white dress and broad-brimmed, chin-strapped hat, rode in an open seat as if insisting that, after all, this was summer. Opposite her, two ladies-in-waiting sat with hands thrust in overcoats, shivering.

The onlookers applauded but the Queen did not acknowledge them. When one of her perfect horses lifted its tail and broke wind, the crowd laughed, but the Queen kept her eyes fixed ahead.

"Think she's deaf?" Lloyd asked.

"Dignified," Fanny said, smiling to herself.

As the crowd dispersed, Fanny followed Louis and Lloyd through the tall doors of the hotel, past the desk and to a small gift shop. Judging by his expression, Lloyd was disappointed by its inventory, consisting only of a rack of post cards, brightly colored umbrellas, plaid tartans and kilts, and some tin boxes of watercolors. Lloyd opened one of the boxes, held the tiny tubs of colors close to a wall-lamp and leaned closer to inspect them.

"Excellent choice," Louis said, digging a shilling from his pocket and escorting Lloyd toward a clerk. He smiled to Fanny. "You, oh trained one, shall be our instructor."

Art lessons in Lloyd's upstairs bedroom got off to a slow start. Lloyd rolled his eyes when Fanny arranged a bowl of apples, set it in a windowsill and suggested that they first try sketching a still-life with charcoal, after which she would show them how to create a wash with the watercolors.

"Perhaps he would rather create something of his own choosing," Louis suggested, sitting in a stuffed armchair with his drawing pad.

Giving her what seemed a triumphant look, Lloyd took his sketchpad to the bed, sat on the far side of it and started scratching with a stick of charcoal.

Louis cocked his head this way and that and said, "hmmmmmm," mugging as if he were studying the bowl of apples from various perspectives. Maybe he was trying to lighten things up, but she felt piqued nonetheless. "I'll go." She headed for the door.

He stopped her and gave her a quick hug. "Nonsense. How could I possibly get my apples right?"

She sat a small folding chair by a far window and stared out. A shaft of sun had penetrated the black clouds in the valley below them and illuminated a swath of meadowland near the river. A good omen? Several sheep ambled into the shaft of sunlight as if walking onstage from the darkened wings of a theatre. She took up her charcoal and sketched the largest one, a proud-looking ram. After she had drawn the animal's shape—she especially liked the posture, the strength in the way he held up his head and horns—she noticed that the room had gone deathly quiet, and turned to look behind her. Louis, slumped in his chair, had fallen asleep with his neck pushed crookedly against a wall and his sketchpad on the floor by his feet. By contrast, her son sitting on the bed seemed not just alert but engrossed in his drawing, the back of his neck taut while bent over his sketchpad.

She set down her sketch, gently roused Louis and steered him to the bed, where he lay down on one side of it muttering, "Need to rest."

Lloyd sighed, shifting further away on the other edge.

"May I see your drawing?"

"No!" Lloyd hugged the sketchpad to his chest.

She pulled Louis's shoes off and covered him with a light blanket. He seemed to be sleeping peacefully, but with each inhale she heard a faint gurgle, and his face was still much too pale. An image crossed her mind of Hervey, dying in her apartment in Paris. She shook her head and walked back to her chair by the window. Outside, the ram had ambled into the distance, and the clouds had closed off the sun. Feeling uneasy and lonely, she silently left the room.

She reached an umbrella from a hook in the hall and tiptoed through the pantry, startling one of the maids who was plucking a pheasant, and walked out a side door to the garden. Crossing the croquet lawn she followed the stone wall that ringed the property until she came to the place furthest from the cottage where the wall came to a point like the bow of a ship. Someone, evidently years ago, had formed a pile out of small stones and topped it with a cross made of sticks, perhaps to mark the grave of a family pet.

Fanny sat in a mildewed lawn chair that faced the little shrine, held the umbrella to protect against the rain that had slowed to a cold drizzle, and wondered if animals thought about loneliness and death. Although she was not especially religious, she offered several prayers: for her children and their safety; for her blended family, that it somehow would last; for Louis, that he might live and thrive, at least through the winter and, if it please God, for many years after that. She remembered hearing a preacher complain that prayers tended to be selfish, and hers certainly were, all of them begging that she not be left alone. But she did not trust her sanity, absent loved ones. The rain got heavier, splatting down on her umbrella, but she stayed for an hour, lost in her thoughts.

When she slipped inside the cottage, again through the small back door, she resolved to have a serious talk with Louis. Being cooped up in the rain with his parents was having a deadly effect on her mood and their fledging marriage. It seemed to be propelling her son further away from her. They were spinning their wheels, and she could not figure out what was going through Louis's head, from hour to hour. Love and obeisance, however oddly expressed, to his father? Defiance? In any case he seemed to have shut himself off to her, and she feared further loneliness and the black mood that would surely envelope her as a result.

Ascending the creaky steps to Lloyd's room, she was met with a message, scrawled on a sheet of sketch paper in Louis's distinctive block lettering and thumbtacked to the door: "Boys Only. All Others Keep Out."

CHAPTER 27
Finding Treasure

Locking her out had been a spur-of-the-moment decision. During his nap, he had dreamed of lying in a hammock on the deck of a square-rigger on a balmy day, looking up at sails puffed-out against a blue sky and feeling happy to be headed to the Caribbean with nothing on his mind but warm days and adventure. The dream had been such bliss that he felt confused and disoriented when he woke in the upstairs room to the sight of rain falling from a gunmetal sky onto the dormer window just above his head.

The scratching sound of charcoal against paper made by Lloyd, bent over a sketchpad a few feet away, quickly brought him back to reality. Pushing up to a seated position, he peeked around Lloyd's shoulder at three cartoon-like sketches the boy had made. In the first one, the Queen sat stiff-backed, chin-up in her black carriage, apparently oblivious to a huge cloud of gas enveloping her that one of the horses with lifted tail had loosed. The second sketch showed a stout man waving a Bible overhead, his collar so tight that his neck bulged over it—a good caricature, Louis thought, of Thomas Stevenson. In a third sketch Louis, thin as a scarecrow, read from an open notebook to a boy sitting in a chair with head slumped and eyes closed as if he had fallen asleep.

Smiling to himself at the boy's devilish sense of humor, thinking it might be a way to bridge their differences, Louis ambled to the chair that Fanny had vacated and looked at her sketch in the grey light from the window. She had drawn only the outline of a unicorn, or perhaps it was a ram, before abandoning the effort. Without giving much thought to what he was doing, Louis took up the charcoal she had left on the floor and added details to the drawing that completely changed it. At some point he must have begun humming, although he was not aware of it.

"What's that song?" Lloyd suddenly asked, frowning from his perch on the bed.

"Song?"

"What you were humming."

Louis, who had been lost in an imaginary world he was drawing, perked up—perhaps he could take Lloyd to that world too, if he did not overplay his hand. "It might have been a ditty."

"A what?"

Louis carried the easel that Fanny had been using to the opposite side of the room and set it on the worn hardwood floor near Lloyd. "Where are those paints?"

Lloyd motioned with a jerk of his blond head toward the tin that lay on the windowsill. "Why do you want them?"

"To lend color to this masterpiece." Louis placed the colors in the easel's tray. He wet his brush in a water cup, swirled it in brown paint, dabbed cross-hatches to depict hills, and then painted green swirls to form trees.

"What is it?" Lloyd asked, his curiosity having apparently drawn him from his perch so that he now stood just behind Louis.

Louis stepped back from the easel. "What do you think it is?"

Lloyd leaned close, his bright blue eyes moving slowly around as if studying the details that Louis had added. "A map of Point Lobos, near Monterey."

"Good guess!" Louis took satisfaction in the boy seeing that Fanny's altered sketch of a ram was now a body of land surrounded by bays and inlets, and marked by cypress trees, hills and rocky bluffs. "Alas," he continued, "it's not Point Lobos, but a far-off place that resembles it, an island known only to the few who survived."

"What are you talking about?"

Louis did not immediately reply, because his mind was elsewhere. As he stared at the map, characters of a story began to appear among the woods and bluffs he had drawn, their faces and bright weapons—flintlock pistols and gleaming cutlasses—peeping from unexpected places as they stalked each other, fought and murdered out of the simplest of motives, greed. Ripping a fresh sheet of paper from the pad, he wrote in block letters "Boys Only. All Others Keep Out." He handed it to Lloyd. "Post this outside the door. Lock it. Will you swear to tell nobody, not a soul, however related, what we are doing in here?"

Lloyd hesitated, his eyes widening. "Nobody."

While Lloyd went out to post the notice, Louis dabbed his brush in black paint and slowly, ornately formed the words beneath the drawing:

"*Treasure Island*"

Louis heard a thumping-sound on the door, and moments later, Lloyd walked in carrying one of his brown leather shoes, explaining, "I used it as a hammer."

"Good, I knew I could count on you." Louis stood and put his back to the low, ancient door. "Besides guarding the entrance to our preserve," he continued, gesturing with a flourish at the low-ceilinged room with its dormer windows, old brass bed, sconced gas lamps, hunting boots stacked in one corner and coats hanging from hooks in another, "you shall be my editorial assistant!"

"Your what?"

Louis paced the worn hardwood floor from the door to the opposite wall, and then back to the bed where he gripped one of its brass posts as if it were a ship's mast. "While I scribble some thoughts, from time to time I'll have questions about things a boy your age would know."

Lloyd frowned. "Like what?"

"Well, for example..." Louis paced, pressing his hand against his forehead as if pondering a hopeless problem. "Let's say your mother ran an inn, and a stranger who came to lodge there had a secret past—he was a pirate who had murdered a dozen men on voyages of plunder in the Caribbean. Let's further say that he seemed to favor you, and proposed to share a secret if you'd vow to keep it between the two of you. Would you run and tell your mother, or hear him out?"

Lloyd knit his eyebrows for a few moments. "Hear him out."

"What I thought. Until I raise more such questions, you may draw more of your fine sketches." Louis smiled at the sketchpad on the bed.

"You snooped!"

"Couldn't stop myself. Marvelous work, but you'd best not show those to your mother."

A rapping on the door, and Fanny's voice: "What's going on in there?"

Louis nudged Lloyd, shaking his head. "Can't say," Lloyd said to the door.

Her voice again: "May I come in?"

"Please read the sign," Lloyd said, putting his hand over his mouth to stifle giggles.

A long pause, then she asked, "Is everything all right?"

Louis nodded vigorously to Lloyd.

"Yes," Lloyd said loudly.

"Louis, are you all right?"

He could easily imagine a frown creasing her beautiful face as it leaned close to the thick wood on the other side of the door. Part of him longed to open the door, let her in on their game and beg her cooperation. But would that destroy what he had created? Louis made a strangling motion on his throat and nodded to Lloyd.

"Yes," Lloyd said, "he's all right, but unfortunately is unable to speak."

Eventually, Louis heard her walk away.

Louis took his sketchpad to a small desk that faced the southernmost window, filled a pen with ink, and numbered down a page from "1" to "15." As sheets of rain pelted the roof above them and Lloyd stared over his shoulder, he dashed out chapter titles. He had never written a novel before—well, never finished one, anyway—and supposed that fifteen chapters would be about right.

In an hour, another loud door-knocking. "Supper is on the table," Fanny's voice called, with what Louis sensed was a note of irritation.

Louis scrawled a note for Lloyd, who read it to the door: "We humbly request that you have two suppers sent here."

Her voice: "Louis. Don't you think you're taking this game a bit far?"

Louis nodded.

"He says yes," Lloyd said.

Louis headed a fresh page, "Chapter One," spaced down a few lines, and began writing. When someone knocked on the door, Lloyd opened it just long enough to take a tray of food from one of the serving-maids before shutting it again.

Louis intended to eat his pork chops, potatoes and peas, write for an hour or so, and then retire to his own bedroom where he would explain everything to Fanny: how he had seen Lloyd's irreverent sketches and seized on the idea of forming a secret society of boys as a way to reach him. How it seemed to be working, and how in the process he had received—either from heaven or, more likely, his subconscious—a story that he simply had to get down.

Instead, he ate half of his meal while uttering phrases of made-up pirate lore to Lloyd, asking questions and cocking his head to hear the boy's answers. Setting the food aside, thoughts racing, oblivious to time or any discomfort, he wrote until long after midnight, at some point turning off the gas lamps when Lloyd mumbled that he was tired, and then continuing by the light of a candle while the boy slept. Candlelight, he found, gave a delicious entrée to the archaic world he was writing; soon, he began hearing the creaking of a mast, the snap of sails as they caught wind, and raspy voices of sailors singing a ditty:

Fifteen men on the dead man's chest—
Yo-ho-ho, and a bottle of rum!

He was dimly aware, at about midnight, of Fanny's voice calling softly through the door, "Louis?" but he was too much in his other world to answer. The grey light of dawn shone through the dormer window when he finally closed the notebook, tiptoed down to their bedroom, slipped under the covers and put his arms around her.

"Cold," she blurted, jerking away from him.

"Fanny?"

Silence; then, her soft feminine snoring.

He woke late and alone. Throwing on his robe, he hurried, bleary-eyed, to the dining room where a breakfast of porridge and boiled eggs had cooled on his plate and the others had finished eating. Margaret dabbed a linen napkin to her lips, seeming to regard his entrance coolly as the maids in their white blouses cleared dishes. Thomas's eyes and frowning brow appeared over the top of his *Aberdeen Journal.*

"Louis was up late," Fanny said flatly, barely giving him a sideways glance from next to him where, dressed for the day in a grey woolen dress, she sipped tea.

Margaret Stevenson frowned at him. "Sick?"

"Art," Louis said, smiling conspiratorially at Lloyd, sitting in his pajamas across the table, who looked up from his bowl and nodded solemnly.

"What, pray tell, have you been working on so feverishly?" Fanny asked.

Louis sipped coffee and shrugged.

"We can't say," Lloyd chimed.

Thomas peered over his newspaper at Fanny. "Louis loves his secret little games. Don't worry, dear, you'll get used to them."

Louis had only eaten half of his toast, but stood. "Come along, Lloyd."

"Wait!" Fanny was giving Louis her sighting-down-a-pistol stare.

He sighed. "All right, I confess, we've been working on a story. We shall share a reading of the first chapter with anyone who may wish to hear it. Said reading to commence in ten minutes in the parlor of the late Miss MacGregor's cottage. Please excuse us while we prepare."

Louis walked Lloyd down the hall and nudged him toward the stairwell. "See if you can put on something without mud on it and then come and get me." In his own bedroom Louis dashed water on his hair, carefully parted it, and dressed in a linen shirt, his cleanest trousers and coat.

At the appointed hour, Louis and Lloyd made a solemn entrance to the parlor, where Fanny waited on the sofa that faced the big fireplace, one leg crossed over the other, chin propped in her hands, squashed between Margaret Stevenson and Mrs. Cunningham and looking none too happy about it. Louis, notebook in hand, yanked the sash and opened the drapes of the big window next to the fireplace, thinking that the view out the window of the Cairngorm Mountains and storm clouds would be a fitting backdrop for his performance. He directed Lloyd to sit in an armchair next to him, and opened his notebook with a flourish.

"Part One," Louis read.

Margaret held up her dainty hand, stopping him, and turned toward the dining room. "Aren't you going to join us, Thomas?"

"Yes," Thomas said from the dining room table, giving them an absent-looking wave while poring over a thick book, either one of his engineering texts, Louis supposed, or a favorite theological tome. When Thomas did not rouse from the chair, Louis shrugged and opened his notebook.

"Part One," Louis resumed, "The Old Buccaneer. Chapter One. Squire Trelawney, Dr. Livesey, and the rest of these gentlemen having asked me to write down the whole particulars about Treasure Island, from the beginning to the end, keeping nothing back but the bearings of the island, and that only because there is still treasure not yet lifted, I take up my pen in the year of grace 17___, and go back to the time when my father kept the 'Admiral Benbow' inn, and the brown old seaman, with the sabre cut, first took up his lodging under our roof..."

Within a few pages, he introduced an old sailor with a white scar on his cheek who sang ditties, drank rum and frightened the story's narrator—Jim Hawkins, a boy of Lloyd's age, whose mother managed an inn—into keeping watch for any appearance of a seafaring man with one leg. He read how the drunken sailor told stories to Jim: "Dreadful stories they were; about hanging, and walking the plank, and storms at sea, and the Dry Tortugas, and wild deeds and places on the Spanish Main..."

He paused to glance over the pages at his audience. The three women seemed to be indulging him rather than engrossed in the story, Fanny with a wry but fixed smile, his mother shuddering every time the captain sloshed rum and swore, and Cummy, who liked tales of bloodshed when the shedding was deserved, so far wearing her usual tight-lipped scowl. His two male listeners showed opposite reactions from each other, Lloyd leaning forward with rapt attention while Thomas Stevenson remained at the dining table, buried in his book and showing only the bald spot on top of his head.

Louis picked up his pace and volume, thankful for a voice that stayed firm with no coughing, and read to the point in the story where pirates storm the Benbow Inn looking for the scarred man and his secrets; shots are fired, one man is trampled to death by horses in the melee, Hawkins and his mother escape, but the frightening man dies of a stroke. Jim finds a key tied around the corpse's neck, and uses it to open the dead man's sea chest. Louis lost himself in the story, pacing the floor and even swaying as if to the rhythms of the sea, until his father suddenly bellowed, "No!"

Louis stopped reading. "Is something wrong?"

Thomas called from across the room, "You read that the boy found boots, powder and shot in the sailor's trunk. A good seaman would never keep such things in his chest."

"He wouldn't?"

Thomas stood. "Boots are too dear to a sailor to be stored in a chest; he'd be wearing them. He'd never keep gunpowder there because it would get damp."

"I see. What sorts of things might a sea dog keep in his chest?"

"Odd things, perhaps trinkets he'd picked up in his travels. A boat-cloak that he'd only wear at sea. Lots of stuff."

"Perhaps you would write a list. You can deliver your list to my associate, Lloyd Osbourne, but I'll need it this evening, so I can write the chapters for tomorrow's reading."

Thomas mumbled something and sat back down.

That afternoon, as Louis wrote more of the story in Lloyd's upstairs room, out of the window he saw his father in a brown waistcoat and hunting boots pacing the perimeter of the garden during a brief appearance of the sun. And later, when Louis fetched a cup of tea from the kitchen, Thomas Stevenson was at the dining table, writing on a legal envelope with a pencil.

Finally, after Lloyd had fallen asleep, this time after muttering "good night," Louis heard footfalls outside the closed door and a rustling sound as an envelope was pushed beneath the door. He picked it up, read what was listed on the back of it and smiled.

Wide awake, Louis surged ahead in the story, spooling out several more chapters, occasionally stretching and pacing the room until new sentences would intrude and demand that he sit and write them. At some point he left his story to daydream, and glimpsed a vision of a magical future with Fanny, although the details remained fuzzy...

Again, it was almost dawn by the time Louis slipped into his own bed and wrapped his arms around Fanny—who again shuddered and pushed away from him. He knew that her patience at being ignored was wearing thin, and could imagine how appalling each day must be for her, making hours of small talk with his mother or being grilled on theology by his father while Louis locked himself away. But he was convinced that for the time being, he simply could not nor should not interrupt whatever was bubbling up from within.

Next morning, when Louis brought his pages and Lloyd into the parlor, Thomas was reading his newspaper by the fire. Fanny brought her own chair from the dining room, leaving the couch for Cummy and Margaret, who strolled in from the dining room. "I'm afraid I must back up a few pages," Louis explained while Lloyd seated himself cross-legged on the rug, "to correct some details of the story."

He opened his notebook and read, "Chapter Four, 'The Sea Chest,' and reread the scene in which Jim opens the dead man's sea chest, this time reading word for word the list that his father had penciled on the envelope for what Jim finds inside: "a quadrant, a tin cannikin, several sticks of tobacco, two brace of very handsome pistols, a piece of bar silver, an old Spanish watch and some other trinkets of little value and mostly of foreign make, a pair of compasses with brass, and five or six curious West Indian shells." He glanced at Thomas, who nodded gravely.

He read for almost an hour, until he got as far in the story as he had written, and closed the notebook. Although he couldn't wait to get to a quiet place and write the next chapters, he took Fanny's hand and tugged her up from her chair. He would walk her to their room and try to explain why he had been ignoring her, and beg her indulgence for a few more days—and hope she received his pleadings well.

"May I steal your husband for a moment?" Thomas suddenly stepped in front of Fanny with his bowler pressed to his chest in a silly-looking show of gallantry.

Louis leaned close to Thomas and said firmly, "Perhaps later, father."

But Fanny dropped Louis's hand and backed away. "But of course you may steal him, be my guest, Master Tommy."

Thomas stiffened. "Master Tommy?"

She patted Thomas's shoulder. "My nickname for you." She turned and walked down the hallway.

"Master Tommy." Thomas grimaced as if from a horrible taste, shook his head—and suddenly, his face split in a wide grin. He threw back his head and laughed. "She's a peach. Oh dear son, you've found a good one there, a *bessom*! What say we have a cigar?"

"Well..."

Thomas walked to a hutch and removed a box of cigars from a shelf. "I'm afraid you need serious help."

"In what realm, sir?"

"Hah. What realm indeed. Your story, of course, what other realm would I be expert in?"

"All of them, I expect."

Thomas laughed. "She's a bad influence on you, a bad one she is, but oh, how funny!"

Louis sat in one of the two armchairs by the hutch while his father got out two cigars and solemnly handed one to

Louis. "Actually," Louis said, "she can be quite serious, and I've been ignoring her."

Thomas waved off the concern with his cigar. "The treasure tale is lively, son, don't get me wrong, but you often go off the mark when it comes to seafaring."

"Oh?"

"I could help you to get it right. If you'd allow it." Thomas held a match to Louis's cigar and then lit his own. The men puffed clouds of smoke around themselves in silence.

Louis felt unexpected tears in his eyes. This squat, bullheaded man whom he loved would not be on earth forever, and it was a rare chance for the two of them to share something. "I would be honored."

After their cigars, the two men retired to Lloyd's room, Thomas bringing with him three thick volumes about sea adventures. There, to Louis's great surprise and pleasure, his father became a boy again, tossing his waistcoat in the corner, loosening his collar, and pacing the floor with his books to extol the fine points: the size of cannonballs, how many cannon a pirate ship would carry, pirate rituals and rules, including how leaders were chosen and deposed. Sitting cross-legged on the bed, Lloyd cared about none of these details, only insisting that the story have as many stabbings, shootings and ship battles as possible. "Be sure," he told Louis fiercely late that night, "to make every chapter exciting. Every single one of them."

Louis had the most fun with the character of John Silver, who rolled easily off his pen because every aspect of his charming, domineering and hectoring personality, and his most notable physical characteristic, a missing leg, were those of Henley. To create any scene involving Silver, all Louis had to do was imagine Henley in the situation, add a knife or flintlock pistol tucked in his belt and "watch" the result.

On the third morning of the readings, Lloyd covered the painting of the treasure map with a blank page and then bore the easel from his bedroom as if it were a sacred battle flag, marching it downstairs in advance of Louis and setting it carefully within the semi-circle of parlor chairs. When the usual audience had assembled and Louis stood ready with his notebook, Lloyd removed the covering page with a flourish.

Margaret clapped her hands.

Thomas smiled and said, "Hurrah!"

Fanny cried, "What did you do to my ram?"

Louis felt his face redden. "I'm sorry, dear, I meant to explain earlier—I thought you'd abandoned the ram, you see, and—"

"Just read. No explanation needed." Fanny's smile was almost as tight-lipped as Cummy's.

As Louis read, within a few pages Lloyd was jumping to his feet to cheer when things went well for Jim, or groan when they didn't. Thomas Stevenson puffed his pipe, smiling when Louis read parts that incorporated his suggestions. He interrupted the reading only once, when Louis read that Captain Flint's former ship was named *Fury*. "That's not a proper ship's name."

Louis sighed and snapped the pages straight. "Have you a better one?"

"Yes," Thomas said, drawing on the pipe for a few seconds and then pointing it at Louis. "*Walrus*."

As Louis nodded and penciled the change, someone knocked at the door.

Mrs. Cunningham let in a balding little man wearing an old-fashioned waistcoat similar to the ones Thomas wore, a straw hat and carrying a suitcase. After an awkward pause in which the family exchanged puzzled glances, Louis plunked down his notebook. "Dr. Japp!"

"Stevenson?"

"Many of us here answer to the name. I'm Louis." He introduced Dr. Japp around, explaining that he had written to the professor some weeks earlier to suggest that he stop by, if he were in the Braemar area, and they could discuss an essay that Louis had been writing about Thoreau.

Dr. Japp nodded at the semi-circle of chairs. "Please forgive me, I've interrupted."

"Louis was reading to us," Margaret Stevenson explained.

"About Thoreau?"

"About pirates," Louis said.

"Oh," Dr. Japp said, taking an empty chair. "Do carry on."

Louis resumed reading his chapter about Jim Hawkins hiding in an apple barrel, where he overhears the sailors plotting mutiny and realizes they are a band of pirates who plan to seize the treasure for themselves and kill everyone else aboard.

Louis looked up from his notebook. "That's enough for today. I'm sure Dr. Japp is tired from his journey."

"Cracking good tale," Dr. Japp said. "You'll read more tomorrow?"

"Perhaps later in the week, when we're done with Thoreau."

The professor waved off the thought. "Plenty of time later for Thoreau. Carry on with the pirates—but I must say, I'm a bit confused. Can you catch me up on the parts I've missed?"

Louis clapped the little man on the back. "No need for that. Tomorrow I'll start again from the beginning."

Fanny rolled her eyes.

Lloyd yelled "Oh boy!"

Thomas settled the issue by nodding his approval.

"Cummy, show Professor Japp to his room," Margaret said, "then go and order more tea and biscuits for our morning sessions."

Watching Mrs. Cunningham tug the dusty little man down the hall, Louis chuckled. "I'd no idea he would actually show. I've scarcely looked at the Thoreau piece, not to mention started on it. Afraid it'll be nose to the grindstone, dear." He kissed her cheek. "You'll have to excuse me." He turned.

The dam broke. "Have you lost your mind?" she shouted.

"Something wrong back there?" Margaret Stevenson called from the dining room.

"Yes!" Fanny yelled, stomping toward the front door.

Louis hurried to follow as she banged outside, startling a cat off the steps. She splashed through the mud to the gate, turned onto the Aberdeen Road and headed into a driving rain toward the white cottages of the village. Both were hatless and dressed for indoors, she in a flowing blue cotton dress and pumps, he in a linen shirt, trousers, and low-cut shoes that squished as he clomped through the mud, five paces behind her. "Fanny!"

Passing the grey steeple of St. Margaret's Church he followed her under its eaves and around a corner, where he found her with back pressed against the stone wall, arms folded over her chest and tears in her eyes. He braced his hands on his knees, gasping, "Fanny, I—"

"Do you have any idea, any solitary thought about why I am so upset?"

"You're bored," he tried. "Have been cooped up too long with my family. With my father especially."

"All of those things. What else?"

"I appropriated your ram," he said sheepishly, "and defaced it."

"What else?"

"I locked you out of Lloyd's room."

"Not just out of his room. Out of the part of you that I love most. I'm your literary advisor, remember?"

"Of course I remember, but—" a fit of coughing seized him and he doubled over, and felt suddenly miserable, exhausted, and with rain dripping off his long hair and down his neck.

"Oh, Louis, look at you!" She was a sight herself, with her wet hair plastered onto her skull, the soaked cotton revealing the exact curves of her breasts, and mud covering her ankles and shoes.

He tugged her to the church doors and inside.

The nave was empty, smelling of mildewed wood and dust, and illuminated only by the dull light of a stained glass window depicting Mary with the Jesus Child. He walked her to a pew, trying not to tread on the names of the dead that were inscribed on the granite floor.

"Goodness, I've made you sick," she said as they sat on the pew.

"No no, I'm fine."

She looked in his eyes. "What am I to you, Louis?"

"My wife."

She turned away, and for a time seemed to be studying the dark grain of the pew ahead of them. "But why did you marry me? Did you need another nursemaid? A second mother?"

Her words felt like a slap on the face, but he tried not to show it. "You didn't like the story I made up for Lloyd," he finally said.

"You're changing the subject. And I haven't said I don't like it. It's a story for boys, that's all. Truth be told, I think you could make it deeper, more allegorical, like *Moby Dick*."

Louis took her hand, rubbed her palm, and smiled into her beautiful brown eyes. "But it *is* allegorical, dear Fanny."

"Oh?"

He put his arm around her. "Does the story of a boy leaving his family and all that is safe behind, and setting sail across the ocean sound at all familiar to you?"

She frowned up at him, but with her eyebrows raised in perhaps the beginning of hope. "Not really."

Playfully, he pushed her away so that he could watch her face when he said, "All right then, just complete this sentence: the boy in the story left everything that was safe, to sail in dangerous seas, to...."

"... find treasure."

Louis grinned and lightly tapped her chest.

She smiled as if she were beginning to like this guessing-game. "Me? I am...treasure?"

He whispered, "The treasure I crossed an ocean for. What I almost died for. You will always be so."

"Good." She leaned her head on his shoulder and snuggled close.

He put his arm around her shoulder. "What am I to you, Fanny?"

She stiffened.

"Is that such an awful question?" he continued.

Finally, haltingly, she spilled out what had tormented her for many months: that her love for him was in replacement for her dead son. How disgusted she had been when, in dreams filled with desire and lovemaking, Louis's face had transformed into Hervey's! She explained how she worried that not just her physical desire, but her entire attraction for Louis had been based on grief—or, worse still, perversion. Realizing this, she had determined to make their relationship platonic, after Louis showed up in California, but had failed. Even her black moods seemed related to these perverse thoughts and impulses.

"So you've been trying to put away your dark side," he said, a bit playfully. "I thought we weren't supposed to do that. We were supposed to embrace it."

"How could I embrace something so awful?"

He laughed. "Oedipus did."

"I'm trying to be serious."

"Why? Fanny, oh dear, dear Fanny, life is so serious as it is, without complicating it by worrying about what some clod of a doctor might say your dream is about. I love you regardless, and in fact feel honored by the thought I could be a reincarnated loved one."

"Not reincarnated!"

"Balls, who cares? What if a dream is just a dream? What else am I to you?"

She peered into his eyes. "You are the one who's never lied to me. The one who is steadfast, who never leaves me. The one who is playful. The one who makes me laugh. The one who puts up with me. The one who Lloyd absolutely loves to be with, now that you've hatched that silly treasure story."

She leaned against him and wept while he brushed wet curls off of her neck and murmured reassurances that were no longer needed. They sat for a long time, looking up at the stained glass. Sun shone now on the window making the figures glow.

Louis took it as a sign that his luck was turning when Dr. Japp and his father took an immediate liking to each other, the professor saying at lunch how "honored he was to be in the presence of the famous lighthouse engineer." Thomas, beaming, moved the discussion to theology—which turned out to be one of the professor's favorite subjects. By the following afternoon, after Louis's reading of the pirate story, his father and the professor set out in hiking boots and knickerbockers to walk through the marshes to see the Linn of Dee. As they clomped out the door, Louis heard them discussing the breakdown in the morals of Scottish youth. Upon their return, Thomas presented Dr. Japp with a copy of what Louis had always considered a ghastly tract that Thomas had written, *Christianity Confirmed*. Red-cheeked, as if having the time of their lives, they squished across the hardwood floor, collapsed in armchairs by the fire and celebrated their day with drams of whisky.

In odd moments, the professor talked with Louis about Thoreau, but the main suggestion offered to improve the essay was to "cite me, Dr. Alexander Japp in a reference section." Dr. Japp enjoyed himself so much at the cottage, in fact, that he extended his stay. Thomas got on so well with Dr. Japp that he cabled his Edinburgh firm that his vital work at the office must wait so that he could spend more time with his family at Braemar.

His father now occupied for much of the time, courtesy of Dr. Japp, Louis wholeheartedly returned to Fanny both in body and spirit. He dashed out new chapters early each evening, telling her it was the easiest writing he'd ever done and that the story was writing itself. Then they would have a glass of wine, bundle-up in sheepskin coats and stroll in the chilly moonlit garden.

"Tell me, truthfully, what you think of the story by now," he said one night as they walked, hand-in-hand, through the thick damp grass that grew along the stone wall.

"Why?" She turned her face up to him, her dark eyes a luminous mystery in the dim light.

He smiled toward the beautiful eyes. "I'm thinking of sending it to Henley. I'll bet he could find a buyer for it."

"Will he appreciate that the villain is a ruthless blowhard with one leg?"

Louis laughed. "That's the best part of sending it, to find out if Henley sees himself perfectly reproduced as John Silver."

"Boys and their games." She began walking again, and their thick rain boots made squishing sounds in the wet earth next to the low wall that, regardless of how inadequate the ancients might have been at other things, had survived perfectly formed for centuries.

"This boy's game could fetch several pounds, and likewise the Thoreau piece. Then, if we're very frugal, we wouldn't need a shilling of father's money. We could go someplace where the living is cheap and the weather is warm, and stay a while."

"Back to California?"

For some reason his imagination was soaring with possibilities. "Much further. We could sail to the South Seas and live on an island."

"How I love your ridiculous dreams." She led the way toward the odd shrine of stones and a cross near the apex of the wall. "But you asked how I liked the story, so I'll answer truthfully. I'm flattered that it reflects your glorious quest to the New World to make me your wife, but still, I think writing an adventure for little boys is beneath you."

"You know what I think? That Fanny Vandegrift Osbourne Stevenson, recently of the Western frontier and originally of the Indiana flatlands, has become a literary snob."

She elbowed his ribs. "I'm serious. You are wasting your talent."

"Lloyd adores the story."

"And I adore you for entertaining him so completely. It gives me confidence that the three of us might make it as a family."

"I suppose that is something." He nudged her with his elbow as well.

She smiled sideways at him. "It is."

"And I've never pleased my father more than with this silly tale. It has been wonderful—no, more than wonderful, it's been amazing—to have him grinning and laughing and slapping me on the back for something of my creation."

They had arrived at the shrine. Both looked down at it as if trying to divine some message, some prophecy about their future.

"Fanny, what if—I mean, just suppose that Henley could get this in print. There might be mothers who read it to their sons, or, who knows, their sick husbands or their senile fathers. Thus women would buy the thing as well as boys.

"I still think the story is beneath you."

Louis sat on the damp lawn chair. "No, *I'm* beneath you!" He yanked her backwards onto his lap, turned her over and swatted her bottom while she struggled, screamed and laughed.

"Is something wrong out there?" his mother called from a window.

Giggling, they crept back to the room, undressed each other and made love.

Louis was happy to find his voice growing stronger as the readings went on. Within a week his cough disappeared. Finally, on the fourteenth day as they assembled in the parlor, Dr. Japp announced that by next day he had to be on his way. "Any chance you'll wind up the story by then?"

"Doubtful," Louis said, smiling at Fanny, to whom he'd confessed that he had no idea how the story would end.

"Today's chapter," Louis announced to the assemblage, "is called The First Blow." He read how Jim Hawkins witnesses John Silver committing murder:

"John seized the branch of a tree, whipped the crutch out of his armpit, and sent that uncouth missile hurtling through the air. It struck poor Tom, point foremost, and with stunning violence, right between the shoulders in the middle of his back. His hands flew up, he gave a sort of gasp, and fell. Whether he were injured much or little, none could ever tell. Like enough, to judge from the sound, his back was broken on the spot. But he had no time given him to recover. Silver, agile as a monkey, even without leg or crutch, was on the top of him next moment, and had twice buried his knife up to the hilt in that defenseless body. From my place of ambush, I could hear him pant aloud as he struck the blows."

Fanny giggled, causing the rest of them to stare.

"I'm sorry, I was thinking of Henley."

The rest of them looked mystified. Louis smiled and read on. When he finished for the day, Professor Japp waited while he gathered up the pages of manuscript. "I've an idea for your story."

"Don't tell me you are an old seaman too."

The professor shook his head. "I can sell it."

Louis motioned for Fanny to sit with them. He called for a pot of tea. Japp explained that he knew a Mr. Henderson, publisher of *Young Folks* magazine, and that Henderson had recently asked if he knew writers who might contribute lively stories. "Henderson will buy it in a heartbeat. I daresay he'd pay a hundred pounds for it."

Louis choked on a sip of tea. None of his essays and travel books had fetched even a fraction of that. "You're joking."

"Not at all."

Thomas Stevenson bounded over from a doorway where he'd been eavesdropping. "This calls for whisky and cigars!"

Through clouds of smoke and with the dusky flavor of Thomas's best single malt on their tongues, they hatched a plan. Louis would outline the remainder of the story that night. Dr. Japp would take the outline and the first fifteen chapters and show these to Henderson. Meanwhile, Louis could finish the story. The professor stood and pounded Louis's back. "You'd best get cracking!"

When they got back to their bedroom, Louis closed the door and sat on the bed.

"What's wrong?" Fanny asked.

"I've already thrown everything in the story I could think of. I'm out of ideas, not to mention a bloody outline."

Fanny kissed his cheek. "Just say that Hawkins gets home with the treasure and all lived happily thereafter, or something like that."

"And I don't feel right about giving him my only copy of the chapters. What if he loses them, or rides off a cliff?"

"Simple. I'll write a copy, tonight."

Louis tore out some blank pages and handed her the rest of the notebook. For hours, she copied while he fretted over his outline. At last she said, "Finished."

"I am, too."

"You wrote how the story will end?"

"Hawkins gets home with the treasure and all lived happily thereafter."

"Certainly you said more than that."

"Not much." Louis began to pace.

She pulled off her clothes, lifted a grey nightgown over beautiful small shoulders and climbed in bed. "Would you please come to bed so we can get a few hours' sleep?"

"I'll tell Professor Japp the thing is stillborn. I'll never finish it. I am one hundred percent blocked. Henderson will hate it. You are right, it's a trivial story. Henderson will laugh. Henley will laugh. Everyone will laugh. I'll be finished. The laughing stock of the writing world. You will hate me. You'll grow tired of poverty and leave me. I'll die alone, miserable."

"Hush," she said, leaning over to blow out the lamp.

THE END

MARK WIEDERANDERS

AFTERWORD

This is a work of fiction based on historical records of the early years of the relationship between Robert Louis Stevenson and Fanny Vandegrift Osbourne. Like other historical novelists, I had to make choices about how closely to stick to what was documented during those years. I invented some events and scenes that did not occur, and dropped other events that actually happened but that seemed to add tedium to the story. In some scenes, I simplified the cast of characters; for example, history records that one of Fanny's sisters, Nellie, lived with her during Louis's year in California but she doesn't appear in my novel. I supplied fictional dialogue, but only after reading dozens of actual letters written by the principle characters for hints about rhythms of speech, senses of humor, degrees of formality and the like.

Some intriguing gaps in the historical record appear to have been intentionally created. In introductory remarks to their eight-volume collection of *The Letters of Robert Louis Stevenson* (1994), editors Bradford Booth and Ernest Mehew described how family and close friends either destroyed or heavily edited letters that, they believed, would leave an unseemly view of the pair. Most tellingly, no love letters between Louis and Fanny survive from their courtship during which Fanny was still (legally, at least) married to Sam Osbourne. We are left to guess at the ebb and flow of thoughts and conversations that led to some big decisions. Why did Louis spend a year in Europe, after Fanny returned to California, before following her there? When he reached Monterey, why did Fanny seem to hold him at arm's length?

331

What events precipitated her moves to Monterey and then back to Oakland? Were the months before achieving a divorce due to Sam's resistance, or did Fanny have second thoughts about a future with Louis? In filling these gaps with invented scenes, I tried to honor what I thought were authentic personality traits of the principle characters: Robert Louis Stevenson's obvious zest for life, passion, irreverence, creativity, and immense human decency; and Fanny Osbourne's pluck, pragmatism and resolute strength. I rejected the notion that they must be presented as saints.

I invented most of the letters exchanged by characters in this novel. Excerpts from a few authentic letters, described further in the Sources and Acknowledgements pages, are shown in italics. There is no documented evidence that Fanny Osbourne spent time in Paris's famous asylum, Salpêtrière, although in a recent (2005) biography, *Myself and the Other Fellow*, Claire Harman thought it possible Fanny had been treated by the famous mesmerist, Jean-Martin Charcot, who practiced at that institution.

Louis's scripting a drama that would nudge Sam to grant Fanny a divorce is also fictional. There is some evidence that the historical Sam Osbourne's Civil War experience left him with what we now call post traumatic stress, which might explain his fecklessness in marriage. J. C. Furnas in his 1951 biography of Stevenson, *Voyage to Windward,* said that Sam's life story "feels like fundamental instability encouraged by the dislocations of war and thenceforth flawing his behavior at crucial junctures." The historical Timothy Rearden did provide Fanny Osbourne with writing lessons and legal help in obtaining her divorce, but there is no evidence that he demanded a physical relationship with her as payment. Biographers have interpreted the relationship between Mrs. Osbourne and Rearden as overtly flirtatious—until Robert Louis Stevenson emerged as the true love of her life.

SOURCES

Graham Balfour's 1901 biography, *The Life of Robert Louis Stevenson*, included a photograph of Fanny Osbourne's sketch of RLS that I used as the basis for this novel's opening scene. The descriptions, places and events in Louis's adventures with Modestine I paraphrased from Stevenson's engaging account of that journey, *Travels with a Donkey in the Cevennes*. Lloyd Osbourne described Louis's haggard appearance and poor state of health when he arrived in Monterey in his reminiscences, *An Intimate Portrait of RLS*. Louis wrote about his collapse in the mountains above Carmel Valley where he was nursed to health by ranchers in letters to his friends. Anne Fisher's 1946 book, *No More A Stranger*, based on conversations with Monterey old-timers, includes a photograph of Anson Smith and the two daughters whom RLS taught to read during his recuperation. Fisher also provided a vivid description of whale-rendering that I used in developing my fictional "Blubbering" chapter.

Isobel ("Belle") Field's memoir, *This Life I've Loved*, provided some wonderful details about Fanny's time in France as an art student (for example, the incident where the instructor chastised Belle for drawing a falsely-detailed moustache). Her book also provided photographs of her father, Sam Osbourne, descriptions of his spit-and-polish style of dress, and the fact that others addressed him as "Captain" long after his military service. Belle's mention of one of his war stories gave me the idea for a fictional scene in which Sam rambles about the battlefield death of a friend: "Once in a rush forward across a field, he stumbled and the man behind him was shot through the head."

Fanny's actual painting of the bridge at Grez was reproduced in the 1968 biography, *The Violent Friend* by Margaret Mackay and now belongs to the Stevenson Collection at The Writer's Museum, Edinburgh. I described the illness and death of Fanny's child, Hervey, using the harrowing details she wrote in letters to California friends that are now in the Robert Louis Stevenson Museum archives in St. Helena, California. Fanny's recurring depressions were recounted in Louis's letters over the years, as were her bouts of what she called "brain fever" which have been interpreted by biographers as having both a physical and a psychological basis. My fictional account of Fanny's treatment at Salpêtrière was guided by Stanley Finger's description of Charcot's methods in *Minds Behind the Brain* (2000).

That Louis literally vaulted into Fanny's life, and the dining room of the Chevillon Inn, was recalled in both Belle's and Lloyd's memoirs. Louis related in letters over several months that he was writing a Western novel, *Arizona Breckinridge*, alternatively praising it and damning it so many times that in my novel the effort becomes something of a running gag. Louis related the exploding pistol incident in his essay about Monterey, "The Old Pacific Capitol". His brief career at the *Monterey Californian* under editor Crevole Bronson at a salary of $2 per week, paid out of collections secretly gathered by Jules Simoneau and other friends, was described in Fisher's book. Roy Nickerson's *Robert Louis Stevenson in California* (1982) identified RLS as the likely author of the November 25, 1879 article about the Bohemia beer wagon. Although I supplied some imagined scenes and details, Belle described her elopement with Joe Strong in her memoir, including the strain this put on the close relationship with her mother.

Stevenson described his Bush Street lodgings in San Francisco, his landlady Mrs. Carson, her son Robbie, and his favorite haunts and routines during the winter of 1879-80 in letters to family and friends. Anne Issler's 1949 book,

Happier for his Presence fills in many details of his San Francisco sojourn, including his search for work as a San Francisco newspaper reporter and his getting paid for a few columns about restaurants. Issler provides details about Fanny nursing him to health in her Oakland home before their marriage, and concludes that Sam and Louis would have encountered each other at the site. Louis described his tiny wedding and his honeymoon in letters and in his book, *The Silverado Squatters*. Their trip to Europe, being met by Sidney Colvin and Louis's parents in Liverpool, and Louis's friends taking an immediate and gossipy dislike toward Fanny was documented in letters exchanged confidentially between his friends. Thomas and Margaret Stevenson's acceptance of Fanny (after they were legally married, at least) and Fanny calling her new father-in-law "Master Tommy" were mentioned in letters of Louis and Fanny to their friends and family.

Louis's letters and poems left a vivid account of his first stay at Dr. Ruedi's spa in Davos, including the milk, exercise, and outdoor-air treatment regimen, as well as the reappearance of Mrs. Sitwell with her dying son Bertie. Stevenson described in a lively essay, "My First Book," how he wrote the first chapters of *Treasure Island* to entertain his stepson while they were pinned inside "the late Mrs. McGregor's Cottage" by incessant rain in Braemar, Scotland. He said that "women were excluded" from the process of creating the story, and related how Thomas Stevenson was drawn in by the daily readings of the tale and became a consultant: "I had counted on one boy; I found I had two in my audience. My father caught fire at once with all the romance and childishness of his original nature." Fanny's lukewarm response toward the story, Dr. Japp's appearance at the cottage, Louis re-starting the reading from the beginning, and Dr. Japp leaving with the first chapters tucked in his valise to show to a magazine editor were reported by Louis in his essay and letters.

STEVENSON'S TREASURE

A note and disclaimer regarding sources: in the above paragraphs and in the Acknowledgements, I have tried to give credit to the sources from which I gained ideas for this work of fiction; any omissions on my part are inadvertent. The museums and libraries who own the original letters and manuscripts that I excerpted on several pages of the novel advised me that because of their 130-plus-year-old age, the items are in the Public Domain. Nonetheless, I honor the memory of the fascinating individuals who once wrote them!

ACKNOWLEDGEMENTS

Many thanks to the Robert Louis Stevenson Museum in St. Helena, California, where staff patiently helped me search through collections of sketches, telegrams, steamer tickets, and other objects from the daily lives of the historical persons on which this novel is based. The California History Room of the California State Library, Sacramento, California, was a fine source of nineteenth century photographs that showed how buildings and locales looked when Stevenson saw them in 1879. With permission I have reproduced some of these photos on my website. Thanks also to staff of the California State Parks museums in Monterey who maintain the Stevenson House (known as "The French Hotel" in the 1870s) and hold informative events related to Robert Louis Stevenson's time in that city.

I am especially grateful to the Yale University Press for their wonderful eight-volume publication, *The Letters of Robert Louis Stevenson*, edited by Bradford A. Booth and Earnest Meyhew (1994). This comprehensive edition of letters written by Stevenson, his family and associates provided me with vital factual information as well as clues to the personalities of individuals who lived 135 years ago. Likewise I am indebted to the Beinecke Rare Book and Manuscript Library, also at Yale, where the original letters excerpted in this novel are preserved.

My appreciation to John and Felicitas MacFie, owners of 17 Heriot Row, Edinburgh, for showing me around the Stevenson family home and patiently answering questions during my stay. Alan Foster's tour of Old Town gave me a lively sense of the sites frequented by RLS during his youth.

Mrs. Doreen Wood at the Braemar Castle was a good source of information about the geography, history, and transportation during the time Stevenson's family stayed at "the late Mrs. MacGregor's Cottage."

Heartfelt thanks to Sands Hall, novelist and creative writing instructor par excellence, for encouraging me to write this story, giving insightful suggestions about some early scenes, and writing a book-cover blurb when the book was finished. Thanks to author Kim Culbertson for the blurb she provided and for her friendship, suggestions and good humor over the years of this novel's development. I am grateful for a long-running critique group in the Sierra Nevada foothills that included Kim, Ann Keeling, Bev Lyon, Brad Hoover, and Jeff Kirkpatrick. More recently, a Sacramento critique group including Deborah Russell, Sandra Briggs, Del Jack, and Jean Clark helped with later drafts.

Thanks to the many friends in the Northern California chapter of the Historical Novel Society for suggestions made at work-in-progress readings, and especially to authors Mary Burns and Persia Woolley for reading the manuscript, providing book cover blurbs, and making astute editorial suggestions. Among HNS chapters in other regions, Sophie Perinot provided suggestions about an early draft and Judith Starkston gave timely advice about submitting the manuscript.

Special thanks to Chief Operations Officer Michael James at Fireship Press, who runs a high-quality ship that publishes an outstanding array of entertaining and informative historical titles. Editor Midori Snyder, a fellow Stevenson fan, first considered the manuscript I submitted and then helped guide me through various steps of the publication process. Thank you also to Christina Paige for providing excellent copy-editing of the manuscript.

I gratefully acknowledge the support of The Martha's Vineyard Writers' Residency, The New York Mills Regional

Cultural Center, and The Vermont Studio Center, where I wrote various phases of the novel during writers' residencies.

Finally, I would never have reached the end of this several-years project without the support and understanding of my wife Esta, with whom life just keeps getting better as we turn each page. To my adult kids, John, Sarah, and Annie, for filling the house and holidays with love, and for helping me keep life in humorous perspective. Loving thanks to my sisters Chris, Jud' and Jean, from whom I learned so many lessons about strong, funny and self-reliant women; and to brother-in-law Robert Markowitz, who encouraged me many years ago to take up the pen and try to tell stories with it, without waiting to quit the day-job.

About The Author

Mark Wiederanders

Mark Wiederanders writes historical fiction about the lives, loves and personalities of famous writers. This interest fits well with his former career as a research psychologist (Ph.D., University of Colorado) who specialized in studies of the criminally insane! An earlier screenplay, "Taming Judith," about William Shakespeare's youngest daughter reached the finals of the Academy of Motion Pictures' annual writing competition and was optioned by a film company. The seeds for writing STEVENSON'S TREASURE were planted when Mark read an account of how and why RLS wrote his first big hit, TREASURE ISLAND. Although the adventure classic is not a love story, Mark considered it more than coincidence that "Louis" Stevenson wrote the book shortly after making an arduous journey of his own. His trip to America had one purpose: to make a married American, Fanny Osbourne, his wife. After deciding to end STEVENSON'S TREASURE with scenes of young Louis penning his timeless story during a tense, blended-family holiday in the Highlands, Mark traced the couple's unique relationship backwards to the time they met.

To research the novel Mark walked the whalebone-studded sidewalks of Monterey, hiked the Carmel Valley where Stevenson collapsed, combed the Calistoga mine-site where the couple honeymooned, studied letters and scrapbooks, stayed in the family's home in Edinburgh and in the Highlands cottage where TREASURE ISLAND was penned. Mark wrote parts of STEVENSON'S TREASURE at residencies awarded by the Vermont Studio Center, the Martha's Vineyard Writers' Residency, and as Artist-in-Residence at the New York Mills Cultural Center.

Currently, Mark is at work on a novel about another famous but eccentric writer and the love of his life. Speaking of which, Mark and his wife live in northern California where they have raised three wonderful children.

IF YOU ENJOYED THIS BOOK

Please visit

FIRESHIP PRESS
www.fireshippress.com

Fireship Press books are available directly through our website, amazon.com, Barnes and Noble and Nook, Sony Reader, Apple iTunes, Kobo books and via leading bookshops across the United States, Canada, the UK, Australia and Europe.

Lady with a Lamp:

An Untold Story of Florence Nightingale

by Marina Julia Neary

A Play with the Power of a Novel

Crimea 1854: Having botched the Charge of the Light Brigade Lord Cardigan is hiding on his yacht drinking himself into a stupor. On shore at the hospital corps a mutiny is brewing. Egotistic doctors, brutish surgeons, and skittish nurses wage mind wars against each other amid filth and chaos. Florence Nightingale, the legendary "Lady with a Lamp"— a saint to her patients and a frigid spinster to her colleagues — finds solace in the company of Tom Grant, a haggard physician with a sinister reputation. Trading grim jokes and scientific facts the two develop a cerebral romance that promises to mark a new era in English medicine. Inevitably Tom's semi-criminal past surfaces, throwing him into the political cross fire between Lords Cardigan and Lucan.

Following Marina Neary's superb novel *Wynfield's Kingdom*, this play is as much a delight to read as it is to see on stage.

Fireship Press
www.FireshipPress.com

www.Fireshippress.com
Found in all leading Booksellers and on line
eBook distributors

A SLENDER TETHER
BY
JESS WELLS

Amidst the turbulent weather of Europe's Little Ice Age, *A Slender Tether* offers three compelling tales of self-discovery, woven into a rich tapestry of 14th century France. Christine de Pizan, daughter of a disgraced court physician and astrologer, grapples with her ambition to be the first woman writer of France. A doctor finds an unusual way to cope with the death of his wife. And opportunity alternates with disasters in the lives of four commoners, yoked by necessity: a paper-maker struggling to keep his business, a falconer with a mysterious past, a merchant's daughter frantic to avoid an arranged marriage, and a down-on-his-luck musician with a broken guitar and the voice of an angel.

Fireship Press
www.FireshipPress.com

Peregrine

by

Mary Ellen Barnes

The true story of one woman's indomitable
spirit, and her love for the hawks she raises
in the time of King Charles I of England,
Cromwell's War, and the forming of the
New Colonies.

Frances Latham, daughter of the royal falconer, is expected to tend her
brothers and marry a farmer's son, but she yearns for freedom to study in
London, to hunt with hawks, and to marry for love. Her spirit will carry
her from a stifling country life to the bustling streets of London, through
the harrowing hell of the plague, and eventually to the shores of the New
World, where Frances struggles to raise eleven children and pass on a
better legacy than the one she endured.

History buffs will become immersed in this panorama of the English
court, country life, the grueling voyage to colonial America, the harsh life
settlers endured on its shores, and encounters with Anne Hutchinson and
Miantonomi, the Narragansett sachem.

WWW.FIRESHIPPRESS

HISTORICAL FICTION AND NONFICTION
PAPERBACKS AVAILABLE FOR ORDER ON LINE
AND AS EBOOKS WITH ALL MAJOR DISTRIBUTERS

For Love of Glory

by

Leslie Fish

Tria Juncta in Uno: "The three joined in one" - This is how Ambassador Lord Hamilton describes himself, his wife, and Admiral Horatio Nelson. But what happens when Emma, Lady Hamilton, returns to England on her husband's arm, pregnant with Admiral Horatio Nelson's child? As the Napoleonic Wars rage on, the three friends form the most famous, and infamous, *menage-a-trois* of British history.

Emma is grateful to William, who had rescued her from ignominy when he married her. But it is Nelson she adores, for the two of them understand the call of glory as no others do. Then Nelson is called upon to lead England's greatest fleet to victory or disaster at the Battle of Trafalgar, and what will become of Emma in the wake of Nelson's destiny?

Fireship Press
www.FireshipPress.com

www.Fireshippress.com
Found on line and with eBook distributors

**For the Finest in
Nautical and Historical
Fiction and Nonfiction**

WWW.FIRESHIPPRESS.COM

Interesting • Informative • Authoritative

CPSIA information can be obtained at www.ICGtesting.com
Printed in the USA
BVOW02s0722060314

346845BV00002BA/4/P